P.

ᵇy

Michaelbrent Collings

cover and interior art elements © Alex Malikov and tratong
used under license from Shutterstock.com
cover design by Michaelbrent Collings

website: http://writteninsomnia.com
email: info@writteninsomnia.com

For more information on Michaelbrent's books, including specials and sales; and for info about signings, appearances, and media,
check out his webpage,
Like his Facebook fanpage
or
Follow him on Twitter or on Instagram.
You can also
sign up for his email list
for deals and new releases.

"A proficient and pedagogical author, Collings' works should be studied to see what makes his writing resonate with such vividness of detail...." – *Hellnotes*

"[H]auntingly reminiscent of M. Night Shyamalan or Alfred Hitchcock." – horrornews.net

"*The Haunted* is a terrific read with some great scares and a shock of an ending!" – Rick Hautala, international bestselling author; Bram Stoker Award® for Lifetime Achievement winner

"[G]ritty, compelling and will leave you on the edge of your seat.... " – horrornews.net

"[W]ill scare even the most jaded horror hounds. " – Joe McKinney, Bram Stoker Award®-winning author of *Flesh Eaters* and *The Savage Dead*

"*Apparition* is a hard core supernatural horror novel that is going to scare the hell out of you.... This book has everything that you would want in a horror novel.... it is a roller coaster ride right up to a shocking ending." – horroraddicts.net

"What a ride.... This is one you will not be able to put down and one you will remember for a long time to come. Very highly recommended." – *Midwest Book Review*

DEDICATION

To...

Joanna Penn, who astounds...

Mom, who amazes,

and Laura, always.

ONE
first hunt

1

IT HAD BEEN LONG since the last *olamiyo*. Certainly longer than Leboo's lifetime, and perhaps longer than that of his father or even his father's *father*, too.

But it did not matter. Because of the lions. Because of their cubs. And because some things demanded a response.

This was, strictly speaking, not even a proper *olamiyo*. Those hunts – the men of the tribe sneaking out at dawn to hunt the lion on the savanna grasslands – were a thing of the past.

Leboo had snuck out with the others, to be sure, each of them knowing somehow that such was right… that it was the only way to do this with any chance of success. The dawn had painted the land, blooded it with reds and oranges as the *empikas* – the men chosen for the hunt –crept out on silent feet, each holding spear in a hand that was dry and steady. Each of the men was *ilmorijo* – there was not a junior warrior among them, and certainly none who was still a child.

They were the proud men of the village, the strong men of the tribe.

Yet, in the end, when the prey had become predator, the hunters the hunted, they ran.

Only Leboo did not run. For he *was* Leboo – named as one born outside the village, one whose mother had not had time to leave the bush when her time came. He was born in this place, born in the savanna, in the wild.

The wild was his birthright.

And now, he feared, it would be his death.

Only the lions kept him from running. Only the lions pushed him onward. The way they were, what had happened to them… it was all so *wrong*. That was why Leboo called the council in the first place, just a few days ago.

The men of the council had nodded. They had agreed. The young men had whooped and shouted – "Of course, of course, we will come, we will right this thing!" – while the older men simply nodded, knowing a nod sufficed, and knowing already that none of the younger men would actually go.

This was a thing of fathers. A thing to avenge the fathers of the pride – and the mothers and children that had been lost.

And so… the hunt.

Begun in dawn, it continued through the day and into the night. Tracking became more difficult. This was a hot place, and the dry season had been long, but nights still got cool at this time of year.

None of the men shivered. None suggested they return.

Then they found their prey.

No. Then they *found* us.

It was night. Torches had been lit, but all knew that the tracking they did was for now only for show. The lions would be watching, and the men had to show them that they would not relent, would never give up this hunt.

In the dying light of the last torch, in the twilight between man's fire and the darkness, Engai Narok – the good god, the Black God – became his vengeful alter-ego. Engai Narok closed his benevolent eyes, and Engai Na-nyokie, the Red God, awoke.

And that was when *they* came.

They were dark as night, almost invisible but for that single moment in the last embers of flame. Then their eyes glowed; twinkled like stars fallen to earth.

But one by one, those stars died. And with the death of those fallen stars began the death of the men.

The screams were not the worst. Nor was it the sense of those falling around Leboo, not the obscene feeling when a man is torn to pieces and a small piece of nature torn with him. It was not even the warmth that splashed across him, which he knew was the blood of his brother, Maitera.

What will Sankau say, when he does not return? Will his wife cry for him? Will she weep?

Will my wife weep for me?

No, the worst was not the blood, not the screams or the death.

It was the *laughter*.

It began an instant before the hunt became a slaughter. A cackling, hungry bark of a laugh. The laugh became two, then five, then ten, then twenty…

Great Engai Narok, how we misjudged.

But it would not have been different had they known the number of their foe. The lions demanded justice, and nature required that evil be punished.

Those who survived the first attack ran. Leboo did not know if any survived. He only knew that suddenly, he was alone. The foe had followed those who ran. Foolish of the other men to flee that way. Here, in this place, in this land where life was measured in years, yes, but also in seconds, it was death to run.

Running was what the food did.

So the men ran, the foe followed, and Leboo was suddenly alone.

And, alone, he tracked in the night. Something had gripped him: a madness, perhaps, or perhaps simply a sense of what must be destroyed, were the universe to return to its senses.

4

He continued forward. He was no longer looking for what he had originally sought. Not justice, not even punishment.

Vengeance.

He would do what had been done to others.

He would kill their children.

The trail was hard to follow. It was night, and nothing was quite so dark or so lonely as night in this place. But Leboo was of this place, and the darkness and loneliness were old friends who did not stop him, but seemed rather to beckon to him, to urge him ever forward.

He followed the trail of the many, to a place that as a child the elders had always counseled him to stay away from. And now he understood why; understood what hid there.

Water sounded, murmuring around him as he went deeper into this place, this gash in the world. A sound that meant life, that meant growth. But here, it was the signal of doom. For of course *they* would shelter here.

He continued, the walls of this place closing around him. The stone on all sides stood silent and dark, blocking what little, pitiful light there had been above.

He continued, the blood pounding in his ears, thrumming through him, shouting, *Run, run, run!*

He continued, and finally found them.

They were up late, the children. Rolling around, wrestling and playing as children will. They were small, and it would be so easy.

He crept forward. He had lost his spear somewhere in the fight – killing the beast that killed his brother? – but he still had his long knife. That would be enough.

He snuck closer. Three paces away from the nearest of the young.

And again Engai Na-nyokie showed his displeasure. The Red God winked, and a sudden wash of moonlight flowed into this place and fell upon Leboo.

The light fell on him, and once more, those starlight eyes glowed. The eyes of the young, who saw him for the first time, and who turned to face him with teeth bared and murder in their eyes. Even now, so young, they would kill – as, indeed, many already had, murdering and sometimes eating younger brothers or sisters as they competed for their mothers' affections.

It was one of those loving mothers he now saw. She was young herself, but already strong and large – as all the mothers were – she had been resting in the mouth of a cave in the walls, watching her children as they played with the others. Now she stepped forward. Now she saw Leboo, as he saw her.

Help me, Engai Narok. Be my hands, and guide my blade.

He heard the lions roar, as clear as if they had been here with him in this dark place, and knew that the good Black God had spoken. Had said, "Go. Fight. Win. You will triumph, and balance will return."

Leboo leaped forward, even as this young mother did. They clashed, blade and muscle, hand and claw.

When they withdrew from that first clash, he saw he had blooded her: her left ear was gone.

She made no sound, though. Not the merest whimper of pain. In her mind, she was still whole. That made Leboo take heart, almost as much as the cry of the lions in his heart. She was too stupid to know she had been wounded.

But I am smart. I am smart, and strong, and I will –

The thought ended abruptly as he realized how warm he was. His groin and legs felt like they were burning. Then his innards spilled from the long slit the young mother had opened in his belly.

6

Leboo looked down. He glimpsed his guts falling in dark, tumbling curls to the brown earth that lapped his blood.

He looked up in time to raise his hands against the next attack. The mother hit him in the center, and now he was not warm, but cold. He fell beneath her, and felt her bury her head inside him, tearing, pulling.

He realized the lie. Too late, he realized the lie.

The lions had not been urging him forward. They had been calling him *home*.

But he would not go easily. He would leave his mark behind.

He grabbed the mother's one remaining ear. Yanked it up and now at last she *did* scream. More surprise than pain, perhaps, but at least he had won that much. And would win still more.

He brought his blade down on her. He slashed from the left, from her now-deaf side. The blade bit into her temple, just behind the eye. She twisted away enough to avoid being blinded, but Leboo felt the knife bite down to bone. He pulled it forward, taking the skin off that side of her head. Dragged the knife forward, through cheek and chin.

Then the knife fell from his hands. The cold would let him do no more.

Strangely, the mother stood back.

Leboo was surprised. It was not these *things'* way to show mercy.

Then he realized what was happening as the mother called her children. Two of them, both girls – of course, the strongest and most terrible were always the girls, and the women they became – stepped forward. As had their mother, they buried their heads inside him, burrowing in and up, following the path of his soft insides, the best and easiest parts to eat.

7

Leboo was on the ground, face to the sky. In his last moments, he saw that not all the young men of the village had been fooled by the dawn departure of the warriors. Someone had followed them. A dark face peered down at him from atop the wall. A face he recognized.

Not a warrior. Not even a man.

Leboo had no idea how his daughter had followed him. How she had survived the attentions of the monsters who had made a mockery of the hunt, then followed and found him here.

Naeku. Naeku, look away. Look away, then run.

But she did not look away. Like the creatures, her eyes twinkled in the night. Not with the fires of death, but with tears.

Look away. Look... away... and...

The final instruction never reached his mind. The first of the children burrowed into his lungs and the breath left his body; then the life left his body, too, as she chewed her way forward, and took the first bite of his heart while it still beat inside him.

The heart stilled.

The lions were silent.

Only the laughter remained.

TWO:
camp

Interlude

THE GIRL IS AFRAID. Afraid, and maybe dying.
They are all dying, and so many already dead.

But the girl is the one closest to it. She has already been touched by it, more than any of them has.

So the woman says the only thing she can think of. She says the opening words to a story:

"Once upon a time, there was a little girl…"

She does not know where the words come from. She only knows that the girl is afraid, and the woman cannot live with that fear. Even if death comes for her, as seems likely, the woman cannot simply watch the fear creep into her.

"Once upon a time, there was a little girl…" The same words. For a moment, it seems as though these are the only words the woman will be able to say.

Then a gate opens inside her. She speaks, and a story is born.

ONCE UPON A TIME –

(a third time these words were said, but this would be the last time, with her and within her and the story was her and it would be told)

– there was a little girl named Gale. She had a family, too: a father named Craig and a grandmother whom everyone called Grams. But this is not their story.

Gale was playing outside, as she so often did. She was a beautiful girl, and usually had many people who wanted to come to her house and play with her. But today she played alone. She had a treehouse, and that is where she went.

Up, up, up she climbed. And when she climbed into the treehouse, she knew immediately that something was different. Something had changed.

10

The moment she climbed up and passed through the door to her treehouse, her world disappeared, and another one was born.

She looked around, amazed to see that her small room of a treehouse had become a vast land. And oh! what a land it was! Mountains, valleys, forests. The land stretched forever in every direction and it was so green and full of life and nothing was dry or dead.

But it *was* strange. How could you call it anything *but* strange when the mountains appear to be giant, towering things made of marshmallow, or the trees clearly made of red licorice, or the river that wound throughout it all so obviously made of strawberry milkshake instead of water?

"Where am I?" asked the girl.

She did not expect an answer, but she got one just the same. "Why, you're in the Magical Land of Piz, of course."

1

Evie Childs woke, as she so often did, to the sound of her own screams, and to the realization that she had successfully caught them before they exploded from her. Stifled the –

(*unborn*)

– screams within her mouth, clamping down on them with jaws strong from years of tooth-grinding, biting them to pieces, then swallowing them again.

They were not dead. Even bitten to pieces, smothered, and swallowed, those scream-children of hers would regroup somewhere deep within her, curled in fetal sleep. When grown old enough, the shrieks of horror would be born again, and would come forth as all living things came forth: with noise. With terror.

With pain.

But not this time. This time, she had smothered those banshee children again. This time, she had made no sound. This time, she was safe. For now.

Thoughts of safety – or the lack thereof – made her look around, as they always did. Checking to see how close danger might lurk.

Once Upon a Time,
a danger lurked.

But no… Bill was not here. Which did not mean she could relax. Relaxing was a sure ticket to a lack of preparedness, and that in turn was yet one more ticket to pain.

It was hot. The air conditioning unit hummed in the corner of the tent, but it had utterly failed to keep up with what everyone said was the driest and hottest season on record –

12

seconded only by the *last* season, which had apparently melted under its own heat, reformed –

(*like a scream*)

– and been reborn twice as fierce, dry, hot.

She sat up, the skin of her back sticking to the mattress for a moment as she did. She looked around again, as though Bill might have appeared in the space between waking and sitting.

He still was not here.

She still was alone.

And how long had she been alone? Twelve years married, and, what… eight of them alone? Or had it only been seven? Seven since he went *away*, though his body remained.

Me. My fault. I killed her, *then* him, *followed swiftly by* us.

Get moving.

She twisted, pushing her feet off the edge of the bed and to the floor. The floor was wood, high quality – nicer than the floors in her home, in spite of the fact that she was now in a tent in the middle of nowhere.

She rubbed her feet against the floor, back and forth, faster and faster, rubbing until her soles heated up and then started to ache.

The ache was good. A reminder that she still lived. An irony: pain had become the sum of her existence, the thing she feared… and at once the only thing that reminded her she still lived at all.

Get moving.

The thought pushed her forward again, and she realized she'd been rubbing her feet on the floor for a while. Minutes? An hour? She didn't know.

Once Upon a Time,
a girl sat uselessly.
She died because of it.

The thought, like all the Once Upon a Times, was useless and next to nonsense. She had once thought of a writing career. Well, no, not a *career*. But maybe a publication or two. Just an article in a magazine, perhaps. She had even written a book, before it all fell apart, before the center disappeared from her life and the rest of it fell into the empty void left behind.

Evie reached for the light cotton button-up shirt beside her, swinging it over her shoulders. The guides had all recommended that guests wear something like this, but few did, opting for t-shirts or tank tops because "Are you kidding? In *this heat*?" or "I don't want a farmer tan!" or just because "Because no." As a result, most of the other guests had so many mosquito bites they almost glowed in the dark.

Evie did not. She had barely any – as though even the mosquitos knew she was tainted.

No. I just wear long sleeves. That's all. I'm not tainted or evil or broken or –

She was falling into a dark place inside herself. The place the scream-children came from, incubating until a moment when she closed her eyes and was weak and they might be born once more. She had to move. She buttoned on the shirt, hiding her flesh from mosquitos and – more importantly – from the eyes of the other guests.

She leaned down, grabbing her shoes off the floor. At home she would have simply slid her feet in, laced up the sneakers, and good to go. Here, she picked up the shoes, held them at arm's length, and shook them vigorously.

Another thing she had not seen any other guest do, even though the guides had everyone to do it. Even after one of the guests had been bitten by a scorpion who took up lodging in his footwear the very first day, she had yet to see anyone check for biting creatures in their footwear.

She waited. Shook again.

Nothing climbed out. She figured any scorpion determined enough to stay in its home despite an earthquake that measured 12.2 on the Scorpion Richter Scale probably deserved a bite of something, so she went ahead and slid her feet in the shoes.

Nothing bit her.

What now?

Look for Bill?

No.

Then what? If she kept sitting here, she might start rubbing her feet against the floor again, or rubbing her hands together to warm them against the chill that was always in her bones. One day she would rub herself to nothing. Just a shapeless pile of ash and char where a pile of ash and char in woman shape had once existed.

Move.

SHE MOVED. SHE WOULD not burn up today. Or at least not this minute.

She stood, then turned and tucked the mosquito netting under the mattress of the bed. It wouldn't do for Bill to find the netting open. He wouldn't like it at all.

The tent was tall enough that Evie could stand fully upright inside. She walked to the flap – double-zipped, and a thick line of Velcro guarding its closure as well, though somehow those mosquitos always made it inside. Zip, zip, rip, and she threw open the tent flap.

The furnace blast of air that slammed into her face and exposed skin gave lie to the impression that the air conditioning hadn't been doing much. She stepped out, the wetness that had dampened her exploding to saturation as her pores went into overdrive.

She closed the tent.

She turned back to the camp. As she did, a voice came over the loudspeaker situated in the middle of camp, the canopies and tents that were Happy Africa Safari Tours radiating out from it like spokes in a wagon wheel. The voice was that of a woman, low and pleasant and with the somehow rounded tones that Evie had come to associate with this place. Naeku's voice.

Evie heard the same things she always heard in that voice: confidence, intelligence. Freedom.

"All guests who wish to participate in the evening drive, we will be leaving in five minutes. Don't miss this chance to see nature in its full glory!"

She heard Bill snort in her mind. Heard him say, *"Nature? As though we've seen a lick of that. I guess shitting in a hole counts, I guess that's natural. Not the type of thing I'd expect to pay for."*

To which she replied, *"But, Bill, we* didn't *pay for it. We didn't pay a thing. We* won *it. I* won it, *actually. I wrote my way to this small freedom."*

This last was in her mind, too. She was not insane enough to say something like that aloud. Stupid? Perhaps. Untalented? Likely.

(Murderess? Definitely.)

But *insane*? Not yet.

Naeku continued speaking: "And we *will* be leaving in five minutes, *sharp*, so don't be late!"

Evie wavered. She wanted to go – if only to be near Naeku. She liked the guide, and she sensed the guide liked her, too. The first friend she'd had in years, and even if that was because Naeku didn't know her the way those back home did

– and so did not yet despise her – it was nice to have that again. To have someone who looked at you with a smile in their eyes, instead of disgust or hatred.

But at the same time, she hadn't checked with Bill.

"Five. Minutes. *Sharp*."

That was what decided her. If only because those were the words Bill said when he was ready to leave, and Evie had been trained to follow them. The Pavlovian response was greater than the terror, so Evie turned toward the center of camp and began to walk.

2

THE COLLISION HAPPENED FIRST. That was not the end of her world, but it began the series of secondary collisions that would send her to the end.

Bernard "call-me-Barney-everyone-calls-me-Barney-but-not-like-that-shitty-purple-dinosaur" Eberhardt was a man who came from money, and looked it. His shoes – expensive loafers worn defiantly in a place that laughed at such weak footwear – were the color of old nickels. His skin was the sallow shade of bills that had seen too many days, been passed between too many hands. His eyes were tarnished dimes, sometimes twinkling when the light caught them just right, but usually dark and sullen.

He was like Bill. Only where Bill had limited his powers to the domination of one person, Barney Eberhardt had sought to rule the world. It had gone dreadfully wrong, somehow, which was why he was here.

If Evie had written stories anymore, Barney would have been a villain, pure and simple. As it was, in real life, he was nothing so dramatic. He wasn't a villain, he was simply evil. The banal kind that our world preferred, who sought sex and power from the weakest, and took what he could get at any turn.

He wasn't Hitler or Mussolini, who were *Evil*, and had the force of will to move masses and cause global catastrophes. Just evil, of the sort that took only from those who allowed it, any number of which were more than willing to allow him to take everything from them on the off chance that he, a powerful movie producer, would give in return.

His kingdom ranged far and wide and deep, but from what she understood it was all falling down. Just one more in

18

a line of dominos that had begun with a similarly large and moneyed man, and who had shone a light on a business rife with corruption and power.

Once Upon a Time,
why was anyone really surprised?

He had spent much of his stay at Happy Africa on the phone, and he was on the phone now. It was a blocky slab of plastic with a stub of an antenna jutting out of one corner, a sat-phone which he wielded like a club, reminding everyone that its presence meant He Was Connected, even in a place designed to sever such connections.

"Jesus, Herb. Just tell the bitches and their lawyers to go fuck themselves and..." Barney broke off, frowning as "Herb" responded. "No, no. Of *course* don't really say that, numbnuts... Yes, of course I know how tenuous... Listen, Herb, I don't care how –"

Barney had just passed by Evie's tent when she left. Now he spun about, his body pivoting with astonishing speed and grace for a man as thick and solid as a barrel full of nickels. His feet drove hard at the ground as though to insist that he was not what moved; that it was really the earth itself that moved around him.

Kick, kick, and before Evie could react – before Barney even seemed to register her presence – he slammed into her. The phone jostled in his hand. It didn't leave his ear, but it jumped a half-inch higher than usual, which was as far from his face as she had ever seen it.

"Je-*sus*, woman!"

Evie did not speak. The impact with the Money Man had driven the air from her lungs. She gasped, managing only a breathy croak in response.

No response was merited or required. Barney simply shoved her out of the way and continued on whatever path it was he had determined was his to walk.

"No, Herb. No, not you. Just some idiot who – look, release another one of the 'I've decided to withdraw to seek counseling and personal healing' things and... Herb? Herb?"

Barney withdrew the cell phone from his ear. Shook it. Glared at it for failing him in the midst of so crucial a sentence – for to Barney Eberhardt, all his utterances were crucial. Money talked, and mortals listened.

He actually growled then – wildlife from a different kind of jungle – shook the phone once more, and noticed Evie was still watching him.

"The hell do *you* want?" he said.

Again, no answer was expected. He kicked the earth away once more. Dirt puffed around his nickel shoes, rising in thin clouds in the hot, dry air. The dust settled on his loafers, coated his dress socks. "Selena?" he called. "Selena? Goddammit, Selena!"

He strode toward another tent. It was larger than hers and Bill's, of course. The Executive Package, it was called. She had not been inside it, but knew from pictures on Happy Africa's website that it held not only a refrigerator, but a chest of drawers, a steamer trunk, and a vanity – all of which looked as though they might have been plucked off the Titanic moments before the luxury liner went down.

Barney was ten feet away from the Executive Suite when the tent flap opened. Zip, zip, rip, and Selena Dancy walked out.

She slipped outside the slit in the heavy canvas, arranging the lack of clothing which famously failed to cover the two main "talents" which had risen her to the top of the Blist, and kept her there long enough to bag a meal ticket named Barney Eberhardt.

She pulled the halter top an inch lower, whether to hide her underboob or expose a bit more overboob was impossible to say, then went on tip-toe to plant a quick kiss on Barney's cheek. Such a kiss could only have been a platonic or even downright matronly action from anyone else. Selena infused it with the famous sexuality that had made her a household name, even before the sex tape that leaked to coincide with the opening of her biggest hit, *Open Drawers.*

Barney flushed. Flushed more as she rubbed against him. "Geez, Barney, give a girl a chance to get ready," she sighed. Like the kiss, the sigh screamed, "I'm here, baby, and whatever you do, I'll... just... *love* it."

Evie couldn't be sure if Barney's flush was born of lust or irritation. He *sounded* angry, even as he wrapped his thick arms around her and pulled her close, their pelvises grinding together hard enough to merit a hard PG-13 in whatever movie they made next.

"You bitched at me to come on this thing for a year, so why are you always late when it's time to go?" he growled.

As though to back him up, Naeku's voice came over the loudspeaker. Jolly, but firm: "Three minutes, folks. And we're leaving. Spots are still open, but they're going fast!"

Selena pouted the pout that was only slightly less famous than her eternal co-stars, Right Boob and Left Boob. "Not like we've actually seen a single animal."

Barney grinned. "You wanna skip the tour? Just... umm... 'stay in'?" A lascivious eyeroll toward the Executive Suite followed the question.

Selena smiled the come-hither smile that had graced gossip mags and saturated the blogosphere since well before the first time she turned twenty-nine (she'd been twenty-nine nearly a decade now). She ground harder against Barney, and his flush could not be misinterpreted.

She leaned in close…

… and twisted away at the last second, nimbly ducking out of his embrace and walking away. Headed toward the center of camp. But she knew how to make an exit. Hips swaying, long legs glistening with sweat that looked professionally-applied, she cast the line: "You coming or what? Maybe tonight'll be our lucky night."

The dust puffed at her feet, too, but none of it stuck to her expensive hiking boots or her legs. It would not have dared.

Barney watched her slink away. His color heightened. "Not looking like a lucky night so far," he muttered.

And he followed her. He always did. Money talked, people listened. But *sex* demanded action.

Evie had stood still during the entire exchange. It was a talent she had discovered early, and had refined and honed to razor sharpness in the last few years. She stood so still that sometimes she thought she might have fallen into the space between molecules. Into the nothing that was so much of everything.

Even after Barney had rounded the corner of the tent where the staff prepped the guests' meals, she stood still. Counting down from ten in her mind.

Ten… nine… eight…

Barney and Selena were going on the tour, and she could do nothing about that. But she could stay out of their way.

Seven… six… five…

Then, in a fit of independent pique, Evie decided to skip the last numbers. She decided to move.

IF SHE HADN'T MOVED right then she might have missed what came next. Her world might not have ended – again – after all. But she started walking early, and right when she would have said, "zero" – the intervening numbers perhaps giving her time to reconsider her decision to go out on the evening "safari," to return to her tent and so miss the thing that happened next – she passed by the Executive Suite.

Zip, zip, rip. The tent flap opened, and Evie turned to see Bill Childs looking out. His free hand was still adjusting his belt, then zipping up his fly before the sight of his wife sunk in far enough to halt his movements.

For a moment, she thought she saw a glimmer of something she had not seen in years – since the third time he slapped her, in fact. She saw shame.

Then the glimmer of shame was swallowed up in the bright fire of anger by which Bill warmed his soul. He finished zipping up his pants, the motion now infused with defiance. The muscles in his arm and forearm bulged and danced beneath the skin. He was a powerful man, an all-state running back who had made the transition from athlete to Normal Human without losing much of his speed, and absolutely none of his strength.

Bill stepped out of Selena and Barney's tent, and that was when Evie's world ended. Not when she saw him adjusting his clothing after visiting a starlet's lair – she had seen that kind of thing before, though he had never managed to reach so high in his other adulteries – and not even when he flexed his muscles in a way that dared her to say something.

It was that moment of shame. The moment she saw the shadow of the man she thought she had married, and saw him murdered by the soul of the man to whom she had *actually* said, "I do." No... the moment *after* that, when the shame disappeared and his eyes returned to their usual disdain.

"There you are," he said. "I've been looking everywhere for you."

The magnitude of the lie should have stunned her. Ten years ago, she might have responded with a clipped, "And what? You thought I might be hiding in a diseased vagina?"

Now, though... she felt shame flood her cheeks with blood. She felt her gaze fall to the ground at her feet. She felt her body slump, her back stoop in the classic posture of prey that knows its time has come, and so knows it can finally relax.

It killed her. Part of her knew it was wrong. Part of her shouted, *Why are you feeling shame? You didn't do anything!*

But, as always, she shoved that part of her back into its dark closet, locked the door, and ignored its cries until it fell silent again. Because she *did* deserve it. She deserved it, and whatever else Bill might deign to deal out to her.

> ***Once Upon a Time,***
> ***a girl killed someone,***
> ***so she deserved what she got.***

"Sorry," she said. She lifted her eyes to his, about to stammer another apology.

She hadn't meant to meet his gaze. It was an accident –

(and more shame blooded her cheeks)

– but she did, and before she could look away Bill whispered, "You better stop staring at me like that, if you know what's good for you."

She turned away. She didn't realize she had done it. If she had, she would have felt even more ashamed – how dare she turn her back on the man who *fed* her, *clothed* her, *protected* her from the Big Bad World – but she heard Naeku's voice speak, "Almost ready to leave!" and followed its sound without thinking.

24

Bill sighed, and his footsteps slapped down on the hardpack behind her. She smelled the musk of his sweat close by. That smell used to bring a smile to her lips. It meant he was home from work. It meant he would hold her and kiss her.

Now, the smell drew her mouth into a thin line. Now, it meant he was near, and would not kiss her, and any touch would bring pain.

She kept walking. Her shoulders pinched together. Bill had never hit her in public, but her body didn't register whether other people were around or not. It just knew where the blows tended to come, and knew that Bill behind her was rarely a good sign.

There was no pain. No sudden explosion of heat followed by the electric rush of a welt pinching out of her flesh.

Zip, zip, rip.

She looked over to see another tent exhale a blast of air conditioning, and along with it Craig, Gale, and Grams Jensen. The Jensen family wore the expressions that typified them, and which had seemed to Evie at once foreign and familiar. It had taken her two days to place the look: they were happy. They loved each other.

As always, Craig had a hand wrapped around Gale's much smaller one. The little girl's father was a software engineer, and looked it: pale skin that spoke of long days below flickering fluorescents, hunched over screens, eyes tracking never-ending lines of code. A small man who looked like he might break or melt or simply blow away if he stepped out of the climate-controlled life he obviously led. But his hands were surprisingly large and strong, and they always hovered protectively near Gale, dancing out every so often, touching the girl's cheek or hair or shoulder as though he could not quite believe that his daughter was there, or that she was real.

The motions baffled Evie. It was not as though Gale gave the impression *she* was going to blow away or disappear.

Gale's free hand held her cane as it always did, the long white length of metal with the red tip darting back and forth like a divining rod that would lead her through darkness into a future that could only be bright.

Evie had been in a tour car with them on the first day. She hadn't stared, of course – Bill would never stand for such rudeness – but she wondered, as no doubt all the rest of the guests did, how much fun the girl could possibly have on a safari designed to let people see wildlife up close and personal.

As soon as Craig began to speak, Evie wondered no more.

"WE'RE GOING THROUGH A long plain," Craig had whispered to his daughter. "It's dry, so dry you can see the cracks in the ground, like tiny earthquakes stirred this place up just before we got here. Scrub is everywhere, dotting the land like... well, like dots. It's dying, everything looks dying or asleep, but it's still beautiful. It goes on forever.

"To the left, the sun is still low. You can't look at it, of course, but it's painted everything yellow and made even the dead scrub look like it might jump up and sprout leaves at any moment. Dying, but ready to be alive as soon as God gives the word."

"Are there elephants?"

"No, sweetie. No elephants. But I bet we find some today."

They hadn't. No animals at all, in fact. But listening to the man whisper to his daughter had made Evie see things she never noticed before: the way the heat waves rose all around, the tiny puffs that signaled a lizard or some other small animal scurrying from shade to shade, the drifting shadows of birds flying high overhead.

The little girl asked about elephants several other times. Evie would have given all she had to give those elephants to the child.

The memory ended with a snap as Grams – the *first-liveliest* person Evie had ever met – bent over to tie a shoe. She grunted as she did.

"You okay, Grams?" asked Gale. Her voice was high and lovely, the chirp of a bird greeting a new day.

"No," said Grams – whose name no one knew, other than perhaps her son, and Craig would not tell – "I'm not okay, sugarplum. I'm old, and my body feels like a sardine truck ran over it." Evie had trouble believing that mere camping – or even a mere nuclear warhead – would do more than momentarily irritate the wiry old lady, who always smiled, and made no bones about ogling the young men among the guides, and was in essence everything Evie wanted to be someday and knew she never could. Still, whether her pique was real or just a show of the dramatic by a thespian of life, Grams groaned as she straightened, then said, "Camping... whoever invented camping should be shot."

"Or run over by a sardine truck!" Gale chirped merrily. Then she turned toward Evie. "Hello, Mrs. Childs," she said.

The girl had memorized the names of everyone in camp on the first day. On the second, she shocked everyone by "seeing" them whenever they were within ten feet of her. On the third, the camp guides had started calling her, "Little Elephant," both for her favorite animal and because, as one of them explained to the girl in the mess tent, "The elephant has the best sense of smell in the animal kingdom, with his long nose. But even with your tiny nose, you might just be the smelliest little creature in all the world."

Now, Evie whispered, "Hi, Gale. Ready to see the elephants?" Her voice was pitched low, and quiet as a worm sliding through the dirt – what she thought of as her Safety Voice – but Gale heard her.

The little girl giggled. "I hope so," she chirped, then oriented on Grams, who still fumbled with her shoelace. "You going to die down there, Grams?"

Grams made dire, threatening noises as she straightened, twin gunshots sounding as both knees popped, but her eyes smiled.

Gale spoke again, her chirp muted this time. "Hello, Mr. Childs." Her tone made it clear she did not like Bill.

Bill ignored her, poking a thick finger into the middle of Evie's back to let her know she was moving too slowly. Evie sped up, but managed to say, "See you, Jensens!" without feeling too guilty at the minor deviation from Bill's unspoken instruction.

Grams and Craig responded in kind. Craig added, "Bill." The software designer's lip curled when he said the word, as though he had bitten into something distasteful.

Grams didn't speak. She just looked pointedly away from Bill, her lips puckered.

Evie appreciated Grams' silence. Craig's scorn would burn inside Bill, she knew. And when the fire got too bright, he would have to vent the heat somewhere.

Her shoulder blades twitched an inch closer together.

She kept walking.

"One minute, folks!" Naeku said on the loudspeaker.

28

3

THE CAMP HAD FOUR Land Cruisers, two trucks for carrying supplies to and from camp, and a conversion van that Evie suspected doubled as a ferry for the guides and other camp employees whenever someone had a day off and wanted to venture back into the dangers of civilized life. All of them bore the camp logo – a widely-grinning lion with the leg of some undiscernible animal in its mouth, its right front paw curled in an improbable thumbs-up – on the front doors and the hood.

Two of the Land Cruisers were currently idling. The Land Cruiser was the vehicle of choice for safari outfits like Happy Africa, and had evolved to a marvel of form and function. The Toyotas' trademark sleek lines were nowhere apparent in these models; instead replaced by a marked blockiness around the fenders and roof that somehow conveyed that its drivers and passengers were tough survivors... but tough survivors who insisted on the amenities. A black bullbar – a cage that covered the front grill, protecting it and the front headlights from any accidental impacts – heightened the impression of "ready to rough it," as did the thick, heavy-tread wheels.

Instead of emptying out behind the vehicle, the exhaust port burrowed through the car's hood, clinging to the front windshield so it could belch smoke above the top of the Land Cruiser – which Naeku had explained would allow the car to ford streams or even rivers much more deeply than a normal car could do.

Most important of all, each of the Cruisers featured a pop top: a roof which, at the touch of a switch, would detach and extend upward several feet. Passengers could then poke their heads out to rubberneck or take pictures of any wildlife they might encounter.

Selena and Barney sat in one Land Cruiser, Barney once more speaking on his phone, gesturing wildly to whatever poor soul had earned his attentions. No one else was in the vehicle, which didn't surprise Evie: who would want to be cooped up in a car with a non-stop screamer?

There was that for Bill, at least: he didn't scream. Indeed, when he was angry he tended to be at his most quiet.

In the other Cruiser, Gunnar Helix had staked a claim on the back seat.

Evie wasn't on the computer much – Bill didn't like it when she was, said it was a waste of time that could be spent on important things like chores and cleaning – but she stole a guilty moment here and there. So she knew what YouTube was, and knew that six million subscribers was nothing to sniff at.

As always, Helix had his camera with him, and was swiveling around in his seat, capturing images that he would beam to the masses of breathless women – and more than a few breathless men – pretending to care about outdoor survival tips in between moments where his shirt would somehow contrive to come off.

"Six million subscribers... one for each can in this here six-pack!" he'd said only moments *after* meeting Evie, and only moments *before* his shirt came off. He laughed and flashed teeth so white and straight there was no way nature had produced them alone. When he went to shake Evie's hand on the first day, Bill inserted himself between the online celeb and The Little Woman. He took Helix's hand instead, and Evie saw Bill's arm muscles bunch and knew the grip was anything but friendly.

30

Helix's own arm seemed to swell. His smile widened, and his "Pleased to meetcha!" seemed genuine, though Evie saw a flash of pain in Bill's gaze and knew Helix must have given better than he got.

Don't hurt him!

She thought it, of course. Saying it might embarrass Bill.

Now, in the back of the Cruiser, Helix laughed into the camera, having obviously told one of his jokes – all of which involved his musculature. His shirt was on now, his million-subscribers-each abs hidden, but even as she watched he pointed the camera at his biceps, grinned, and laughed to the swooning hordes who would see this when he got home and updated his channel.

As she watched, the Jensens piled into the Cruiser with Helix. Grams sat in the back with the online star, and Helix obligingly took a shot of both of them, his arm around her shoulders. The old woman laughed and slugged him in the ribs, both of them obviously enjoying one another's company. Then the camera swiveled to Craig and Gale. The two waved gaily, though Evie thought she saw something pained flicker in Craig's eye.

She had seen that look a few times, always when he looked at his daughter. Evie didn't think he was the type to mourn over her lost sight – the family was too full of light for such a dark pity to take much hold – and worried that the girl might be sick. She knew the Jensens had enough money to be comfortable, but not enough to toss thousands of dollars at this kind of vacation. A huge expense, especially given the fact that there had to be other places that might be more fun for a blind girl to experience.

It had the feel of a last wish, and given the little girl's obsession with seeing the elephants, the father's sad looks in her direction… Evie was worried the last wish was Gale's. She

31

hadn't asked, though. To hear the little girl was sick, even dying was not something Evie would be able to handle.

The world was too dark already. It needed such bright souls.

A JAB AT HER shoulder encouraged Evie to move toward the Cruiser with Selena and Barney. Bill wanted that Cruiser. Probably to ogle Selena.

Would he even bother hiding it from her? Probably. Or if not from her, then surely he would prefer not to have Barney know that his girlfriend/longtime ingenue/sexual business partner was enjoying getting plowed by another man. Particularly someone as lowly in his eyes and – just admit it – as poor as Bill.

He wouldn't care about *her* pain, Evie knew. Just as she knew that it was right for him not to. It was probably her fault Bill was stepping out. He'd done it before, and she'd tried to be better for him.

Better for him? You should kick him in the junk so hard he can never use it again and has to pee through a tube for the rest of his life.

She flushed, even as she stumbled toward the Cruiser where the Hollywood power couple waited.

That's not true. I shouldn't think such things. Bill is good and protects you and pays for you to live and even if he didn't and he was simply capital-E Evil…

… it'd be no more than you deserve.

She sat down. Buckled in.

No sooner had she done so than Bill said, "Shit, I forgot my wallet."

He didn't say anything else. He didn't have to. She unbuckled her belt, then got out and ran to their tent. A hurried search turned it up quickly: a simple billfold of light brown, well-worn with use. She had given it to him right before they got married. It came with those empty plastic sleeves meant for photographs of loved ones, and she'd put a picture of herself in there and said, "So you can carry me wherever you go."

"On my ass?" he asked, and laughed.

"Well, it's where you spend most of your time," she laughed back.

That was when times had been good. She had no idea whether her picture was even in there anymore. She didn't dare look, either. A few years ago she had gotten his wallet to pay for a pizza he ordered. He was off his chair in an instant, grabbing the wallet and tearing it out of her hands so forcefully it ripped two of her nails away.

The pizza man saw it, and looked away as though to say, "If I can't see you, you can't see me." That was how most people reacted to things like this.

She didn't know if he would have reacted differently to what came after, as punishment for touching Bill's wallet. Maybe. Maybe he would have called the police. Maybe they would have come to save her.

But she would have turned them away, because this life was hers. She had earned it and could not allow someone else – no matter how well-intentioned – to take her away from it.

She brought the wallet back to the Land Cruiser, throwing herself in. She held out the wallet to Bill, but he didn't take it. He didn't even notice it; he was too busy stealing not-very-covert glances at Selena.

She put the wallet in her pocket, so she would have it should he require. He didn't mind her holding it – or anything else, she was good at holding things – so long as she didn't open it.

After putting the wallet in her pocket, her gaze settled on her hands, clasped in her lap. It was the safest pose to assume.

4

EVIE HEARD A LAUGH and looked over to see inside the other Cruiser, where Grams now held Helix's camera, aiming it at Gale while Helix made a stream of quarters fall out of the girl's nose. The little girl couldn't see the magic trick, but she laughed so hard and loud it broke Evie's heart.

She's just a little sick. She'll be fine.

Another lie.

Movement drew her eye from the small, bright family and their small, bright play. Legishon appeared out of nowhere, as he always seemed to do, and hopped into the Cruiser where the magic show played. Legishon (or "Leg" as he preferred to be called) was a Maasai. He spoke little, even on the outings. The cars were equipped with a radio and sound system that allowed one guide to provide patter for everyone, and it was usually Naeku who provided the running commentary. Leg was a silent one, but fire sparked his eyes: the eyes of someone who knew always where he was, what he was there to do, and the best way to do it. He was a warrior who had left his village, but could not quite bring himself to leave the wild.

He was short and thin. Not much of him, but what there was all muscle and bone. Evie suspected he could outrun a cheetah, outclimb a monkey, and arm wrestle an elephant to a tie. Every movement - even simple ones like getting into the Cruiser – was marked by an almost balletic grace and economy of motion. She had seen him on the first day, whittling something with the large knife he carried at his belt. The motions were sure and swift. He was carving an elephant for Gale – which had delighted her, as all things did –

(not sick even, just her dad misses her mom or something, not sick at all not her and definitely not dying)

– and his knife moved so quickly and surely it was as though Leg was less carving and more reigning in another living creature. It was not hard to imagine him skinning an animal with that knife, eating the meat, using the bone for needles and the tendons for bowstrings, wasting nothing, and all the while speaking not at all but taking everything in with eyes that flickered with silent fire.

He saw her looking and grinned. His teeth were whiter and straighter than Helix's, but unlike the YouTuber's grill, Evie figured that the Maasai's teeth were one-hundred-percent homegrown.

She found that satisfying, for some reason. Nature *should* do a better job than a Beverly Hills orthodontist. Or at least be *capable* of a better one. And in Leg ("My name is Legishon but you can call me Leg because obviously I am ten feet tall," he said with one of his rare grins), nature had proven such to be the case.

He waved. Evie dared a half-smile, then felt Bill watching her and dropped her gaze to her lap again.

Leg's door slammed.

Time to get going. Obviously none of the other guests wanted to miss dinner on the off-off-*off* chance of seeing some evening wildlife. Evie spared a glance and could see that the rest of the camp seemed to be milling around the mess tent like omegas around a fresh kill, waiting for the moment when they would be allowed to feed.

Evie knew about alphas and omegas. She had researched them during stolen moments before the trip. She knew which she was.

36

THE DRIVER'S DOOR OF Evie's Land Cruiser opened, and now Evie fully raised her gaze, because she knew who would get in. Naeku. And Evie could never help but stare at the young woman.

Like her brother, Leg, Naeku was thin and short. Anyone else with her frame would be described as petite, but Evie found it impossible to describe Happy Africa's lead guide this way. Not someone who flowed from place to place, utterly at ease and seemingly knowing everything about every animal that had ever lived, and every event that had ever happened within a hundred miles in every direction. Not someone who could tip back a fifty-gallon water can and roll it into place behind the food prep tent without the least expression of effort.

Naeku smiled. Her teeth matched those of her brother. She wore the khaki shorts and shirt that all Happy Africa's employees wore, but over it she wore a red and yellow shawl that hung off her shoulders like an off-center superhero cape.

Evie thought of the woman as a superhero. She knew from her research – the same that had taught her about alphas and omegas in animal groups – that it was rare for a Maasai woman to escape her village. The social pressures, the poverty, and a lack of prospects outside that world all kept the women in the village. Most Maasai women were circumcised – a vicious experience where they would be feasted and feted at night, and the next day a woman of the tribe would walk into the girl's mud hut with a razor blade and remove parts of the girl's clitoris and often much of her labia.

It happened without anesthetic. It happened when the girls had reached puberty. And if it didn't, the girls would never marry among their people, and would be ostracized by most.

Evie wondered if Naeku had left the village because she refused to let such a thing be done to her. It pleased Evie to

37

think that was the case; to picture the young but already-powerful Naeku staring down the elders of the tribe, or grabbing the razor blade away from the woman who would mutilate her, then running. It was an easy image to conjure, since Naeku was everything Evie was not: smart, well-spoken, *strong*.

Evie would have let it happen. But not Naeku. No, not someone like her.

Naeku got in the car. She turned to face the four passengers and smiled broadly.

"We ready to go?" asked Naeku. Her voice in person was even more beautiful. Honeyed, rounded, without the hitches or quivers that Evie so often heard in her own voice.

Strong.

No one answered Naeku's question, but Evie bobbed her head up and down. Naeku's smile widened as she faced forward. "Then let's go."

NAEKU HELD A RIFLE in her hands, the same one Evie had seen her bring on every one of the expeditions. "They're for your protection," said the camp manager on the first day, "but we've never had to use one." The guides/drivers were actually guides/drivers/guards, which was why Naeku was clipping the rifle into a rack attached to the middle of the front bench seat. Just in case.

Evie thought she would be frightened of the rifle that went out in every car on every safari expedition – she could see the barrel of Leg's own rifle in a similar holder on his seat as well – but the weapons didn't bother her at all. In Naeku's hands it seemed no more dangerous to her than a stove flame. Something to be used, to be respected, but never to be feared.

38

Naeku withdrew the mic of the CB radio that hung below the front dash like an electronic bat. Clicking the button on the side, she said, "Ready?"

Leg's voice came back, the same rounded, honeyed tones with a touch of bass that made it beautiful in a completely different way. "Of course." Then he rattled off something in Maa, the lovely language of the Maasai.

Evie saw Naeku's eyes in the rearview mirror. They narrowed to slits. The expression of displeasure fled as fast as it came, and when she answered in the same language it sounded calm, almost bright.

But Evie knew what hidden pain sounded like. Leg had just said something his sister didn't like. And judging by the long pause between her last words and his response – a clipped "Let's go then" – she had given as good as she got.

No more words.

It was time to go.

THE LAND CRUISERS' WHEELS bit into the ground and they lurched forward, heading to the gate.

Evie had been excited to win the all-expense paid safari trip, but she couldn't help wondering: if they were going to a wild place, full of wild creatures, would staying in a tent be safe? What would keep a lion from clawing its way through the canvas and making a midnight snack of her?

The answer proved to be elegant in its simplicity: acacia.

The guides called it a shrub, but it looked more like a tree to Evie: some of the specimens she'd seen were nearly twenty feet tall. Naeku had told them that the branches, all of which spread from a tall, thin central trunk, giving the plant a vaguely umbrella-like appearance, were usually covered in green this time of year.

"The giraffe graze the lower branches, a beautiful sight," she had said.

Though as with everything else, the acacia were bare, denuded limbs thrust upward like worshipers offering prayers to whatever sky gods might provide them rain and allow them to survive.

But a lack of leaves did not strip them of the one feature which made them excellent at keeping animals out of camps. The branches sported one-inch spines that, when the branches were woven together in a tall *boma*, or wall, around the camp, became Africa's answer to barbed wire. Evie had ventured to touch one of the thorns at one point. Just a light pressure had drawn a thick drop of blood from her skin.

The *boma* was six feet tall, and wrapped completely around the Happy Africa camp, broken in only one place by a metal gate exactly large enough to allow two Land Cruisers through it, traveling abreast about a foot apart.

The gate was now closed.

In front of it stood a few Happy Africa employees, lounging against the metal gate and not bothering to hide the glances they kept shooting at the employees' mess tent.

In front of *them:* the camp manager, Regina Heronen. Evie thought the Brit was about fifty, but her sun-leathered face obscured her true age. She could have been younger or older by ten or fifteen years. She always wore a low-hanging cap with the New York Yankees logo, further hiding her age. Evie had thought – almost madly – the first time she saw her that the only way to really *know* how old the woman was would be to cut off a leg, count the rings, and multiply by two. It was appropriate, because Regina seemed – in form at least –

less a woman than a block of wood roughly carved to resemble one.

She was kind, though, despite her tough outer appearance. When Leg finished the wooden elephant for Gale, the camp manager wouldn't let the Maasai warrior provide the gift without "a proper wrapping," which turned out to consist of a beautiful piece of cloth woven in much the same way Naeku's ever-present shawl had been.

In the stories Evie no longer wrote, but could not help but think, Regina would have been a wizardess. A creature wise and strong, who did not often meddle in the affairs of the less-wise men and women she protected, but when she did she changed the world. Powerful, but a power tempered by the kindness she had learned at her mother's knee while learning spells and potions and magics that had made her what she now was.

Here, in the real world, the kindness that had shone when Evie saw Regina talking to Leg that night was gone. Regina had been leaning against the gate, browned arms crossed over her flat, wide chest. When the Cruisers got within a few feet she stepped away and walked toward Naeku's vehicle, gesturing for her to roll down the window.

Naeku did, leaning out to talk to her boss. A whispered exchange occurred. Regina spoke Maa, though the words sounded clipped and ugly when she spoke them, not at all the dancing curves of Naeku's speech. She spoke it now, heightening Evie's suspicion that this was bad news.

She hoped she wasn't telling Naeku that the outing was cancelled. Bill wouldn't like that.

Evie glanced at her husband and, sure enough, he was frowning. Quiet, but she sensed the anger roiling under the surface. Saw it in the way his fingers kept opening and closing, like he wished he could squeeze the life out of something.

Bill would never do that to her. Sure, he roughed her up from time to time, but he *did* protect her. He wouldn't –

"What's going on?" he asked quietly.

Evie's gaze jerked to Naeku. What the guide said might well determine whether Evie's night was unpleasant, or *very* unpleasant.

What I deserve. No more than I deserve.

Regina flicked a glance at Bill, scowled – didn't seem Bill had many friends at Happy Africa – and walked back to the gate without a word. She raised a hand and waved her forearm in a circular motion.

The gate opened, just like it would have opened for a wizardess making that same sign. Here, it was Happy Africa employees who did it, but in Evie's mind she could plainly see the great gate of Castle Africus opening under nothing more than the force of will of the Great Regina.

The story ended. Real life intruded. Naeku spun to face the passengers. "Good news!" she nearly shouted. "Rain is forecast later. If it rains too hard, we might have to turn back, but –"

"How is *that* good news?" barked Selena.

Naeku continued smoothly, as though the interruption had not occurred, "– rain might draw out some wildlife."

Everyone heard the word she did not say: "Finally."

Her smile redoubled. "And even if the rain *does* fall hard, so much the better for our chances tomorrow!"

Barney's turn to bark, "Right. Like that's gonna happen. This has been the deadest live animal safari ever."

Naeku's smile never faltered. "Nature lives on her schedule, not ours."

"Tell that to the money I spent on this colossal fuckup of a time waste," muttered Barney.

Again, Naeku acted as though she heard nothing. "I am so excited," she said. "I feel like this trip will be the lucky one!"

The smile was wide. Sincere. But just as Evie knew what tension sounded like, she knew what a smile looked like when it was used as a blanket to hide a lie rather than a window to the truth.

Naeku was lying. She didn't think the trip would be a lucky one. And, though none of them knew it, she was right.

It was now just after six p.m., which made it a little less than four hours until the first of them would be killed.

THREE:
contact

Interlude

THE GIRL RELAXES IN the woman's arms. Not the relaxation that comes with danger passed. This is a deeper, more frightening relaxing. The inertness of a dead thing. The woman feels her. The girl is dry of sweat, which terrifies the woman. It is so hot here, and to be so empty of moisture that you cannot sweat... the time is coming short. The end is coming, and the woman would have known this even without the bringers of that death being so close.

The girl cries out. The woman cannot tell if the little girl can even hear her anymore. Delirium is a more likely alternative.

But the story is still there. A weak thing, perhaps, but it is all the woman has.

GALE TURNED AROUND, AFRAID for a moment of what might be behind her. As she turned, she immediately realized two things: first, that the door of the treehouse which she had just come through was nowhere to be seen, as was the treehouse, the tree, and anything else of her world. There was just more of the great, strange place in which she had suddenly found herself. More marshmallow mountains, candy trees, spun sugar bushes dotting the landscape as well... and all of it leading to an ocean in the distance that she suspected was unlike any ocean she'd ever seen, because even at that great distance she could tell it was all orange soda (her favorite!).

The second thing was even stranger, for though Gale *had* seen a snowman before, she was certain she had never seen one made of peanut butter.

"Who are you?" asked Gale.

The creature gave a funny little bow, one thin chocolate arm crossing its center sphere (its body?), and it said, "I am the Peanut Butter Snowman." Then a jelly tear squeezed out to its cheek. "I've lost my mommy and daddy. Can you help me find them?"

"Of course!" answered Gale, for she was a good girl who loved to help others. "I'm sure we'll find them easily."

"Oh, no," said the Peanut Butter Snowman. "I have looked all day, everywhere from the FlufferNutter Range to the Deep Fanta Sea. I can't find them."

More jelly tears came – he cried grape from one eye (his eyes were Reese's Peanut Butter Cups, of course), and strawberry from the other.

Gale drew a handkerchief from her pocket (Grams said never to leave home without a hankie!) and dried the Peanut Butter Snowman's tears. "Well," she said brightly, "you *may* have looked. But you *definitely* didn't look with me."

She held out a hand, and the Peanut Butter Snowman took it with his own. He was Enchanted, the girl knew, so she would not have melted chocolate in her hands, which was good because that would be quite sticky.

"Let's go find them," she said.

1

THEY HAD NOT QUITE left the camp when the Land
Cruisers jerked to a sudden halt.

Evie was afraid of most of the people in the camp – so
many things scared her, which was just one more reason she
needed Bill – but two of them did much more than that. They
terrified her on a level that not even Bill in his worst, most
silent moods could hope to match.

The rest of the camp's visitors were all white: mostly
from the United States and Canada, but there were also three
Germans and a couple from the Ukraine. The final two,
however, the two who scared her the most, had skin every bit
the dark match of Naeku's, and walked with the assurance of
people for whom nothing on the safari was new, or
unexpected, or even much noticed.

Why they would come to Happy Safari, no one knew.
The guests had all speculated, but only when the two men
were not near. As soon as they entered the mess tent, or even
just walked by, people fell silent. The silence remained until
the two men left.

They had come late to camp, shuttled in on one of the
supply runs a day after everyone else arrived. Apparently that
was a habit more than a one-off, because Tharcisse and Jean-
Paul were late for this jaunt as well. They were running for the
Land Cruisers, not waving or calling, but the expressions on
their faces making it clear they intended to go out on the
nighttime excursion... and they would brook no dissent or
alternate outcome.

Their names were Jean-Paul Shabani and Tharcisse
Ntiranyibagira – the latter of which Evie could only remember

because it sounded a bit like "Bagheera," the name of the black panther in Disney's *The Jungle Book.*

Evie figured either of them could have killed such a creature with nothing more than a look.

Jean-Paul, the one running in the lead, was thin as Leg, just as wiry and muscled, but where Leg had a grace of motion and form, Jean-Paul seemed to be all hard edges and angles, all knees and elbows and teeth. Even his earlobes were slightly pointed, giving him a diabolical appearance that was not helped by the hand-rolled cigarettes he smoked, and which surrounded him with an eternal cloud of foul-smelling darkness. His eyes never rested, constantly on the move as though always trying to gauge where the nearest escape route lay, or the nearest weapon should he choose to stand and fight.

His first name had surprised her, but Naeku told her he was Burundian, and many people there had French names – a legacy of Belgium's occupation of the country after World War I.

Still, Evie could not think of him as a Jean-Paul. The name conjured up svelte men who spoke quietly of wines and art, philosophizing over cigars and brandy in parlors devoted exclusively to such things. Not this angular, angry-looking man. Not this man whom she feared so deeply, for reasons she could not understand.

There was only room for one additional person in each of the Land Cruisers, which meant that Jean-Paul and Tharcisse would have to split up if they really meant to go out.

She hoped Jean-Paul would get in Naeku's Cruiser. That he would come with Evie's group. But he veered to the right and got in Leg's car.

A moment later, Tharcisse opened the passenger door of Naeku's car. He got in, moving with the easy silence of a born predator.

Tharcisse made Jean-Paul look about as intimidating as one of The Wiggles.

He wasn't as big as Bill or Helix or even Barney, but Tharcisse somehow gave off an impression of being more massive then all of them put together. Certainly his musculature rivaled Helix's. But where Helix's muscles imparted the same impression as his teeth – something not totally natural, but rather crafted with great care, assiduous routine, and a ridiculous disregard of expense – Tharcisse's muscles were as natural and imposing as granite walls. They bunched under the jeans and gray t-shirt he always wore, as though angry at the indignity of such confinement. His knuckles were whitened by scars and callus, and what looked like knife wounds had forever marked his arms.

Not that those were noticeable on first inspection. No, what Evie noticed first – and what she suspected *everyone* noticed first – was the thick line that passed across Tharcisse's neck, just under the point where his square jaw met either side of his throat. It stretched from one side to the other, and there could be only one reason for such a feature: someone had once cut Tharcisse's throat.

How the man survived such a gruesome wound was a mystery, and none of the other guests speculated on it. At least out loud.

In the story Evie told of him , the ongoing fantasy she stole away to whenever she dared, he was an assassin supreme, on a mission from some Dark King in a tower, waiting for his moment to strike a blow that would lay an end to all peace and bathe the world in war and blood.

"Welcome," said Naeku –

(another lie another hidden truth, she doesn't like this man any more than I do, doesn't like him at all)

– to which Tharcisse utterly failed to respond. He looked straight ahead, which meant that Evie could not see his face, since she was seated directly behind Naeku and he was seated in the front passenger seat, but she suspected that if she could she would have seen him staring out the front windshield. Staring, but actually *seeing* nothing at all because nothing out there interested him in the least.

"Okay," said Naeku. "Here we go, then!"

She put the Cruiser in gear and it lurched forward. Leg's car followed, and now they were beyond camp. The wild had them.

GRAMS DIDN'T LIKE SEEING the two men sprinting their direction. At least it was the little one – Jean-Luc, was his name? – who was headed for their car, rather than the hulking creep who ran close behind.

"What is it?" asked Gale when the car stopped. "Why are we stopping?"

Grams opened her mouth to answer, as always feeling the pull of knowing what was coming. Knowing that it wouldn't be long before *it* happened. And when it did, the family would be done.

Don't think that way. Enjoy what you have. Enjoy your family in the now that remains.

"It's two of the guests," said Craig. "I guess they didn't hear the announcement that we were leaving."

"Which guests?" asked Gale. Then, lowering her voice as though imparting a terrible secret, she added, "Is it the mean ones?"

Helix snickered in the seat beside her even as Grams barked, "Gale! Manners!"

Gale hunched, embarrassed. "Sorry, Grams."

Grams – and she was Grams to everyone, even her own son; had been since the day Gale was born – sniffed. "You should be. Always respect your elders, Gale." Another sniff. "So it's *Mister* Meanie and *Sir* Angry McBossypants to you."

Helix's snicker was replaced by a full-throated laugh. "You are a cool ol' broad," he said.

It wasn't often that Grams was glad Gale was blind – she had lost her sight when she was six, to a disease with an unassuming Latin name but which Grams more properly referred to in her mind as That Sonofabitch – but she had to admit that her blindness made a few things easier. The blindness made it easier for "cool ol' broad" Grams to coolly flip Helix the bird.

Craig frowned at her, of course. He was a good dad – the best she'd ever seen, which made the moment blindness came to his daughter such a double cruelty, because her son would feel the pain of it just as acutely as her granddaughter.

And what of the second cruelty? The one we're trying so hard to avoid out here?

Crueler by far. Yet somehow she'd known it was coming. As hard as she'd tried to leave her past behind, she'd known it would happen – Jack Jensen would reach out his cold, dead fingers and stir up her family again.

The stirring came on one of their group trips to the doctor. It was a tradition Grams began on a day, early in her blindness, when Gale was afraid to go alone. Craig offered to take her, and said he'd even have a physical himself. Gale brightened a bit at that, but it wasn't until Grams said *she'd* go, and get a physical as well, that Gale finally agreed to leave the house.

It worked out well, not least because Grams found she liked Dr. Kalighi. He was in his mid-thirties, which meant he was old enough to know what he was doing, but young enough that he still worried about messing up, so was double-careful with everything. She had her own GP, of course, but Dr. Kalighi was too much to resist. She had to admit that it wasn't just his medical acumen that attracted her, either: he was handsome. Balding, but he was one of those lucky few for whom baldness is more blessing than curse – like that one actor with the over-square jaw who was always beating up bad guys who generally managed to yank his shirt off before he destroyed them.

She *liked* that actor. And she liked Dr. Kalighi. So at the end of Gale's appointment Grams signed papers to have her info turned over to his practice and that was that. He was careful, thorough. He smiled as well. Even when looking over the parts of her she'd just as soon not have people look over much, his smile remained.

He wasn't creepy – she knew *that* look all too well – just pleasant. He poked and prodded with the best of 'em, but somehow it didn't seem nearly as bad as it had with her old doctors.

And after she got dressed again, he kept up that smile and sometimes she felt taking a bite out of him. Maybe not a small one, either.

She was under no illusions: she was old. She was wiry in a way that was off-putting to many, the kind of thin that puts people in mind of crotchety folk who shake canes and yell at "those darn whippersnappers" to get off her lawn. But when she smiled at herself in the mirror, every so often she still saw the traces of the beautiful woman she had been.

Old? Sure. But she still kept a rubber in her wallet – which she had stolen out of Jack's pocket that last day, an act of rebellion she carried with her everywhere – for the same reason she kept her joint and lighter with her: because you just never knew when there'd be a moment to grab some fun.

Once in a while she thought about jumping Dr. Kalighi. She had no idea how she'd go about it, of course, but it was fun to dream, and all the dreams ended with both of 'em naked in bed, smoking that one joint – she'd even managed to smuggle one of 'em out here! – passing it back and forth and remembering what had just happened. Then Dr. Kalighi would turn to her and ask, somber, quiet, if she would do him the honor of scheduling her next breast exam as soon as possible and the whole thing would start up again.

Foolish old woman.

She often thought it. But the lighter and joint always rode in her pockets, and the condom always reminded her that, old or not, she was strong. Her world might fall to pieces – and actually had done so more than once – but she always rose up. Built back what had been lost.

She was proud of that fact. Proud that she had created a new world, where Craig turned out to be a magnificent man, and he chose an equally magnificent woman to be his wife. Lord, Grams had cried when Janey died, how much she had cried.

Most important, Craig had raised an astonishing girl. Gale was the best, kindest, sweetest sugarplum of a girl in all the world. Which made that last visit to Dr. Kalighi all the more cruel.

Just physicals for all of them. And though Craig and Grams and Gale each took polite leave at appropriate times when one of the adults needed to get undressed for part of their exams, they mostly just sat in the same exam room together, waiting for their turn.

Dr. Kalighi was quieter that day. That was the first thing Grams noticed, and the thing that put her on edge.

Ashes, ashes – is it all about to fall down again?

He was quiet with her. Usually she liked to go last – she had discovered that at her age, anticipation was more fun than actuality in most cases – but this time he said he would examine her first, and something in his face told her this was less request than necessity. Dr. Kalighi barely spoke, only the occasional, "Breathe in," or, "Okay, you can sit up," marring the silence.

He was even quieter during Craig's exam. And quietest of all with Gale.

The girl noticed, of course – she noticed more things blind than most sighted people could manage. But she didn't ask anything about it. She matched Dr. Kalighi's silence with her own, waiting for him to say whatever he would. Such a good girl.

Dr. Kalighi said nothing. Not a single word the entire time he examined her. But he kept glancing at her, with eyes that were so very sad.

It wasn't a surprise when he gave her an extra lollipop and asked if she'd be willing to sit in the waiting room for a minute after the exam. Gale was terrified, so Craig glanced at Grams and Grams nodded and went with the frightened girl.

Grams was frightened, too.

CRAIG CAME OUT OF Dr. Kalighi's office with a look of despair she'd never seen on his face before. Not even when Janey died.

He kept looking at Gale. Kept drinking her in. He smiled at his daughter, but the smile was shallow, as was his voice as he tried for a semblance of jolliness for the tense little girl.

"What did he want?" Gale asked.

He shook his head at Grams, and the words in his eyes were just as clear as when they asked her to wait with Gale.

Don't say a word. Don't ask a thing. Later. There'll be time later.

But not much, as it turned out.

She drove back home with them – with her sweet sugarplum and her amazing son whose thin cheer she could have scratched off with her pinky nail. He took them to a restaurant on the way home.

"I've been thinking… we should go on a safari."

Gale brightened up, her dark mood swallowed in delight. She'd loved animals since she was just crawling around in diapers. No dog was too big for her to pat, no cat too ornery for her to charm.

She especially loved elephants. Babar stories had been her favorite as a very little girl, and they still held a treasured space on her bookshelf, between the braille versions of *Stuart Little* and her *Magic Treehouse* books.

Gale was so happy at Craig's suggestion, but Grams' fear only grew. It grew through the day, which turned out to have a surprise expedition to the zoo that Craig "had been planning to surprise them with." The first time he ever lied to her, which she would have known even if he hadn't stolen away for a moment to call the office on the cell phone; even if she hadn't heard the whispered request for a half-day off.

The fear crescendoed after Gale was in bed, smiling despite the upset tummy she'd suffered after being plied with enough cotton candy, chocolate-covered frozen bananas, and churros to send an army battalion into diabetic shock. Grams was there, of course. She lived with her family, and since Craig paid the rent and took such good care of them both she did her best to respect his obvious wish not to talk about what he'd learned.

55

Her attempts ended as soon as Gale's door was closed and they were in the hall.

"Craig, I've never laid a hand on you, not as a babe and not as a boy. But I swear to Heaven I will lay you over my knee and swat your ass hard if you don't tell me right now what's going on."

He gestured for her to follow him into her room. He had her sit on her bed. He told her.

She had to bite her lip to keep from screaming.

She would remember that blood-taste to the end of her life. Knowing it signaled the countdown to that end, in so many ways.

"Do we tell her?" she finally asked.

Craig hesitated. "No. Not yet." He thought again, then repeated, "No. After the trip."

The trip should have been impossible – safaris usually booked years in advance. But it had been a bad season or two, she gathered, and a lot of the outfits were taking all comers, no matter how late the booking.

Happy Africa. The name was almost a slap. Because how could it be a happy thing when they were going for such a sad, sad reason?

Gale very quickly realized something was wrong, of course – so much sight from a girl who could not see – but never asked about it. And Craig never spoke of it again. Neither did Grams, though it broke her heart every time she saw Craig looking at his daughter in a way that told her he was saying goodbye to the most important thing he would ever lose.

NOW THEY WERE HERE, and the safari was a bust. Or should have been. But somehow it was all right that they hadn't seen any animals. It was all right, because time was short, and short time means it doesn't matter where you are. All that matters is those final minutes.

Happy Africa. And in spite of the dryness, the heat, the utter lack of any sights other than dead grass, trees, and scrub, Grams found the name accurate. Because Craig – and especially Gale – made this place a happy one. Sadness was there. The sadness of parting, and of a disease that would destroy what they had enjoyed – that was *already* destroying it, as old Jack reached out and put the disease that had killed him into another. Destroying even from the cold grave.

But she would not let him win. Not completely. She would be happy. She would show Gale a good time – even if it was the last truly good time.

She would smile at the guides, and make friends. She would play Uno in the tent with her family every night, announcing each card as she played it so Gale would know what was in play and could lay down a card from her own hand – all of them marked with points of braille Grams and Craig had carefully punched in each – in turn.

They openly conspired to let Gale win more than she lost. *Much* more.

It was good, it really was. But it would be over far too soon.

It would all be over.

Why? Why someone so young, when an old coot like me is just muddling along, healthy as an ox and with a heart that the bald and dashing Dr. Kalighi says would be the envy of any thirty-year-old?

She had no answer. She saw Craig was thinking equally dark thoughts. But they laughed. They smiled.

And yes, she would even take every opportunity to waggle her eyes at the not-at-all-bald but still delicious-looking Gunnar Helix. And, should he make a crack about her being a "cool ol' broad," she would definitely flip him the bird.

That was the kind of thing good people did, when tragedy loomed. They fought its reality at first, and after the reality sunk in they fought to *love*. Love, to the very last. And nothing said love like being your best self.

CRAIG'S EYEBROWS RAISED, OF course. Sighted or not, he believed Gale would somehow know when Grams made a rude gesture or rolled her eyes. She probably did, too, but Grams wasn't raised in a nice house or a nice neighborhood. She'd been raised in a very ugly part of Detroit, and she figured that Craig was lucky she'd at least managed to stop openly saying the f-word by the time Gale came along.

Helix raised his eyebrows, too, but not in reproach. He laughed, delighted at her spunk, then laughed harder as she nodded at him and told Craig, "Boys will be boys. And women will always be around to remind them how very sad that is for them."

"What does that mean?" Gale asked, even as Helix roared anew, camera covertly pointed his way so he could use this moment, Grams right in center-stage if she signed a release form, center-stage with face blurred if she didn't (though she knew she would).

"It means next time Grams says to respect her elders, she doesn't mean herself because she clearly has growing up to do," said Craig.

Grams flipped *him* the finger. Craig couldn't help but laugh. He had once told Grams he didn't know if he was more excited or terrified to find out if Gale was going to take after her.

And now you'll never know.

She forced the thought back. Buried it deep under the laughter that he piled on thick as dirt over a coffin.

A moment later, still obviously unsure what had happened or why it was funny, Gale laughed as well.

Her laugh was always bright, tinkling. A tiny bell that rang for people; only instead of ringing them to a meal or to serve, it was a ring that told people now was time to laugh, to play, to *live*.

Six months. Maybe less.

More laughter. Bury the thought. Bury it deep.

Grams responded to Gale's laugh with one of her own, creating the sound as much by force of will as by need, and was still laughing when Jean-Luc or Jean-Paul or Jean ValJean or whatever his name was got in. Laughing hard enough she barely noticed the hard look the man got in his eye when he heard the entire carful of people – even the sullen-seeming guide, Leg, was chuckling now – laughing.

Be honest. You barely notice anything anymore.

Six months. Six damn months.

IN ACTUALITY, THE TIME left was much, much shorter. Grams could not know that, of course. She wasn't God – as had been so recently, so ruthlessly, proven to her. But if she *had* known, she would have laughed all the harder, and held her family close. Because that's what people do when they're about to lose something.

2

REGINA WATCHED THE LAND Cruisers move away. A huge trail of dust followed each, billowing in the wind of their passage, then gradually settling back to its bed as the lack of any other wind left them solely in gravity's sway.

Please, let them find something. Anything. Even a lame antelope who does nothing more interesting than eat a piece of grass and take a shit. So long as there's something they can take a picture of.

Pictures were where it was at. Pictures were the lifeblood of an outfit like Happy Africa: pictures posted on Facebook with happy faces tagged so their friends could see how close they were to the *real live animals*; pictures tweeted out with hashtags like #onsafari or #lovinlife and even occasionally (and best of all) #happyafricarulz; pictures shared at work amongst people who *ooh*ed and *ahh*ed and *oh*ed and then – most important – went home and booked a reservation.

There had been no pictures to speak of for weeks. Months. Only bare-text blog entries or terse Facebook posts or tweets that all boiled down to: "Didn't see shite. Ripped off. #HappyAfricaSucksBalls."

Happy Africa didn't suck balls. Regina was very proud of the camp, proud of the guides and cooks and other employees. She was proud of the outfit in general, and immensely proud to have landed a job better than any she could have dreamed of.

She had come to see the sights. She had stayed a woman in love – not with any man, but with the wild, often ravaged beauty of the land all around. She had been eighteen. At twenty she was a camp guide, and now... she was the manager of Happy Africa. It was *hers*. Oh, sure, some faceless company that had tentacles in everything from entertainment to pharmaceuticals actually owned the place. But she had raised it, and that made it her child far more than it was theirs.

And it would all come to an end if they didn't have a few pictures, and a few happy guests. That was what she had told Naeku before she left.

"You have to show them some action tonight. No matter what, find something." Regina's Maa wasn't great, but she was one of the few people around who hadn't been born to it who took the time to learn. Even if she'd only been able to string a few words together, she would have done her best with them, because she didn't want the guests to know how close Happy Africa was to death.

One or two more bad trips. No more reservations by jealous coworkers and friends. Happy Africa would tear down its tents, sell what it could... and a week later Uncaring Africa would have reclaimed the space Regina had worked so hard to carve out.

Naeku, as always, smiled, though she had to be surprised Regina had come to her like this. It wasn't usual for the camp manager to brace any guide at the gate. One more thing Regina was proud of: she was careful, she had an eye for detail. She planned ahead. Normally if she had to say something to a guide about an upcoming jaunt with the guests, she told them well in advance, in the privacy of the tent that doubled as her living space and office.

Normally.

She hadn't had anything to say to Naeku before the guide left tonight. There was a rainstorm projected (finally!), but Naeku knew to turn back if it got bad enough, and knew what that turn-back point would be – probably better than Regina. Nothing to say she didn't already know, nothing at all. But when Regina heard Naeku's voice on the loudspeaker,

61

telling everyone that they were heading out, she was gripped by a sudden certainty: this trip would make or break them. This one outing with only half the guests would mean the difference between Happy Africa's continued happy survival and its most unhappy demise.

When she actually intercepted the Land Cruisers at the gate, she still didn't have much to say. But she had to say *something*, so after only a moment she settled on the obvious: "It might rain. You have to show them some action tonight."

Naeku's reaction, predictably, was to smile through her surprise and say, "I'll try. But with the rain maybe coming tonight... and nature –"

" – does not live for us, I know," Regina finished. "But I also know we won't survive another season of angry customers."

Naeku's eyes flicked back, taking in several of the passengers. "They're already angry," she answered, the Maa curving gracefully from her lips, the smile never leaving her face.

Regina glanced back as well. She loved her job, but she did not love all the people she met. Some of them were pains in the arse. Some were unpleasant, joyless duffs who existed to ruin moods.

A few – a very few – were right bastards. Bill Childs and Barney Eberhardt – or the two Big Bloody Bastards, as Regina had taken to calling them in her mind – were some of the worst she'd seen. Predators if ever she saw them. Barney was a straight-up prick who would sell his gran for a penny, and Bill... Regina was fairly certain Bill beat his wife.

It hadn't happened in front of anyone; the man was cautious about it, that was certain. But if it did, Regina would gladly cover the man in gravy and leave him outside the *boma* for a night.

Some very bad things hunted at night.

But that hadn't happened. Yet. For now, the Big Bloody Bastards were paying customers. And they, along with the rest, could sink Happy Africa. With just one or two more negative posts, they could kill off the last hopes of the camp.

So two facts remained:

First: Naeku was right: she couldn't control the animals. She couldn't control the weather.

Second: It didn't matter, because tonight was *everything*. Regina just knew it.

"Do your best," she whispered, imparting as much emotion as she could through the filter of a language that constantly tripped her tongue.

"There is no other way to do anything," Naeku replied. Her smile was still there. Her voice was carefree.

But Regina knew she was scared. The Maasai woman didn't have anywhere else to go. She wouldn't go back to the village, she was certain. She would die first.

Happy thoughts.

Regina didn't know if she was mocking her own dark mood or telling herself to buck up. She mulled that question the rest of the night. Long after the Land Cruisers had disappeared from view, and much later, after she became occupied with greater questions – like where the guests and guides were, hours after they should have returned; and why no one was responding to her calls on the radio – that question repeated with grim tenacity in the back of her mind.

3

"HEY, BUDDY, YOU LOSE your watch?" Barney said. Evie had known it was coming – there was no way someone like Barney would let anyone inconvenience him without at least a small jab. Tharcisse had interrupted Barney's personal schedule, if only minutely, and such an affront would have to be avenged. But Evie knew Barney's jab would miss. He was fighting out of his league.

Barney had had the air of someone who had gotten his way every day of his life. Not because it was given him, but because he *took* it. Because of that he not only believed he was invincible, but he failed to note the rare occasions when someone more powerful than he entered the ring.

Evie knew what power looked like. She knew it as an incoming fist, or an open mouth that could point out every flaw with a quiet earnestness that would reduce her to tears – mostly because they were always so right.

She knew the power of pain, above any other. And while Barney held that power in his hand, but Tharcisse had made it a part of his soul. Barney was a tough customer, but when he took something from someone, Evie knew that person would still be alive. Barney would tell himself that was because he wanted whatever poor victim he had crushed to know, and to *live* with the knowledge, of his or her defeat. But the reality was there were lines few men or women would cross.

Tharcisse, she sensed, had never seen a line he was afraid to vault over and land far beyond. He had the same air of someone used to getting his way… but with the added edge of someone who would not take what he wanted from cringing people. Corpses did not cringe, and Evie thought Tharcisse

64

was the type to kill anyone who got in his way, then peel what he wanted from their dead hands and do nothing but smile as he did so.

She shifted her story of him: he was no assassin, he was a demon brought up from the Nether Kingdoms for a nefarious purpose. No one knew what it was, only that there *was* such a purpose, and they would likely suffer for it. But since he was a demon who looked like a man, and since the people of this land believed in live and let live, and the wizardess would not punish even a demon until he showed his fangs, he lived among them. Which did not change how dangerous he was to any who might stand against him.

Evie hadn't stood against him. She did not intend to do so in the future.

But she watched him as the Land Cruiser bounced and jounced its way toward the set of ruts that served as something of a road during the safaris. She was amazed at her courage –

(What if he turns around? What if he sees me looking?)

– but she couldn't help it. Her eyes returned, again and again, to his powerful, thick neck. To the broad muscles of his back that bunched and relaxed with every up and down of the Cruiser. To the scar that peeked at her from around the curve of his neck.

Her danger sense, honed over the years, started pinging away like a sonar in one of the World War II movies her father had adored. Movies like *Das Boot* or *The Enemy Below*; even newer ones like *The Hunt for Red October* or *U-571*. Dad had loved the underwater thrills, the sense of hunter and hunted. Most of them featured that same ping she heard in her head now, that flat electric tone that repeated faster and faster as unseen dangers closed in.

Ping… ping…

The Cruiser bounced hard. Tharcisse grunted, the first sound he'd made on the trip. Everyone else complained about the heat, about the flies. Bill kept looking at Selena, and Barney kept fiddling with his phone which – blessedly – had stopped receiving or sending calls. Motion, noise.

Not Tharcisse. He sat and stared and made no sound and the *ping... ping...* in her mind continued. Then with the grunt, something changed. She thought she saw him shift in his seat. Thought she saw him reach for something she couldn't see.

Pingpingpingpingping...

The sonar was loud. Something was going to happen. Something was coming.

THE MOMENT ENDED ABRUPTLY when Selena said, "Can we pop the top?"

Evie breathed out as she saw Tharcisse relax a bit. Or maybe he hadn't even tensed in the first place. Maybe it was all her stupid imagination.

Stupid imagination. Hardly the words of someone who fancies herself an author – even a terrible one should be able to come up with something better than that.

"Can we?" Selena repeated. "It's all cooped up in here."

"It will let the air conditioning out," said Naeku pleasantly. She was already flicking a switch, though – obviously she'd realized that Selena Not Getting What She Wanted was a much less pleasant traveling companion than Selena Satisfied.

An electrical whirr slid through the passenger area as the roof of the Cruiser lifted away from the body of the car. The structure looked feeble, the struts and stands that supported the roof resembling nothing so much as a kid's first

Erector Set construct. But it worked. The lid popped off the Cruiser, and just as Naeku had said, the cold air popped out as well.

The blast furnace outside seared its way in, but Selena didn't seem to mind. Apparently she wanted more, actually, because no sooner had the pop top clicked to its maximum height than she was standing on her seat, looking around with a near-manic look on her face as the wind of the Cruiser's passage somehow contrived to whip through her hair without mussing it in the slightest.

"Please, Miss Dancy, sit down until we stop moving. It's not –"

Selena cut off whatever Naeku had been about to say with a terse, "Hey, shut up!"

"Miss Dancy, it's simply –"

"I said, *shut. Up.*" Selena remained standing, staring down at Naeku from her lofty perch.

Barney chimed in. "Your website said we'd see miles of animals and we haven't seen a single thing, so unless you want to be on the ass-end of a lawsuit, you let her do as she pleases."

Evie saw Naeku's lying smile slip back into place again. The chinks were showing, though: Evie thought she could see anger in the other woman's eyes. "We cannot predict the wild, Mr. Eberhardt. It's the end of an exceptionally dry season, which sometimes means –"

"That the animals are out hunting, lots of wildlife, but the dry season's been so long a lot of the animals have died off blah blah blah." Barney settled back in his seat, his tarnished-dime eyes hooded and spiteful. "We heard this yesterday, sweetie. Don't you have a new –"

He never finished his sentence, because the just then the Land Cruiser hit something. It flew a foot in the air, then slammed down with audible screams from the chassis, springs, and passengers.

4

SELENA FELL BACK WITH a screech and thought about a single fact that had followed her through life: it was no *fair*.

Her being angry about it didn't matter, of course. Lack of fairness, by nature, didn't care about your anger, or about anything but its own spread. And spread it did. It was woven into life – or at the very least, into hers. She had learned that a long time ago: in her last life where she lived in a two-cow, one-farm town where her beauty turned her not into an object of affection but a freak.

Her pa was a good man, she supposed. Or if not generally good, then at least good enough to know that she was "in for a rough row, and a lot of hoeing" (she laughed every time she thought of that last wording, given where she had ended up and what she now did for a living), and to take pains to hide his daughter's nature from the rest of the world. She was a farmer's daughter, the daughter of a farmer's wife, and in the eyes of her widowed pa, that meant she must be a part of the land.

The land was an ugly thing there. Dry and dusty. She saw pictures of Idaho once, and asked why her pa didn't move someplace like that, somewhere the land actually grew things without them having to fight up through hardpack and a thick layer of dust atop it all.

Pa laughed at that. "How?" he asked. And that single word with all the hopelessness of poverty – the kind of poverty that allows for survival, but no more – was enough to dash any hope of going someplace beautiful.

The land was ugly. A farmer's life was ugly. So, according to Pa's logic, *she* would be ugly. If not by nature, then by practice and habit.

He began dressing her in, plain, gray dresses long enough that they dragged in the ever-present dust until the gray shaded to a dingy brown that never completely washed out. Long sleeves, high collars. Victorian sterility in a shapeless smock of despair.

Pa pinned her hair back, then bobbed it, then brushed it so hard it lay utterly flat and shapeless against her head, moving from one t'other as each fashion proved useless in turn. She was too beautiful – her curse.

She went to school, of course. That was The Law, and though Pa hated losing his one and only farmhand for so many hours a day, he would not cross The Law. At school she saw nothing but lustful looks from students and teachers alike. She knew those looks well, since she helped her pa breed horses for the very rich Mr. Hoffer just outside town. Dirty work, disgusting work, but it was also some much-needed money on the side, and it taught Selena well how to spot the horses who were the early finishers, the ones who would do as they were told, and the ones who might well try to break their tethers and anything else they found until sated.

She stayed away from the latter, as much as possible. She succeeded, too – as much as possible, given who she was, what she looked like, and that rotten luck she was already coming to understand was her lot in life. Which, in a place like Rail Heights meant she made it through middle school before the wrong kind of stud found her.

SHE WAS ONLY FOURTEEN the first time she was raped. "So beautiful," murmured the boy who did it – Hank

Cremmins, whose father was so low he actually looked *up* to
Pa, if you could believe that. Hank was a year older than she,
and drunk on the Orange Alert homebrew his own pa made
out of corn and insults, and which was designed not so much
to dull its drinker, but to bludgeon out any thought of where
the drinkers were or what they were doing.

She understood the need to drink the stuff – she wished
she could go through life without knowing where she was or
what she was doing, too, and if Pa hadn't been such a teetotaler
(more bad luck!) she might even have been drunk, too, and
might not have remembered what happened.

But she *did* remember. She remembered the feel of
Hank's arms when he yanked her behind the bleachers after
she stayed late at school, trying to eke out a few more moments
away from the farm. She remembered his breath, hot on her
neck, then her cheek as he swung her about, already fumbling
with himself one-handed as he whispered, "Beautiful,
beautiful, want, want…" over and over.

She remembered his pants around his ankles. She
remembered his red shirt, which stayed on the whole time. She
remembered the awfulness of the actual act; him forcing
himself on her and then belching, farting, and falling asleep
within seconds of finishing.

She stayed there, crying on her back, wondering if he
would sleep if she crept away, or if he would wake and want
more. She worried about the latter the most, because he was
one of those last horses. Wild eyes, a dark need that was
beyond merely animal, that descended to places of sulfur and
heat and destruction.

He would destroy her if she tried to leave, she was sure
of it. He would take her again, then kill her.

She calmed when she finally realized this. Her shivers
abated.

Would death be so bad?

She put her clothes back to rights as much as it was possible. She stood. She stomped out from under the bleachers. She took no care for silence in any of it. She hoped that Hank would wake. She wouldn't let him do that *thing* again, nosiree. She would fight, and she would force him to kill her.

She had answered her own question by then. *Would death be so bad?*

No.

When she finally made it home – walking hurt, so it was full dark by then – Pa was standing in front of their rickety clapboard house, arms crossed. A statue he must have been since finishing the chores. Pa wasn't the beatin' sort, but she thought she might have gotten a whuppin' just the same had she not been such a fright, and had she not told him what happened.

She did tell him. There was no beating, but in a way what came was even worse. Pa shook his head and she could tell he believed her – but could also tell that he thought she'd asked for it in a strange way, looking the way she did. More than that, he could tell that they were barely hanging on as it was, and how could he afford to lose the work if he followed this through to the end? There would be police, a hospital visit. Maybe even court in Steel City, the county seat.

How could he do all that and not lose what little they had? How could *they*?

She tended herself until the bleeding stopped, and it wasn't fair.

She went back to work, and that wasn't fair, either.

She had cried the words –

(it's not fair why does this happen everything happens to me?)

– over and over since the moment Hank grabbed her. And it *was* crying, though the weeping happened only in her mind. But as the hot water of the shower poured over her and washed dust and blood and hopefully any traces of Hank Cremmins down the drain, the cries went from powerless wails of pain –

(*it's not fair*)

– to angry shrieks of resentment.

IT'S. NOT. FAIR!

She was a freak. Fine. She was so beautiful she made men – and more than a few women – crazy. Fine. She would *use* her freakishness.

She tried it first with rich Mr. Hoffer. It wasn't much, just a smile and a tilt of the head. But she put *meaning* into it. Old Mr. Hoffer was in his sixties. A grandfather who had been married – happily, by all account – for nigh to thirty years. But when she smiled, and cocked her head, he flushed bright red and left.

He called her as she and Pa were packing up and leaving. As she knew he would. As she knew he *must*.

"You're a good girl," he said.

"I try to be," she answered.

Silence. He fidgeted. Then, at last, moving almost as though hypnotized – which she supposed he actually was – he drew out five twenty-dollar bills. He pushed them into her hands in a moment Pa had his back turned.

"Take it," he whispered hoarsely. Then he turned away and never once did he show his face to her after that. Which was fine: she had what she needed, at least to start.

She should have saved the money, which was more than she'd ever seen in one place at one time in her life. Pa – and the universe itself – had taught her the importance of thrift. Of saving for a rainy day.

She once pointed out that rainy days hardly ever came to the farm, and that was part of the problem. Pa smiled a sad smile and said, "Every day, in every way, a little rain will fall."

But she didn't believe it. No, not no more. She was *done* with rainy days.

She used the hundred dollars. She bought six miniskirts, seven too-tight tees, and three pairs of shoes at the Goodwill store in town. The shoes were all of a sort that Pa had called CFM shoes when she once asked about them. She still didn't know what that meant, but decided it would stand for "Can Fix Myself."

She hid the clothing in a hollow log in the woods on the road between home and school. She changed from her shapeless gray/brown skirts every day.

Her grades went up first. It didn't take much.

After that, she paid a visit to the biggest boy in school. *That* didn't take much, either – it was the same thing Hank had wanted, but this boy had the dumb look of the horses who would do anything you wanted in return for what *they* wanted, and the added shade of an early finisher, and all the better for that.

After, she mentioned casually that she didn't much like Hank Cremmins. The next day, Hank didn't come to school. Never did after that, either, and she heard he was in a special place where they could tend to people whose backs were broken, and whose jaws were shattered to so many pieces that they would never eat solid food again.

She was glad. That was all. Partly because of what had happened to Hank, but mostly on account of *she was the one who did it*. Sure, the boy – she thought his name was Thad – and his friends had done the actual dirty work. But it had been *her* who made it happen.

Grades kept going up. She ascended through the ranks of the school until everyone – *everyone*, even the ones who hated her – wanted to be her or screw her or both. She gave what she would in return for what she wanted, and was happy.

Though it couldn't continue of course. That damn rotten luck. The *not fair* of her life.

THE SECOND TIME SHE was raped wasn't, strictly speaking, a rape at all, though not for lack of his trying. She saw that angry, animal look on the side of the road as the bigger boy lumbered out of a row of corn as she walked by. She was lugging groceries back from the small store that mostly carried eggs, milk, candy, and – of course – enough liquor to sink an aircraft carrier. She was already in her gray outfit, ready to see Pa once again.

She didn't know the young man by name, though of course she'd seen him around town. One of the many who made it out of high school by the skin of a hen's teeth on the vague promises of Something Better Around the Bend, and who then drifted aimlessly when they got out and realized there were already as far Around the Bend as possible, and instead of Something Better they were ass-deep in As Good As It Gets.

She saw the look, and she knew what would come next. She'd thought of nothing else in the two years since she'd been taken by Hank: the moment where it would happen again.

But this time, she knew what to do.

Her eyes went wide, and instead of struggling she fell into him, breathing into his ear, "I hoped you would do something like this… ever since I saw you…"

He was grinning and fumbling at his belt. She helped him. And when she found what was down there, she grabbed him with hands that were strong from hauling crops and pitching hay and guiding randy horses home. She squeezed as hard as she could. He screamed.

That was when she noticed he was wearing a red shirt. Just like Hank. And suddenly she wasn't squeezing, she was *pulling.* The muscles of her forearms corded, something she'd never enjoyed seeing before but now she loved it and willed more strength into her hands, her arms; then her legs and back, too, as she yanked at the man harder than she'd ever pulled on anything in her life.

The red shirt was all she saw. It got redder the harder she pulled. A dark, spreading red that surprised and delighted her.

She didn't stop pulling for a long time.

Then she went home, dropped off the groceries, and went to find Pa. He was in the barn, and when she found him she didn't tell him what had happened, or how the blood came to be on her hands and all over her gray-brown dress. He didn't ask, either. He pointed at the nearby pump, then went in the house without a word.

Selena washed her hands as best she could, then went inside and changed her dress. Pa's door was closed, and she heard him moving things in there.

She went back outside, because she did not know what else to do and felt wildly, insanely, as though Pa was probably waiting for her to get her chores done.

She waited, and ten minutes later Pa came out again, too. He was holding a packed bag and more money than she'd ever seen in her life. It beat what Mr. Hoffer had given her by three dollars and seventy cents, though it barely covered the price of the ticket on the bus that trundled into town once a day to fuel at the gas station that was the last one between Around the Bend and Just T'other Side of Hell.

"THIS'LL GET YOU TO the city. Carol will meet ya there," he said in the twang of what he called His People. She hated it, and had copied the accents (or lack thereof) of the beautiful people she saw on TV, in much the same way that she copied their hairstyles whenever she could, always flattening or combing or teasing it back to whatever horrible concoction Pa had settled on for the week before going home.

So it was with a proudly twangless voice that she answered, "Who's Carol?"

"Your aunt," he answered, and that was the last he thing he ever said to her. He took her silently to the bus stop in their very not-silent thirty-year-old Ford truck, led her silently to the stairs of the waiting bus, and kissed her on the cheek with such a quiet air that she cried as she had not done since Hank.

She got off the bus in the city. A woman was waiting there, who rushed up and kissed her and said, "Oh you poor thing" over and over. Aunt Carol – Selena hadn't even known such a person existed. Pa had never mentioned he had a sister, and since Ma died when Selena was only three, she certainly had no memory of her speaking of such a thing, either.

It was easy to see why, too: Aunt Carol was a freak just like her. Beautiful, and she had dared educate herself. She had actually gotten *out* of Around the Bend, and settled in Heaven.

Aunt Carol was a lawyer – a concept so far beyond Selena's sphere that it took nearly a week to understand that the woman wasn't pulling her leg. In fact, she was a full partner at the second-largest firm in the city, a shining star whose future as a litigator showed no prospect of dimming.

77

After the initial barrage of *poor things* had ceased, Aunt Carol looked at her. She went silent as Pa had, and fear froze Selena's spine. What was Aunt Carol – this bold, brassy woman whom Selena already liked more than anyone she'd ever met – going to do?

Aunt Carol phoned a cab. Selena was sure she would pass another wad of cash her way and send her packing as Pa had done. But Aunt Carol got in first, motioning for Selena to follow.

They went to a place called St. John, which sounded like a hospital but which was in fact a clothing store of a kind Selena had never seen. Aunt Carol gestured wordlessly to a woman who worked there and who dressed nicer than Selena imagined the Queen of England probably did, then pointed wordlessly at Selena.

The woman managed not to wrinkle her nose. She just took the girl in hand and walked her to displays of dresses that weren't quite Queen of England level, but definitely a few steps above Princess.

Aunt Carol bought five of them, for just over three thousand dollars. All for Selena.

Then, still without a word, she took Selena to a place called Burberry. She bought her two scarves and a handbag. Cost: twelve hundred dollars and change.

Off to a place simply called The Cut, where beautiful women with beautiful hair and outfits cut and styled other beautiful women's hair until it was more beautiful than it had started. The price of Selena's wash, cut, and style: an even three hundred, not counting tax and tip.

And finally, still with no words spoken, Aunt Carol took her to a place called called La Perla and for a hog's hair under seven hundred dollars bought Selena some of the dirtiest, most revealing, completely *lovely* underwear (the lady who sold it to her actually called it *lingerie,* just like on the TV!) she had ever seen.

Still not a word.

It didn't much matter by then: Selena didn't know what she could have said that would have made a lick of sense. She was too overwhelmed, and that feeling persisted as Aunt Carol spent yet more money on yet another cab to take Selena to what must surely be the tallest building in the universe.

A man dressed like a guard or a general – the doorman, she supposed; she'd seen a few on the TV, just like she'd heard the word *lingerie* – greeted Aunt Carol with a "Ms. Dancy," bowed slightly, and opened the door.

Aunt Carol nodded back. She still said nothing. Nothing in the hall, nothing in the elevator ride that made Selena's stomach lurch so bad she worried she might get sick.

Nothing when she took Selena down a long hall to a door with the number 15D on it, nothing when she unlocked that door and took Selena into an apartment whose front room was bigger than Pa's house.

Nothing when she marched Selena into a bathroom that looked like a palace, all marble and brass and not a spot of rust or even so much as a hard water stain anywhere to be seen. Nothing when she drew a bath in a tub twice the size of Selena's bed, and still nothing when she pointed from Selena to the bath, then to the neatly-wrapped packages that held all her new clothes.

And, finally, nothing as she walked out and shut the door.

Selena bathed quickly – the only way she knew how – being careful not to splash her new hairdo. She dressed in the plainest of the dresses Aunt Carol had bought. She could not bear to try the lingerie. She wore her old panties and bra.

She walked out to find Aunt Carol sitting on a sofa, dabbing at her eyes as though she had been crying. Aunt Carol turned to look at her, smiled, and finally spoke:

"Now, my dear, *that* is the real you. And don't you ever forget it."

SELENA HAD BEEN WRONG in her first assessment: this was not Heaven. Heaven would have been a step down.

Aunt Carol enrolled her in a private school. There she spent six months among girls who were so cultured they might as well have been aliens, but so kind and polite they did not make fun of the ignorant creature in their midst.

When Selena marveled at this, Aunt Carol said, "Beauty does that to people." Then she added with a smirk, "Or at least to most people. Makes them kinder than they should be, more trusting. Easier to move around." For the first time, Selena noted in Aunt Carol not just striking beauty and intelligence, but cunning.

No horsey, empty look here. Aunt Carol might be a princess – maybe even a queen – but she had more than a bit of wolf in her, too.

Selena loved her all the more for that. That, and the clothes, and the insistence that she take care of herself and learn learn *learn* all she could. Not just at school, but about the world. About "real life," which, it turned out, was more than sewing seed for crops, then doing the same with horses.

Selena's grades were poor at first. But they went up – some because she continued the practice of trade for trade, tit for tat, she had practiced at her old school. Partly because she found she actually enjoyed the learning.

She thought Carol knew both things... and that she approved of both, too. For all this and more, Selena loved Aunt

Carol. That love grew to something like adoration. Which made it all the worse when, six months after she arrived in Heaven, the queen of all suddenly crumpled in a deposition and was dead of a heart attack less than a minute later.

SELENA FELT WORSE THAT night than she ever had in her life. Not even Hank compared; his violation had been nothing compared to this rape of her heart. She was adrift, and worse. Most people adrift had at least some idea where they were, and where they would prefer to be. Selena had neither.

Aunt Carol had changed her will to make Selena the sole beneficiary – "Better that than your cornholing father," she said when she did it, and for the first, last, and only time Selena heard a hint of the twang of His People in her aunt's voice – but it turned out that all the high-priced lawyer's income had been very nearly equaled by her expenses. The car belonged to the Firm, and even the apartment was a rental.

Selena was left with six thousand dollars and change, all of which would be held in trust until she was eighteen. She was also told by "her" lawyers – friends of Aunt Carol's at the place Selena knew only as The Firm that she would be returned to her father.

Selena ran away.

She ran the only place she could possibly have gone. She ran to Hollywood.

AUNT CAROL HAD MENTIONED it a time or two. "I'm a stunner," she said once, "but you're an absolute *knockout*. You better study hard or you'll end up an actor, and what would I do with you then?" and she laughed.

Selena had liked hearing that. She liked the word Aunt Carol used: *actor*. Not act*ress*, act*or*. Like Selena was as good and strong as anyone else, and so deserved no softened version of a job title.

The day men were to come for her, to take her back to Pa's house and the town where she suspected she might meet a dark comeuppance given what she'd done to that boy the day she left, she ran. She had a thousand dollars in that same Burberry purse – ten times more than Pa's savings, which Aunt Carol had given her as a combination of "mad money" and "just in case." She went to the bus stop again. This time she didn't take a rickety claptrap, but a proper bus. A Greyhound, with excellent air conditioning, a nice bathroom in the back, and a movie playing on several screens at all times.

She took it to the only place she could. She took it to Los Angeles. She became an actor.

WHEN SHE GOT OFF THE BUS, she wasn't worried. *It's not fair*, which had reared its ugly head in the hours and days following Aunt Carol's death, had returned to its counterpart *IT'S. NOT. FAIR!*

She was angry. And she got what she wanted when she was angry. Bad luck or no.

It was five days before she landed her first job. It was as a walk-on in a commercial. Just background. But it was on a studio lot, and she saw a large man watching from behind the director as she walked back and forth behind an actor talking about expensive perfume (a sample of which she had decided to get from the prop boy, who had been staring at her, too).

The big man didn't stare. But his eyes flicked to hers constantly. She wasn't surprised when he took her away from the commercial before it was finished. No one said "boo" to him, either. He whispered something to the director, then took her by the hand and walked her out.

She had just met one of the most powerful producers in Hollywood: she had just met Barney Eberhardt. And that day Barney Eberhardt took her to lunch. He followed her into the bathroom of the nice restaurant, and made it clear he *would* have her.

But he couldn't. Because she gave herself before it came to that, and took from him in return.

She had sex with Barney Eberhardt, in the bathroom of a fancy French hotel, and willingly did anything he wanted and more.

The next day, Barney Eberhardt cast her in her first movie. And then her next movie, and three movies in, she was the first name after the title, and two movies after *that* she was the first name on the screen, period.

SHE DIDN'T FORGET WHAT her father had done. *Any* of it. Which is why she sent him a hundred and three dollars – and seventy cents – every week. A reminder of what he had done, and that she had not forgotten. It was enough to elevate his survival at Around The Bend, but not enough to shift survival to actual *life*. And she knew he would know that. She knew, too, that he would know how much more she could have done. It would gall him, and maybe send him weeping to that same old store to buy enough booze to kill himself with.

He sent her a postcard one day. She had no idea how he'd found her address – she lived with Barney by then, in a palatial mansion where there were as many servants as had been in her class at high school – but she got the card, saw who it was, and tore it up without reading it.

Then she thought better of it. She sent it back to him, with the words "I didn't even read this" scrawled over the near-illegible scrawl of his own. She put it in an envelope with one hundred and three dollars – and seventy cents – and that was the last money she ever sent.

She got a notice in the mail not long after. The bank that owned the mortgage on the farm letting her know it was to be auctioned as part of an estate sale. She ripped up the notice and sent *it* back (sans money), too.

Life was perfect.

But still no fair.

IT WAS NO FAIR that every movie came with Barney's requirements, which grew stranger and sometimes painful as time passed. It was no fair that people constantly whispered that she had gotten to where she was by sleeping her way there. That rankled, because *anyone* could sleep their way to the top; what she did was far more subtle, and devious, and powerful.

It was also no fair that she was getting older.

Barney had dallied with other women, which was fine at first, when she was the one *allowing* it. But when he did it on his own, before getting the go-ahead from her, that was just no good.

But she had lost her ability to make him do exactly as she wanted. And at last he showed himself to the wrong person, molested the wrong barely-legal kid. Now the world was crumbling down around him, and she'd gotten far enough into it that she worried it might destroy her world, too.

Not fair. So very much not fair.

THE SAFARI HAD BEEN her plan. They booked it over a year ago, and she had hoped then that it might renew her power over him. Then the lawsuits happened, and the investigation, and now she just hoped it would keep them out of the public eye long enough to hit the sweet spot: enough time that the storm passed and things returned to Business As Usual, but not so much that people forgot the beautiful and talented (yes, *talented*, dammit!) Selena Dancy.

The safari turned out not fair, too. No animals, no good-looking guides – the only one worth banging was Bill, and that was only because there was nothing better and she felt like if she didn't keep her hand in, so to speak, she might get rusty. She manipulated him in small ways, just to keep in practice.

But it wasn't enough. Barney barely paid attention to her – always on that damn sat-phone, talking to his lawyer, Herb Something-Jewish-Or-Other. When he *did* come around, she turned him away, because if she couldn't have it on her own terms he sure as hell wasn't going to get it on his.

For the first time, it barely phased him. He didn't like it. He grumbled. He even yelled a time or two. But his heart wasn't in it. He just didn't care the same as he used to, and Selena felt her power disappearing all around.

And now *this*.

NO ANIMALS. NOT ONE. Zip, zero, nada, donut. And now she was *falling* for Chrissakes'. Not one of the lovely falls she engineered on the red carpet, either, which always showed just enough leg and just enough boob to assure front-page coverage on the gossip blogs and the websites where "REAL CELEBRITY SEX" was much-touted, if rarely shown.

The bitch Naeku did it. She hit that pothole on purpose, Selena was sure of it (though, in truth, she wasn't sure it was a pothole at all, because did they even *have* potholes on dirt tracks in the middle of Butthole Africa?), and now she tumbled gracelessly back into Bill's arms.

He copped a feel, squeezing her ass with one hand, her right tit with another. She'd make him pay for that later –

(But will I? Can I anymore?)

(it's not fair)

– but for now there was nothing to do but right herself. She tried to push up. Couldn't at first. She saw Bill's wife – a pitiful woman, who granted had little to work with but obviously wasn't even *trying* to move her husband around like a chess piece, the way she should've done – looking away as hard as she could. She knew, of course; they always knew.

"Gotta be more careful, sweetie," Bill said

He squeezed. It *hurt*.

She screamed. Not because of the squeeze – it was because of what she saw outside.

"WHAT IS IT?" SHOUTED Naeku, and the Land Cruiser jounced to a halt.

Selena was vaguely aware of the other Land Cruiser stopping, too, its passengers – all but that blind girl, Gale, whom Selena had to admit to liking, if only to herself – pressed against the windows, trying to see whatever was happening.

She put herself to rights, scrambling out of Bill's clutches and pressing against a window herself.

"Out there," she whispered.

"Did you see something?" asked Naeku. "Maybe it's our lucky night!"

The Land Cruisers were equipped with several spotlights, each of which could be rotated in wide arcs that allowed nearly three-hundred-sixty-degree coverage. The light had waned as they drove, and the sun was a bare glimmer on a faraway horizon, so Naeku turned on the lights and swept a bright cone of over the dead land.

"What did you see?" asked Evie Childs.

Selena surprised herself by responding to the woman with the tone of an equal, instead of the hauteur of a queen. "I thought I saw…"

"What?" asked Barney. "What was it, babe?"

She pressed harder against the glass. Naeku kept sweeping the light back and forth. It illuminated scrub, some bushes that looked thoroughly miserable –

(No fair for them, either!)

– and not a thing more.

The man beside Naeku, Selena noted, the strange, frightening man who had arrived late with his strange, frightening friend, was the only one who did not turn. He did not look. He just… waited.

No matter.

"What did you see?" Naeku said quietly.

Selena peered out the glass. Looking for what she had seen – had thought she had seen.

"What was it?" asked Barney again. He was already punching numbers on his sat-phone. Apparently even satellites didn't get coverage here, because he grimaced and finally put the thing away. "What was it, honey?" he asked again, with slightly more feeling.

"Nothing," she finally managed.

A moment later, she returned to her seat. The Land Cruiser started rolling again – though to where, she had no idea. There was nothing out here. Everything was dead.

For the first time, that thought comforted her.

Nothing out there. Nothing at all. Everything's dead.

So I couldn't have seen that shape.

87

And I most certainly couldn't have seen all the other shapes, running through the dark beside us.

LATER, HANGING ONLY A few feet above her doom, she would have time to think that in a life paved with lies – to others and to herself – that thought was the single greatest whopper she'd ever told.

5

GRAMS SMILED AT HELIX out of the corner of her eye. Lord, he was a pretty one. She didn't get the impression he was much of a thinker, but with that smile, that face, and those big hunky muscles, he didn't much need to be, either.

He swung his camera from side to side, aiming it out the windows, moving with the easy fluidity of someone who knew his way around both sides of a camera. It was already dark enough that Grams doubted he was catching much, but perhaps he thought that the mere sound of his voice would turn his audience to quivering masses of jelly.

"And over here," he said (camera right), "we see nothing. While on this side," (camera left), "we see more nothing." Then he swung the camera toward himself and added, "Nevertheless," (close-up, smiling), "whenever you watch The Survival Helix, the view is spectacular."

Grams smiled, because Helix *was* entertaining, in much the same way as candy entertained. Her son, however, was a five-course meal. He had started speaking to Gale, describing the world around them, and within moments she fell into his words with abandon.

Craig had a surprisingly deep voice, the kind of voice you might hear reading the news or an audiobook rather than the one you expected from a software engineer. Strong, too. That strength was important, given what he had to do and be every single day. For Gale. For what was coming.

"It's dark out, dark inside," Craig whispered. "I suppose it should feel lonely, but it doesn't. It feels complete, like we're the only people alive, but also like that's the way God made the world, so us here is the right thing, and the only thing we have to worry about.

"Leg's light splashes ahead of it – that's the right way to say it, too: *splashing*. It moves ahead of us, but the grass and brush break it into little pieces of brightness that reflect off them, then those little pieces break to smaller pieces, just like the surf gets thinner and thinner the farther it goes up the beach. The light gets thinner, going from white to gray, and then the black is all there is forever."

The cab was dark, the better to allow them to see outside. Leg made no attempt to provide any patter. What would he say, anyway? "And over there... tree. And there... tree. To the left, in a huge change of scenery... several bushes."

Helix was taking it all in with his fancy, expensive camera that no doubt took eighteen-billion-megapixel pictures, allowing his viewers to get hot flashes over the sight of every one of his pores, and night vision so they'd miss nothing of him even on a dark night like tonight.

But he wasn't filming himself now, Grams realized. He had pulled himself away from the vision of himself and was now filming Craig: paying attention with the most important eye he had, which was the perfect round one at the center of his camera. That was how entrancing her son's voice was when he spoke like this – so full of magic that it could cure even Gunnar Helix of the most serious case of self-love Grams had ever witnessed, if only for a moment.

"Over to the right, the sun still hasn't fallen completely, and that one little speck of light so far away makes it seem like the plain goes on forever. Everything's a vast blank canvas."

"Like a painting being erased," whispered Gale, the child caught in the wonder of this moment, which broke Grams' heart anew.

"Maybe," agreed Craig. "But it's okay that it's being erased, because the painting will be drawn again in the morning, new for anyone to enjoy." He paused, then, in a rare moment where he admitted to such things: "I wish you could see it."

Gale answered perfectly. She snuggled up to her dad, wrapping her arms around his neck. She still wore her dark glasses, but even so it seemed like she was looking right into his eyes. "I *can* see it," she said, and kissed Craig.

Grams gently pushed Helix's camera down. Such things were not for YouTube subscribers. Such moments were sacred.

Helix seemed to realize it, too. He didn't so much as blink, just settled the camera to his lap, and looked away. He still listened, but who could blame him for that? When magic spoke, you *had* to listen, didn't you? The world, Grams believed, was full of magic, but rarely was it so open and so easy to recognize.

"What about... *them*?" Gale whispered to her father. In the dark cab, the whisper seemed to come from everywhere and nowhere at once. The voice of a kind spirit, a guide. "Are there any elephants?"

"Still haven't seen any of those, honey," said Craig.

Gale shrugged. "There's still plenty of time."

Craig smiled a smile Grams was coming to know all too well – she saw it all the time on him now, and felt it on her own face.

"Yes. Plenty of time," said Craig, lying with the smoothness and sincerity that only sociopaths and good parents can muster.

IN THE OTHER LAND CRUISER, Naeku swung one of the spots back and forth, trying to catch anything. Regina's words kept crowding into her mind. "Do your best," she had said.

Naeku was doing just that; as she had told Regina before leaving, her best was the only way *to* do something. But sometimes, she knew, even one's very best couldn't change things. Nature was the queen of all, and it was useless to pit your will against her.

Nature said when you were born, when you died, and how those things would happen.

Nature certainly did not succumb to the will of a mere person, even one as strong as Regina Heronen.

But Naeku would do all she could. Back and forth, back and forth went the spot. She wondered what her father would have said, if he could have seen her, driving along in a Land Cruiser and sweeping a bright light from side to side in hopes of catching sight of something wild.

He would have laughed.

That was true enough. Father had often laughed. That was the memory she had taken with her when she left. The other memories she did her best to leave behind. They came all the same, clinging to her like mosquitos, sucking her dry and leaving an itch in her mind as each flew away and was replaced by another.

He would have laughed.

She focused on the laugh.

Another memory pushed in: the laugh she had heard at the last. Not his – he only screamed. The laugh of the Other. The laugh that had been born of hunger and pain and ended when she saw her father disappear under a blooming flower of blood that sprayed so high she felt its drops on her face.

She swatted at the thought. It flew away, and before another parasitic memory could replace it in her mind, Naeku filled that space with Regina's words, spoken over and over in an unending loop: "Do your best, do your best, do your best."

"That is the only way to do anything," her father had always said. "Do your best, or do not bother. The world will never let you survive unless you do your best."

But you did your best, didn't you, Father? And we know how that ended.

She kept sweeping the light left, right, left, right.

Nothing.

Usually she found the last glimmers of day a beautiful sight. Not tonight. The darkness had seemed to smother the sun, squeezing and pressing until finally the light took a last gasp and died, falling into the infinite darkness of a forever night.

Now the sun was gone. Only the stars still shone.

BEHIND NAEKU, THE NATIVES were getting restless.

She had heard that phrase once, in an old "jungle movie" that Regina sometimes played in her tent. Naeku tried to watch it once, but found it too painful. Too many things about it were wrong, down to the very plants that had pretended to be wild things found in Africa but which she could see were transplanted from pots and jammed into infertile soil for purposes of the old black and white picture.

The "natives" of the movie were ridiculous, too. They were the right color – mostly – but as dark as they were, they also somehow seemed pale and ghostly. Perhaps some of them had been born in the wild places, but they now possessed only the soft bodies and listless eyes that she saw in the faces of most "civilized" people.

But as bad as the movie had been, as much as it made her frown and cringe, she laughed loud and hard when one man said it: "The Natives are restless." She couldn't get it out of her head, and said it over and over for weeks until Regina finally cornered her and threatened to dock her pay if she said it anymore, because there Had Been Complaints. Few things were as bad as when there Had Been Complaints, so Naeku stopped. She didn't think Regina would really dock her pay, but what if she did? What if she *fired* Naeku?

Where would she go then?

Nowhere. She would go nowhere. Perhaps just walk into the wild and keep walking until she lay down and stay laying down until she died, one way or another.

Certainly she would not go back to the place where she had been born. That place was dying by the time she left, but even if she had left it a vibrant and growing place, why would she *ever* return to the spot where she had lost so much? Indeed, in her mind it had ceased being a *real* place long before she left. It was only a tattered thing whose last frail threads of existence were defined less by themselves than the gaping holes left behind by all she had lost: her parents, her sense of self. Even parts of her own body had been taken there.

No. Never the village.

But if she did not find something tonight, then tomorrow she would certainly find there Had Been Complaints. The Natives were restless, and must be satisfied were that outcome to be avoided.

She would do her best.

And still nothing, nothing.

A mile further on one of the many dirt roads that crisscrossed this part of the land, and now Barney and Selena were muttering loudly to one another. Bill Childs had fallen into a silence so dark and thick it rivaled even that of this infinite night.

His expression worried her almost as much as did the plight of Happy Africa. Naeku didn't care much about his happiness; if there Had Been Complaints that originated with him, she likely would have smiled. She thought Regina would, too. The older woman despised him.

Naeku knew men like him. In the village, it was common to beat a wife. That was one of the reasons she had left. She was marriageable – old Zawadi had seen to that, coming to Naeku not three days after her first time of blood had stopped, and making her bleed far, for more. She was given time to heal, though that was a joke; such wounds rarely healed completely, and most of the women suffered near-constant pain in the form of infections, incontinence, and abscesses, not to mention the discomfort of the sex act itself.

Naeku knew it was coming. Even without mother or father, she saw it coming and determined to fight it. To keep anyone and everyone from doing what they all said must be done for her to truly become a woman, and to find a husband.

Her resistance did not matter. Zawadi entered and held her down; struck with her razor before Naeku had time to realize the moment was *actually here.*

After it happened, Naeku's future in the village became a thing of stone. She would be taken by one of the men – probably a fourth or fifth wife, since as an orphan and a notoriously headstrong child she was unlikely to have the "honor" of being first among many. She would have children – assuming she was able, after what Zawadi did; many women never could, after that.

Then Naeku would grow old and die as "the wife of" whatever man deigned to take her. Not as herself, merely as a lesser part of him. He would beat her if he wished.

That was her future in the place of her birth.

So she did all she could do: she snuck away, as her father had so long ago. And like him, she would not return.

Leg found her as she was leaving. Of course he did, with his nose always in her business. But as much as he annoyed her, she was glad when he decided to leave with her. That feeling lessened as soon as she realized he was only going so that he could convince her to stay.

"Come back," he kept saying. "What are you out here? You are nothing."

And at the village I would be less even than that, she thought, though she never actually spoke the words. Why bother? Leg was stubborn, and in the face of such stubbornness, silence was best.

They drifted for years. They passed from place to place, traveling long stretches between cities and towns. She was surprised to find, when they entered one town, that the people there knew them.

"Ah, the Two Spirits," said an old woman near the *boma* that surrounded the place.

Leg laughed when he realized she was speaking of him and Naeku, and that they had become something of a legend. Two wild children who would come suddenly and leave twice as fast. Who would work for a day, take what food and money was offered, and be gone without a trace before anyone woke the next morning.

Naeku did not laugh. She did not want to be a spirit. She had barely had a life as it was.

Now, though, she was alive as she had never been in the village – at least not since Father died. She loved being a guide for Happy Africa. She loved driving, even if Father *would* have laughed at the sight. She loved the spotlight, and the tents. She loved the people, who had become her tribe. Regina was not exactly a mother, but very much an aunt of the type who would scowl constantly... but would also protect you with her life and give you her whole heart.

96

Naeku was happy here. She rarely thought of the village anymore.

A lie.

One of the mosquito thoughts landed. It sucked a bit of her dry, leaving the itch of memory: a razor in a hut.

Another mosquito: the remembrance of blood-sprayed walls and her father's eyes losing their light.

She forced her thoughts back to this place, this moment. She *would* find something to show the restless natives. If for no other reason than because she suspected Bill Childs would take any frustration he felt out on his poor wife.

Regina would not stand for it, Naeku knew. But she could not stop it if she did not see it, and this man was very careful indeed.

As though the camp manager had felt Naeku thinking of her, the radio below the dashboard crackled, and Regina's voice exploded from it. "All guides, all guides!" Her voice was so excited that Naeku knew what she was going to say before she said it. "Lion sighting!"

Naeku snatched the mic from under the dash. "Where?"

"Mile 19, east of camp."

Of course. Nowhere close, which meant their chances of seeing the lion was slim. He would stay where he was, no doubt, but it was unlikely they would get close enough to see it. Not with what would be in their way.

Do your best, Nae.

Her father's voice spoke inside her. And he was right. "Leg?" Naeku said into the CB.

Leg's voice crackled over the monitor. Even he sounded excited. She suspected he had come to love Happy Africa as well, if not as much as she. He would go back to the village at her first whisper of assent, of that she was sure. But the love *was* there.

97

"I heard," he said. His Land Cruiser moved off the trail they were on, and she cranked the wheel of her car, too, shouting, "Hold on, everyone," as she veered off the road.

Riding off the marked trails was a fine idea, so long as you knew where the dangerous areas were and knew to avoid them. Most places could be traveled with fair ease, but there were a few hidden dangers that could stop a car – even one so tough and well-designed as the Land Cruiser.

You did not want to be stranded in a place like this. Staying inside a stopped car would mean baking in the oven it would become without air conditioning, and leaving... that carried far worse dangers.

But none of those dangerous places lay near here, which Leg knew, so Naeku wasn't surprised that he took the shortcut. Hopefully, if they hurried, they could be among the first there. Hopefully they would see something that would make the guests happy.

Hopefully...

6

NAEKU'S WORST FEARS HAD come true.

She had once seen a picture of Los Angeles. One of the guests brought it to show her "the hellhole he was getting away from." The picture surprised her: no buildings, no beach from the movies, no Hollywood sign. He referred to the thing in the photo as "the 405," and finally managed to explain that it was a highway, though one unlike any she had ever seen. She believed at first that it was a vast car park, one built by a madman who thought a long, thin design would be the best way to cram as many cars into as tiny a space as possible, with the one small drawback that the cars, once parked, would be crushed between one another and no one would ever be able to leave.

"Nope, freeway," said the guest. His name was Marlon, a lawyer who had the most perfectly round paunch Naeku had ever seen. It looked like he was smuggling a melon under his sweaty shirt.

"But… where are they all going?"

Marlon shrugged. "To an early, hypertensive grave."

She didn't understand that. But the image of that strange 405 stuck with her the same way the image of the ridiculous man saying, "The Natives are restless," stuck with her.

Now she sat in Africa's version of the 405 and thought she might finally understand Marlon's joke/not joke about a hypertensive grave. Her heart pounded, anger flowed liquidly through her brain. She needed to get to the front but there was no way she could. She felt like beating on the steering wheel in a rage, and if the guests had not been with her she believed she would have done just that.

Occasionally, when a "hot sighting" happened, there was a cluster of vehicles that made it impossible for anyone in any other car or truck to see what they were seeing. It happened, and it was a fact of life. But it had never been as bad as this –

(No season has ever been as bad as this before, either. Not since the one when Father died.)

– with what looked like every car, truck, or van from every safari outfit for a hundred miles clumped around the sighting Regina had told her about.

Naeku had no doubt there was a lion – maybe several – at the center of the African 405. She had no doubt they were supremely uncomfortable, as well – surrounded by tons of steel and glass, and more tons of sunburned tourists *ooh*ing and *aah*ing as they each leaned out of their pop tops to take pictures of the Vicious, Wild Animals to show their amazed friends back home. Vicious, Wild Animals who were no doubt terrified by the massive attention and wanted nothing more than to piss themselves and run.

Even lions got scared. She had seen it.

THE NATIVES HAD VAULTED from restless to furious. Barney and Selena carped shrilly while Bill muttered darkly.

Evie and Tharcisse were silent, but such silence served only to highlight the angry sounds the others made.

"The *hell*, lady," screamed Barney. "Where are the damn –"

"We aren't going to see *anything!*" wailed Selena, her own voice drowning out that of her companion.

With all their noise, Naeku shouldn't have been able to hear Bill at all, but his murmurs somehow threaded themselves between their words, and she heard him plainly.

"Some vacation. Waste of time. We spend good money and –"

Naeku shouldn't have been able to hear him, just as she shouldn't have been able to hear Evie's whispered, "Honey, we won the trip. Remember? And I'm sure Naeku is doing everything she –"

Quiet, Evie. Do not speak. Not now.

Evie fell silent, as though she had heard Naeku's thoughts. It was too late. Bill turned his dark gaze on her. "*Honey,*" he said, intentionally repeating the word she'd used, to threatening effect, "you ain't helping my mood."

Naeku decided she would sleep on the ground outside the Childs' tent tonight, rain or no rain. She felt sure Bill was going to beat his wife tonight. Naeku would stay close, and if there Had Been Complaints the next day... well, she could deal with that if it happened.

For now, she could only do her best with the situation at hand.

She cast her gaze forward again. She still saw nothing but vehicles with people jutting out of pop tops and in some cases even standing on roofs, iPhones and cameras held high overhead in the hopes that they might catch a lucky shot of the lions.

Full night, but there were so many cars and so many lights that it looked like the middle of the day here. The natural order was upended, and no way would any other wildlife come here.

A lion roared. The sound rumbled through the area, moving through the air, the ground, even the bodies of everyone around. It was a frightening sound, but also strangely pleasant. The lion did not kill for sport, or even in rage. It killed out of need, and in its roar Naeku usually heard, "I must stand proud, and will do what must be done. But I bear you no ill will, and I hope you bear none toward me."

This roar was different, though: Naeku heard in it only heard pain and fear. The lions knew nature had been perverted here, just as much as she did.

Leg's voice clicked onto the radio. "Nothing is going to happen here," he said in Maa.

"I know," she answered in the same tongue. "Do you have any good ideas?"

"Sure," he replied in a voice that with him passed for cheery. "We can go back. Drop off the guests, perhaps beat a few who deserve it, then go back to the village secure in the knowledge that Happy Africa is gone at last and you can finally get married if any madman will still have you."

"The only part I like of that is the beating of the guests."

"Sorry, but that only comes as part of the rest." He waited a moment, then sighed and said, "Shall we go back to camp?"

Naeku knew they probably should, if for no other reason than because she could smell a storm coming, and it felt like it would be a strong one. Perhaps not a long deluge, but strong enough to make some places between here and camp near impassable.

But Regina's eyes had been so desperate when she met Naeku at the gate. Desperate... and correct in that desperation. Tonight might well end Happy Africa.

So Naeku did not go back. She turned the wheel and shouted again, "Hold on," and rode away from the place where nature had been perverted.

She knew a place. A wild place. It was not a place she liked to go, but now... it was the place she *must*.

7

SELENA WHOOPED IN EXCITEMENT as the Land Cruiser arced away from the glut of other vehicles. Barney allowed himself a quick smile and even put his arm over her shoulder like they were a normal couple in love.

Naeku was smiling, too. Tharcisse did what Tharcisse always did: nothing. Staring straight ahead like his neck had been welded into a straight, unchanging bar.

Evie took these things in, noted them, then disregarded them as unimportant.

Only Bill mattered.

She reached for his shoulder. It was awkward, but she managed to massage his shoulder, her small fingers straining to rub hard and deep. It was the way he liked her to massage him – when he allowed it. It made her fingers hurt every time, because his muscles were so thick she felt like she was massaging a stone wall. But she did it, because sometimes – *sometimes* – it made him happy.

Or at least less mad.

This was not one of those times. He tolerated it for less than five seconds, then shrugged her away. His stare never wavered from her face. She turned away from it, of course, but she could still feel it burning into her.

Your fault, those eyes said.

And he was right. If only she'd ignored the contest. But it seemed like such a little thing. "All-expense-paid trip to Africa!" the magazine said. The rules of the contest were simple: write a one-thousand-word story for their Halloween issue, and the winner would get two round-trip tickets and a safari... *free.*

Bill didn't like it when she wrote. She had shown him her first and only book, *A Paper Princess*, soon after she finished it – which she did soon after their marriage turned dark. He got halfway through before proclaiming his life "too busy" to waste on such things.

Still, he let her send out queries to agents and publishers for a while. Even that ended, though, one day when she came home late from work to find him waiting, angry, fuming. She didn't know why, only that that had been a very bad night, and that he had put an absolute stop to her sending out queries and tried to stop her from writing at all.

When Kindles came around, and then Nooks and the iBooks store and the rest, she screwed up her courage one day and asked if maybe, just maybe, she could publish her book there. Bill pointed out that would just be a waste of time: what would it take away from her responsibilities in the home? And what would she likely get out of it?

She almost did it anyway. Bill showed her the error of her decision, a more strenuously this time, and she agreed not to do publish the ebook she had hoped for.

So no more queries. No new writing.

But sometimes… sometimes she stole away to her Once Upon a Times again.

Sometimes she wrote in secret. Five minutes here, two minutes there. She kept it all in a file in the computer labeled "Bills and Income," which she knew Bill would never look at because he didn't care for the details of such things.

The stories weren't good. The words were junk. But for some reason, when she saw the call in the online newspaper, she wrote a story. She sent it in.

And was shocked when Bill stomped in from getting the mail and waved the open letter at her.

"The hell did you do, Evie?" he demanded.

He probably would have gotten even madder, only... it *was* a vacation. They hadn't had one in a while. Ever, actually. And, she mused, he could tell the guys about it at Clancy Muldoon's, the bar he went to with his coworkers most nights before coming home

The guys, she thought, were what decided him.

And she was happy. Happy because it might mean a chance to fix things. Happy because it might mean he would enjoy himself.

But happiest of all, she admitted to herself, because it meant someone had liked what she wrote.

"Maybe I could write something else," she said that night in bed. "Maybe I could even make some extra money for us, Bill."

"You saying I don't make *enough*? That I don't *provide*?" The last word of each sentence came out hard and fast – always a bad, bad sign.

"No, no, no, sweetie. Not at all." Her voice was low, penitent.

It mollified him that time. There would be no more talk of new writing.

But he didn't know of the Once Upon a Time in her mind.

> *Once Upon a Time,*
> *a girl gave a boy all she had,*
> *and in return he gave her...*

She did not know how that story ended.

BILL WAS STILL STARING. No doubt still thinking dark thoughts about Evie and about how this was all her fault. He was right, too: it was all her fault that they had come all this way, and spent all the money they had. The trip was paid for, but there were vaccinations to be had, passports to acquire. Several hundred dollars, at least.

All for what, this?

Evie looked around, trying to avoid the heat of Bill's righteous glare. She looked out the side window.

For a moment she thought she saw a glint in the darkness, like a star had fallen to earth. Then it winked out and was gone.

She still felt Bill's eyes on her.

Evie looked forward. Naeku's face was a mask of concentration as she hurtled the Cruiser over land designed to thwart such things.

Tharcisse…

Evie jerked in her seat. For the first time, the man with the scar bore an expression other than boredom or disdain. He was smiling. The grin was wide enough she actually saw it stretching around the side, to the profile she could barely see.

The man's scar, always livid, now seemed to glow, and the tip of it curled upward as his cheeks bunched. He was smiling *twice* now.

She liked neither of the smiles. They were here to see wildlife outside, but what would happen if something wild were to gain entrance to the vehicle? What if they opened the doors and invited it in?

She thought about saying something. Thought about leaning forward and whispering in Naeku's ear and telling her to watch Tharcisse; that he was up to no good.

It was only a thought, though. Even if it were true – and it surely wasn't – Naeku would have spotted it already. She was smarter and noticed more things than Evie, so if there *was* something to her thought, Naeku no doubt knew it already.

Selena had stopped whooping with joy. Apparently she'd decided that the five minutes they had already spent bouncing along sufficed.

"Where are we going, exactly?" she asked, the petulance in her voice thin and sharp as a blade.

"There is a place my brother and I know where animals sometimes gather, even in the dry times."

"Then why the *hell*," Barney barked, "didn't we go there in the first place?"

Naeku's voice returned. "Because there are certain places it is better not to disturb."

Evie didn't think anyone caught the tension in her voice. No one but herself: the other woman who understood that there were places best avoided.

GRAMS WATCHED THE DARKNESS flow by outside, then watched Helix for a minute or ten. He was dozing, but even with his mouth lolling open, his head bouncing lightly from side to side, he was a delicious snack of a creature.

Craig and Gale were silent in front of her, and Grams thought they might have been dozing, too, until Gale suddenly said, "Why do they call you Leg?"

The guide in front laughed. Grams had only heard him laugh twice now, and both times it was in response to Gale. She was magic, that girl.

"It is my name, little one," he said. "Legishon, actually, but it is easier for many people to remember me as Leg, because of how tall I am."

Grams could hear the frown in Gale's voice as the little girl said, "But you're not tall at all. Daddy said you're pretty short."

Grams snorted so hard she thought she might have blown snot all over the back of her son's head. But he didn't flinch, and Heaven knew he had little enough hair that he would have felt such a thing, so she felt her dignity was intact.

Leg, surprisingly, laughed again. "And that is why my name is so easy to remember, you see?" he asked.

That frown still sounding, Gale answered, "No."

Now Grams heard a tone in Leg's voice, one she had never heard at all: embarrassment. "Sorry," he said. "I – I didn't mean... I mean... umm..."

Grams knew what he was experiencing: she herself had never realized how often she said the word "see" in normal conversation, until she had a granddaughter who absolutely *couldn't*. "I see," or "you see?" were so much a part of normal vocabulary that hardly *anyone* noticed normally. And even with a little girl who wore dark glasses and waved a red-tipped cane in their midst, most still didn't notice... until after they actually said the words. Then they reacted just as Leg now reacted. Apologies, embarrassment, stuttered words that all came down to the unspoken, "I'm so sorry, I didn't mean to talk about *you*."

Gale responded as she always did. "It's okay, I know you didn't mean to be mean." She giggled as she always did, too, which she had told Grams she did because "mean it to be mean" sounded funny to her.

Grams saw Leg in the rearview mirror. He was smiling.

Magic little girl. You're pure magic, and you don't deserve what's coming your way.

None of us do.

"Well... anyway..." Leg was smiling, but his embarrassment was still palpable. "My father was very tall. He was the tallest man for miles and miles. So it also makes me

108

happy to be called Leg, because then I think of him, and that *does* make me tall."

Grams didn't think Gale would understand that. But the little girl was magic, and magic's one consistent characteristic was that it surprised you. Gale said, "Because when you remember him, you're part of him and he's part of you. And he was tall, so when he's in your brain you can't help but stand up taller, too."

Grams saw her little sugarplum look up at her daddy –

(See? There I go again. She's not looking at him, really. How could she?

But then… how could she not? She sees so much, and sees so well.)

– with such naked affection that Grams' vision blurred for a moment. She didn't wipe away the tears, and they didn't spill over her cheeks. They just hung in front of her eyes like a gauzy curtain, making everything ripple as though in a dream.

Life is but a dream, and row row row until you can't row anymore and you ship your oars and wait for the end.

"Yes," said Leg. His voice was quiet. "My people are always in my mind, but when I think of my tall, tall father, I *do* stand taller."

"Where does he live?" asked Gale. "Do you ever visit him?"

"No, child. I do not visit him," said Leg. Grams could tell that Leg's father was dead. She expected him to change the subject… but magic, again, surprised her. "He went to his ancestors long ago."

"How did he die?"

"Bravely. As a warrior." Leg's voice was proud. He actually did look taller at that moment. Grams wondered if Craig had ever felt like that; if he'd ever thought of her and stood a bit taller or felt a bit stronger.

She hoped so.

"The job of a parent," she'd once told a friend who was struggling with feelings of inadequacy as a mother, "isn't to raise a perfect child. They come down perfect already, so our job is just to try as hard as we can to not screw them up too badly." She meant it, too, and not as a hopeless thing, but as one that brought peace. Parents all messed up, constantly. To try for perfection was laughable. But sometimes... sometimes you could find a way to channel the goodness of a child. Sometimes you could teach him how to find his own strength and goodness and let it shine.

She thought she had done that with Craig. No, she *knew* it. Because how else could he handle so well the tragedy that hung over them all? How else could he wake up every morning and go to work and come home and smile broadly at his child and hug her at night and tell her with his every move that all was well and would be well for a long, long time?

Yes, she'd been a good parent. She'd gotten out of the way of the great man inside him. And yes, he would stand taller for that. For as long as he could, he would stand tall.

"I bet he *was* brave," said Gale. "'Cause you're brave."

Another laugh from the guide – tonight had become a rare feast of gaiety from him. "And how do you know that, child?" he asked.

"Because you just are," she said. And Leg said nothing, because nothing more needed be said. Gale was right: Leg *was* brave, if for no other reason than because she had pronounced it so, and the magic of the little sugarplum then made her pronouncement become true. "What does *Naeku* mean?" Gale then asked. "You call yourself Leg because you're so tall, so why does she call herself *Naeku*?"

"It means 'born in the evening,'" said Leg.

110

"That's very beautiful," said Grams. She cursed herself the instant she said it, because the spell that Gale and Leg had woven together was suddenly torn apart.

"Yes, it is," said Leg. The laughter left his voice, leaving it subdued and almost sullen. Silence blanketed them, deep and dark as the night.

8

"THERE! I SAW SOMETHING!"

Selena's voice was so loud and shrill that Naeku very nearly jerked the wheel to the side. That would have been a bad move, given that Legishon had drawn his Cruiser even to hers, and now hovered only ten feet or so away. He had done this when they were children, as well, running with her, matching her stride for stride wherever she went. She always found that funny, and more than a little endearing. Leg was serious so much of the time that such rare glimpses of humor were all the brighter for it.

But if you don't move over, one of these days I'll run right into you. And where would we be then, dear brother?

"Didn't you hear! Stop the car!"

The follow-up to Selena's first pronouncement was just as loud, just as painful. At least Naeku was ready for it this time.

She slowed the car, cursing herself. Even if Selena *had* seen something, it wasn't good that she was the one to do so, and not the "expert wilderness guide."

No matter. Focus now, *and do your best.*

Leg's Cruiser slowed even beside hers. His voice crackled over the CB. "Something?" he asked.

"Hell yes it's something," said Selena. She was nearly astride Barney, searching out his side window.

"Come in, dear sister," Leg said on the CB.

Naeku sighed and spoke in Maa: "Maybe. The woman who dresses like she is in heat says she saw something."

Naeku swiveled to look at Selena when she said this. Selena didn't draw away from the window, but she frowned. "What'd you say to him?" she demanded.

112

Naeku kept the CB mic in front of her mouth, more to cover her smile than to be ready to pass any information on to the other car. "What direction did you see it?" she asked. A lame question, given the direction Selena was obviously pointing. Like the position of the mic, it was more to cover Naeku's amusement than anything.

Selena pointed. "There," she whispered.

Naeku had never heard the woman speak in such a low, utterly real voice. Every word she had said in camp was painted with scorn, or lust, or rage so ostentatious it had to be an act.

Not now.

The pop top was still up. Now Bill, Barney, and Selena stood. Evie did not, of course.

Neither did Tharcisse. The guy beside her was starting to spook her, though she covered it up just as she had her amusement with Selena.

Naeku grabbed the handle of the side-mounted spotlight and twisted it, sweeping the light across the grasses that had somehow conspired to survive in this place – at least in the patch that surrounded the car. A moment later, Leg's own spot began sweeping as well, matching her movements fluidly: they had done this many times. One more reason that she loved him even though –

She stopped her spotlight. She had caught something. A momentary shadow, a glimpse. Then gone in the grass.

But it was *something*. It was real.

Sometimes your best suffices for the job at hand.

Father's voice in her head, drowned by Selena's shout of, "A lion! Was it a lion?"

Naeku frowned. That *was* why she had come here – if wildlife were to be found anywhere at this time of night, it would be here, but…

113

She froze. Every muscle tensed, so much so that she knew anyone who saw her would be able to spot it.

The light had captured something. Just one more quick glimpse before the thing disappeared into the darkness, but it was enough to tell Naeku what hid nearby. A shadow with a loping run – born of front legs a few inches longer than the rear ones.

Naeku could not show what she felt. Could not show how quickly the sight of this creature had thrust her back to *that* moment. To Father, to his blood.

She had seen these animals many times since that night, of course. You could not avoid them out here. But seeing them always had the same effect.

For once, Barney's attentions were a blessing. Selena was absolutely *riding* the big man, her thighs splayed wide to straddle his huge girth, which he was clearly enjoying. But not so much he couldn't shift to the side, focus on Naeku, and say, "Well?"

"Not a lion," Naeku whispered. It penetrated her fear that Selena would not like this answer. Lions were, along with elephants, leopards, rhinos, and the Cape Buffalo, part of the Big Five that people came to see. Naeku would have to phrase the next moments carefully. Which was hard, given the way her heart beat all the way through her, a nearly crushing pulse she felt everywhere, as though a giant held her in its clenched fist, which he tightened then relaxed in turn.

"Not a lion," she whispered once more. Then, adding a touch of awe to her voice – easy, since fear and awe were so close to being the same thing – she added, "I think it is a spotted hyena."

She thought no such thing. She *knew*.

114

Selena's response was immediate and predictable. "Eww, gross. Aren't they carrion eaters? Just a bunch of corpse-stealers?"

Naeku forced a chuckle. "That is a myth. Actually..." She pressed the button on her mic, allowing her voice to slide into the other car as she fell into some of the patter she had memorized. After thousands of these drives, one started repeating the same information every time a certain animal was sighted. Despite her fear, this one was no different, and she felt her voice strengthen as she took comfort in the familiar patterns. "If we have found a spotted hyena, then we have found the most successful predator in Africa."

(father, papa, where is your heart? they have eaten your heart, so what will you love me with? how will you protect me?)

Continuing, she said, "A spotted hyena will eat carrion, yes, but over seventy percent of her food comes from fresh kills, as opposed to the lion. The 'king of the jungle' eats fifty percent of his own kills, but fifty percent of his diet *is* carrion. In fact, the lion is more likely to steal food from the hyena than the other way around."

She was picking up nothing in the spotlight now. Unsurprising, really, but –

There! Another shadow in the grass – or perhaps merely a shadow caused by the grass itself. But it made the shadow because it had *moved*. And on a windless night like tonight, that meant something was there.

She continued speaking, still hiding in her mind, cowering behind words that hid her from her fear. "The hyena can eat anything, from skin to muscle, even waste. It uses it all. Even bone: a hyena's jaws can exert over a thousand pounds of pressure per square inch, enough to crunch every bone in your body, consume anything of value, and leave nothing but splinters behind."

115

She cursed herself inwardly. She never said, "every bone in *your* body" before. It was always "the body of a full-grown Cape buffalo," or even, "the body of a baby elephant."

Barney harrumphed. "Still a glorified dog."

Naeku tried – with some success – not to glare at him. His ignorance was stunning, and not just with respect to animals. He knew nothing of things like basic courtesy or appreciation for others' expertise.

Still holding down the mic button, speaking to everyone even if she now looked only at Barney, she said, "Most people will say that the hyena is a glorified dog, but that is because they know little of the realities of life and death out here. First of all, the hyena is closer to a cat than a dog, and she is the most frightening cat alive. She is one of the few animals that can chase a lion away from his kill. The spotted hyena also has one of the most complex social systems in the world, every bit as complex as most primate species. In fact, the only group that has interpersonal interactions on such a high, complicated level, arguably is we humans."

"So it's smart," Evie said. She was looking out the window on Selena's side, her face a mixture of fear, excitement, and...

Naeku searched for the term, and finally came up with the only one that fit: *life*.

She wondered what Evie would have been without the man beside her, crushing her down. Something very special, Naeku suspected.

"Yes," she said, her own voice just as low, just as reverent. "She is very smart."

Bill had picked up on something none of the rest of the passengers had. "You keep saying 'she.' What, are all hyenas chicks?" He packed the last word with such scorn that Naeku could not let his derision go unchallenged.

"No," she said coolly. Then, in clipped tones, she added, "But the 'chicks' rule." She spoke this last to Bill. She pressed on the mic and spoke to all. "Among the hyena pack, the lowest female is higher in rank than the highest male. The 'chicks' rule completely." She smiled at Bill. Not a Western smile: this was the smile of a Maasai on the hunt: tight-lipped, no teeth. A smile that spoke of their intent to track, find, and kill. "The males exist only at their pleasure."

Bill shifted under the power of her gaze. Then responded by grabbing his crotch and doing his best to stare her down. "I don't think that'd last long if *I* was in the pack."

Barney chortled. He must have seen and, of course, approved.

Naeku didn't lose her smile. It only widened. "Good luck with that." Into the CB, she continued, "The spotted hyena is unique among mammals in that she has no external vaginal opening. Instead, the female has an elongated pseudopenis which she uses for urination, copulation, and reproduction." She let go of the mic, again speaking mainly to Bill – and to Barney, whom she knew was cut of much the same ugly cloth. "In other words, the female has a penis-like member through which she urinates, and through which the male must copulate, which it literally cannot do without her active approval and cooperation."

"Why the hell not?" demanded Bill.

"Because it would be like trying to rape someone through a ten-inch tube sock. Not possible, even if your penis were long enough." The meaning she put into "your" was every bit as obvious and derisive as Bill's utterance of the word, "chicks."

You'd be the smallest dick in the pack.

Bill bristled. Looking at Naeku with pleading eyes, obviously hoping to change to a safer topic, Evie asked, "You said reproduction, too?"

"Yes," said Naeku. She looked away from Bill, again peering out her window to see what she could capture with the net of her light. Speaking on the CB, she said, "Cubs are born through the narrow opening of the pseudopenis, which usually ruptures in the process."

A collective hiss from the men in the Cruiser. That happened every time, which Naeku always found amusing given the fact that they were of the gender that could *never* feel such a thing.

Naeku continued her spiel. "Up to twenty percent of new mothers die in the birthing process, and among those that live, up to two-thirds of their cubs are smothered to death during the birth process. Even after birth, if two cubs are born alive – litters are usually two or sometimes three – the larger will often kill its smaller sibling so she will have access to more of her mother's milk."

"Mean sons of bitches," Barney said.

"Daughters of bitches," Naeku corrected him. Into the CB: "This means that every cub who survives is born strong, and every mother who lives is one of the toughest of her species."

She swung the spotlight sharply to the right, catching nothing more than another swaying patch of sunburnt grass.

How many are out there?

"Are they dangerous to us?" asked Evie.

Naeku wanted to answer, "No they are not. Not everything is dangerous, Evie. Not even most things, and if you would just run from the animal you have taken in, you might know that."

Instead, she said, "Not as long as we stay in the car."

118

"Come *on*," Selena wheedled. "I want to see something!"

Naeku thought a moment. Then she said, "Turn off the lights," into the CB.

The lights on and in Leg's car switched off. Naeku flipped the switches and turned the knobs that would do the same in her own car.

The blackness inside and out was complete. Had Naeku not known the layout of the Cruiser's dashboard, she would have had trouble finding the key in the ignition.

There was nothing so dark as night in this place.

GRAMS FELT MORE THAN saw her granddaughter suddenly jerk in her seat. At first Grams thought all the worst thoughts. Death had come at last – at last, though far too soon.

But it wasn't that. The little girl had seen what no one else could.

This is her world.

The thought sent a thrill of fear through Grams' spine. It also sent a charge of pride into her mind. There sat her granddaughter, seeing more than anyone else thought possible, and certainly more than most of them would ever hope to experience.

Beside her, a green glow winked to light: Helix had turned his camera to night vision. Grams could see the small screen beside it. It illuminated the world in the gray-green of such scopes, an odd color palette that made everything sickly and cancerous. It turned the normal into the freakish, and sent our world spinning into an alien dimension.

He swung the camera to the side. A patch of grass... moving...

How, with no wind?

119

"Anything?" Craig said from his invisible seat in the black.

"No," Helix whispered. He sounded tense, though whether from anticipation, frustration, or fear Grams could not have hoped to guess.

Gale's voice was low, the voice not of a girl but a specter in the night:

"They're out there."

NOTHING… NOTHING… THEN, A howl. Just one, but that one walked an icy path up Evie's spine. The howl ululated across the world, covering all with a wave of fear, of need.

Hunger.

The word erupted into her mind. She knew there were worse things than Bill – Tharcisse came immediately to mind.

(he hasn't moved why hasn't he even moved?*)*

But now she knew that even that man was far from terrifying, when he stood beside the embodiment of fear.

The howl seemed to last for several minutes. But what came next seemed even longer, an eternal sound fed by an infinitude of hunger:

The laugh.

It whooped and bounced a painful path through Evie's mind. Up and down, and now the laughter came in painful slashes and jags.

The laugh continued. And was joined. One more. Two. A dozen.

More.

Evie fought the urge to cover her ears. Tamped down the desire to grab hold of Bill. He wouldn't like it if she grabbed

120

him, and would like it even less if she sought safety with anyone else.

> *Once upon a time,*
> *a girl was afraid,*
> *and knew that no one*
> *would ever rescue her.*

From the invisible, faraway place that was the front seat, Naeku whispered, "Let's see if we can catch them."

For a moment Evie thought the guide was going to get out of the car and ask everyone else to do the same. She had a mad image of the civilized creatures inside the car getting out, fanning out among the dead and dying grasses, calling for the hyenas to come.

It would be the fly, intentionally flinging itself into the web and then yelling for the spider to come and finish the job.

Naeku spoke into the CB. "Leg, turn on your spotlight on three. One... two..."

Don't do it! Evie screamed in her mind. *Just let's go back can't we —*

"Three!"

Twin spots turned on, their light so sudden and bright it had actual weight. Illuminating a broad swath of...

... nothing.

But the laughs silenced.

The spotlights swung right and left, trying to capture some sign of the spectral creatures that had just sounded like they were right outside the Cruisers' windows.

We're hearing ghosts.

Another ghost sounded in her mind. A ghost that had never had a voice, but which screamed inside her every day.

No. Not here. Don't think of that here.

(murderess)

She focused on Bill. She could barely see even him, even as close as he was. But she could smell his breath, foul enough she wondered when the last time he had brushed his teeth had been.

Not the only carrion eater out here.

She felt movement. Something up front. Tharcisse?

She glanced at him. He was looking somewhere other than straight ahead for the first time. He was looking out the side window, staring at Leg's vehicle. She followed his gaze and saw Jean-Paul in front of the other car.

The other man was staring right back.

The two men nodded.

Things happened very fast after that.

JUST AS EVIE HAD done a moment before, Naeku sensed movement, and was surprised to see Tharcisse turn in his seat. Borderline *shocked* to see him looking out the window.

In the next moment he turned back toward her, and she saw something in his hand: a gun. He held it low, almost in his lap and surely out of sight of the passengers. But Naeku saw it, and knew he had intended her to see.

"Drive," he said in Swahili – no Maa for him, but he obviously knew Naeku would understand this language well enough, and that the passengers would not. "If you speak a word, I will kill you."

She did. Without question, not even bothering to turn off the spotlight, she put her car in gear and started forward.

Leg's car moved forward as well. In fact, it did so before hers did, which she knew could mean only one thing: the same thing happening here – and she had her suspicions what it was and kicked herself for having them too late – was happening in the other Cruiser.

"Follow him," murmured Tharcisse. She fell in behind her brother's vehicle. As she did, she glanced at the rifle between her and Tharcisse. It was secured by a plastic strap, yes, but the strap was made to be easily loosened in case –

Tharcisse was staring at her and must have seen her intent. Or maybe what came next was just part of the plan, because when he snatched the rifle away, rolled down his window, and tossed it out, she thought she saw something tossed from Leg's car ahead of her.

Yes. They are acting together. They have planned and practiced it. Maybe done it before.

A new fear gripped her. She hoped it wasn't right, but if it was...

A crunch and pop as Tharcisse reached below the dash. His muscles bunched for a moment – though the gun he held never wavered for a moment – and then he pulled the CB away from its moorings, trailing broken cables that he had ripped apart with brute strength.

He tossed it out the window. Again, Naeku saw something else fly out of Jean-Paul's window ahead of her.

The Natives aren't just restless anymore.

THE OTHERS IN THE car were finally starting to notice. Naeku could hear a few murmurs, could feel the nervous shifting that was now taking place. They might not have seen Tharcisse's gun, but they must have seen at least the CB fly out his window.

Tharcisse knew it, too. He half-turned in his seat. Naeku glanced in the rearview mirror, realizing for the first time that Selena was still astride Barney, and that at some point Bill had half-risen from his own seat.

"Everyone sit," said Tharcisse. "Get in your seats, and do not move." No one moved. "Your seats. *Now.*"

Barney snorted. "Listen, asshole, I don't know who you —"

Tharcisse shot him.

9

A FLASH ILLUMINATED THE other car, and with it came a sound so loud that even separated by layers of metal and glass, it hurt Grams' ears.

She clapped her hands over them, knowing that it was useless, that the sound had already come and gone. Her body didn't care. It just knew that something far too loud had just happened far too close.

A gun. Someone's shooting!

In front of her, Gale had her own hands over her ears, and was screaming in pain or fear or both.

"Shut *up!*" shouted Jean-Paul –

(That's *his name: Jean-Paul!*)

– and that was when Grams realized what was happening, at least partly. She had wondered what was going on when Leg suddenly lurched the Land Cruiser forward, sending everyone in the car rocketing back. Grams had bounced sideways, which she thought was lucky at first since it sent her sliding into Helix, but now she knew that luck was a thing fled far, far away.

Jean-Paul had a gun, which now peeked around the side of his seat, swinging back and forth from Leg to… *Gale!*

"Shut her up!" he bellowed again.

Craig immediately shoved his own body between Gale and the gun. Grams had to resist an urge to toss herself forward to add another layer of protection.

Lord, let this not be the end. Not so fast. It was already coming fast enough, so please don't do this.

Gale was still screaming, and now Craig spun in place, facing her even as he put his back to the gun pointed at them both.

"Shh, shh, *shhhhhh*." Craig wrapped Gale in his arms and rocked her, whispering into her ear. The girl's screaming stopped –

(Thank you, Lord!)

– petering into whimpers which then grew low enough they almost disappeared.

It wasn't enough for Jean-Paul. "Shut her up, or I will kill her."

He moved so fast that Grams thought at first it was the end. But no, it was just the man turning toward Leg, cocking his gun as he did so. Leg's hand, which had been inching toward Jean-Paul, froze in midair then returned to the steering wheel.

Jean-Paul barked something at Leg. It was in what sounded to her like Swahili, which she certainly did not speak, but even without any knowledge of the language the tone was more than clear: "Try that again and I'll turn your head into a canoe."

Leg nodded tensely. Jean-Paul turned back to Craig – and Gale. Grams gasped as the gun pointed at them.

"Hey, man, easy. We can –"

Jean-Paul cut off Helix's words with a growl. A *growl*, like he was no man but instead an animal capable only of the base communications of death or survival.

Just as well, Grams thought. Helix thought he was hot stuff, but she had heard the unmistakable quaver of fear in his voice. And bargaining with a man with a gun while you were openly terrified could never end well.

She squeezed Helix's arm, not sure if it was to comfort him or reassure herself.

WHEN GALE FIRST WENT blind, first had to learn how to navigate a world so suddenly and completely dark, she had fantasized about regaining her sight. Or maybe something better – perhaps if she got hit with just the right amount of toxic waste she could be like the Daredevil, the comic book hero who was blind but could hear so well that he could karate chop the crap out of bad guys.

Maybe toxic waste. Maybe bitten by a radioactive bat. Perhaps lightning would do it; that gave superpowers didn't it?

She clung to those thoughts for a long time. Eventually they faded, though they never disappeared completely.

Now she was glad the lightning option hadn't happened, because when the horrible explosion went off somewhere close by, she knew that it was the scariest thing that had ever happened. And if she had been frightened by that sound, what would *lightning actually hitting her* sound like?

What was it? What was that, Daddy?

She waited for him to answer, but he didn't, and she only realized a moment later that he *couldn't* answer her because she hadn't said anything. She was screaming, and couldn't stop until Daddy whispered in her ear. "Quiet, sweetie. You have to quiet down. Daddy will get you through this but please, please, *please* quiet."

The third *please*, which was the closest she'd ever heard Daddy to begging, was what silenced her.

She knew several things in her life:

First, that she wanted to see.

Second, that it would never happen, so she might as well make the best of it.

Third, that Grams was the second-greatest person in her life.

Fourth, that *Daddy* held spot number one by a mile.

So if he was telling her to be quiet, and that it would be okay if she was quiet, and please please *please*... then she would be quiet.

She managed to close her mouth, and in the next moment heard, "Just do what we say, and stay quiet. No one will be hurt if you follow those rules."

"Daddy, what's happening?" she whispered. She probably shouldn't have; the man, whose voice she recognized easily as belonging to Sir Angry McBossypants, had told everyone to be quiet.

But she couldn't *not* ask. She didn't know what was happening, so she didn't know what to do to keep herself and Daddy and Grams safe.

No answer came, really. Grams just said, "It's okay, sugarplum," while Daddy murmured, "We'll be fine. Just don't worry, we'll be –"

"Shut up!" shouted the man in front.

Why are you so mean? I don't even know your name.

This time Gale didn't ask the question. Sir Angry had said to shut up, and this time she would listen. She knew Daddy and Grams would both die to protect her, and since the thought of either of them dead was unbearable, she would do whatever she needed to to keep them safe.

She supposed she would die for *them*, if it came to that.

Please, God, protect Daddy and Grams.

And, if you still have time after you're done with that, watch out for me, too.

"I'M SHOT! HOLY SHIT, I'm shot, someone call someone!" screamed Barney, and Selena was amazed at how loud he was, and how much blood was coming from him.

(red shirt and then red in her vision and then red on her hands as she squeezed-twisted-pulled)

Barney had clapped his hand over the wound the moment it happened, but blood poured between his fingers, soaking his shirt, and she could see a dark stain spreading across his back.

She reacted instantly, without thought. Well, she did think the perennial "No fair!" (because it was true, so what else could she think?), but after that moment she pressed on his back with one hand, while the other went to his belt.

She was very good at getting his belt off him. She did it now, sliding the expensive leather out of its loops. But for once she didn't follow that with a variety of interesting and highly athletic motions. She just flicked the belt under his arm, around the corner of his shoulder, passing over the wound on both sides, and pulled it tight.

Barney yowled. What a baby.

"Shut up," she snapped. It was the first time she had said such a thing to him. Felt good.

"Help! Help, someone call someone!" Barney was still screaming. "I'm dying, I'm –"

"Shut up." Tharcisse's voice penetrated quick and deep, all the way to her heart with a still, silent sound. Just like the Holy Spirit Father O'Donnell always talked about in church when Pa used to take her. Only Tharcisse was most definitely flesh and blood and muscle and bone, all of which were oriented on Barney.

Barney managed to bring the yowling down to a whimper. Selena thought that might not suffice; that Tharcisse might shoot him anyway. But the man up front gave a little nod and Selena let out the breath she hadn't realized she'd been holding.

She risked looking away from Tharcisse and the ten-foot well of darkness that the muzzle of his gun appeared to be.

Just a gun. Pa had bigger ones.

But never pointed at you.

In front of her, Bill looked like he had collapsed in on himself. His shoulders hunched to his ears, his head turned away like someone who screams, "I didn't see anything, not your face or anything, and I won't tell the cops, I *promise!*" in the movies. Selena herself had delivered similar lines in *Count to Ten* and *Deathcall*, so she knew how such a thing always ended, which was not well at all.

Evie was cringing, too, though she had not looked away as Bill did. She was facing Tharcisse, watching for signs of where the next danger might come from, figuring out the best ways to appease him.

Selena looked at the rearview mirror. Naeku was driving, holding the car steady on its nightmare run across the rutted landscape, but her eyes kept flicking upward, taking in the passengers, especially Barney.

She'll get us out of this if anyone can.

Then Tharcisse was speaking and, like Evie, Selena watched him and only him.

"I have no wish to hurt anyone else, but I obviously will if my instructions are not followed perfectly."

For a moment, Selena felt weirdly as though she were listening to more patter like Naeku provided on the trips.

"To your left, you will see a tree that has been there since Father Time was a glint in his father's eye. To the right, grass. Up front, the rare sight of homo homicidus, who is armed today. If we're very lucky we might even get to see him hunt!"

"Pass up your cell phones now," Tharcisse was saying. "You have ten seconds until…"

130

"… I START FIRING," SAID Jean-Paul.

Grams was fumbling with her cell phone before he even spoke. So was Craig, pulling his own phone from his pocket even as Gale pulled out her own – a prepaid phone she used only in an emergency, to call Craig, Grams, or emergency services.

Helix hesitated, and Grams couldn't be sure if he had been stunned to inaction, or if he was just refusing to turn over such an important part of his communications network.

Either way, Jean-Paul swiveled the gun so it was aimed at Helix. Then he changed his mind and pointed it at Gale's face. "Now," he said.

"No!" Craig was shouting, moving himself to better cover his daughter.

"Stop," hissed Jean-Paul. "Move and I kill you both."

Craig froze in place. Grams didn't wait for more. She reached for the pocket where she knew Helix kept his phone. He glanced at her as she dug in his side pocket, but said nothing.

Jean-Paul took the phone. He looked at Leg, who dug out his phone as well, and the radio on his belt.

Jean-Paul rolled down the window with his free hand, then tossed the phones out the window.

Behind her, Grams could see the other car. The window rolling down and small objects flying out in almost perfect sync with Jean-Paul's own removal of all communications.

They've done this before, thought Grams. How many times?

That wasn't important, though, was it? All that mattered was the next question in that chain: *And how many people lived through the process?*

131

NAEKU WATCHED AS THE passengers passed up their cell phones. Tharcisse pointed his gun at Barney, and said, "Yours, too."

"I... can't reach..." began the fat man who was an Important Person in another world and nothing but a blubbering, bleeding mess in here.

Tharcisse shrugged. "Then I'll kill you and have someone take it off your body."

Barney mewled pitifully, then groaned as he used his good hand to dig the sat-phone out of his pocket. He handed it forward with another groan that made it sound as though the loss of the phone hurt him worse than the bullet had.

Tharcisse took the phones, then gestured for Naeku to hand over hers, along with the radio she wore on her belt. She did. She saw no alternative at the moment. She knew that she'd have to do something, though. Whatever this was, their chances for survival went down with every rotation of the Land Cruiser's wheels, with every foot they traveled away from the normal lanes of traffic, and further into the wild places beyond.

EVIE WAS SURPRISED AT the calm that fell over her within moments of Tharcisse's takeover of the car. She was afraid, yes, but after the first moments of almost painful terror the fear seemed to recede. Still there, but as the bed of a deep lake: it lay under all, supported the things you saw, but could only be seen indirectly. Buried.

She knew this was a sign that her life had gotten worse than she was willing to admit. What kind of life could it be if the sight of a madman with a still-smoking gun just seemed like one more awful moment in an unending string of the things?

Is it that bad?

(you know the answer to that)

Once Upon a Time,
the Princess began to wake.

The words rang true, and something inside her opened its eyes, stretched, and looked around in horror at what the world had become while it slept in the dark spell cast by the man who now sat at Evie's side.

It was not awake. Not fully. But...

But nothing. Watch. Appease. Survive.

"I'm bleeding to death," Barney whispered hoarsely.

Tharcisse smiled. As before, the smile made his scar curve up. Two smiles, and Evie couldn't be sure which one was worse.

"Bleeding to death," Barney said again.

Tharcisse shrugged, the smiles never fading. "If you speak again, I will stop the bleeding permanently," he said.

Barney moaned, but said nothing.

Beside Evie, Bill moaned as well. The bravado she had known her whole life was gone. The thing inside her saw it. Its eyes opened a bit more.

In front, Naeku caught her eye in the mirror. She gave a tiny shake of her head, and Evie realized that Naeku had been worried *she* would make some kind of move against Tharcisse.

She almost laughed at that.

(well why not? why not try?)

Evie suddenly didn't know what frightened her more: what was happening around her, or the voice that was speaking within her – the voice of the thing that had so long slept, but now was waking up.

133

THE LAND CRUISERS HURTLED through the night. They rolled beside one another, flattening brush and grass for a while, tires spinning extra revolutions as they found loose sand from time to time. Dust plumed behind them.

That was not the only thing, either.

The dust hung in the air for as long as the light of their passage illuminated it. Then it began to settle, an actor that had no need to show itself once the lights faded and the audience disappeared.

Then the dust was no longer settling. It exploded, shattered away from its cohesion by what followed the two vehicles.

There were many of them. They loped strangely, strong front legs digging down, claws grabbing the earth with more purchase than any man-made vehicle could hope to match. Their shorter but still-strong back legs followed suit, pushing the creatures forward, forward.

The Land Cruisers were moving fast – faster than they should. A few of the creatures who followed could not keep up. They fell behind.

All those who faltered were male. They fell behind because they were smaller, weaker, and had no pride to keep them in the hunt. Whatever the pack found, they would eat last of it anyway, and then only if the Queen suffered them to do so.

The dust, pounded to its constituent pieces by the creatures' passage, fell in sad-seeming nothings behind the beasts. Even the dirt was afraid of the hyenas.

The hyenas thrust themselves forward, driving themselves to follow the things they had seen and smelled. Not the machines – those were not of interest. And the things inside them might not have been, either, until the loud noise came. With it, an unpleasant odor. Something burned, something foul.

But under *that* smell: something lovely. Something wet and red and salty. Something that would mean life for the pack.

The hyenas followed. The one at the front – Queen, she who had led them for years now, and would continue to do so until she was deposed in blood and pain, just as she had deposed the last matriarch of the pack – bayed. The others followed suit.

Then she laughed, and her pack laughed with her.

Blood had flowed. The hunt had begun.

And oh! how beautiful it was.

FOUR:
predation

Interlude

"IS SHE BREATHING? I don't think she's breathing!"

Did she say that? Or was it the other woman, the other survivor? Perhaps no one said it at all; perhaps it was just a voice in her mind.

The woman does not know. She cannot answer, either, because to speak such things would mean a stop to the story. She cannot do this, because the story is life, and to stop the story means the girl will not survive.

GALE AND THE PEANUT Butter Snowman traveled quickly. He was a pleasant companion, and of course she was a kind, bright girl so she was no bad company herself.

They talked of things they liked to do (Gale loved to read, while the Peanut Butter Snowman liked to ski down the FlufferNutter Range on the cinnamon-stick skis his parents had given him for his Tenth "Best If Used By" birthday). They talked of people they knew (Gale's parents and his, mostly), and of places they had seen (Gale had once been to Disneyland, and even a place called Africa, while the Peanut Butter Snowman had seen so many amazing sights that they cannot now be listed).

They also spoke once of his name. "Aren't you more of a Peanut Butter Snow*boy*?" Gale asked.

At this the Peanut Putter Snowman looked at her with wide, serious eyes. "Parents do not name a child for what he or she *is*," he said. "The baby comes empty, and so the name they give is what they hope the child will someday *become*."

Gale had no answer to this, for it was true. So she nodded and remembered it, as one must do with all true things.

They traveled quickly. In fact, they traveled so quickly it almost seemed like magic. When Gale told this to the Peanut Butter Snowman, he laughed and said, "How *else* would a person travel in the *Magical Land* of Piz?"

That made sense, so Gale thought no more of it. She just enjoyed their travel. She skied the FlufferNutter Range with the Peanut Butter Snowman (or Pebes, as she was starting to think of him). She swung from Twizzler Vines in the Taffy Forest. She even floated down Strawberry Stream on a floaty Pebes fashioned for her.

This last nearly went dreadfully awry, for Pebes made the floaty out of spun sugar grass, which immediately began to dissolve in the fast-flowing milkshake stream. Luckily, he was able to grab a passing cotton candy cloud and weave it into the floaty so Gale was fine, though surprised that the cotton candy didn't dissolve, too – until Pebes laughed and said, "It's a cotton candy *cloud*, and how would it ever rain its life-giving fruit punch if it dissolved when wet?"

The girl had no answer for that. Though she realized she was suddenly very, very thirsty.

"I don't feel so good," Gale said. And she thought she heard a laugh – something far away, but something she felt was the first and perhaps only dark thing in the Magical Land of Piz.

"I know where we have to go now," Pebes said. "It's a frightening place, but... I think you're sick."

"I think so, too," said Gale. She was a good girl, and very wise. But now she was also afraid.

138

1

EVIE DID NOT UNDERSTAND the details of the situation, but she did understand the *whats* and the *whos* of it.

What: *a man is holding us at gunpoint, urging Naeku further and further into places I can tell she does not like to go, just as I can tell that he has done this before.*

Who: *the scarred man and his friend, both of whom have had murder in their eyes since the first moment, though none of us realized, or at least wanted to admit it.*

Selena spoke suddenly, the sound the first one that anyone had uttered since Barney stopped whimpering and slumped. He was awake, Evie suspected, but had no energy to support the belligerence that had been his primary go-to until a few minutes or hours – but certainly at least one lifetime – ago.

"Please, sir," said the starlet. "We'll give you what you want." Selena produced a purse from somewhere, a clutch embroidered with gold sequins that shimmered even in the dark car. "I have money…"

Evie wanted to tell her to *shut up*! because speaking at a time like this was unwise. Dangerous. Perhaps even deadly.

Tharcisse's face darkened, but to Evie's surprise he laughed. "I know you do. Anyone who can afford airfare from America, then hotels and travel to get here, then a trip like this," he said, gesturing all around him with his gun before returning it to the position it had held for some time now, which was pointed squarely at Naeku, "can afford to part with some cash."

Naeku spoke as well. "So that's it? A ransom? Who are you? FPB? This is *not* the way to aid your cause." Evie didn't know who FPB was, but she felt how Tharcisse shifted when

Naeku mentioned a ransom. The guide's words had hit close to home. Evie's heart lurched, though she knew her face did not show it. That was something Bill had given her: the gift of silence, of always looking as though she would accept what came next with good grace or gratitude.

That skill stood her in good stead now. Once the initial takeover had happened, Tharcisse swung his gun from passenger to passenger before aiming it at Naeku... but he never pointed it at Evie. She was beneath his notice.

Which is right. How could he be as bad as I am?

(That's not true, and you know it.)

The thing inside her continued to wake.

Then the moment was broken by Tharcisse's snarl. "You know *nothing*," he barked at Naeku. He said something in another language – not Maa, she was sure, the words were nowhere near lovely enough – that made the guide go red with embarrassment or rage or fear. Then he added in English, obviously for the benefit of everyone: "All you need to do is drive and do what else I say. Refuse, and die."

BEHIND THE LAND CRUISERS, the shadows still flowed. More joined them, then more still. Now they did not merely flow – that was a thing that rivers or streams did. This was neither. It was an ocean of darkness.

As though bowing before the Queen and the darkness she led, the stars began to wink out, one at a time.

Darkness above, a greater darkness below.

GRAMS LOOKED AT CRAIG and Gale. She had tried to reach up, to hold her child and grandchild, or even just to touch them, but Jean-Paul gestured and she knew that to complete the motion would be death for one or all of them.

She leaned back and did not lean forward again.

How far have we gone? How much farther are we going? And what happens when we get there?

Her hands ached, and she realized they were clenched into tight fists at her sides. She forced her hands to relax – what good would it do her to make her arthritis flare? Things were already bad enough without that.

But only moments later she felt the dull ache again and saw her hands had returned to their hard curls of bone and skin. She opened them, rubbed them against her thighs. Even that small movement drew a look from Jean-Paul. She froze, then risked another motion. She put her hands in her pants pockets because she knew if she didn't she was going to keep making fists, keep moving, and sooner or later Jean-Paul would shoot her.

Or maybe not. Who knew what these madmen wanted? Grams didn't, and really didn't care. She just needed to get Craig and Gale to safety. And it didn't matter that such safety would itself be short-lived. Even if they all got through this, death was coming fast, fast, and far too fast.

Her hands were aching again. She had clenched her fists right in her pockets. Each was curled around something, too, which somehow made the ache worse. In her right hand she held a joint, in the left the lighter she had planned to use on it.

Weed was awesome. She had discovered it long ago, when trying to find a way out of the terror and pain in which she found herself. Even Jack, as big a waste of skin as he was, hadn't minded her lighting up from time to time. It gave him an excuse to take a puff or two himself, which in turn was all he needed to move onto the harder stuff.

At the end, he'd looked like a monster, with sallow skin and sunken eyes and only half the teeth he started with, and she could never be sure if it was the disease that ate him away, or if it just finished the feast the drugs had begun.

Grams never moved up the drug ladder with Jack. But she'd never given up the weed, either. It was easy to get, even before it was legal in California, and some nights she needed a toke to get through. Then when she stopped needing the drug to calm her enough to leave the house, she just enjoyed its effects.

She'd never smoked it in front of Craig, and certainly never in front of Gale. Her son knew, she was sure – you didn't light up *that* much incense unless you were covering up a certain smell, and it didn't matter whether the person doing it was a rebellious teen with an ironic Rolling Stones t-shirt or a woman with more than six decades on her odometer and a Rolling Stones shirt she'd actually purchased in 1969, when as a preteen she'd seen them in *SOME GIRLS*, at their classic Forth Worth, Texas show.

Craig knew, and he was all right with it. He knew why she'd started, and why she still did it. The official reason behind her medical marijuana card was "arthritis pain" – a reason that her doctor wrote without blinking (another reason she liked Dr. Kalighi, apart from his action-star looks and sex-me-now eyes). But the real reason was far different, and brought with it a lot more pain.

She hadn't meant to bring any weed with her on the trip, of course. She wasn't an idiot, and she had no desire to rot in some third-world cell on a drug possession charge in a country that for all she knew would cut off your nose for such things. But she *was* getting old, and she missed things from time to time. She hadn't realized the old gasper was even in there.

Now she was suddenly glad. Soon as they got out of this, she'd hug and kiss Gale and Craig to a state of unconsciousness, then she'd get as blasted as possible on the one stick she had.

She loosened her grip on the joint – what good would it be if she crushed the thing to a pile of sweaty junk in her palm? Not much.

She forced her shoulders to relax. The adrenaline was wearing off, which was good and bad. Good because they'd been alive long enough for that to happen. Bad because… it had been a while. Who knew where they were now, and how would they find their way back?

How could anyone find *them*?

Helix reached out – carefully, below the level of the seat and so out of Jean-Paul's eyesight – and gripped her arm. "Don't worry," he whispered. "I'm an expert in this stuff. The government has trackers. Someone will –"

Grams appreciated the kindness behind his reassurance, but she wanted to scream at him to shut up before they got killed.

Jean-Paul beat her to it. "Quiet!" he shrieked. Gale let out a small, surprised yip. It seemed to enrage Jean-Paul. "Shut her mouth now or *I will do it for you!*"

His voice was shaky. For the first time Grams wished that the other one had been the one to take control of this car. He was scarier by far, but he also didn't seem the type to crack under pressure.

People who *did* crack, as Jean-Paul seemed on the verge of doing, didn't tend to *just* crack. They tended to explode, raining shards of pain on everything and everyone around them.

"Shut… *up*," Jean-Paul whispered hoarsely.

"Okay, okay," Craig said. He held a hand toward their captor. Not too close, just an open palm a few inches in front of him, showing surrender while at the same time putting yet another layer between the gun and Gale.

Jean-Paul's gun jittered in his grip. He was so jazzed – by fear, by excitement, by the prospect of violence, it didn't matter which – that he couldn't keep still enough to do a good, solid job of aiming anymore.

Up front, Leg glanced at Jean-Paul. At the gun. Grams saw it and knew what was coming even before the guide whipped out a hand, grabbing Jean-Paul's gun and pushing it up toward the roof.

Jean-Paul reacted instantly. The gun went off, the sound deafening in the confined space. Jean-Paul didn't let go of the gun. Neither did Leg, but that meant the smaller man was at a disadvantage, because his other hand was on the wheel while Jean-Paul had a free hand.

Jean-Paul slammed his fist into Leg's face. The Maasai twisted at the last second, so the fist hit him glancingly. Glancing or not, the shot rocked Leg's head sideways and blood exploded from his mouth and spattered a thin paint trail against the windshield. Had to have hurt like crazy, but the guide didn't make a sound. He just let go of the wheel for a moment, long enough to send a shot back Jean-Paul's way.

The hit connected. Jean-Paul *did* scream as Leg's fist hammered his nose to a flattened pulp against his face. Then again as the Land Cruiser hit a bump. Without a hand guiding it, the vehicle shimmied sideways, a hard turn that tossed Jean-Paul backward, his head slamming into the window.

Leg brought up his strong left leg, seeming to swivel impossibly on his hip as he kicked. He caught Jean-Paul in the gut and the gun went off again. Grams had lost track of where it was in the struggle, but the deafening crack sounded,

144

followed by a shout from Leg. More blood spattered the windshield in front of him.

Leg didn't let go of the gun. But it started to drift toward Gale. Craig roared in front of her and threw himself forward, adding his own strength to Leg's. The gun swept forward and went off twice. Holes appeared in the dashboard. A moment later the engine coughed and a thick cloud of smoke belched from under the hood.

Jean-Paul sent a thundering punch into the side of Craig's head. Craig cried out and fell back, dazed. Gale somehow felt him tumbling back and was holding him as soon as he was back in reach.

Surprisingly – or maybe not, given what she knew of her granddaughter – the little girl didn't scream or even let out a small cry at any point. She just held her daddy.

Grams lurched forward. Her only thought was to get up there, to grab the gun, to save her family. If it meant Jean-Paul shooting her with every bullet that remained in the magazine of his gun, she figured that would be a legitimate way of disarming him – anything that would save her wonderful, loving, doomed family.

No saving them. Not completely. No matter what.

Shut up. Doesn't matter. Do something – anything!

She was half over the seat in front of her when Helix wrapped his thick arms around her chest and yanked her back. Her breasts flattened painfully, her ribs seemed to collapse even more painfully under the force of his embrace.

"You'll get us killed!" Helix shouted.

In the next moment she didn't hear anything but the wretched shriek of metal on metal, and saw nothing but a world gone mad. A moment after that she saw nothing at all.

NAEKU SHOULD HAVE KNOWN that Leg would try something. He wouldn't wait to see how something played out. He would act. So the instant she heard the shot, even before she glanced over and saw her brother struggling with the man who had taken him and his passengers hostage, she knew what she would see.

Her brother pounded at the other man. She thought she saw a kick. Another body entered the fray: Craig Jensen. She wouldn't have wanted guests to put themselves in danger, but now that Leg had committed them she was glad her brother shared the car with someone brave. Someone good.

Naeku spotted Gale. The girl had slid sideways, avoiding the violence she could not see. She lifted her cane and unfolded it halfway, and Naeku realized with shock – and more than a little awed admiration – that the little girl was contemplating getting into the fight as well.

Two more shots went off. Naeku heard a follow-up sound, a grinding hack that was itself followed by a thick mushroom of smoke growing from the hood of Leg's car.

She saw blood on his windshield. Saw his grimace and knew he'd been shot.

She also saw Tharcisse, who had swung around and was now bringing his own gun to bear. In the next second he would be able to fire through his own window, right through Leg's. He would kill her brother.

Naeku glanced in her rearview mirror. Her senses seemed to heighten, taking in every single detail. The blood still seeping from Barney's shoulder, the thickness of the fingers still pressed against the front of his wound. The terrified sparkle in Selena's eyes, the way she clutched her gaudy purse to her chest. The snuffling sounds Bill made as he tried to imagine himself somewhere far away, somewhere safe.

146

She saw Evie. White face, lips that were blue with terror, but those only serving to highlight the glowing red points on her cheeks. A fevered light behind her eyes, like a furnace stoking itself to a frenzy.

Will she burst? Will she lose control and do something that will kill us all?

No. Evie's eyes met hers, and Naeku realized in that fraction of an instant that what she'd taken for fevered panic was no such thing. Evie was taking it all in – perhaps in even greater detail than Naeku herself. She was absorbing it all, tamping down the fear and cultivating only a survival sense that would tell her what to do.

That sense told her now. In the instant that their gazes met, Evie seemed to know what Naeku would do – what she *must* do to save her brother.

Evie nodded. She grabbed her seatbelt from where it hung beside her. Guests rarely wore the seatbelts. It was the rule that they should, but given how often they tended to shift around as they looked for wildlife, most of them refused and the guides generally didn't enforce the rule.

More's the pity.

It meant that no one would be ready for what was coming. No one but Evie, who slid her seatbelt across her chest in a fluid movement. The retractor whirred, a low-level hum below the madness of the moment, followed by the telltale click of the tongue sliding home in the buckle.

All in only an instant. A movement so fast and sure that Naeku could barely follow it. Which was good because Tharcisse had a bead on her brother and she couldn't wait any longer.

She jerked the steering wheel as hard to the side as she could.

EVIE'S HEAD JERKED TO the side so hard she thought she must have broken her spine. Pain speared up and down her back, pins and needles stabbed her buttocks, daggers dug into the back of her skull as the sudden force of the car's turn strained her body to its limit.

Behind her, Selena and Barney both screamed, both screams speaking loud and clear the thoughts both must be having: *Please don't hurt me!*

Bill made no sound. Just hunched deeper into the posture he'd assumed since the moment after Tharcisse shot Barney.

He's not wearing a seatbelt!

The thought brought with it an instant of the shame that followed every time she let her husband down. A spike of psychic pain easily the match for the shooting agony in her back and neck. She tried to reach his seatbelt. She had to buckle him in! What would happen if –

Centrifugal force drove her away from her husband as Naeku's swerve continued. A loud crash, then a shudder rode through the Land Cruiser. Evie knew somehow that the sounds meant that their car had slammed into the other one, but instead of rebounding the two cars stuck like glue. Something had caught, twisted metal locking tight in an embrace that would let neither vehicle escape.

Tharcisse was tossed to the side in the violence. His hands flew up, then hit the windshield an instant after the two Land Cruisers collided. His gun fell from his hands, dropping against the dash. It discharged, and the bullet passed so close by her that she felt the heat of its passage against her scalp. Glass crashed behind her as the bullet continued on and blew out the Land Cruiser's back window.

An inch lower and I'd be dead now.

Another shriek sounded, and the world spun around her. She saw a water bottle seem to float upward like something you'd see on a space station in a sci-fi movie. Then the world sped up, everything happening at a thousand times actual speed. The water bottle zipped up – or was it down? – slamming into the side of Bill's head. He rocked sideways, water splashing over him.

His body was floating, too. Just like the water bottle.

More glass crashing. The windows of the Land Cruiser blowing out. Darkness outside, but she knew if she could have seen it the horizon would have been spinning madly around them, disappearing on one side and reappearing on the other as the Land Cruiser flipped end over end over end.

Bill's body jerked to the side.

She saw it fly out one of the windows.

Then she saw nothing as something hit the back of her head and everything went black.

Once Upon a Ti –

2

DARKNESS. SO THICK THAT even thought was swallowed up. Darker even that that black lie that had taken hold of Evie –

(you're nothing you're less than nothing it would have been better if you'd never lived because at least then you couldn't have killed her)

– and so thick that she felt it moving around her. It pressed in, scraped and scratched with claws equally unseen.

Sounds came, welcome in the darkness. Crackling, dry pops that made her think of fingers breaking, of a belt slapping flesh with the dry-wet *snap* it always made.

Evie blinked. She knew she blinked, and that her eyes were open, but still she saw nothing. More blinking, and now she felt wetness on her cheeks.

Blood? Is that blood?

Maybe. Or maybe just tears as her broken eyeballs tried to lubricate themselves into a semblance of functionality.

More blinking. The *snap-crack-snap* sounds continued, then grew. Another sound came as well: a sloughing, rough sound. Sandpaper on wood? A match striking?

Open your eyes!

She did. At first the only thing she saw it was a flickering mélange of dark and light, but gradually the shadows and bright spots drew up battle lines and withdrew behind them, allowing her to tell at least where one left off and the other began.

Another sound intruded. The crackling was still there, as was the sound of rough-on-rough. But through it all, a drum beat. Tympanic *boom-boom-boom*s that made her head ache even more than it already did.

She blinked again. The eyes closed on that stirred-up brew of light and dark, and opened to sight. She understood what the sounds were:

The drumbeats were her own blood, pulsing through her head as she hung upside down from her seatbelt. The Land Cruiser had come to rest on its roof. The pop top had been closed, she was sure of it, but had it always been so *close*? It seemed like it was only an inch below her head, crumpled and buckled in odd places.

The snapping, crunching, crackling was flame. She couldn't see it, but the orange, flickering glow could only be the light of a fire. A big one, too. Far enough that she couldn't feel its heat, but would it come closer?

She didn't know. She didn't want to find out.

The scraping came again, a dry sound that made her muscles clench. She turned her head – it hurt to do so – and saw four boots shuffling back and forth in the parched dirt above/below the Land Cruiser, just a few feet from her. Still muddled by the crash –

(Oh, that's right, we crashed!)

– she couldn't place what she was seeing at first. She looked away from it, the burning bands searing her neck and the base of her skull. She twisted and saw two lumps behind her. Barney and Selena. The two were draped atop each other. Blood puddled on the roof of the Land Cruiser where they lay.

"Hello?" she said. Her voice sounded muffled and far away, like she was speaking into an old-fashioned megaphone. She giggled. It seemed the right thing to do.

Neither of the lumps moved.

She turned again. Saw the front seat.

Tharcisse was a curled ball on the roof of the Land Cruiser. His eyes were closed and Evie noted with a strange absence of real interest that the gun he had used to capture everyone was nowhere to be seen.

Dead? Maybe.

Hooray!

Evie giggled again.

Beside Tharcisse, Naeku hung from her own seat belt. Evie couldn't see her face, but did see the blood trickling from a cut on her scalp. It dripped through her hair, which was damp with it, the wet mass reflecting the bright flame outside in oddly beautiful shimmers.

Naeku groaned.

She's alive!

The happiness of that thought was there but, like Evie's voice, it felt like a faraway thing, something that belonged to a stranger.

She looked to her side again. Beside the Land Cruiser, the shoes were still doing their strange waltz. The pair on the right were hiking boots, stained brown by long periods of time walking on dirt. The others were a scuffed pair of black boots that laced up high to a point well above the ankles. They looked military.

A grunt sounded. One of the owners of the boots had just been hurt. That fact snapped Evie to full consciousness, and she realized she was looking at the feet of Leg and Jean-Paul. She couldn't see the details, but as the feet moved back and forth, shuffling, kicking, she knew the two men were locked in battle. One of them had just been hurt.

It all seemed strangely distant, like she was watching the scene through binoculars. Another distant sight: seeing Bill rocket through a broken window, disappearing into the night. But that couldn't have been real, could it?

Yes. It happened.

I failed him. Couldn't get the seat belt on in time.

Another grunt drew her attention back to the Mysterious Dancing Boots – she giggled again – and a spatter of blood fell to the dark ground below. The parched earth lapped it up, and the wet disappeared almost instantly.

That was all right. More came.

A groan pulled Evie's gaze forward. Tharcisse was moving. His eyes fluttered. Even addled by pain and shock, she knew that he was waking up, that he would see what was happening outside the vehicle, and that he would join his co-conspirator in the fight.

Leg didn't have long.

Then a third pair of boots entered Evie's view. The same kind of hiking boots Leg wore, but a few sizes smaller. A scream sounded, a primal shout of challenge and hatred. The sound told her exactly who owned the new set of boots.

Naeku.

Evie turned forward for a moment, and sure enough, the Maasai woman must have woken, seen what was happening outside, and struggled free of the car to help her brother. Evie hadn't noticed any of it – stark proof that her brain was misfiring, and maybe broken in some important way.

Where's Bill? I have to find him!

Naeku must have jumped, because her feet soared upward. They didn't come down again. Evie wondered absently if Naeku knew how to fly. It wouldn't really surprise her, she supposed. Naeku was amazing. A real warrior-princess like Evie had always enjoyed writing about, even if her stories never went anywhere.

A sharp jab of pain drew her back – again – to the present. Her mind sharpened a bit each time it whipsawed back from shock to reality, and now had enough of an edge that she understood what had just happened. Naeku hadn't

153

learned to fly, she had leaped onto Jean-Paul's back, and now hung to him, attacking him as she and Leg tried to overpower the lone enemy between them.

A cough sounded nearby, in the Land Cruiser with her. Tharcisse. His eyes were open, though blurred with the pain and shock she supposed must be visible in her own gaze. He looked around. Saw the shoes.

Unlike Evie, he quickly jerked himself back to full understanding, total wakefulness. He looked around and, apparently not finding his gun, drew a long knife from a previously-hidden sheath on his belt.

Tharcisse turned to look at his surroundings. The front windshield had blown out, and the frame had collapsed around it, leaving an opening far too small to wiggle out of. His own window, the front passenger side, had followed suit, though not to nearly such an extent.

He began wiggling out the hole. Wriggling toward the fight.

Watch out, Naeku! He's coming!

Evie's mouth did not move. She wanted to scream or cry or both, but that broken part of her brain wouldn't allow it. She giggled instead.

GALE'S HEAD HURT. SHE smelled something sharp, too, like the smoke Daddy made in large amounts every time he tried to make bacon. Daddy was many things – all of them good. But he also *wasn't* a few things, and definitely wasn't a good cook.

Was this bacon she smelled?

No. It was sharper, tangier. It had an edge that burned her nostrils.

She thought it was burning her skin, too. The smell was *that* strong.

It's fire.

She hadn't been fully awake or aware to this point, but now her brain seemed to *pop*. Not like a balloon, but like a car that was starting up after a long time not being used. *Pop... pop-pa-pop.*

She remembered. The sounds of the man in front shouting about killing people. The louder sounds of a gun going off, with the *pla-tink* of bullets hitting something hard. She remembered Daddy's screams, and the moment where she felt him leave her side for a moment. Another sound –like a bone breaking, but covered in a wet blanket. Then Daddy reeled into her, crushing her against the seat.

The world had jerked away from her, the Land Cruiser veering to the left, then hitting something with a crash of metal. The grinding as it tried to move back to its previous path.

And through it all, so much shouting.

She had a vague memory of the car starting to shimmy, then in the last moment before another loud crash signaled the pause in her world, she felt Daddy grab her seatbelt and click it over her.

That was why her chest hurt, she thought, only realizing in that moment that it did indeed hurt. They had crashed, she now knew. So that pain made sense.

But why did her cheek feel like it was sunburned?

Something popped with a dry, brittle crack. She knew that sound, as she knew so many others. It was the sound of fire.

Her cheek was hot, because the fire was near.

Daddy groaned. She realized he was still next to her, and had to try hard not to cry. "Daddy!" she managed.

"Honey?" Daddy's voice was slow, lurching. He sounded like he'd been taking drugs or something. Not that Gale knew what that would sound like, but if she *did* know what it sounded like, she thought it would sound like Daddy did now.

"Daddy, we have to go," she said, pulling his arm. A sharp intake of breath told her she was hurting him. She let go of his arm, but didn't stop saying, "We have to go!" over and over.

"Okay," said Daddy. His voice sounded clearer, which was good. Her cheek was getting hotter, and the crackle of flame was louder. The sharp smell that greeted her on waking slashed into her nose. She finally placed it: gasoline. The car was on fire. Would it explode?

She grabbed Daddy's arm again and yanked it. Another hiss, and Daddy said, "Ow! Sweetie, stop –"

"We have to *go!*" she shouted.

"I know." The sound of something shifting.

"Let's go, Daddy!"

"I can't." A long, horrible silence before her daddy said, "I think I'm stuck."

"Grams? Grams, help!" shouted Gale.

Grams didn't answer. And Gale's cheek felt like it was blistering.

NAEKU SAW HER BROTHER, a bloody mess, cuts from the car crash striping his skin everywhere. He had other wounds, too: long gashes across his arms, a deep slash that had split his cheek open.

Knife wounds. She knew what those looked like –

(the razor coming down the pain the blood)

– and her heart pinched to the size and hardness of a pebble as she realized how close her brother was to losing the fight against Jean-Paul. The other man held a long, thin blade in his hand. She could see its razor edge even from here, as well as the blood that coated it.

Leg was weaving on his feet, exhausted from shock and loss of blood. Jean-Paul was doing better, but it was clear that Leg had given an accounting of himself, even wounded and unarmed.

Naeku felt a moment of pride. The scum had dared to brace a Maasai warrior! He would pay.

Leg stumbled. Jean-Paul seized the opening and lunged with the knife. Leg barely got his hand up in time to block the thrust. The knife punched right through his palm, impaling Leg's hand up to the hilt. The point, hung with gobbets of flesh and coursing blood, stopped only an inch from Leg's chest.

Jean-Paul grunted and leaned forward. Pressing into the earth, into Leg. The point of the blade moved toward Leg's chest. It touched him, then slid forward another quarter-inch. Leg screamed.

So did Naeku. She shrieked – a wordless sound that nonetheless conveyed her agony, fear, and most of all her rage – and rushed Jean-Paul. She leaped into the air and landed on his back, one arm going around his throat and the other raking at his face with her nails.

Jean-Paul screamed. Screamed again – louder this time – as she found one of his eyes and pressed as hard as she could. It felt like pushing her fingernail into a grape, only no grape would explode in wetness the way his eye did. His shrieks grew so loud that she thought for a moment he would faint. He would faint, wouldn't he? Surely no one could withstand all that had happened in the last few minutes without succumbing to unconsciousness.

But Jean-Paul did not faint. Instead, he seemed to go mad, tearing at her, making her turn her face away lest she suffer the same fate as he. He yanked his blade out of Leg's hand – her brother gasped and weaved, his eyes rolling back in their sockets so far that only white showed – and reversed his grip so the knife pointed backward.

Naeku had a moment to realize that, far from ending the fight, she had pushed Jean-Paul to heights of animal madness that made him more dangerous than ever. Then he slammed the knife backward, and she felt it enter her.

The pain was fleeting. She bit it down. Ate it whole as she had that day, the first day she had felt an edge bite her flesh. That day she had screamed and cowered. She would not do that today.

She flailed at Jean-Paul's face, trying for his other eye. Her side tore, as Jean-Paul whipped his head about, keeping her from completely blinding him.

Jean-Paul's hand found the handle of his knife and he jerked it out of Naeku's side, wringing a scream from her. A moment after that another scream sounded. This time it was Leg. He leaped forward, grabbing Jean-Paul's knife hand with his own wounded, bloody one. Jean-Paul struggled, but Naeku's searching fingers finally found a target. She felt two fingers slide into something warm and moist, and yanked back and to the side.

Jean-Paul screamed a lopsided scream a she tore his cheek wide open. Her fingers had caught his mouth like a fishhook, and now that mouth was an extra three inches long on one side. Jean-Paul shrieked as he had not even at the loss of his eye. He dropped the knife, both hands going up to clap against his cheek.

Leg was an irritating nit sometimes, but Naeku loved and admired her brother. And never more so than now, when he caught Jean-Paul's knife before it even touched the earth below, and in the same fluid motion slammed the knife home.

As it had a moment before, the knife sunk hilt-deep into flesh. Only now it was Jean-Paul's neck that had been perforated. The would-be assassin gurgled, his hands flapping back and forth between neck and cheek as though unsure which to first attend to. Naeku felt blood cascade in thick sheets over the arm that still hung to his neck, wetting her forearm from wrist to elbow.

Jean-Paul stiffened suddenly, then slackened just as fast. Naeku did not let go. She felt the body tumble below her and kept holding, intent on riding the corpse to the ground, and maybe pummeling it into a violent semblance of burial for what he had tried to do to her brother.

Her fall was arrested halfway down, however. She felt something hard as steel wrap itself around her own throat, jerking her back. She saw something whip past as she flew backward.

Tharcisse. The big man had fought free of the car she herself had come from, and now tossed her behind him like she weighed no more than the wooden elephant Leg had once carved for a little blind girl.

Leg shouted and rushed Tharcisse, but the man had his own knife, and Naeku saw it but Leg did not. She tried to shout, even as she fell back, but she slammed into something hard and the breath left her and she could not even scream her despair as Tharcisse almost calmly slashed.

Leg stumbled back. He grabbed his throat, his body trying to somehow hold it together.

He cut Leg's throat. Now Leg will look like him!

The thought swirled insanely in her mind, even as Leg's eyes went blank. Still on his feet, he weaved for a moment, his body trying to obey the final instructions of a brain that had suddenly cut off all communications.

Tharcisse's heavy boot shot out. It caught Leg in the chest and Naeku thought the big man would kick him down, then kick her brother to death. But the touch was strangely soft, more a nudge than a kick. No kicking was necessary, because Leg was already dead.

Her brother crumpled to the ground, a thoroughly ignominious collapse rendered somehow obscene by Tharcisse's final touch. The murderer hadn't been content to kill Leg; he had *humiliated* her brother at the last moment by sending him to earth with nothing more than a tap. As though to say, "Let no one misunderstand: this Maasai was no match even for my lightest touch."

It was too much to bear. Naeku knew that the wave of rage that rose inside her was as much to cover the sudden, shooting pain of her brother's death as it was real anger, but she didn't care. She rode the wave, let it push her to her feet, and shrieked as she crested it, then dropped down its breaking face. The wave drove her into the man who had killed her brother.

She reached out her hands, barely feeling her bruises or even the knife wound in her side, though it stretched and tore as she lurched forward.

Tharcisse grinned. The scar on his throat rose as well. Two smiles, and she realized he was two people: one a mere man, the other a demon called from the darkest places in Hell. She did not know if she could kill the demon.

She would have to settle for killing the man.

EVIE PUSHED FREE OF the wreckage. She managed to stand, but had to lean on the Land Cruiser to do so. She felt something sharp bite her hand, realizing dispassionately that she had cut her palm on a piece of metal that jutted out of the car.

Better not bleed on the floor. Bill wouldn't like that.

!

She remembered again: the sight of Bill ricocheting around the inside of the Land Cruiser, then disappearing out the window with all the speed and flair of a stage magician dropping out of a magic steamer trunk, crouching below the stage while the audience cheered and whooped.

Only this was no trick. Bill *had* disappeared.

Evie turned, marveling at how bright it was. It was night, wasn't it? So why...

She saw why a moment later: the other Land Cruiser apparently had managed to avoid flipping over as hers had done, but it was in worse shape nonetheless. Flames licked out of the engine, curving around the buckled hood and reaching bright fingers toward the main body of the car, toward the...

Oh, no. No!

The car was on fire. Smoke plumed, black and acrid and nearly impossible to see through. Nearly. But she could see through it enough to glimpse movement in the back of the Land Cruiser. Someone – perhaps everyone – was still in there.

Gale!

3

LEG IS DEAD. MY brother is dead. And I am going to die, too.

The thoughts slammed into Naeku like fists, driving her down, making her want to curl in on herself and simply *end*. But she could not do that, could she? She was the last of her line; there was none other to stand and seek the justice that must be done. So she forced herself upright. Forced herself to stand tall.

Then she flung herself at Tharcisse.

She ducked her head, feeling her side tear with every movement. Her hip was suddenly warm and wet, and she knew that running like this was making her bleed. She did not have long before blood loss weakened her too much to do what must be done.

Tharcisse did not move aside or even seem to brace himself. He faced her with the same eerie calm on his face that he wore when he killed Leg. He slashed at her, the knife that had ended her brother seeking the same fate for her, but she stepped to the side at the last moment. Slid around the knife, pushing Tharcisse's arm away with one hand while she punched his throat with the other.

He was strong – so very strong. Pushing his arm felt like shoving the back of a Cape buffalo. It did not want to move, and had she not hit him exactly right with her closed fist, she knew he would have ignored her strength, overpowered it, and finished her off with one powerful thrust of his knife.

But she *did* hit him exactly right. His arm muscles relaxed as he gagged. He didn't let go of the knife, but the other hand went to his throat, clawing at it.

He wasn't dying: she had felt his neck muscles clench and knew that even the direct blow had not managed to crush his windpipe. Bruised him, yes – perhaps even permanently damaged his larynx – but he was still full of fight.

She moved from one attack to another. A flash of pain, this one brighter than ever, curled her to the side. She did not fight it; she followed the pain instead, dipping down on that side and finding the target that presented itself. Tharcisse still held his knife, and rather than try and push it away again, this time she simply latched onto his arm with her teeth.

She ground down, feeling blood splash into her mouth. She tried not to gag, and mostly succeeded. She would kill this man, this fiend. She would kill him and leave his body for scavengers.

Tharcisse roared, the sound strangely loose and gasping – good, she *had* hurt his larynx, *had* bruised his windpipe – then reached down with his free hand. He grabbed the nape of her neck as though she were a kitten, then tossed her away from him again.

He followed as she tumbled back, grabbing her by her throat, squeezing, choking the life from her.

Now he will stab me. Now it will end.

(daddy, where are the lions?)

But he did not stab her, and with strangely sharp vision she saw his knife lying in the dust several yards away. He must have dropped it when she took that wild bite out of his arm. Not that it mattered – her vision was still sharp, everything standing out in high contrast, but equally sharp edges were pressing in on the outsides of her sight. Black blades sheared through her vision, growing thicker as they cut away her vision. When they joined, she would lose consciousness and that really *would* be the end.

163

She grabbed Tharcisse's hand, trying to pull it away. She failed. He was too strong. A moment later the hand on her throat was joined by its mate, and the shards of darkness closed in tight. She was going, going...

In one of the narrow places between darknesses, she saw Evie. The woman was watching her, eyes darting back and forth from Naeku to other things, things which must be terrible as well, but which did not matter much to her in the face of her own impending death.

"Help!" she said. *Tried* to say. Tharcisse was truly choking her, and when a person is being choked there is no wind for speech. The only sound that came from her was a moist *hrk... hrk* as her jaw opened and shut, blood and saliva spilling out over her teeth and lips.

Her eyes felt like they were going to explode. Thunder roared in her ears. Then she heard nothing but the last beats of her heart.

Evie stared at her. She took a step closer, then halted. Naeku knew this was it. Evie would not act against the hulking, dangerous figure Tharcisse presented. There was no one to stand for her, no one to protect the last of her family line.

Darkness closed her vision. Naeku felt herself grow limp. Going... going...

(*daddy where are the lions, i cannot hear them at all*)

Gone.

GRAMS WASN'T SURE HOW she got out of the car. She must have, though, because here she was, wandering around and feeling dazed as she hadn't since the first time she smoked a joint. Only then everything had seemed so funny – her fingers were *hilarious,* she remembered – and now nothing was funny. Not at all.

What happened?

Smoke swirled around her, rising on eddies of heat then thinning into lighter and lighter clouds that were eventually swallowed by the night sky. She watched one of them, a dark thing shaped like a dragon, whirl in on itself until it was no longer a dragon but a writhing gray maggot. The maggot churned. It held its shape for a moment, then puffed into nothing.

She heard a strange sound. Not the *crackle-crick* of the fire that lit this area. Not the pop and ping of overheated metal that strained against its own shape. It was a pained sound.

She looked. She saw the source of the noise. Shock constricted her brain to a pinpoint, and the only thing left was the sight of Naeku, feet dangling in the air, the life being choked out of her by a man Grams knew yet whose name she could not remember.

Sir Angry McBossypants.

Yes, that was it. That was his name.

No it's not.

And it doesn't matter that it's not.

Grams took a step forward, her thoughts coming into focus as she realized that Naeku was dying. She had to stop it, had to help. But what could she do? Even at fifteen feet away she could see the way the big man's muscles bunched, the way they rippled in the light of the fire that licked around the Land Cruiser –

(Isn't there something in that car? Shouldn't I be worried?)

– and knew that attacking him with her bare hands would do nothing for Naeku.

Weapon. I need a weapon.

She looked around. Saw nothing useful. A few bits of plastic, curling into blackened discs as they burned. A stick –

too short to be of use, and it looked brittle as glass to boot. A few small shrubs. The omnipresent scorched grass.

Naeku gurgled.

There was nothing Grams could do. She saw Helix's camera, flung loose when the Land Cruisers crashed –

(Is that what happened? Did we crash?)

– and laying on the dirt at her feet. A red light was blinking, and for a moment she had the insane urge to pick up the camera, look in, and say, "Calling all YouTubers! Emergency! Send help! Call someone! Call the Ghostbusters!"

The camera was in her hand now, though she had no recollection of picking it up. The red light on its front was blinking. Watching everything, recording the soon-to-occur death of a good woman.

EVIE WATCHED NAEKU DANGLE. She knew she should help. Naeku's eyes kept flicking over to hers, and Evie knew the other woman was asking-begging-*pleading* for help.

Evie took a step toward the tableau, the death that must come.

Once Upon a Time,
a Princess knew she must do the rescuing.

Only she was no princess, was she? Not even much of a woman.

That thought reminded her: where was Bill?

Part of her knew that she was in shock, and that if she didn't get her act together – and soon – that Naeku would die and it would be her fault. But more of her knew that Bill was gone, and that was her fault right *now*.

"Bill?" she called.

A sound. She spun toward the metallic *klonk*, thinking it must be Bill. He was back, and he'd smile the way he used to, and hug her and let her know he was going to help, was going to save her and –

But it was not Bill. It was Naeku. Her pedaling feet had found the side of one of the Land Cruisers. She tried to find purchase, to push against it and perhaps free herself from Tharcisse's clutches. But Tharcisse simply took a step back and all Naeku managed were a few more of those hollow sounds as her feet pattered against the car.

Tharcisse was grinning. That grin penetrated Evie's haze. She stepped toward him. She didn't know what she was going to do, only that she must do something.

Tharcisse heard or saw her. He turned his head slightly, his gaze falling on her. The smile widened.

Evie froze, one foot hanging in the air mid-step. The moment of strength passed. Naeku was dying – *would* die – and she could do nothing.

Another person dead because of me.

A ball of gray and pink exploded from somewhere. Evie had a moment of shocked clarity in which she recognized Grams, all wiry limbs and knobby joints, barreling straight at Tharcisse. She had something in her right hand, which she pulled back like a pitcher about to loose a burner right over home plate. She brought her hand forward hard, but didn't let go of what was in her hand and at the last moment Evie saw that the old woman was holding Gunnar Helix's very expensive camera and then the camera was gone, disappeared as it slammed into Tharcisse's head and exploded.

Tharcisse reeled to the side, dropping Naeku as a hand went up to hold his head. Grams had hit him in the temple, and Evie thought she saw his head dented strangely there.

Tharcisse took a pair of halting steps. Naeku scooped something off the ground, straightened, and buried a knife in his right eye. The blade was long and thin, the point continuing right through his skull and peeking out the back side of his head, the man's thick hair shoved aside to allow the point to just show.

Tharcisse stood there, frozen – or perhaps held in place by Naeku's death grip on the knife. Then she let go and he sunk to his knees. He fell forward, straight onto the still-jutting hilt of the knife and now the point wasn't just peeking out of the back of his head, it showed a good inch-and-a-half.

Evie turned aside and vomited so hard her back spasmed, pinching her spinal cord which reacted with panicked jolts of pain that ran down the sides of her legs.

She couldn't be sure if she was vomiting because of the violence, or the grim look of satisfaction on Naeku's face, or simply because she had frozen in place and made not a move to help a woman she respected and admired.

If it hadn't been for Grams, Naeku would be dead now.
The wrong people always die, don't they?

4

A SHOUT CAME FROM inside the other Land Cruiser, the one that was still upright but on fire. The sound felt like a pinch to the base of Evie's spine, because it brought the realization that she had seen Grams, Selena, Barney. But no Craig. More important, no Gale.

That was Gale's voice she heard, too. Screaming, "Please, help me! Help my daddy!"

Grams was holding the remaining bits of Helix's camera, staring at it dully. Evie realized the old woman was in shock –

(We all are.)

– and even though she'd just saved Naeku, she didn't look up to doing much more.

Naeku heard the shout, too. She took a step toward the source of the screams, then cried out and bent in on herself.

Evie moved at last. Her feet took her toward the Land Cruiser, toward Gale and toward Craig and maybe Helix – but Gale most of all, Gale couldn't die, not Gale!

The fire that had mostly been confined to the Land Cruiser's engine gouted upward. Flames leaped ten feet in the air, and Evie saw the paint on the hood blacken and blister. She was running now, enveloped in thick, almost painful smoke.

In movies and television shows, the smoke was always barely visible. Even in the middle of an inferno, the actors could be seen easily. They coughed to let you know it *was* smoky, but Evie realized as she plunged into billowing clouds of gray-black smoke that she rarely saw the smoke itself.

Not like now. Now, she was blind. Even if the smoke hadn't burned her eyes so badly that she had to shut them just to function, she wouldn't have been able to see through it.

Nasty, black stuff that singed her nose and kept her eyes streaming an unending current of stinging tears.

She felt for the Land Cruiser. Found the side of it, buckled and bent. She felt for a handle. If she could only get it open…

She found one. It was hot, but she didn't let go. She yanked on it. It pulled in her hand, but the mechanism felt strangely loose and the car door didn't open.

She moved on. Gale was still screaming. "Daddy! Help my daddy!" At least it wasn't the wordless shriek of someone on fire. Evie had time to get there. To save her.

She felt along the back of the Land Cruiser. She still couldn't see a thing. Something bit her hand. A piece of broken glass or jutting metal. She couldn't tell, just knew it hurt but not so much that she couldn't keep going.

Around, around… the blind trip around the side of the Land Cruiser seemed to take a year. Two years.

Happy birthday to me!

The song sounded in her mind; kept ringing over and over as she felt her way hand over hand along the side of the Land Cruiser.

Happy birthday to me!

Gale was still screaming, but the words were gone. Just shrieks now, empty of any meaning but terror and perhaps pain.

Evie felt along. Found another handle.

Happy biiiiirrrrrthday, toooooo…. meeee!

She yanked the handle. Like the first one, it pulled easily, loose as the day when it drove off the lot. Unlike the first one, the pull was followed by the rewarding *tunk* of the doorlatch letting go. She pulled the door. It didn't open easily, seeming to hold tight to itself like it was afraid to let go, like the car knew that to open would be to show the death inside.

Evie pulled harder. Metal ground against itself with dull rasps. The door opened.

A monster loomed in front of her.

NOT A MONSTER. JUST Helix.

She probably wouldn't have known what it was that nearly bowled her over in its haste to get out of the car, but the smoke suddenly puffed aside and her eyes blinked open at the same moment, the two events conspiring to provide her with a good look at the burly young man. A far cry from the together, calm creature of only a few hours before. His eyes were crazed, glossed over by pain and fear. He held his left arm in his right hand, and Gale saw yellow bone jutting out through the skin of his left forearm. The skin around it was black with soot, but even in that moment, even through the grime, she could see the caked blood and the purpling bruise that covered his arm from wrist to elbow.

"Help! Help me!" he shouted. Without waiting for reply he pushed the rest of the way past her. That was fine with Evie, because it opened the way for her to slip into the car.

She realized only a moment after entering that in opening the door, she had let out what clean air was trapped inside the space escape. Smoke so thick it looked like Hefty bags curled its way inside with her, only giving her a moment to see what was happening.

Gale was there. She could move freely, but obviously had no intention of leaving. Not without her father, who was crammed into a space far too small for a man his size. He had been sitting on the side of impact, directly where the two Land Cruisers had slammed into one another and then locked together. Evie didn't see any blood on him, but he was slumped and unconscious.

171

Gale must have heard her come in, or perhaps just hoped someone had. She turned toward Evie, who noticed another odd detail: somehow the girl had kept her dark glasses on through the crash, and their lenses were streaked with grime and the residue of burning smoke.

"Help my daddy!" she screamed. "He was awake but now he's not and I think he's stuck!"

"I'm here!" shouted Evie. Then she didn't know where "here" was as the smoke cut off all sight. She shut her eyes tightly, the never-ending river of tears redoubling in size as she felt her way to Gale. She grabbed the girl's cane first, not trying to do so but somehow managing to find it in the torrential clutter of the car. She yanked on it, thinking perhaps to give it to the girl, perhaps just to toss it aside. Her thoughts swirled like the smoke, and like the dark clouds they billowed, split, reformed, and fell apart again. Nothing held but the darkness and tears.

The cane wouldn't come free. She yanked again, and this time it moved forward but it was still caught on something and it was only after feeling her way up the cane that she realized it was caught on Gale herself, the wrist thong wrapped around the little girl's wrist. Evie took Gale's hand in her own and pulled, hoping to shove her through the open door she herself had just entered.

Gale resisted. "Not without him!" she screamed.

Evie didn't have to ask who Gale was talking about. But she didn't have time to argue the point. She hauled the girl forward, grasping her in her arms. Gale hadn't stopped screaming – *"Not without him not without Daddy!"* – and kept screaming until a second set of hands suddenly reached past Evie and held the little girl's arms as well.

"Let Evie get him," shouted Grams. Evie hadn't heard the woman come into the Land Cruiser, and didn't see anything, what with her eyes closed. She barely heard her now, over the terrified screaming of a little girl and the snap-crackle of burning fuel –

(How long before this whole thing just explodes?)

– and her own heartbeat that sounded like machine-gun fire in her skull. But Gale must have heard her clearly enough, for she immediately stopped screaming and then clambered past Evie.

"Save him," she whispered as she passed. Evie nodded, knowing the girl wouldn't see, but believing she would know that a promise had been made just the same. She couldn't speak, because the smoke that pressed in was now so close and thick she worried that opening her mouth would be the last thing she did. If she let that noxious creature into her mouth, down her throat, it would kill her.

She heard Grams pull Gale out of the car. She turned back in what she hoped was the direction Craig was in. As soon as she did, she heard him say, "Is she gone?"

Craig must have woken from his dark sleep just as Grams entered. Must have known that if he showed signs of wakefulness then Gale would want to stay with him – she was that kind of person. She wouldn't want to go regardless, but to leave when she knew her beloved daddy had just woken up? Never.

Evie nodded – another useless gesture in the cloying blindness that had become her world – but did not speak. Somehow Craig managed, though coughing turned the words into a stuttering jumble of near-nonsense sounds.

"I'm... pi-pinned. Somehow... how... the-the-the seat... Get out. It-ih-t's okay. Just w-w-watch out for Gale an-an-and..." Then he spoke no more. Only coughing.

Evie realized she'd been holding her breath. Realized, too, that between the smoke and the fire and the fact that the

173

fire must rapidly be burning its way to the fuel tank meant they didn't have much time to act.

And he said to go. That it was okay.

She did her best to ignore that voice. She was good at ignoring things, wasn't she? Ignoring her life, and what it had become?

Maybe you'll die this time.

Ah, but I've been dead for years, remember?

She found Craig's arm in the darkness. Pulled. He howled with pain and strain but didn't come free. She felt along his body. There was space between his legs and the seat he was on and the seat ahead of his. He wasn't pinned there.

She felt his back. Ran her hands around to his chest. That was the problem: the back of his seat had collapsed forward, and he was pinned between it and the seatback of the Leg's seat before him. She pulled, straining as hard as she could, trying to loosen the seat's grip on Craig.

The fire's pops and cracks sounded louder now. They had been cap guns when she got in, but had graduated to starter pistols, firing off at random but deafening intervals. Metal pinged all around her, the heat of the fire shifting it, bending it to its will.

Not long now.

"Pl-pl-please…" Craig dissolved in a coughing fit again. She knew what he was saying: "Please leave. Please save yourself."

She risked opening her mouth for a moment. It almost undid her just as she had thought it would. The pouring smoke instantly coated her tongue and palate and made the universe not just sound and feel and look like an apocalyptic nightmare, but *taste* like one as well. She started coughing, of course, but managed to gag out the two words she had wanted to say: "Sh-sh-shut *up*."

174

Craig coughed but said nothing.

She felt a surprising satisfaction – both that she'd managed the words and that they had had their intended effect.

He probably just can't talk anymore.

Well, there was that, too.

She pressed against the front of Craig's seat, trying to push it back, trying to give him the space he would need to wriggle free. It didn't work.

She clambered over the seat, into the very back row. She felt around until she found the headrest of Craig's seat. She managed to cough out, "Push now!" then she yanked as hard as she could. The seat didn't come free, but she thought she felt it wiggle. "A-a-a-again!"

She heard Craig grunt through fits of coughing. The seat didn't budge.

She felt fingers on her own and thought Craig was grabbing her, pulling her away and telling her silently to go. To leave him.

"Wh-wh-wh-"

Coughing followed the unsuccessful word, but not before Evie recognized the voice: Grams had come back. She had taken her granddaughter to safety, and now had returned for her boy.

With sudden clarity, as though the smoke had parted in a last, surprising grace, Craig screamed, "Get out of here!"

"Not w-w-without y-y-y-" Grams choked the last; could not finish. Evie kept pulling throughout the exchange. Yanking on Craig's chair from behind at every angle she could manage.

"I don't matter, Ma!" Craig shouted. Again he managed to speak with impossible clarity. He bit off each word, letting each syllable stand as its own complete moment, its own powerful creature. "I. Don't. Matter."

Grams didn't respond. Evie, still pulling, thought she was mulling over what the man had said. That was crazy, though, because Craig *did* matter because he had a daughter and that daughter was beautiful and even if she *was* sick that just meant that she needed her daddy even more and Craig was a good daddy so that meant –

With a surprisingly high *tink*, the seat Evie had been pulling suddenly let go. For a moment she felt as though she were falling, as the resistance she had anchored against disappeared.

Evie knew Grams had gotten out of the Land Cruiser, even though in a state of shock. Now she found out how, just as she found out what had bitten her hand before. The rear windshield of the Land Cruiser had been blown out, the frame on the side where Grams had been sitting widened so much it was almost a door. When Evie fell back, she fell half out the newly-created exit, and her body took over from there. She flipped over, though she felt glass bite into her stomach in a series of tiny nips that would no doubt become searing dots of pain once shock and adrenaline left her system. She wiggled forward and then fell out of the Land Cruiser. Her shoulder hit the hard ground below, and it hurt badly but she barely noticed because her body was too busy sucking in the air that still ruled at this low altitude.

She crawled forward, elbows digging down and yanking her trailing body the rest of the way out of the Land Cruiser.

Snap-snap-sn-CRACK!

The starter pistols had grown – .22s now. A tiny gun, sure, but more than enough to deafen and to kill if used without care.

She dragged herself a few feet, then turned, still on her stomach, to round the Land Cruiser and get back in. She thought she might have loosened Craig a bit, maybe enough to –

"Evie! Evie, are you –"

Grams' voice again dissolved into spastic coughing. But Evie could hear it from her right side – the side *away* from the burning Land Cruiser. Which meant Grams must have gotten clear of the vehicle, which in turn meant she must have gotten Craig out, too.

Evie turned. She kept crawling, this time away from the heat and the small-caliber pistol fire. A few feet into her escape scuttle, she felt hands grab her upper arms and start dragging her. Craig had her on one side, Grams on the other, pulling Evie away from the smoke and fire and toward the girl who waited in a patch of clear air, her arms outstretched, fingers splayed wide as though adding her strength to that of her family.

It worked, after a fashion. Evie saw the girl, and the strength stolen from her by smoke and panic found its way back. She kicked harder, pushing into a semblance of uprightness, then stumbled with Grams and Craig to the still-reaching little girl.

5

ONCE THEY REACHED GALE, Craig picked the little girl up and covered her with kisses as they continued in the one direction that mattered most: away from the burning Land Cruiser. Though when Evie glanced back, she saw that the fire that had seemed an inferno when close up now looked pale and pitiful. Even as she watched, it dimmed and lowered. The .22 was a cap gun again, apparently having bypassed starter pistol status in its eagerness to rest and then to die.

Another thing that wasn't like the movies: apparently not all burning cars exploded.

"Get away! Get over here before it blows!"

Evie turned her head and saw Helix, Barney, and Selena standing about fifty feet away and to the right. Barney was the one screaming, and he kept on screaming as Grams turned toward the group, drawing her family and Evie along with her like the force of nature she was.

"It's going to blow! It's –" Barney swallowed in the middle of his sentence and weaved on his feet. Blood painted the side of his head, the thick dark line of a gash on his scalp. His shirt was soaked with red from the bullet wound in his shoulder.

He no longer looked like money. His nickel-colored shoes had darkened to a sooty brown, his skin gone from "old dollar bills" to a sickening gray. His eyes were no longer tarnished dimes, but stained windows on an abandoned home, little left inside and nothing at all of value.

He stepped backward, and nearly fell. Naeku caught him – Evie hadn't even *seen* the woman until she moved, so still and silent she stood – and gently lowered the big man to the ground. It was easy to see Naeku wasn't in great shape herself, but she maneuvered Barney into a sitting position without a trace of complaint or even much expression. Indeed, she wasn't looking at him at all. She was looking beyond, past Evie and the Jensens, to the Land Cruisers.

No. To her brother.

Evie didn't want to look. She didn't want to look at Leg and she wanted to avoid the wounded look that had appeared in Naeku's eyes even more. She did what she always did when she was afraid, lowering her gaze and trying to take in as little as possible, and to give out even less than that.

Invisibility was a refuge, and if you couldn't manage invisibility, then absolute subservience was a close second.

So Evie looked down and saw Gale. Craig had put her down, and the little girl was holding fast to his hand. As Evie watched she reached out with her other hand, encircling Grams' leg. Grams patted her absently on the head.

Craig swung her hand back and forth in his own, the absent motion of a parent who knows the simple rule: when in doubt, move. Get Out Your Wiggles. Then he seemed to remember himself. He leaned down to Gale, wincing as he did so. Apparently he *had* been pinned around the legs as well as chest and back: his right leg was streaming blood, and simply kneeling nearly sent him sprawling. He righted himself, though, not seeming to care about his own injuries but feeling Gale's head, her neck, her shoulders.

"You okay?" he asked. Gale nodded. "You hurt anywhere?" She shook her head. "Are you –"

"Dad, I'm fine," said Gale. Her voice was so tiny in the vastness of the last hour or so that it made Evie ache inside.

"What about you?" asked Grams.

She hauled her son to his feet and gave him the exact same treatment Craig had just given Gale. He even responded, "Ma, I'm fine," in the exact tones his daughter had used. Grams

179

gazed pointedly at his leg. Craig grimaced, but his eyes flicked toward Gale as he said, "Really," and Grams nodded.

Evie smiled for a moment. Everything was awful, but that family was still –

That thought made her remember. Made her brain seem to slip sideways in her skull. She spun in place, shouting, "Bill? Bill!" into the night.

The darkness around them had been pushed back by fire, but the Land Cruiser's flames were dying. The night pushed back.

"Bill?" Evie wandered away, hearing her own voice sound through the echo chamber of empty night.

SELENA EYED THE CRAZY woman as she wandered away, her steps the uneven zig-zag of the average field sobriety test administered on Sunset Blvd. after two a.m. Evie wasn't all there, Selena realized. Her husband was missing, and that meant the woman had lost the one thing that, for better or worse, told her what to do every moment of every day.

Selena remembered that feeling. Four in the morning: wake, dress, go to the bathroom. Four-fifteen: cows need milking. Once done with that: feed those same cows. After that: breakfast. After that...

She hadn't liked the schedule. Hated it, in fact. But she also remembered that the first few days with Aunt Carol, she had felt something missing. A limb whose amputation she had not even noticed, but which sent a dull, phantom ache through her every moment of every day. It was almost a week before she realized the ache came of not having someone there to tell her what to do with every second of every day.

Over time, she learned to enjoy a life where she had free time and answered to no one but herself for how she chose to use it. But at first she felt lost. She walked straight enough, but her mind did the same zigzags Evie was now doing. She didn't call for her father the way Evie shouted for Bill, but Selena shouted nightly to God, wondering if any such person existed but willing to take the chance if it meant that dull ache of *not being told* would just leave.

It left. She didn't think it was God. But she knew that if Evie was left to wander, she might well get lost in every possible way.

Selena stepped toward Evie. Barney, a tired lump on the ground beside her, grabbed at her arm as she stepped away from him. "Don't," he whispered hoarsely. His eyes glowed, reflecting the flame that was burning down on the Land Cruisers. "Don't go, they'll explode."

Selena jerked her hand away from him almost angrily. Without a word she went to Evie. "Come on, honey," she said.

"Bill. Where's Bill?" whispered Evie.

"I'm sure he's fine," said Selena. She didn't believe it for a second, and believed maybe Evie was far better off that way, but it seemed to have the desired effect. Evie's eyes came a bit closer to reality, and she allowed herself to be turned back to the group.

Selena glanced behind them as they walked, noting how close they had come to walking beyond the demarcation between firelight and... nothing at all. Beyond the dwindling circle of illumination, creation simply ended. Nothing beyond, the Flat-Earthers were right about what happened if you went too far and if she walked beyond that line she would fall and fall forever.

She shivered and drew Evie along faster.

Naeku turned away from what she'd been looking at –

(Don't think about that Selena it's not your job and you got better things to worry about then a buncha dead bodies crisping in the heat or a red shirt and eyes that wanted to have and hold and hurt forever.)

– and limped over to Evie. "Where was he going when you got out?" said the Maasai.

Evie shook her head. "I don't know. I saw… I saw…" Her hand clapped over her mouth as though capturing what she had been about to say. She shook her head and started to wheel around again. "Bill! Bill, where –"

"Good God!" Barney thundered. The big man struggled to his feet. He lurched toward Naeku, seemed to think better of it, spun toward the Jensens and Helix for a moment, then back to face Naeku again. "We have to leave. That car could blow! We have to –"

Naeku's voice slashed through Barney's. In cold tones she said, "This isn't one of your movies, Eberhardt. Nothing is going to explode."

Barney looked away, but even in this moment he couldn't resist gloating. "Hear that?" he said to no one in particular. "She's seen my movies."

For a moment, Selena thought those words might drive Naeku into a fit of hysterical laughter. The guide's face shifted as she sought to keep herself under control. She took a deep breath, exhaled, another deep breath, then turned a slow half-circle, looking at each of the survivors in turn. When she got to Selena, the actress wanted to fall back under the force of her look. She stood her ground, but it cost her.

This is power. Not the ability to molest a hopeful actress, or even to kill. This woman is going to decide what to do, and damn well do it.

Selena broke contact first, something she would have kicked herself for only a few hours before. Now it seemed only right, to show deference for the Person In Charge.

Naeku looked at everyone once again. Just as slowly this time, as though they weren't in the middle of nowhere with a bunch of dead bodies and –

"I'm hurt." Helix stepped forward when Naeku's gaze turned to him. He thrust out his arm, and Selena felt faint as she saw the bone jutting through his flesh. "I need medical attention."

This time it was Selena who had to will herself not to laugh. The words were idiotic. Of course he needed medical attention – who *didn't*?

Barney lunged at the man. "No!" he shouted. "We gotta… gotta get away…"

He gestured wildly, more flinging his hand to the side than pointing, but the gesture was clear: we gotta get moving!

"Sit down," Naeku said. Her voice carried a note of command that Selena hadn't yet heard. All traces of the jocular guide were gone, replaced only by the hard edge of someone who meant to live, no matter what.

Barney must have heard it too. Or perhaps he was just too weak to keep himself upright. He slumped back to the ground, his huge ass providing plenty of padding as he dropped. It also provided enough roundness that he rocked back like one of those punching bags some kids had – the inflatable kind with the weighted bottom that made the toy right itself every time it was knocked down.

Barney's good arm windmilled and, sure enough, he managed to right himself. Selena had the sudden impulse to punch him in the face, to knock a tooth or three down his throat, enjoy his startled face as he rocked away, then repeat the motion when he lurched upright again.

183

Naeku looked at the Jensens. "Are you hurt?"

"No," said Grams and Gale as one.

Craig shook his head, then shrugged and pointed to his leg. It didn't look nearly as bad as the bullet wound or the bone doing its Groundhog's Day impression. Naeku didn't seem to think so, either, because she glanced at Barney, then at Helix. When she turned to Selena, she shook her own head and said, "We're fine, too," realizing only after she said it that she had spoken for Gale as though they knew each other; as though they were *friends* for Heaven's sake. She also realized she was holding Evie around the shoulder, a draping embrace that she never would have done in any other circumstance.

She didn't move though. She stayed there, one arm around the standing woman she'd despised and staying far away from the slumped man whom she'd ridden – literally – to the top.

Naeku suddenly turned and marched away. Not into the darkness, but straight into the center of what remained of a crash and a fire and the death that had intermingled with it all.

"Hey! Where you going!" Selena shouted.

No one else cried out. Like they all *knew* what Naeku was doing. Like Selena was the only one in the dark. She didn't like the feeling, and ground her teeth together to keep from saying anything more. She wouldn't ask again; *she* wouldn't be the dumb one!

Smoke billowed, momentarily obscuring Naeku from view, then she was back again, carrying a box she must have pulled out of the non-burning Land Cruiser. The red cross on the white box made it clear what she had brought back, even before she cracked it open to show the well-stocked first aid kid inside.

Helix shoved forward, holding out his arm. Naeku ignored it. She pulled some surgical scissors from the case and cut away Barney's shirt.

Thing cost three hundred bucks on Rodeo Drive. Wonder if he feels like he got his money's worth.

Again Selena had to bite down, this time to keep from laughing. And bit down harder as Naeku cut away Barney's shirt and exposed rolls of fat and man-boobs nearly as ponderous as Selena's own enhanced pair of tits. All of it was slicked with sweat and blood, and more blood oozed from the bullet wound on his shoulder.

Naeku looked at the wound, then started pawing through the first aid kit. Selena expected her to pull out gauze and medical tape. But the object she withdrew was nothing of the sort.

Selena's eyebrows bunched. "What the hell?" she said, staring as Naeku unwrapped the Tampax tampon she now held, pulling the plastic applicator out of the thin paper. "He's not on his period, he's been *shot.*"

Naeku ignored the outburst. She shoved the applicator deep inside Barney's wound. He screamed and weaved, looking like he might pass out, but managed to stay upright and awake.

He screamed again as Naeku pulled the tampon applicator, leaving the tampon in the wound and the string dangling out of him like he was an unfinished blanket someone had gotten bored with making.

Naeku turned to Selena. "These things stop bleeding like nothing else, don't you think?"

Selena thought the words were odd, but recognized the tone a moment later. "*You're not helping here,*" Naeku was telling her. "*So get with the program or shut up.*"

185

Strangely, this didn't upset Selena at all. She felt oddly like bowing her head.

Beside her, Evie started turning in Selena's arm. "Have to... find Bill," she mumbled. She shrugged out of Selena's grasp and took a few stumbling steps toward the darkness that had slid closer with every passing second.

"No." Naeku was there as if by magic, pressing a roll of gauze into Evie's hands. She turned the other woman around until she was facing Helix. "Bandage his arm," said the guide.

"But Bill..."

Selena surprised herself again. Getting with the program wasn't her way, but she found herself sidling over to stand by Naeku, found herself saying, "Your husband is either fine or he's not. We don't know, but we *do* know that people need you here, now."

For a moment Selena was sure her words had no effect. Then Evie nodded slowly and walk-lurched toward Helix. Her steps strengthened and straightened as she walked, and by the time she had reached the YouTuber she seemed totally awake and aware.

Naeku glanced at Selena and nodded a quick thank you that made her feel warmer than she had when she got her first and only Golden Globe nomination.

EVIE WRAPPED THE GAUZE around Helix's arm. He weaved as she did so. "Easy," he barked.

"I know what I'm doing," she said. And she did. Bill wasn't a fan of emergency rooms – there were always too many questions and too much paperwork – so much of the medical attention that occurred in their little family was of the "DIY" variety.

Evie's fingers moved quickly and efficiently as she wrapped the gauze around Helix's arm, coming as close as she could to the bone jutting out of his skin without actually touching it. When the roll began to run out she carefully laid a few more strips across the bone itself – Helix yelped but didn't tell her to stop – then tied the whole thing off loosely enough that it wouldn't bring too much pressure on the wound, but tightly enough to leave the bandage secure.

Helix grinned at her. His hair was a fright, he had small cuts all over his face, and he was *still* the handsomest man Evie had ever seen. "Good job," he said.

She flushed, though she didn't know if it was because of the compliment, because of his smile, or because noticing those two things meant she was being somehow unfaithful to Bill.

She suspected the latter, and for some reason the thought made her feel sick. Shouldn't she feel bad about that? Like she was committing adultery, if only in her heart?

And shouldn't you be looking for him?

She took a step away from the group. A single step was all it took to draw even with the point where flickering light left off and perfect darkness began. She stopped there, toes hanging into the abyss, then turned back to the group.

Bill was alive or he wasn't. That was definitely true.

"OW! DAMMIT, DON'T YOU know who I *am*?" Barney shouted, drawing Evie's attention. Naeku had pushed Barney forward to give her better access to the exit wound on his back. Now she pushed another tampon in the hole there, shoving the top forward, twisting, then withdrawing the plastic shell while leaving the absorbent cotton inside.

Evie couldn't help but notice the way Selena was watching her lover/meal ticket. A gaze that held anger and satisfaction, but also a deep sadness Evie suspected had

187

nothing to do with him and everything to do with the starlet herself.

Naeku began bandaging the wounds, taping gauze right over the tampons, sealing them under layers of cotton and medical tape. "Do I know who you are?" she mused. The Maasai woman seemed to mull this over, as though deciding if she wanted to say what she had in mind. Finally she shrugged, a "screw it" motion Evie often saw when Bill was about to lose it in front of someone he really shouldn't lose it in front of. "For now, you are a paying customer. But if you'd rather be a corpse, by all means keep on screaming at me; I'll be happy to let you bleed." Then she added, with no small amount of satisfaction on her face, "At least it'll be quieter."

Selena muffled a chuckle. Grams, Gale still clinging to her leg like a baby monkey, didn't bother to muffle hers. It wasn't a chuckle, either, but a guffaw that drew a glare from Barney. Evie covered her mouth, stifling her own laughter.

Oh, how she wished she could be more like Naeku – honest and forthright and never hiding from anything; or like Grams, brave in so many similar ways, with an additional *joie de vivre* thrown in for good measure.

Barney's expression went from pained to enraged to something small and weak and pitiful. Before he could say anything, Naeku pointed into the night. "We go that way. Southeast."

Helix, who had been feeling around his bandage and grimacing every time he touched something tender, now exploded, "What? Have you lost your –"

Then everyone was talking at once. "Middle of the night and –" Selena shouted, while Barney half-moaned, half-shrieked, "We'll get lost or eaten or –" and Grams shouted, "Let her talk, let the woman talk if you –" while Craig leaned down and whispered something to Gale, whose little-girl face

188

seemed both more fragile and somehow older than it had when the group left Happy Africa.

"Everyone... just... *shut... UP!*" The rest of the group fell silent, all turning to Helix as he continued, "We wander off southeast or any other direction and the only thing that happens is we die, *tonight.*"

Naeku pursed her lips, and Evie was surprised how quickly the smile of a professional guide for whom The Customer Is Always Right seemed an eternal motto crumbled and disappeared. "Oh. I see," said Naeku. "You are an expert on this part of the world."

Helix bristled. He took a step toward the Maasai, one hand jabbing a finger her way. It was the finger on his bad arm, though, and the action made him grimace. He handled it with the aplomb of any actor dealing with an ad lib; just switched hands without missing a beat, the new pointer punching holes in the air as he said, "Lady, I do a YouTube channel about *bush survival.* I have six million subscribers, and the Discovery Channel wants me to host my own show. So yes, I *am* an expert. Enough to know that we went far enough off the beaten path that the camp'll be looking for us. And that," he added, now switching from point to thumb-jerk as he gestured at the still-burning Land Cruiser, "is the closest thing to a Bat-Signal we're likely to find. It can be seen for miles and –"

"And it won't matter at all. The fire will burn out in the next few minutes and no one will see it."

Helix harrumphed. He put his hands on his waist in what he no doubt thought of as an imposing stance; he had probably practiced and documented it – *Vision of Beautiful Confidence, #12 on Gunnar Helix's All-Time MOST VIEWED Position Videos!* But Evie saw it for what it really was: fear. He was puffing himself out the same way a small animal might hunch up to appear larger, even though it had no chance to survive what was coming. "So now *you're* an expert on fires?" he demanded.

"No," Naeku said, "But I am an expert on the stars."

Helix looked up, frowning. "What are you talking about? I don't even see any st –"

"Clouds," said Evie, surprising herself with her audacity.

What am I thinking? Bill isn't going to like –

Bill's gone. What he likes doesn't matter at all. If it ever did.

Helix's eyes jerked over to her, drawing her away – thankfully – from that line of thought. At the same time, Naeku nodded approvingly at Evie before turning back to Helix and saying, "It's going to rain soon. We thought it might, but the clouds are so thick up there… it's going to rain hard."

"The fires will go out," said Selena, realizing what Naeku meant as well.

"No one sees the Bat-Signal," said Evie, nodding in agreement. Selena smiled at her. The smile was genuine, like the smile of a new friend who has suddenly discovered that she had the same favorite band, movie, and food as Evie.

Naeku shifted her attention from Helix to the darkness beyond them. "It's worse than that," she said. "Not just the fire, but –" She broke off, her face a mask of thought. "I can smell the rain. It's coming, and it's going to come down hard. That means that the light here will be gone, yes, but that is not all. Any tracks we left on the way here are going to disappear." She looked around, person to person, face to face. "We're on our own," she said.

All that sounded appropriately scary, but Evie got the feeling that the disappearance of all sign of their passage wasn't what the guide had been about to warn them of.

6

GALE LIKED HELIX. DADDY had told her, "He's like an over-muscled child who knows exactly how cute he is," and Grams had later said, "He's a tasty morsel, and if he's not careful I might just set my sights on him… at least long enough to take a good big sample bite," which Gale didn't fully understand. But both of them spoke of him with the kind of laugh in their voices that Gale generally heard when they spoke of people who exasperated them, but they liked just the same.

The reason Gale liked him was simple: he rarely acted different around her. A lot of people avoided a little girl with dark glasses and a red-tipped cane, or compensated for her handicap in a variety of strange ways. People would constantly offer to do basic things for her, as though she still needed help to get a drink or find the bathroom – forget about blind, she wasn't a *baby*. Worst of all were the ones who found out she couldn't see, then spoke in a louder voice every time she was around.

She always wanted to scream, "I'm blind, not deaf! What, do you think you'll *yell* my eyes into working?" She actually *had* hollered that one time, a few years back. Daddy explained that others' ignorance didn't forgive her rudeness, and the gentle words stung more than any spanking possibly could have.

But Gale didn't need to keep herself from shouting at Helix. Whenever he showed up, he treated her as one-hundred-percent normal. He didn't speak to her first unless it was appropriate – another thing too many people did, like they were announcing themselves so the poor little crippled girl wouldn't die of a heart attack at the sudden appearance of their

191

Big Scary Voices. And when he *did* talk to her, it was always at a normal volume, asking her the same questions he asked everyone else. The only thing he *didn't* do was constantly ask her if his hair was all right, which she'd heard him do a dozen times to other people. That was fine, she figured.

So yes, she liked Helix. But she didn't like the way he was talking, or what he was trying to get everyone to do. There was no question that Naeku knew more about this part of the world – she was a *warrior*, Evie had whispered to Gale, and something called a Maasai, which Daddy had explained to her was like a Native American, which he had in turn explained to her was like an Indian in the John Wayne movies he liked. So how could someone like Helix think he would know more than she did?

The thing that most convinced Gale of the difference between them was their handshakes. Both of them had firm, dry handshakes, neither of them seeming to pull away from her or handle her like an already-broken doll. But where Helix had hands with a bit of callus, a sense of minor scraping as his skin rasped in places against hers, Naeku's hands were *made* of callus. It was, Evie imagined, like she was shaking hands with a rhino horn. Helix had the hands of someone who worked out religiously, and for whom the feel of dirt and sweat were no stranger. But Naeku had the hands of someone almost *made* of dirt and sweat and even the huge thorns in the wall around Happy Africa, one of which Gale had found in a most painful way that still made her thumb throb when she thought about it.

Daddy told her the thorns were there to protect her and him and Grams and all the rest of the people at Happy Africa, which made Gale's thumb hurt a bit less. But she also knew the reason the thorns protected them was because they were *dangerous.* Just like Naeku was dangerous. Helpful, protective, but again, hard in a way Helix was not. He enjoyed life in the wild. Naeku was a wild thing herself. She knew this wild place, because she was *of* this place. And now it seemed like this self-centered but fun and kind man was thinking about ignoring her advice.

So when he said, "I'm staying," in a voice that would allow no disagreement, she couldn't *not* disagree.

"Please, you have to come with us, Mr. Helix," she said, "or –"

She heard the soft grinding of dirt under someone's feet and knew it was him. He was walking away from them. Not into the night, but back toward the area she herself had just come from. He was walking to the center of the crash site. She didn't worry that the bad men were there – she hadn't heard their voices, and Daddy would have tried harder to stop Helix if he'd been walking into obvious danger, but Naeku didn't want him going there, and that was enough danger in itself.

Why doesn't he understand that?

Gale also realized that there was one more voice she hadn't heard since the moment the Land Cruiser seemed to explode around her.

Where's Leg?

Then she realized something she'd missed to this point. Naeku's voice had been different since she showed up. Gale had thought it was just adrenaline – Daddy had told her about adrenaline, and Gale figured that was what had her own limbs shaking near-constantly – but now she recognized it for what it really was: grief.

Leg is dead.

She tried not to cry. They were far from help, according to what everyone was saying. And Naeku was acting like they were still in great danger. It wouldn't help anyone if she started bawling now. But she couldn't help but cling harder to

Grams' leg on one side and hold Daddy's hand even tighter on the other. Grams patted her head, which normally Gale hated since, again, she wasn't a baby.

But this time the pat was welcome. The pat meant she was alive, and not alone. The pat meant she was loved, and she decided never to mind such pats again, not if she lived to be a thousand years old. Just so long as Daddy and Grams were the ones patting her, because that would mean they were all still alive.

NAEKU SAW HELIX WAVERING and couldn't do anything about it. She had seen the look on his face before. Guests who insisted that they *could* go for a morning run outside the *boma* always had that expression. "I've gone running every day my whole life," they would say, "even when I lived in *New York* and ran through Central Park in the middle of the night. I don't think there's anything out there that can hurt *me*." As though living in any city was enough to guard you against the dangers of this cityless place. Helix was acting the same way, and though he did have a lot of experience in wild places, nothing could possibly compare him for what lay in their future.

Naeku herself wasn't prepared, for that matter. But at least she had seen what was coming –

(*"What happened to the lions, Daddy?"*

"Something terrible, my evening star. Something we must avenge.")

– and that gave her an edge. Enough to survive? Perhaps. Enough to lead the group to safety? Less likely, but she would try, and she was their best chance.

If Helix decided to stay, she wouldn't be able to stop him. She couldn't waste the time or energy, but she would leave him behind knowing that was the last she would see his face. So he had to come. She had to convince him.

Helix had already gone close to the center of the crash site. He leaned over and picked something up. Naeku couldn't see what it was, but from his "Sonofa*bitch*" she knew it was something important to him, and that meant he had just found his camera – or at least what remained of it after Grams used it to save Naeku's life.

Helix held the bits of plastic aloft. "Who did this? Huh?"

Grams stepped forward, her chin jutting out as she said, "*I* did it."

"You know how much this cost? I could sue –" He broke off the threat with a sound of disgust, tossing the camera away from him.

"Please, come with us," Naeku began. But his "I've run in *Central Park,* lady" face was firm. He looked around. Leg's Land Cruiser –

(no, not Leg's, just the Land Cruiser, nothing special nothing that would break her heart at all)

– was still burning, but the flames were almost gone. The light along with them.

Helix seemed to decide they were low enough he could stay close without any problems. He went to the other Land Cruiser, the one Naeku had driven and which now lay upside-down, and slid inside it. She understood what he was doing: he believed her when she said that it would rain, and was taking shelter inside the place that would keep him from getting his hair wet.

"Maybe… should we stay, too?" said Selena. She took a halting step in Helix's direction.

Naeku had to put a stop to this. Otherwise the whole company would end up wanting to stay, and that meant *she* would stay, and that would be just one more body. A body never found, because what was coming would destroy them down to the tiniest pieces.

Turning to Selena, Naeku couldn't help but scan the night behind the woman. She saw nothing. But she knew that *nothing* was the last thing out there. The night was full, and waited only for the last of the firelight to die.

Barney nodded. Of *course* a man like that would side with Helix over her. He would side with a brain-damaged quadriplegic over Naeku, so long as said quadriplegic had a penis. Barney was of the terrible, frustrating sort for whom penises were the ultimate decision-maker.

"That man is a *fool*," Naeku hissed at him. "Perhaps he knows how to dig for water or avoid poison oak. But this is *Africa*. There is no YouTube audience here. There is only the wild, and that which does not belong to the wild. There is only predator, and prey." She tried hard to convey exactly which group everyone here belonged to with her eyes; no sense further scaring the already-terrified little girl whose face was so white it neared translucency. She turned to each of the remaining guests – the *survivors* – as she spoke.

She didn't even realize that by the end of her sentence she was openly staring into the darkness beyond them. Eyeing it the same way she had eyed everyone else. Because it, too, was a living thing. And it, too, had to be convinced that no matter what, this group *would* survive.

EVIE SAW NAEKU'S LOOK. She saw how dangerous their situation now was, and saw as well the way the Maasai woman stared at the darkness.

Stared down *the darkness.*

Naeku looked like she had locked eyes with a dangerous creature; one for whom strength was the only thing

196

worthy of respect. Evie would have been dead in a second if that had been the case, and she the one who had to face down the danger. It had been a long time since she faced anything. Bill had done that for her. He was the one who –

(beat punched hurt hated*)*

– protected her.

Now he was gone.

Evie felt her chin raise. She looked into the darkness, too. Stared at it with Naeku. But she could not do it long. She dropped her gaze a moment before Naeku turned and stalked to the center of the crash site. She leaned down beside the Land Cruiser Helix was in. His legs stuck out almost comically, but there was nothing comical about Naeku's expression, or the tone of her voice as she spoke to him.

"You have to come. You will die here."

Helix's voice dripped scorn – *Look #18 On the Beautiful Faces List, check it out and be sure to "Like" and Subscribe!* – as he said, "Nope. There's food and water bottles here, and –"

Naeku leaned down even farther. She whispered something to Helix, her voice low enough that it could have been the wind rustling the grass. Helix's voice returned, still scornful but now much louder than it had been. "I don't see anything like that," he said.

Naeku jerked her eyes toward the rest of the group, as though worried they had heard that, which of course they had. Then she turned back toward Helix. She whispered again, but this time Evie thought she heard her. "And yet… it *is* there," she said.

Helix's legs shifted, and Evie got the impression Helix was relaxing. Laying back, perhaps propping his head on a loose bag or something that would allow him to recline without getting *too* dirty. "I'll take my chances," he said.

Naeku stood so still she seemed a part of the landscape. Not a living thing, just an outcropping of rock the earth had thrust upward for no discernible reason. Then she animated again, walking away from the Land Cruiser – from Helix – and stalking toward the rest of the group.

It began to rain.

GRAMS COULDN'T BELIEVE THIS. As Naeku approached her, Grams said, "He just going to sit there like a spoiled child?"

Naeku's expression was more than enough answer. Grams sighed. What was *wrong* with some people? But she'd seen that look on his face. Jack had gotten it, too, so long ago: that look that said, "My mind's made up and the fact that you're an idiot who doesn't know what's good for you isn't my fault or my problem. Just don't get in my way."

Thick drops were falling all around. They were huge, and each one that hit the dirt sounded like a penny tapping on a window. *Tik-tik*, they went. When they hit Grams they exploded into a smaller set of drops, making it seem as though a mist enveloped her from all sides even as water fell from above. The rain wasn't falling hard yet, but drops this big meant the clouds were pregnant and overdue for a violent birth.

Two years was what they had said. Two years with almost no rain – that was global warming for you, she figured – and now the rain was coming. Even she, a thoroughly citified woman if there ever was one, could feel a storm brewing.

The fire atop the Land Cruiser, already dying, now began to sputter and steam, licks of flame leaping upward like angry fists, then falling low and disappearing.

Naeku beckoned for the group to come closer. They did, all but Barney, who was staring at Helix's legs. "Sounds like he's the only one with an actual, *workable* plan," he said.

He looked at Selena, looking for all the world like he was staring at a dog whose loyalty had been unquestioned for years, but who had for some unaccountable reason suddenly decided to leave a fresh brown turd on the middle of the bed.

Selena's expression was half confusion, half the desire to obey.

Poor girl doesn't even know she's been in a gilded cage. Maybe now she's seeing, a little.

Grams had known women like that – one of them intimately – and knew how hard this must be. Selena had come from a damaged place, and had her wounds bandaged by a man who pretended to be good, never suspecting that he was just healing her now so he could fatten her up and consume her at his leisure.

Maybe she's seeing.

Then Selena shook her head. "Plus maybe we stay with him we get on his YouTube channel," she said. The words started out haltingly, but gained strength as she went. She was closing the door on that gilded cage, shutting herself inside because the cage, with all its torture, had become less frightening than the unknown world outside.

Barney chuckled. "Small potatoes. After we sell the movie rights to this whole shitstorm and get you cast as yourself, maybe Cruise as me or maybe just Hanks, I haven't decided yet, the sky's –"

"This is the first rule."

Everyone swiveled to look at Naeku. Her low tone seemed a part of the night, her eyes alight with strength, with knowledge… and with fear.

"What did you say, Miss Naeku?" asked Gale. Poor thing was reverting to her Sunday-best manners. She was always polite, but in the face of all that was happening she seemed to be backing into the uncertain concern of a toddler.

"The first rule," repeated Naeku. "Do not run."

"The fuck are you talking about?" asked Barney. He pushed to his feet, brushing absently at his knees with one hand as he did.

Naeku didn't look at him. Just Selena, then the good ol' Jensens.

What's that old saying? 'The family that gets in a hostage situation and crashes in a ball of flame in the middle of the Dark Continent stays together'?

Sounds about right.

She wanted to laugh. Didn't, because she knew if she did she probably wouldn't stop. Not a good time for laughter, this.

Naeku waited a moment, as though knowing Grams needed a few seconds to get herself under control. Then she said, "We are going now. We will stay quiet, and stay close to one another. We will *walk*." Grams didn't like the emphasis she put on the last word. Why did she do that? Did she think the group would *jog* across half of Africa? With a blind kid; an old woman; a man who was now standing almost sideways, he was favoring his leg so much; and another who was shot?

"We will walk," she repeated, as though in answer to Grams' unspoken question. "We will not run, because that is what the food does... and there is nothing we can outrun in this place anyway." Naeku's voice was steady, calm. Like she was saying, "This is how you turn on the television," instead of words that boiled down to, "Stay calm or you'll get eaten."

As if the world hadn't been a scary enough place already, the Maasai now turned on her heel and walked away.

The terrifying thought gripped Grams that Naeku had realized as she spoke how far along Shit Creek they had floated, and finally noticed that she was the only one holding a paddle. No question she'd get along better without the rest of them, so maybe she had –

No. She wasn't leaving. She just went back to the Land Cruiser Helix had staked a claim on. She didn't speak to him, though Grams heard Helix say something.

She can't hear him, because you can't hear a dead man.

The thought made Grams' tongue go dry, even as sweat burst from her pores. Or maybe that was just the rain, which was no longer *tik-tik-ticking* its way down. The droplets had linked arms and now fell in a sustained rumble that sounded like faraway applause in a city-sized stadium.

Naeku went around to the back of the Land Cruiser, and Grams saw her bend down. A moment later, she was heading back to the group, her face a stony mask. Her sure stride faltered for a moment. Grams looked toward whatever the other woman was seeing. The darkness was almost complete, the last guttering flames atop the Land Cruiser throwing up final prayers and then dying completely.

Naeku was among them now. "Walk," she said urgently. Her voice was a stage-whisper, the sound of barely-contained terror. "Walk."

Still a hint of light. Still the glow of embers deep in the blackened vehicle a few feet away.

Barney shook his head. "I don't think so. I'm not getting anywhere like this." He pointed at his wounds as he took a step toward Helix. He stopped, turning his gaze on Selena. The actress bit her lip, looking from Naeku to the surging night to him. She took a hesitant step in his direction.

"Please," whispered Naeku. "Please just walk. Follow me."

Selena smiled. Grams supposed the look was meant to be haughty and imperious, but the sick fear behind it ruined the effect. "Why? You worried we get rescued here and you won't be able to grab any good publicity? I get that, but..."

The actress' voice petered out as she realized that Naeku was no longer listening to her. She had her back turned to the crash site, and stared into the darkness. She motioned for silence, though no one was speaking.

No one spoke, but Grams heard a voice just the same. Gale's words, when they had stopped the Land Cruisers to look for something that did not want to be seen.

"They're out there."

7

AS THE LAST FLAMES died, Evie saw Naeku point a gun at Selena, and knew that the warrior was going to kill them all. Not out of anger or hatred, but mercy. Whatever was out there was worse than any bullet could be. There was death, and there was *painful* death, and the Maasai knew this.

Then she saw the gun continue its upward arc. Its muzzle pointed up, and Evie saw it wasn't a gun. It just looked like one. But the thing Naeku was holding was the wrong color.

Then she saw nothing at all. The light was completely gone. Night swallowed the world, allowing only for the rustling susurration of rain on dirt that was rapidly slicking into mud at their feet.

And something else. Another sound, beneath the rain. It sounded almost like the purring of a cat. The low tone of contentment... or of knowledge that contentment will soon arrive. Satiation anticipated and enjoyed in advance.

A third sound: Naeku, her voice a whisper. "Do. Not. *Run.*"

Then a fourth and final noise: the *fshwttt* of the flare gun Naeku had been holding. A bright trail of light shot upward, at first illuminating little. The contrail of the flare dimmed, then died. Then a star seemed to appear overhead. A twinkle that became a sun, brightness exploding around them.

The flare illuminated the survivors, hunched in a tight group with Gale at their center, reminding Evie of nature shows that always featured herds circling to protect the young in their midst.

The light illuminated the Land Cruisers. It illuminated Helix's legs.

And it illuminated the three dozen spotted hyenas that had crept to within feet of the group.

One of them was closer than any of the others. She was a terrifying sight, her muzzle drawn back to expose teeth stained dark with the blood of thousands of kills. Her skin shone through much of the mangy fur, slack and loose with long seasons of hunger. Her ribs showed, somehow conveying starvation without stealing any of the sense of power she exuded.

It *was* a she, Evie knew, in spite of the massive member swinging freely between her legs.

No, not a she. The She.

Once Upon a Time,
the Princess faced a Dragon.

Only that's wrong, too, isn't it? She's not a dragon. She's the queen. That's what She is, and the only name She's ever known. She is Queen.

Queen's face was a mass of scar tissue, one side of it roughened by keloids so thick they turned that side of her visage into the rough stone of a statue begun by a mad artist who found beauty only in destruction. Her ear on that side was gone, the spot where it had been marked by an obscene hole in the middle of her scars.

As though she heard Evie's thoughts, and loved the fear they held, Queen's pseudopenis twitched. It lengthened and pointed forward instead of down. The signal of dominance so complete it took Evie's breath away, and she had to fight the urge to kneel. To bow her head and present herself willingly to Queen and her pack.

Queen barked. The bark – *oh-oh-oh-ohhh* – lengthened into a howl.

The flare had begun its descent. It winked in and out, the rain still pounding it to an early death.

Queen's howl now became a stuttering *oo-oo-oo-hi-hi-hi-hi*.

She was laughing. The pack laughed as well. They all stepped forward. Twenty feet away. Less.

"Stay still," said Naeku. Her voice did not waver. Evie froze, and felt the others do the same. The smallest motion would mean death.

Ooo-oo-hi-hi-hi...

The laugh was thicker, pushing aside the rain like a curtain. The rain itself, which had turned momentarily to a cascade of diamonds in the light of the flare, seemed to part as the hyenas approached.

Naeku spoke once more, the words separated by small infinities in which Evie took in a thousand details, a million bits of information. "Do..."

The rain fell. Diamonds dimmed to smoky quartz. Mud puddled and squelched below Evie.

"... not..."

The light dimmed further, the flare sputtering and gasping like a drowning man. The sun-dried grass all around waved in the rain and Evie couldn't be sure if it was calling the hyenas forth, or reaching to catch the rain, or simply bidding a fond farewell to the people who were about to disappear forever.

"... *run*."

The hyenas surged forward. No one screamed, which was good; Evie knew that if they had made even a single sound, it all would have ended.

Silence ruled among the survivors. Even Gale, who had seen nothing and must surely be terrified beyond comprehension, made no sound.

No one twitched. No one made a sound. Not until the hyenas were so close any of the survivors could have reached out and touched them, and even then the only person who moved was Craig. Gale still held to Grams' leg, and now Craig hunched protectively over his daughter, covering her with his body, holding onto his mother at the same time, giving his back to the beasts in the obvious hopes that they would take him, and leave his child and mother.

In the next moment, Naeku moved as well. She stood between Selena and Barney and the onrushing pack. A knife – the same knife she had used to kill the man who killed her brother, which she must have recovered at the same time she got the flare – extended into the night like a living thing, seeking the blood of any who dared cross it. The power couple nearly fell into each other, grabbing for one another and trying at the same time to hide completely behind the Maasai.

And Evie... no one held her. No one clutched her in embrace or stood between her and death.

She was alone. More than ever before, she had nothing to hide behind. In the moment before the hyenas swarmed over her, she realized that not having anyone to hide behind was strangely freeing. In the moment before they were upon her, she smiled.

EVIE WAS SURPRISED TO find that she wasn't dead. She expected to die, praying only that it would happen to her before it did to anyone else, especially Gale. Selfish, she supposed, but she didn't want her last sight to be of the little girl dying.

It wasn't. The little girl didn't die, and Evie herself was not torn apart as she expected to be.

The hyenas rushed forward, their longer forelegs giving them a lurching, hunched stride that made them appear vaguely deformed, but they were still fast, so fast. The creatures streamed toward and around the group, so close that Evie felt ghost-touches where their hair brushed her hands. The sensation was drowned in the smell, though: thick musk, the scent of mating and killing – the one leading to the other, as often as not. It was a disgusting, rank smell… but there was no denying its power. Heavy, cloying, it thrust itself into Evie, penetrating her brain and saturating it. She was panicked, more terrified than she had ever been, but that smell almost made her want to step forward and lay down and just wait for the end.

The pack split apart as they got to the tight-knit group of survivors. They rushed past so quickly Evie barely had time to ask and answer the one question she had: why not us?

The answer, of course, lay on the ground only a few dozen feet away. Three bodies, flesh torn and blood still sending its own powerful scent into the air. The pack would fight for their food if necessary, but why fight when there were such easy pickings to be had?

As the beasts parted and ran around them, Evie thought she saw one – Queen – stop. The matriarch's muzzle turned toward her, its teeth still bared in a forever-smile of malice. The snout wrinkled, a rictus grin that seemed to promise:

"Not your turn. Not yet. But soon."

Hi-hi-hi-oooo! Queen laughed, and the others laughed with her. They were in the middle of the crash site now, and Evie saw the animals making for the dead. They waited, though, until Queen turned back and strutted over.

The hyena sniffed a pair of arms jutting out from behind the blackened husk of the burnt Land Cruiser. Jean-Paul's limbs, splayed in death. Queen chuffed, and a pair of hyenas surged forward. Evie noted that each of the newcomers had a trio of white spots on their right side – spots that Queen had, too.

The princesses and heirs-apparent.

Queen's daughters disappeared around the side of the Land Cruiser. A moment later Jean-Paul's arms began a macabre, twitching dance as their owner was torn to bits.

The flare was dim now, almost dead. The rain had plundered it, stolen all it had. But with the last bits of light, Evie saw Queen go stiff. She sniffed the air.

She turned toward the overturned Land Cruiser. Evie realized that Helix's legs had pulled back as far as they could. Still visible – the big man obviously hadn't been able to fully press himself into the wreckage – but hidden as much as he could manage.

Queen turned toward another one of the bodies. Took a step. Then a step in the opposite direction. She seemed confused.

Then, at last, she oriented fully on the downed Land Cruiser. On the still-visible feet and legs.

The flare breathed its last. In the end it sputtered and grew bright, railing against its own doom. Evie saw Queen take a step toward the Land Cruiser and the man inside.

Darkness fell at last. The demons that hid within the night bayed and yowled and laughed. Evie heard snarling, and tearing cloth. She could imagine the hyenas, ripping clothing and flesh with equal ease, shredding the soft parts of the bodies and crushing the bones in their jaws.

She jumped as a pair of hands touched her shoulders. Naeku's voice sounded in her ear, throaty and breathy as she whispered as loudly as she dared: "Come."

The night seemed to ooze and roil like an oil slick. Shadows in shadows, darkness hiding even greater darkness.

A yelp sounded. Pain. Was Helix giving an accounting? Would he survive?

His screaming began. It was loud and surprisingly high-pitched. A falsetto tone so clear and bell-like it would have been the envy of any castrati.

Evie backed away. She felt as much as heard Naeku moving from person to person in the group. Another hand touched her shoulder: Craig, the next link in a chain that now stretched into the night as the survivors backed away from the sound of torn flesh, spilled blood, and angelic screams.

8

NAEKU HAD NOT HEARD the lions for many years. There were individual lions, of course, but never were they *the* lions, the ones she had heard in her youth. Never had she heard since then the low rumble of a strong pride on the hunt. Not since before her father left.

So why was she hearing them now?

She led the survivors into the night, moving as quickly as she dared across a land that was treacherous at the best of times. The rain lashed them, turning dirt into mud and making every step a trap that had to be escaped. Thunder rolled in the distance. The survivors grunted and gasped as they made their way forward.

In all of it she heard the lions. She heard their sighs, their growls. She heard them purring, and most of all heard the great lament as they found the beginning of their end. The howls of despair as they looked upon what remained of them and knew their fate was sealed.

Thunder rolled in the distance, and she heard the lions screaming in pain. Not roaring this time, but *screaming* as any parent would if forced to witness the ultimate agony of their own child's death.

Naeku gasped. The sound was so real, so heavy, she felt it. It was the cry of a ghost, but ghosts live in the past and so have a reality and importance that no present can match. Regret, the memory of pain… it twists us and makes us into its image, no matter how we fight.

She remembered so much. She remembered her father's eyes.

She stumbled, grimacing as the movement tore her side. Hands pushed against her, keeping her from falling. They were strong hands, and she thought Craig had helped her until she heard Evie say, "You can't keep going."

The touch – human touch, *now* touch instead of the baying of ghosts and the touch of blood in memory – brought Naeku back to herself. She straightened and kept walking. "I have to. Whether I *can* or not is irrelevant."

Behind her, she heard Barney wheezing. The man hadn't been a pillar of fitness to begin with, and now that he'd been shot, flipped ass-over-feet in a car crash, knocked unconscious, and forced to walk it off he sounded every bit as much a ghost as the lions who called in Naeku's mind.

"Gotta… gotta take… a break," the big man managed, gasping out the words in painful chunks.

Naeku forced her pain down. Pushed it to where it did not matter. It was still there, but locked in a place where she would keep it in solitude until she was ready to take it out and deal with it. That was what a warrior did.

And I am a warrior. I have been since my father stared at me and died, even after what was done to me in the village. I stand tall. I bring life and light. I refuse to give up.

She straightened walked over to Barney. The man was still on his feet, but his knees wobbled with every step, and he stumbled every few paces as his feet slid out from under him. He went down to his knees at last, his great bulk displacing so much mud he continued to sink far after it seemed the ground should have stopped him.

"Five minutes," he said. "Just… wanna… take a break…"

Naeku pulled at his arm. He yanked it away. She cursed – a perverse part of her insisting that she do so in Maa; it would not do to survive this and then find out that, due to her profane mouth, there Had Been Complaints – and reached for him again.

The rest of the group watched, and as Naeku struggled with Barney, Evie stepped forward. That surprised Naeku; she would have expected Selena or the Jensens to speak their mind, no matter what – but not Evie.

"Naeku?" Evie said quietly. "Why can't we stop?"

"They're still out there," Naeku said through gritted teeth, still straining to get Barney moving.

"Why would they follow us?" Evie asked. "They can't be hungry. Not after all that… um… food."

Naeku had managed to capture one of Barney's forearms in her own strong grip. At the last word, *food*, she stiffened. Her hand clenched so hard that Barney yelped.

Food. Not Tharcisse or Jean-Paul or Leg or even Helix, still alive and waiting for one of his fans to save him. Not people, no names other than the most basic one, the one Evie used. Food.

"The 'food' they ate… it won't be enough."

"Bullshit!" Selena screamed shrilly.

"Yeah," agreed Barney. He reached for Selena's hand, but she turned away. Scowling, he turned his gaze back on Naeku. "They just ate, what, like six hundred pounds of food?" His glassy gaze tried unsuccessfully to focus on the math problem that presented itself. "Maybe seven hundred, right? They were big guys, except the little guide guy."

Naeku almost killed him right there. She still had the knife in hand – the one she had used to kill the man who had himself killed "the little guide guy," her brother. She gripped it so hard her palm hurt, and through gritted teeth she said, "A hyena can eat thirty pounds in one sitting."

Barney crowed, "That's my point! There were maybe twenty of them, right? So that's thirty pounds each, which is more than enough for that pack of bitches, right?"

Naeku turned away. She had to, or she would lose control and kill him.

Just do it. We'll stand a better chance of survival.

She pushed that thought away. They were being hunted – had been, she suspected, since that long-ago moment when they stopped to look for something that hid too well to ever be found on anything but its own terms. But just because they were being hunted did not give her license to become a beast herself.

She began walking again. Her free hand had clapped itself over the wound in her side without her realizing it. She felt the tearing there, and knew she was losing blood far too fast.

Over her shoulder, she said, "That wasn't the pack. That was the advance party."

A queer sound rose into the night. Barney moaned, a sound that oddly mimicked the hunger-laugh of the hyenas: *oh-oh-ooooohhhhhh.*

Naeku looked back at him. He had his hands clasped over his eyes. That made Naeku think of Gale. The little girl had not complained once, just moving with alacrity through the rain and mud and terror. She was holding her father's hand, and looking back through the last minutes Naeku realized that the little girl had been leading her father, not the other way around.

Of course. We are in her world now.

Evie tried to help Barney to his feet. She stared at Selena, who reluctantly moved to the producer's other side. Both women heaved, but neither was able to lift his bulk.

Evie looked at Naeku. "How many of them are there?" she asked.

Naeku felt a twinge of admiration for Evie. *Clever girl. You cannot force him to walk, but you can show him the thing that follows us, and that will consume him if he does not.*

"I do not know. Some packs grow to a hundred strong."

213

The laughter sounded then. Far away, weak. But there were many of them. A hundred? Perhaps.

The laughter died. Then came again. It sounded louder. Naeku had no idea how long they had been walking. She knew where she was going, but the chances of getting there...

The laughter grew, as though its owners constantly shared with one another the greatest joke of all: that life was only a short waystation between darknesses.

Evie jerked in place as the laugh sounded, and a hardness came over her expression. She yanked at Barney's arm so hard he shouted in pain. Evie didn't seem to care, just kept pulling as she shouted, "Get up! Get... *up!*"

Barney yowled but didn't move until Evie punched him in the shoulder. His yowl turned into an agonized wail, but he struggled to his feet. He swayed as he faced the woman who had shown not a trace of spine through the entire time Naeku had known her. Then stepped back as she moved close to him and stood on tiptoes so she could growl in his face, "Get moving, you fat piece of shit."

Craig moved his hands over Gale's ears at that, a movement so perfectly ordinary and so utterly out of place that Naeku laughed. Grams did, too, and apparently at the same thing, because she whispered, "Bad language is the least of our worries, Craig."

Craig looked abashed. He took his hands away, and Gale said, "It's okay, Daddy. Grams says words like that all the time."

Grams' turn to look embarrassed. "Tattle-tale," she muttered.

Naeku laughed harder. At the same time, she turned and began walking again. Laughter was good – it was a light sound, a life-sound. It meant people had not given up, for laughter and despair cannot exist in the same space. Hysteria, yes. But not simple laughter in the face of all reason.

Then the hyenas' own laugh lilted its way across the world.

Maybe laughter and despair could coexist after all, thought Naeku. Maybe some kinds of laughter *feed* on it.

CONTRARY TO POPULAR BELIEF, a blind person's other senses did not somehow step up to make up the difference for the loss of sight. Gale hoped to be a superhero, but for now her senses of hearing, taste, touch, and smell were the same as everyone else's.

At the same time, the fact was that the loss of sight meant that that instead of one-fifth of her attention going to each of her senses, one-quarter did. So while she didn't hear any more than she had when she still enjoyed her sight, she definitely paid better attention to what she *did* hear.

Just like she was paying attention now. She could taste the mud in her mouth, splashed up in microscopic bits by the rain that splashed down so hard it sounded like a million tiny explosions, coming over and over again and sending dirt and dust flying in wet particles that coated Gale's teeth and tongue.

The rain itself had a clean, free taste, a feel on her skin that reminded her of rainy days when she came home from school to find Grams waiting with a tray of hot chocolate or some cookies that she laughingly insisted she had "made" – in spite of the fact that they all tasted exactly like Chips Ahoy, and Gale could hear the crinkle-crunch of the plastic tray in the bag as Grams put the remaining chocolate chip cookies back in their package and sealed it tight until it was time to "cook" again.

The rain was good. The mud was foul. The dark itself did not scare her, any more than the sound of her own breathing or the feel of her favorite jeans. The dark was both a thing she felt and a place she lived. It wasn't good or bad, it just *was*.

Everything else here, though, terrified her. She knew the ins and outs of her own block intimately, and even the neighborhood Albertson's where Daddy did all their grocery shopping held no mystery or fear. But this place, this wild place, was a thing made one-hundred-percent of the unknown. The grass that swished and sighed as they passed through it created a strange pull each time she waved her cane in front of her. It made it harder for her to distinguish obstacles, things she could step over or things she would have to swerve to avoid.

The sounds were strange and loud. She heard the hum and chirrup of insects. She heard the panting of Mr. Eberhardt, the muttered curse words Miss Dancy kept grinding out between clenched teeth. She heard her father's small noises of pain, and felt him cant to the side as his hurt leg threatened to go out from under him.

She heard Grams, too. She was breathing hard just like Mr. Eberhardt, only with Grams, Gale worried that the breathing might signal something worse than just being out of breath. Grams was super-old, and who knew how long she could put up with this?

That was what decided Gale to move forward, no matter what. She took hold of Grams' hand and led her on at a pace that rivaled any speed she would have risked in the comfort of their own home. She would not stop, because if she stopped then *Grams* might stop, and if Grams stopped... well, Gale worried she might not start again.

So she moved fast through the grass, feet slipping and sliding in the mud, but always somehow managing to find themselves again before she fell.

Above all other things, she was afraid of the laughter. The hyenas had followed them, and followed them still. She didn't know if the others could tell, but each time the laughter sounded, it was closer. The animals weren't coming fast – they weren't running, perhaps because the rain had dampened the group's scent or confused the trail in some other mystical fashion that Gale could not understand. But they *were* following, and they *were* gaining on the group.

And now this: Mr. Eberhardt refusing to go further. Gale wanted to kick his fanny. She didn't, though – partly because Daddy wouldn't approve, but more because she doubted it would do much good and besides, she didn't want to miss and end up kicking him in the goodies. That would be *so* embarrassing.

"Get up," Evie was saying. "Get *up*."

More sounds. The laughter threatened to drown all, even the rain, but Gale *paid attention* and made out the sound of someone large heaving himself through mud.

Mr. Eberhardt is moving again. Good.

The mud squelched as someone else slid across it. "Damn rain," said Ms. Dancy, letting Gale know that it was the starlet who stumbled.

"The rain is good," said Naeku.

Gale jerked, startled. She never heard Naeku moving – the woman was one of the few people Gale had met whose entrances and exits were always a silent mystery. Grams must have seen her jump, because her hand tightened on Gale's, and then she let go, her old, soft hand replaced by Daddy's. "You okay, sweetie?" he said.

"I'm okay."

217

"Why in Christ's name is the rain good?" demanded Selena. But Gale heard the *thwuck thwuck thwuck* of footsteps in mud and knew the woman was at least moving.

Naeku said, in the low voice of someone obviously hoping "not to frighten the poor little blind girl," said, "They hunt less in the rain."

So, of course, the rain started thin. It went from a downpour to a drizzle so fast Gale figured God must be turning off some Heavenly Faucet somewhere, and turning it off fast.

Maybe Mrs. God caught him wasting water.

The thought wasn't the kind of thing she would have mentioned in church, but it stole some of the fear Naeku's words had imparted, so she figured God (and Mrs. God, if there was such a thing, which Gale kind of hoped there was!) wouldn't mind.

"Let's go," said Evie. "Keep moving."

Gale didn't know who she was talking to, but noticed another thing: Evie's voice sounded different. She had always spoken like a mouse, quiet and worried that a bad ol' cat might come along and steal its cheese. Just like her husband – Bill, whom Gale did not like at all and missed even less –

(Sorry, God! Sorry, Mrs. God!)

– always sounded like the bad ol' cat in question.

But the mousey voice… it wasn't gone, but it wasn't exactly there, either. It was almost like a voice *in* a voice. Like the mouse-voice had covered up something underneath it, something so long hidden that people all thought it had disappeared.

But it was coming back.

Gale didn't know what *it* was, really. But she knew that the voice under the voice – the non-mousey one – was fighting its way free. She wondered what Evie would sound like when the mouse was gone.

9

THE STARS WERE BACK in force. On the one hand, that was nice; Evie hadn't enjoyed the time – it seemed like hours and hours – that they had spent slogging through the rain. *Less* nice was the memory-voice the starry sky brought with it:

"They hunt less in the rain."

Everyone heard it, Evie knew. It was in their faces: the wretched, desperate expression Selena wore; the mask of pain that stretched over Barney's haunted eyes; the grim determination of Naeku as she put one foot in front of the other and never made a sound of pain even though her side was still bleeding through her clasped fingers; the weary worry of Grams and Craig, who still looked at each other and at Gale with that strange sadness, though that sadness was less desperate now.

Evie knew why. Whatever tragedy they had come to Happy Africa to forget or avoid, it loomed less large now. The fact was, that unnamed calamity lay in a future that none of them might even live to see.

Once Upon a Time,
the Princess was a whiny baby.

Now *that* was a story that rang true. It also reminded her that where there was a Princess, there must also be a Queen. Evie shivered as she remembered that scarred, malevolent face.

The laugh came again. It lilted strangely, sounding almost light-hearted. Not the call of hungry creatures closing in, but the jeer of friends who are just having a fine old time, like college students laughing over a beer and kidding themselves that *they'll* be different; that *they'll* never grow up and have mortgages or pay taxes or get wrinkles.

It was a Peter Pan laugh: ageless and whimsical. But Pan was a thing of chaos, wasn't he? And at his heart, he kept the Lost Boys in a strange captivity, forcing them to play his game over and over, each day different yet the same.

We are in Neverland.

The mud no longer sucked at her feet. Another good/bad sign. The walking was easier, but she knew their trail would be easier for the hyenas to find and follow. It was getting hot, too, and Evie realized that her mouth was parched. How long had they walked? And how long could they *keep* walking without water? Food, too, though she knew that lack of water would be a far larger problem far sooner.

She looked at Gale. The little girl continued to forge forward without a sound. She was holding Craig's hand now – she had alternated between Grams and Craig every twenty minutes or so, and smiled each time father replaced grandmother or vice-versa.

Craig caught Evie looking. He smiled the melancholy smile she hated, because it meant this beautiful family was destined to lose itself. She didn't know how, but one way or another, Craig had already planned the end of things.

Naeku stumbled, hissing in pain as she went down to one knee. That sound frightened Evie nearly as much as the hyenas' laughter. If Naeku was hurting so badly she had stumbled, if she hurt so badly the pain was actually showing, then she wasn't just hurt, she was seriously injured.

The laughter swelled, as though the hyenas saw her and laughed – what a great joke! Hilarious pratfall!

Grams darted forward and caught Naeku with surprising – or not-so-surprising, given how lively the old lady was – adroitness. "No rest for the wicked, dearie."

The hyenas stopped laughing. They howled. Evie's buttocks tightened, her shoulders drew together. She was waiting for a beating, knowing that this time it wouldn't be Bill who administered it, and thinking for the first time how sad that was, if only because the alternative was so much worse.

They're going to find us soon, and nothing we can do about it.

PAIN. SO MUCH PAIN and she couldn't seem to focus on anything else.

Even what Zawadi had done had not hurt as badly as Naeku hurt now. Not just the stab in the side, either – though that was bad enough. She hadn't realized it in the heat of the moment, the adrenaline rush that took over as she fought and killed Tharcisse, and which continued as they began their long walk to what Naeku hoped would be safety.

Now the adrenaline was gone. A heavy fatigue had settled into her bones, and she realized only then that she must have broken several ribs during the car crash. Or maybe it was after, struggling with Tharcisse.

What was *he doing? Was he really FPB? Was this really just about kidnapping us?*

She didn't know. Certainly the FPB – and other "freedom fighters" in neighboring Burundi – weren't above stealing the freedom of a few rich Americans in the hope of an influx of cash for their cause. She hadn't heard of such a thing happening during a safari expedition, but then there was a first time for everything. Certainly there had been other such kidnappings in other places, and would it not make sense for this to occur in a place with less security – and more American visitors – than Burundi itself?

222

She didn't know, and it really didn't matter any more than it mattered exactly when her ribs had broken. She had coughed once or twice. She didn't do that again. Not just because it hurt so badly but because she felt wetness on her lips after she did it and tasted the copper tang of blood in her mouth.

She was bleeding, inside and out.

Stop complaining. Be strong.

In her mind, she saw Zawadi come in with her razor. Saw the old woman pinning down small, fatherless, motherless Naeku. In her mind Zawadi cut her, only this time she did not stop when she finished with Naeku's private parts. This time she dug the blade into Naeku's stomach. Entrails fell from the wound, coiling about her like slick serpents. The old woman laughed, and as she did her face lengthened, her nose pushed out into a snout. She laughed, and the laugh was a hyena laugh.

"Don't move, child," she said. "It won't hurt as much if you don't fight it."

Then she leaned down and began eating Naeku's innards and then picked something off the floor – bloody bits that Naeku realized were her own flesh, recently lost to Zawadi's knife – and ate them, too.

The old woman buried her head inside Naeku, chewing upward as Naeku watched her own blood arc into the night, caught in the moonlight which was impossible *because she was in her hut wasn't she wasn't she in her hut then why were the walls gone why was there rock on all sides and the burble of water and the cry of the children –*

She stumbled. For a moment, she didn't know where she was or what she was doing. She was caught in a place between fevered, agonized dreams and a far more frightening reality.

"No rest for the wicked, dearie," said the woman who had caught her. Naeku stared at her, wondering what Zawadi was doing here.

Zawadi is dead. She must be by now, mustn't she?

Naeku realized it wasn't Zawadi after all. It was Grams, pulling her, dragging her along.

Naeku forced herself to stand taller. These people – they all needed her to live. They were counting on her to survive, because only by surviving could she help them live as well.

"You okay?" Grams said under her breath.

No. Of course I'm not okay. None of us are.

Naeku smiled, though she felt the smile turn into a grimace as the laughter swelled behind them –

(So close they are so close too close.)

(i hear the lions, father!)

– and the pain in her ribs sharpened..

"Ma," called Craig. Grams looked back, as did Naeku. Craig waved to his mother. "Stay close to Gale, okay?"

"Dad?" said the little girl. She sounded suddenly afraid, though even the fear that came through in her voice was much less than Naeku would have expected.

She would have been a great warrior. She would have hunted many lions.

She blinked, confused. The lions were dead, weren't they? And women did not go on the hunt.

Grams was gone, though Naeku had no memory of the old woman going to Gale. She only knew that she had blinked, and Grams was there. Another blink, gone. A third, and now Craig was half-supporting her as she stumbled along.

"I'm not going anywhere, Gale," he called. "Just helping Naeku."

224

He took the arm opposite her wound, lifting it over his neck and shoulders. Naeku's eyes widened as even this "help" brought more pain, but she managed to bite back any sounds.

She saw Craig glance over his shoulder, communicating something to his mother. She was holding Gale's hand already, and now she began to pull the girl forward. "Let's move up ahead, shall we? We can blaze a trail."

The girl forced cheer into her voice, overpowering her fear by the strength of her desire to *not* be frightened. "Sure," she said. "But you'll have to keep me moving in the right direction." Her head swung from one side to the other as though she were trying to spot anyone who might be listening in, then she whispered – very loudly, "I can't see a thing out here."

Grams laughed. She kept pulling Gale forward, passing both Craig and Naeku and continuing ahead of them, but as she did Naeku saw that her eyes smiled not at all.

She is a warrior, too. And her son. A family with strength and honor.

They would have avenged the lions, too.

Her thoughts jumbled. She was in the hut staring up at Zawadi, she was in the wild staring down at her father's dead eyes.

No. None of those places. I am here. Now. These people depend on me.

The laugh that followed them all pulled her back to herself. Terror rode her spine, clenching her chest, sending flashes of pain through her ribs, and the pain would not let her escape even into the confines of terrible memory.

Craig looked behind, the empty night all he would see. "They're still coming, right?" he said.

Naeku shook her head. Not a "no," but a gesture of futility. A gesture of defeat. "They prefer to hunt the lame, the very old and very young, the wounded. Usually they have to cull such from the herd. But with us..." She pried her hand away from her side long enough to gesture all around. "With us, the whole herd is lame or wounded or old or young. The whole herd is prey."

Another chorus swelled. She could hear individual voices now, the baying and calling of each hyena as it raced toward them.

They have picked up the scent. Surely they have, and just as surely will find us too soon.

"Where are we going?" asked Craig.

Naeku hesitated. She knew where they were going, of course. It was the only possible place, the only place where they might find help before they died of injuries or thirst. But saying it aloud made it real. Real, and terrible.

I'm going back. I swore I never would, but I am.

"Naeku?" Craig said. She focused on him and saw concern in his eyes. "Where are we going?"

"There is... a village."

"Will we make it there?"

She did not answer. That was answer enough. Craig's jaw clenched, his temple pulsing as the muscles contracted and loosened, contracted and loosened. "What can we do to stop them?" he finally said.

"Only blood will stop them."

"And how far to this village?"

Decades. Decades and a long path as one of the Two Spirits, and a willingness to lose part of yourself in the most intimate and horrible way.

Aloud she said, "A few miles."

Craig smiled the smile of someone who had heard what she did not say: a few miles might as well have been a hundred. "Are you sure?" he whispered.

226

She nodded. She knew this place intimately, though she had not been here for a decade. You never forget a place where you have lost yourself, just as you never forget the moment you find yourself once more. "Yes, I know this place. The village is close enough that –"

She did not finish. She would not tell the lie to this man. "Close enough" had disappeared from their world as soon as the hyenas found their trail once more.

The laughter sounded. The night was alive, and coming for them.

Craig pursed his lips, obviously thinking hard about something. "Mom!" he shouted.

Grams stopped. She and Gale were about twenty feet ahead, and Naeku gasped as Craig abruptly let go of her and ran the distance between himself and his family.

"Son, wha –" Grams couldn't finish the thought. Craig engulfed her in a hug that Naeku thought might have broken a lesser woman than Grams right in half. Naeku limped forward, thinking she knew what was happening, and that it could not should not *must not* be.

"Mom," said Craig, "there's a village a few miles up. I need you and Gale to move fast. Carry her if you need to, but *move.*"

Naeku saw it dawn in Grams' face. Saw the old woman realize what was happening, even as Naeku herself had understood. "No, son, don't –"

Craig ignored her. He knelt before his daughter and hugged her even harder than he had done with his mother.

"Dad, you're squishing me," the girl whispered.

Craig withdrew with a strained, sad laugh. "Listen to Grams, okay? Keep her out of trouble."

It had been terrible to see Grams realize what was coming for her family. Worse by far was the sight of Gale suddenly understanding as well.

"No!" she shrieked.

"You can't possibly stop them," Grams said. Her voice was tight, the kind of control necessary to keep terror from overwhelming a person. "You can't possibly."

"I'm not going to try," he said. He smiled. The smile, unlike so many of his previous ones, was real. No darkness behind it, no sadness.

The smile lit the night.

"But I bet," he continued, and wiped a tear from Gale's face, "I bet I can slow them down a little. Enough."

"There has to be some other –" Grams began.

Craig didn't seem to hear her. He hadn't let go of his daughter, and now he leaned in close to her. Held her, breathed her in. Naeku was aware that the others had come close; that Evie was watching with tears in her eyes, and even Selena and Barney seemed to be struggling against emotions which they did not understand.

Craig looked at his mother. "We both know this makes sense, Mom. This was our last trip together, and it was a goodbye. We all knew it." He kissed Gale's cheek. "It's just coming a few days sooner than the doc told me it would."

SHOCK RODE THROUGH EVIE'S body, setting it on fire. It felt like the pins-and-needles sensation of an arm or a leg, cramped in a bad position for so long it's numb but now was coming awake again. Only the part of her that had been numb wasn't a limb, it was her mind. Her *self*. Pins and needles, and with them a return of sensation, a cessation of sleep.

I'm waking up. At last.

She saw everything happening in slow motion: the rise and fall of Gale's shoulders as she began to weep, the hand that Selena rose to her mouth, the way Barney looked away. She saw it in the slow closing of Naeku's eyes as the Maasai mouthed something that only she herself could hear. All of it vivid; bright even in the darkness of this long, long night.

And under it all, the thought: *It wasn't Gale who was sick. It was her father.*

She understood it as soon as Craig told his mother that this trip of theirs had been a goodbye. The send-off had been for him – a last set of memories for a child, so that she would have something grand and wonderful in her mind. Memories that would carry her and let love survive within her as her father left.

Evie, alive Evie, *awake* Evie, felt it all. Her cheeks were wet, and she wanted to stop herself from weeping – hours without water now, and every drop was more precious than gold. But she would not profane the moment. She would weep, because the moment demanded it.

Craig kissed his daughter again, then pulled away far enough to look in her eyes. "Did you know you were a miracle?" he said. She shook her head and he said, "Six months before you were born, the doctors told me I'd be gone in three. Three! But Mommy and I prayed... so very hard. And our prayers were answered: I got to see you born. Then I got to see you grow up to be who you are today. This fine, beautiful, *miracle* of a girl who went blind and somehow still managed to see with better eyes than anyone I've ever met."

Laughter rolled across the world. It was a dark thing, trying to snuff out the light Evie now saw. But Craig just smiled as though there were no darkness at all, and his smile made it so.

"Instead of missing you by months," he said, "I saw you, and you kept me alive. You gave me hope. After Mommy died, you gave me a reason to live a few days longer, then a few days after that. The thing they said would kill me went away, and it went because of you." He laughed, a runny, choking laugh as the tears began to come fast and hard. "I got sick again, and it wasn't even the same thing, you know? Totally new thing, but this time the doctors said it wasn't going to go away, and that…"

He stopped talking, voice dissolving to a jerky hiccup. The light was dimming, the darkness pressing in. Craig wiped his eyes. He wiped Gale's too. He raised his eyes skyward, perhaps seeing past the twinkling stars to whatever lay beyond. "I lived for longer than I should have. Something – some reason – kept me here. And now I finally see what the reason was." He took Gale's face in his hands. "You made every day an adventure," he said. Then he let go of her, turned her in the direction they had been walking, and said, "Now run."

GRAMS KNEW IT HAD to be done. Craig was right – that was one of his gifts, God bless him, to see so much of right and wrong, and to have the strength to actually *do* the right thing. He was dead already, whether tonight or in a month. She knew that logically, but her heart didn't want to believe.

The heart, in the final analysis, is a thing of weaker reason, but stronger will by far than the mind. So Grams wouldn't turn away. She wouldn't play any part in this, no matter how noble.

And then, quite suddenly, she realized she would. It was the moment her son whispered, "Now run," and for the first time in months she saw him look at his daughter not with sadness or fright, but with hope.

230

He had been so afraid that he would leave only a void, and that the little girl's tender heart would collapse around it. But now he was leaving her not with that empty hole, but with a chance to live. He was leaving her with the hope Grams saw in his eyes.

She touched his arm, then took Gale by the hand. She turned, and Gale turned with her. The little girl turned back almost immediately, and Grams worried she might have to force her granddaughter to come along. But Gale was not resisting the plan her father had set for her – she just hadn't done something important.

She ran back to her still-kneeling father and reached for him. Not to hold him – that moment was passed, that thing already done – but to touch his face. She ran her fingertips over her father's cheeks, across his brow. She touched his forehead, his nose, his mouth, his chin.

She was looking at her father for the last time, and wanted to remember his face.

Then the girl turned back to Grams. She was no longer weeping. She would do so later, Grams knew –

(*If there* is *a later.*)

– but for now she would obey her father's last wish. She would run. She would do all she could to live.

Now Gale started pulling *Grams*. Her cane waved back and forth, back and forth, a metronome that ticked off the remaining seconds of her father's life.

The rest of the group ran, too.

NAEKU DID NOT MOVE, though she knew she should. Barney and Selena passed Craig. Selena ran silently, her face the hard mask of someone who knows they have witnessed something special but unknown to them. The mask

231

of a woman for whom masks had become the last and best refuge against that great monster Reality.

Barney ran without saying anything, but he made noise. He huffed, he grunted with pain. He had been shot, and he was far from being in the kind of shape that would allow for a headlong run through the night. But the man was a survivor.

Evie went to Craig and, watching the fleeing form of Gale, said, "We can stay with you. We can –"

"Gale really likes you," Craig interrupted. "She'll need someone. Grams is there, but… keep her safe. Keep my little girl alive."

Evie seemed to freeze. Then Naeku saw her straighten from the half-inch hunch that had always pressed her down.

Something is different now.

Evie nodded at Craig. "I promise," she said. Then she, too, ran. She caught up with Grams and Gale and took Gale's free hand. The cane dangled from its thong, the plastic band wrapped around Gale's wrist, but Naeku knew she didn't need it now. Not with the two strong – and yes, they were strong – women who had taken her in hand and would die for her.

Naeku turned to Craig. She held out her knife. Craig ignored it. He looked around and saw a stick on the ground. Picked it up. Swung it a few times. The thing looked light, a sun-dried husk. He might hit something with it, but Naeku knew the limb would explode on impact and that would be the last of it – and him.

"Get them to that village," Craig said.

Naeku nodded. Still did not run. One more thing had to be done. She touched his shoulder, then leaned forward until her cheek rested on his own. Sweat and blood mingled as she whispered into his ear, "You will be remembered as a great warrior."

His voice whispered back to her. "Just as long as I'm remembered as a decent dad." He shoved her away from him. "Go."

She ran, seeing him take a few pitiful swings with the stick. But in his eyes she saw something she had not seen since her father's last day, his last look. The determination to do right, to sacrifice even his own life and will his child to live.

Craig turned to face the night.

Naeku looked over her shoulder every so often as she ran, and each time his shadow was farther and dimmer. Then one time she saw him not at all, and no longer looked back. She would move forward. That was the gift he had given, and she would not let it go to waste.

10

RUNNING. RUNNING THAT LASTED forever, but forever was nowhere long enough. It took them nowhere near where they needed to go.

Evie, like everyone else, was exhausted, bruised, and bloody. But she still ran. She put one foot in front of the other.

It was the laughter that stopped her, of course. That damn laughter, the hungry chuckles of the hyenas as they hunted. Naeku had been right: six hundred pounds of food had not been enough to assuage their hunger. They would keep coming and coming until no one remained.

And the worst part: to the hyenas, it would mean nothing. The deaths of women and men and a child would be forgotten in the next moments as they turned to their next hunt, their next prey.

Evie slowed, the laughter weighing on her. Then, suddenly, it stopped. She felt a moment of elation, the thought coming that if they no longer laughed, perhaps the hunt had stopped.

Then the scream came. She knew whose it was, and what it meant. She looked at Grams, who had not stopped moving. Her hand was over her mouth, the old woman clamping down on a scream that would undo her.

Grams did not slow. She pulled harder, faster. She dragged Gale along, and Gale in turn pulled Evie.

Grams and Evie had been so careful, even as they ran. They moved around obstacles that might trip the girl. They lifted her into the air, like parents might lift a toddler as she screamed, "Up! Up!" and swing her back and forth in higher and higher arcs until the happy terror of the child grew too strong and she now screamed, "Down! Down!"

They had been so careful of Gale. But now Grams was in a place where she could only see her son dying, her brave son buying them a few seconds at the cost of the life that remained in him.

> *Once Upon a Time,*
> *a Princess met and married a man*
> *she thought was Prince Charming.*
> *But he was cruel, and selfish.*
> *He took and took and took,*
> *and the Princess was blind to it all.*
> *Until she saw a **real** Prince, and knew*
> *for the first time that such a thing could exist.*
> *He died in that moment:*
> *the moment she saw him*
> *and knew what he was.*

The story – the longest one she had really felt inside herself for years – changed her. Craig had changed her. Not just with his selflessness, but by the simple act of telling Evie that Gale liked her, and with the simple charge that she protect his child. His own Princess, whose Once Upon a Time was now in danger of ending without its Happily Ever After.

The story beat in her veins, and made Evie feel stronger than she had in a long time. But the magic of it also blinded her for a moment. So she ran blind at the same time Grams disappeared into herself.

And Gale fell.

The little girl tripped over some brush, and Evie came back from Once Upon a Time to Here and Now in time to stop the girl from falling headlong into the mud.

Grams had let go. She had both hands over her mouth now, but she turned back to Gale when the girl slipped, and one of those hands reached for her granddaughter.

> *Once Upon a Time,*

> **the Princess saw a star**
> **about to fall from the sky.**

No. That part of the story was not true. Evie would not *let* it be true.

She caught Gale, then pulled the little girl fully into her arms. Gale clung to her in silence. Grams' eyes, so full of tears, offered to bear the burden.

Evie shook her head. "I've got her," she said. That was enough for Grams, who turned back to headlong flight once more, old hands still clapped over her mouth, tears glimmering over her cheeks.

Evie ran, too. But the run was nearly at its end. It turned to a shambling, lurching jog; and from there it was only moments to a shambling, lurching walk.

The laughter sounded louder than before, then it became a howl. Evie heard their voices, in unison and as individuals.

Night had fallen hours ago, but the *real* darkness was now upon them.

WORDS SOUNDED IN NAEKU'S mind with every footfall, every step a stabbing pain that turned the words to strangely-cadenced exclamations: *NEVER! make it. We'll NEVER! make it.*

She tried to ignore the thought; to convince herself that it wasn't reality, just the pain turning her body into a thing that could only counsel defeat.

Her feet slowed. Selena passed her, drawing even with Gale, Grams, and Evie. A moment later, Barney passed her as well, sounding like a dying steam engine as he puffed and gasped his way across each foot, each inch.

That was what got her moving again. She was damned if that bastard would outlive her.

She pushed herself to move, managing only a quick walk, but even that was enough to draw even with the man, then pass him. He grabbed at her as she passed, a drunken swipe that she knew would steal the last of her strength away if it connected.

She avoided his hand, pulling ahead of him.

The laughter and howls mixed. Melded in her mind.

NEVER! MAKE! it. We'll NEVER! MAKE! IT!

The agonized exclamations were coming faster. There was no way she was going to make it to the village, with its protective *boma* and women who knew how to heal a wound and – more important – how to send for help.

None OF! US! WILL! MAKE! it.

Truer thoughts than she had ever had. The hyenas were too close. The village too far.

She thought about turning as Craig had done. Perhaps she could buy a few more seconds.

But that was foolish. They were miles away from the village. Too far for her to buy near enough time with her death. And what would the rest of them do then? They didn't know where to go, or – just as important – that one place that they absolutely *must* avoid.

They would die without her. So she would have to survive.

But how?

She saw the answer at the same time as the question. Hyenas were strong. They were fast. Their jaws could crush bone. Their legs could tear and rip and push them so very fast and hard.

But those legs…

Those legs cannot do one thing. And that might save us.

237

SELENA DANCY, STAR OF the silver screen, a woman who had for over a decade been the toast of a town that measured careers in terms of six months, maybe a year, knew she was going to die.

She remembered the way Aunt Carol looked at the funeral. It had been held in some church – Selena didn't know its name, and doubted Aunt Carol had ever set foot in it. She thought it was the church of one of the other partners in her firm. They had set the whole thing up, those gray- and silver-haired men, those women with expensive dye jobs and the occasional even-more-expensive surgical tightening of skin that gave them an appearance they fooled themselves into believing would pass for youthful.

Aunt Carol had told Selena about them all. Not about their cases, but about their infighting, their hatreds, their affairs and the way they constantly used and climbed over each other.

Selena had ended up sitting next to Ralph Foggerty, who in turn sat beside Eileen Genesse. The two of them were married, but their spouses had stayed home. Foggerty and Genesse didn't mind this, Selena knew – they'd been having an affair for over a year. Or as Aunt Carol had put it, "They're banging each other harder than Judge Herd bangs his gavel every time I raise an objection in his courtroom. And that is *hard*, baby. I don't know how Genesse manages to stand at all, let alone walk past the bar for law and motion arguments."

Selena did not want to sit next to them. She didn't want to be here at all. The thoughts of running away, of finding her fame in the tinsel and dreams of LaLa Land were already blooming inside her, and she tried to focus on that instead.

She couldn't. Because Aunt Carol had become the end-all, be-all of her world. The woman had been expertly rouged and glossed. Her eyes had been carefully sewn shut – it wouldn't do for them to be open and staring so everyone could see the shriveled grapes her eyeballs must have become by now. Everyone said she looked so peaceful.

That was the worst. The absolute most wrong thing they could have said to a teenager grieving over the loss of the greatest woman she'd ever known. Aunt Carol had been many things, but she'd never once been "at peace." She had never been content to stay with the way things were – there was always bigger, better, richer, more powerful.

"At peace" was not Aunt Carol. "At peace" was just an empty corpse that now kept eyes closed and hands crossed and screamed silently at the universe.

"At peace" was just a pussy way of saying, "dead."

Now, as Selena ran through the long, empty land between the death behind and the nothing before, she started to feel *at peace* herself. The blistering monotony of one foot in front of the other… breathe, breathe, breathe – one foot in front of the other… breathe, breathe, breathe… had lulled her. Had dulled her.

She wasn't running anymore. Just sliding forward a foot at a time. She wasn't afraid anymore. She was *at peace*.

She would have lain down in another moment. That was what you did when you were *at peace*; what you did when you were dead. And it didn't matter that your brain hadn't fully caught wise to that fact. It just mattered that your *at peace* moment was here, and such a moment tended to last forever.

The thing that saved her then was Naeku, suddenly shifting her direction. They had been moving in a straight line this whole time, heading for the village Naeku had mentioned. No longer. Naeku was turning.

The breath caught in Selena's throat. *At peace* wavered.

"Where are you going?" Selena rasped.

Naeku looked back. "Run!" she shouted.

Selena looked back, too. *At peace* fled completely, running ahead of her with a scream on its ghostly lips, frightened to movement by the motion both it and Selena could see behind them.

The night had grown legs. Flashes that could only be teeth. Those fallen-star glints of eyes that saw far too much, yet at the same time saw everything as one of only two things: something to flee, or something to hunt.

Selena had no illusions about which of those narrowly-defined categories she belonged to. The knowledge pushed her forward, and she was running once more.

Behind her, she heard Barney shout, "Hey! Where are you – Wait up!"

Naeku didn't wait. Neither did Selena. Not even when the man screamed, "Help! Selena? Help!"

She had always thought of herself as the hungriest dog in a dog-eat-dog world. Now she knew she had only been half right: she *was* a dog, and certainly Barney was, too. But she was the latter half of the eat-dog equation. And the thing at the front wasn't actually a dog. It was something much worse.

She heard Barney behind her, weeping, cursing. His voice grew quieter with every step she took, every inch she added to the space between them as she outpaced him and left him behind.

"Where are we going?" screamed Gale, just ahead. She was in Evie's arms, her head poking above the woman's shoulder, her face white and pinched.

Selena's mouth had been dry for a while. Now it felt packed with sand. The sand moved down her throat, choking her.

Breathe, breathe.

No, can't. Can't.

(why not be at peace?)

She saw Naeku, answering Gale with a gesture that she had apparently forgotten the little girl could not see. Or perhaps she knew it, but the gesture was all she could manage. Selena didn't know how the Maasai woman was still alive at all. Her knife wound had never closed, and her pants were soaked down to the knees with her blood.

Selena admired her almost as much as she did Aunt Carol. This Maasai woman would never be *at peace.*

Naeku was still gesturing ahead, finger jabbing into the night as she moved forward in something that now resembled an endless loop of falling then catching herself in the instant before tumbling to earth, then pitching forward and catching herself once more.

But that finger never stopped pointing.

Selena followed it. At first she saw nothing but more darkness. Then she realized that the darkness had *gathered* in one spot.

She made out what it was. "You gotta... be... shitting me," she gasped to no one in particular.

The tree looked like the hand of a dead giant, buried alive and managing to claw only this far out of the grave before dying. But the effort had stripped the flesh from its bones, leaving a withered, bare skeleton hand outstretched into the night sky,

The hand did have a few more than five fingers, and that was good... but they were all grouped together, the pinkie finger only five feet off the ground, max. Not fingers alone, the branches were also ladder rungs that would allow the survivors to climb up them, but would offer no safety since anything else could climb them as well.

Selena knew this. She knew about animals climbing into trees and killing people – she'd researched it in the hopes of landing the lead in *Wilder*, which went to that bitch Julianne Moore, whom Selena hoped would choke to death on the Oscar she eventually won.

And now that same damn movie was going to bite her in the ass again. Figuratively, of course – the hyenas would do the *actual* biting – with the horrible knowledge that their safety would be anything but, and their deaths all the more horrible for the false hope that would precede it.

"They'll just jump up and kill us," she said, in her voice a disturbing whimper that she had not heard there since that first time, since Hank had dragged her into the darkness below the bleachers, and his red shirt covered his chest while his pants sank below his knees.

Naeku's voice tore the vision away. "No," she said, her own voice thick with the breathlessness of the run, and damp with the blood that made her lips shimmer in the starlight. "Hyenas can't… climb… at all. Built… wrong…"

Selena ran faster.

EVIE LOOKED BACK BECAUSE sometimes *not* looking back was impossible. Also because Gale was peering that direction.

No, she's blind. She isn't looking at anything, and thank God for that.

But Evie remembered the little girl's voice in the Land Cruiser. She had seen the hyenas before anyone else, though her sight was a dark kind that relied on other senses to create its images. And now Evie had the odd sensation that the girl was "looking," again, and perhaps seeing something that would capture them all before they made it to the bare tree that seemed to run from them, drawing two feet away with every foot the group slogged forward.

Selena was almost abreast of them. She'd slowed quickly during the run/walk/stumble of the night, but every time Barney drew even with her she seemed to find a buried reserve of strength. Now she was drawing on those reserves again, pushing forward, gaining on Evie and Gale and Grams.

Behind Selena, Naeku tumbled. She looked like she had lost most of her body mass during the night, and now looked light as a brittle autumn leaf. Behind Naeku came Barney. His eyes were clouded, staring at something no one else could see, every ounce of his remaining strength devoted to the off-kilter cadence of his run. His bullet wound had soaked through the gauze and tampons –

(*Obviously they weren't Tampax Supers, because those things* last!)

– and his upper body looked as though it had been painted. Not bright red – the night was too dark to allow such fine color distinctions – but a mottled gray. He was a zombie, stumbling mindlessly forward, motivated only by his need to survive.

A monster? Yes, Barney was that – in all his forms. But the monster he was paled beside the demons behind. The night had been moving, like a black blanket that hid writhing snakes below it. Now the animals burst through the covers and Evie saw them.

Foam dripped from their mouths, though Evie could not tell if it sprang from wells of pain, thirst, hunger, or simple madness. Their front legs punched them forward, their shorter rear legs seeming constantly on the verge of losing purchase, yet somehow always finding a place on the ground that pushed the beasts forward faster, faster.

The pack ran as a group. An ameboid mass that had sensed food, and now must follow that food to its end. As Evie watched, the mass extended three appendages. All of them had the same spots on their backs. Two of them were younger beasts, their skin tighter, their faces more youthful than that of the thing that ran before all.

Queen. Older, yes, but stronger and quicker than the others. Evie got the sense in that quick glance she spared that the matriarch only ran so close to the pack because that was what such a creature was expected to do. She suspected that, had Queen been alone, she already would have overtaken the survivors.

Evie faced forward. She realized that Gale was holding her tighter, so tightly it was painful. Then the clench tightened to the point that Evie's breath – already a gaspy, windy thing of so little substance her head felt light – started to wane even further.

She tripped, and only the thought of Gale tumbling to the ground, a tumble she knew would end in both of them dying in the mud, kept her from falling completely. Somehow she managed to run. Somehow she managed to keep on, for the sake only of a girl and a promise.

She arrived at the tree. Grams proved the speediest of them all despite her age, and by the time Evie got to the tree the old woman was already on the lowest branch, reaching down to grab Gale as Evie thrust her upward. Gale didn't know what was happening – how could she? – and she screamed and clutched at Evie so hard that her nails drew long gashes in Evie's neck when Evie finally managed to tear her away and send her into her Grams' waiting arms.

"Take her. Take her," she said over and over, a prayer-like litany that was rewarded by the lightness of the little girl being pulled up by her grandmother.

Evie waited a moment to make sure Gale was secure –
or as secure as could be, given the circumstances. She wouldn't
let the little girl fall.

She needn't have worried. She knew that Grams
probably heard Naeku's breathless assurance that the hyenas
couldn't climb, but was glad just the same when the old
woman took Gale to the nearest limb, hooked the little girl's
hand over it, and shouted, "Keep going, sugarplum! Climb!"

Gale, who had held her tears for so long, now sobbed.
"I can't. I don't know where – I can't see –"

"You're doing fine," Evie said. Her voice was calmer
than she would have expected, and it seemed to calm the girl
as well. Gale's panicked shivering slowed. "Keep going, Gale."

The little girl did. Grams waited a moment, watching
her granddaughter just as Evie had done. Then she turned
back and held out a hand. Evie took it, surprised at the strength
she felt as she half-climbed onto the low-hanging limb.
Perhaps less than half-climbed; Grams seemed to be doing
most of the work, and that was fine with Evie.

She had barely gotten onto the limb when she saw
Selena. The actress had beelined to another branch, one higher
than the one Evie now rode. When she got to it, Selena
practically ripped herself from the ground. She was astride the
branch in less than a second, and then continued upward.

Naeku followed close behind. Evie started to crawl
across her own branch, intending to help the injured woman
up, but even winded and wounded, battered and bruised,
Naeku negotiated the climb quickly.

That left only Barney, a wounded beast followed by
creatures whose power and rage dwarfed his own.

Evie watched as he ran. He was only ten feet from the
tree branch. But the hyenas were only twenty feet behind him,
Queen baying as she felt the scent of blood all around, as she

245

saw her next kill lunge forward, almost fall, right himself again.

Evie watched Barney run. She made no move toward him.

He looked over his shoulder. A thin mewling escaped his lips. The sound fell into darkness behind, and the snapping jaws of the hyenas consumed it and he fell silent and faced forward and Evie saw death in his eyes.

He reached the branch, maybe six feet ahead of the hyenas. He jumped, grabbed it with his one good arm. He screamed as the branch hit his bullet wound, but didn't let go.

More sounds from his mouth. *"Lll, lll, lll!"* he shouted, and Evie realized he was screaming "Help!"

> ***Once Upon a Time,***
> ***an evil creature***
> ***begged the Princess for help.***

Evie considered just leaving him to die. But only for a moment. Then she saw Queen, the ruined side of the hyena's face seeming more devilish than ever in the night. The teeth visible through the scarred holes that had been ripped in her cheek clamped down, opened, and clamped down again in anticipation of flesh.

Evie threw herself across the tree limb. She grabbed Barney's arm, his shoulder. He screamed again. She didn't listen. Didn't care. She pulled. His legs pedaled, grabbing for something that would let him push his bulk upward to safety, finding nothing but air.

He switched his grip suddenly, letting go of the branch and grabbing Evie instead. The motion almost pulled her down with him.

Queen leaped, and her teeth clamped down on the man's calf. Barney screamed louder, and Evie felt herself tearing away from her tenuous hold on the branch.

"Don't let go!" Barney screamed. "Don't, please, don't!"

Evie couldn't have let him go if she wanted. He was holding her too tightly, and she felt herself drifting downward as he pulled them both over the edge.

She saw the man's calf tear in Queen's jaws. Trailing gobbets of flesh ripped away from Barney's fat leg, and blood rained to the earth. He screamed, but the injury actually helped him because though Queen's jaws were still locked around part of his calf, now that part was no longer attached to his body.

Evie pulled. Barney fell another inch; she was too tired to lift his enormous weight to safety. Instead she began to tumble down with him.

Queen spit out the meat in her jaws. Her daughters pounced, each trying to beat the other to the appetizer before the feast. They snapped and snarled, rolling the bit of flesh in the dirt and seeming to care not at all that they were fouling their food.

Queen turned back toward Barney. For a moment, Evie locked eyes with the pack's leader. She felt herself falling into that gaze, then realized she was falling in actuality.

A hand darted out, catching her. Another reached out and pulled at Barney's collar. Grams and Naeku had both leaped to this branch, and now Naeku had one strong arm encircling Evie's waist, her other hand gripping the next branch up. Grams had a similar grip on the branch as well, pulling Barney one-handed, yanking him up with a shriek of pain and exhaustion and anger.

The branch they were on creaked and cracked, but none of the women let go.

Queen leaped...

... and her teeth clicked down on the very air that Barney had been trying to climb only a moment before. The big man lay across the branch, exhausted. His bad arm hung below it, blood dripping from his outstretched fingers and puddling below.

Queen leaped, and her teeth crashed shut only inches from Barney's fingers. Another of the hyenas jumped, and this time Evie saw its snout knock into Barney's middle finger. The barest hint of a touch, but it must have communicated danger to Barney, because with a final, exhausted heave, he pulled his hand upward and laid it across the branch ahead of him.

Then he closed his eyes.

Evie sagged in place, sensing the others doing the same.

They were safe. And yet not safe at all, because they were atop a tree that was the only high point in a flood of hyenas. She remembered seeing news reports of people on rooftops, waiting for help as the water rose all around them. And perhaps this particular flood could reach no further than it already had, but the water itself was not the only danger.

Evie realized then just how badly she was sweating. She looked around and saw Grams' face shiny with sweat, and even Selena's skin had lost some of its translucent perfection under the panic- and fear- and exertion-sweat that sheeted her face.

Naeku: sweating and bleeding.

Barney: sweating and bleeding. Droplets on his fingers now making their way around the branch he rested on, then falling to the waiting jaws of the hyenas below.

Gale was high up in the tree, for which Evie was grateful. But even without being able to see the details, she knew that Gale had to be sweating, too.

Sweat, blood. They both had the same major ingredient: water.

How long since any of us has had a drink?
How much longer can we last without one?

248

Below, Queen settled on her haunches, her head cocked up so she could stare at Barney's bulk. *She* knew she could afford to do the one thing the survivors could not: simply wait.

11

REGINA STOOD AT THE open gate, looking into the night.

They should have been back hours ago.

At first she had been able to fool herself, to tell herself that Naeku or Leg or both had just decided to go the extra mile. Or, even better (and more fantastical), they had found a pride of lions or a herd of elephants and stayed too long, letting the guests drink in the sights of an Africa suddenly come alive in the night.

They would have radioed.

That was the clincher, the thing that worried her most, of course. The radios were silent. The last communications had been from Regina to them, telling them where the lion sighting was. Nothing since, certainly nothing in the only direction that mattered: not from her to them, but vice-versa. She needed them to call, and when they did not Regina set Kip, an Aussie kid who was keen on being a guide but still too wet-behind-the-ears for such a thing, to keep calling them on the radio.

After ten minutes, Kip found her in the mess where she was working her way through what was obviously a thermos of water and less-obviously (but more realistically) a thermos of vodka. She tossed a mint into her mouth as he entered; vodka was supposed to be the perfect drink for any boozer trying to keep her secret safe at work, but she didn't believe that for a second. *She* could taste it, and out here in the middle of the place she sometimes thought of as The Beautiful Nowhere – always with affection; nowhere was just the right place *to* be, more often than not – every sense seemed sharper. That was one of the things that happened out here, one of the reasons the guests all came, and the reason she herself had never left. You were more alive out here.

Until you're not.

Still crunching the mint, she said, "Anything?"

Kip shook his head. "No," he said, though it always sounded like, "Nah," when he said it. "Not a squeak."

She sighed. "Give it ten more minutes." Kip turned to go, and she shouted, "Wait!" Kip turned around, waiting for instructions. She was silent, all her attention focused suddenly on several facts.

1) Happy Africa is in trouble. It's dying.

2) One more problem and it's dead.

3) This is definitely a problem.

These three thoughts were followed quickly by a fourth thought that was more an explosion of rationalization:

But it's not the kind of problem that matters if none of the guests know about it. If we fix this fast enough, and everyone has a fine old time and the animals cooperate… we might get through this. The rains came, so we're going to weather the great bloody lack of a storm if we can just get through this night. Naeku can take care of herself, so she can get them back and then we'll find out everything was gravy and Happy Africa will survive and I won't lose the job that I've worked so hard for for the last twenty years.

All bullshit, she knew. But the kind of bullshit that grows more attractive the longer you look at it. Because what were the stakes, *really?*

On the one hand: Happy Africa's certain demise.

On the other: giving Naeku a few more minutes, just a few more, that's all, to get back.

Attractive bullshit is still bullshit.

Regina was one of the few female camp managers in this kind of outfit in the whole world. She had scraped and scratched and struggled her way here over a period of decades.

251

This place was her first real home, and the only one she had ever wanted to have.

All that ran through her mind, and all of it combined to make the only possible decision. She sighed and said, "Get Busara on the phone."

Kip frowned, knowing what that meant. "We bring in a rescue chopper and there's no hiding this. We're telling the world we're in trouble."

Regina nodded. She opened the thermos and tossed back a prodigious swallow of liquid courage. Sure enough, she saw Kip's nostrils flare; he knew what she was doing.

What does it matter? I'm about to lose my job anyway; might as well enjoy the ride.

"Get me Busara," she repeated. Kip nodded, turned away once more, then turned back again as she said, "Wait." "Don't bother getting me when you get Busara on. No need for a chat, just tell her to get her chopper here ASAP and pick me up."

Kip nodded again. His eyes flickered to the thermos she still held. Yep, he knew what was in there, she thought. Everything's so very alive in this place.

She carefully – and more soberly than she would have thought possible – poured the rest of the Vodka on the floor.

Everything's alive here. Until it's not.

FIVE:
suspended

Interlude

IT IS HARD TO tell a story such as this. Not just because it comes in the middle of flight, in a foreign place where life is so cheap and danger waits at every turn. More than that, it is because the story has become much more than a simple tale. It has become a True Thing.

The woman keeps telling it, because she knows this. She knows that the True Thing is not really about the Magical Land of Piz at all. It is about Here, and Now. It is about a princess.

The woman does not know if the princess will survive.

She can only tell the story.

GALE WORSENED, AND PEBES knew why, though he did not tell Gale. He knew that the Land of Piz was a place of magic and light… but that light sometimes threw a shadow. Such a shadow had been thrown in the Land of Piz, but it had long kept itself far away, in dark places and deep ones where no one traveled and so were things no one needed to fear.

Now, though, the shadow was on the move. He should have known it already, because why else would he have lost his parents? And why else would Gale be walking slower and slower?

Pebes knew, too, that the girl herself had triggered the shadow's movements. She did not belong here, not completely. And things which did not belong to a place could not help but make that place either better or worse. He suspected – no, he absolutely knew, as much as he knew he was a Crunchy (the Creamies were also Peanut Butter Snowmen and Snowwomen, but not nearly so pleasant or smart) – that Gale would make the Magical Land of Piz into an even more Magical place. She had brought more light, and so the shadow was afraid. It had to stop her from her quest.

254

It has cast a spell.

Indeed it had. Gale had started to suffer a great thirst. The Peanut Butter Snowman had brought her to the Sprinkle Star Falls near Milkshake Bay, but the girl had refused to drink either from the Bay or the Falls themselves. She shook her head, and tried to speak but could not.

She pointed at her mouth, then her tummy. She was thirsty, not hungry, but that was all she could think to do.

Pebes knew he must take her to the Great Fanta Sea. It was whispered that a drink from a certain place where the Great Fanta Sea flowed and mixed with the Sugared Sands, could heal any wound however great or small. He must take her there.

Only… it was in the Cove of Creation: the oldest part of the Magical Land of Piz. It was the place from which light had first flowed, and that meant it was the first place of Shadow. It was the place the shadow now pursuing them had been born.

They were going to its home. But it was the only way Gale could survive, so he would take her there. He would brave the shadow, for her. He was a child, but he was also a Peanut Butter Snowman of the family Crunchy, and no shadow would stop him from saving his friend.

1

NONE OF THEM HAD a watch, which struck Evie as odd, and yet totally unsurprising. The guests all relied on phones to tell them what time it was, where they should be, what they should be doing, and whom they should be doing it with. Naeku had a watch, a thick chunk of plastic called a G-Shock, but she never wore it on her wrist. She said it gave her a rash sometimes, so she kept it cinched to one of her belt loops – a belt loop that had ripped at some point during the night.

It didn't much matter. When Evie asked if anyone had a watch, after getting all the "no"s and the explanation from Naeku – her voice was so weak and bubbly now – the Maasai then looked at the starry sky and said, "Four a.m.," and Evie believed her without question. She suspected a nuclear clock could take pointers from the woman's time sense.

Of course, that same internal clock had also just told them that they had been driving or running or hanging from a tree for nearly ten hours.

Barney still hung from the lowest branch, one hand flopped limply downward on either side. He had tried to remain upright for the first hour or so, but exhaustion and blood loss got the best of him and he finally slumped. The hyenas took a few more leaps at his dangling fingers, but none came as close as they had in those first moments, and Barney's eyes closed.

The hyenas' only attempts to capture the tantalizing morsel of hanging meat seemed half-hearted to Evie. Strange, until she realized that Queen had taken up position just below the man. As though she knew he *would* fall, sooner or later, and was content to wait until that happened. To show too much desperate interest, to leap for him and then miss, might be a sign of weakness. It might damage her standing.

The hyenas rested. The central mass of them – it had to be at least fifty, though they moved about so much it was hard to tell – gathered around the base of the tree, while a few outsiders walked the perimeter. Males, Evie guessed, based on the jealous, hungry looks they kept sending the survivors' way. That and the fact that they were smaller than the rest of the hyenas, and obviously hungrier.

And, true to Naeku's earlier words, they had the smallest penises in the pack.

Evie kept thinking that, and kept having to concentrate to keep from braying laughter. The adrenaline pumped out by the night's headlong flight from death to darkness to death again had worn off, and with it the giddy need to laugh or cry or both. But the exhaustion that seeped into her bones was worse, because it brought with it only a tired wish to let go of the tree, to fall.

They all needed rest.

We need water.

She glanced down. The sky was lightening, and she could see that the ground below them had already dried. Not even sunny out, and the heat of the night had wicked away every last trace of water that hadn't managed to flee somewhere deep underground. Barney's wounded shoulder had stopped bleeding, but not before unfurling a thin ribbon of red that wound down his hanging arm to fall from the tips of his outstretched fingers.

The hyenas had reacted to the blood with short-lived excitement, trying to lap it up, a few taking one of those indifferent leaps for the producer's fingers, but the excitement died quickly as the blood dripped to earth... and was gone in less than a second. The land drank it, and what little the land missed, the heat evaporated.

As Evie watched, Barney's eyes opened. They were unfocused, not glazed exactly – glaze was impossible when everything was dust-bone-dry – but filmed over with pain and the madness of impending death.

She didn't like that look.

Evie looked away from him, taking in the rest of the group, noting their positions – a ridiculous thing to do, given that none of them had moved for hours. Madness, she had once heard, could be defined as doing the same thing over and over and expecting a different result. If so, then madness was very close.

Probably here already.

How long before we get too thirsty? Before weakness makes one of us fall, or desperation drives us to try a useless escape?

Or will we just hang here? Arms and legs dangling like Barney's, looking like gruesome ornaments on the world's grimmest Christmas tree?

The image was so vivid she shook her head.

Not dead. We're not dead, so we're still alive.

Another giggle-moment. It was welcome this time, keeping her from thinking of Barney as a round, red, glass ball hanging on the tree; of Selena as tinsel (obviously) wrapped lasciviously around the limb of her choice; of Naeku and Grams as plastic gifts dangling from bloody loops; of herself as one of the nondescript ornaments that falls every year, that breaks and no one much caring that it does because such things are cheap and meant only to fill in the cracks between the ornaments that matter.

And on top of it all: a once-shining angel, looking around but seeing nothing at all behind her dark glasses, only knowing that she is alone, and destined to fall.

It won't come to that.

Her laughter was gone now, replaced by desperation. Gale *couldn't* die like that. Not alone like that, in the dark and not knowing what would happen next.

Evie wouldn't let that happen. Never.

A new image: herself climbing to the top of the tree, taking down the darkening angel, and breaking her in pieces. Cruel, yes, but how much crueller to leave her to die alone?

NO.

The scream in her mind was the loudest she'd ever heard. Louder even than the one time she *had* killed someone.

"You all right?"

Evie blinked, trying to remember what she was doing, where she was.

"You... all right?" Naeku asked again. This time Evie heard the words and understood them.

She laughed quietly and looked at the other woman. Unlike Selena, Grams, and Gale, Naeku had remained on a lower branch. She had pressed herself against the trunk, wedging herself into the crotch of the limb and the tree. She had lost her bright red scarf at some point during the kidnapping and crash, but there was still plenty of color to her ensemble. Once completely done in various shades of khaki, her shirt and pants now sported a mottled shell that was the brown-black-red of congealing blood.

Blood is the new black.

That laugh threatened to return. Evie kept it at bay by going to Naeku. She straddled the woman, the only way she could get close enough to do what she wanted. Naeku grimaced, but seemed to know what Evie was doing. She let her clenched fist fall away from where she had been holding it against her wound, and Evie carefully lifted the ruined edges of Naeku's shirt.

"Wooh! Take it off! Show us your tits, baby!" Barney shouted. His voice was slurred, faded. No longer the voice of a man in control of a vast empire, he now just sounded like a transient who had realized drugs and alcohol were the closest thing to a home he would ever know.

Naeku grimaced as Evie looked at the knife wound. "Is it that bad?"

Evie did her best to control the horror she felt. What had started out as a knife wound had opened farther and farther during the night. It had torn across part of Naeku's belly and begun to curve around her side. The pressure of her fist there had kept her from bleeding out, but the thick plug of coagulated gore that remained made it look as though some alien cancer was consuming her.

"No," said Evie. She tried to think of something else to say, something that would sound hopeful without being an obvious lie. "No," she said again.

Naeku smiled tightly. "Of course not," she said. Evie knew the tone: it was the one she used whenever she was at an ER, and a doctor took her aside and asked in a low voice if there were any "problems" he or she should know about.

"Ah, shit, man." Barney's voice was thicker. "No tits. What kinda goddam trip is this?" Evie swiveled to look at him. The big man had pushed himself into a sitting position. Now he hunkered down, then pulled forward, hunkered down, pulled forward. The fattest caterpillar in the world lurching across a dry branch, looking for something smaller than it could consume.

Below him, Queen, who had looked for the last hour as though she was asleep, finally roused herself. She followed directly below Barney, jaws hanging open. Ropy saliva sagged from her mouth, and Evie was oddly – madly – jealous of the thing.

She's *still got spit. How's* she *still got any spit?*

Queen's mouth opened wider as Barney suddenly lost his balance and almost lurched off the branch. The ruined, split side of her mouth opened further than the unmaimed side, a disgusting mismatch that Evie couldn't look at for more than a moment.

Barney grunted and managed to right himself. He didn't look at all steady, and surprised Evie by not only not falling, but standing on the limb and grabbing the next-highest branch. She wouldn't have thought he could do that – not with a bullet wound in his shoulder and a chunk of his calf missing – but Barney not only stood, he hauled himself up higher in the tree.

Selena was on the branch Barney now occupied. She scooted toward the trunk as the limb crackled. "Get off, Barney! Shit, get *off!*"

Barney looked toward her, blinking and only seeming to see her now for the first time. "Hey, babe… Help a guy out, yeah? Need to… to… get higher…"

Without waiting for a response, he lunged up and settled the rest of his weight on the branch. He lurched to the side once again, and now it wasn't just Queen following him. Her daughters walked below as well, and like their mother they drooled thick lines of white. Their jaws opened then crashed down with audible *click-clacks*, like they were already tasting the man above.

Selena slid to another branch. She looked at Barney with fear, with revulsion. Barney looked up. Grams and Gale were a few branches higher – the old woman had settled there long ago, singing quietly to Gale for a while, cradling the girl as best she could and whispering, "Sleep, sweetie, sleep," as the girl wept herself to sleep.

Barney didn't seem to be looking at them. He stared at the sky, like he thought he might climb right into it and nestle safely among the stars if he could only get to the top of the tree and reach out his hand.

He'd likely fall trying. And Evie found she didn't much care.

Barney seemed to realize for the first time that Selena was nearby. His hand stretched out, reaching for her. The actress shied away from him and in that moment Evie saw right into Barney's soul, the fire in his eyes burning her, the ugliness he carried with him more revolting than any bleeding cancer on any knife wound. She recoiled, and at the same time felt Naeku shift and heard the woman hiss.

She sees it, too.

Selena did as well, Evie could tell. She could also tell that, unlike Evie and Naeku, Selena had seen this part of Barney before. She knew him. Knew him, and had used this darkness to her advantage.

Barney's still-extended hand closed into a fist. The fist extended one finger and as he flipped Selena the bird he said, "Ungrateful hag."

Then the clarity in his eyes faded. The stupor of oncoming death sheeted his expression. He looked up again. He climbed higher. Toward the stars.

UNGRATEFUL HAG. UNGRATEFUL HAG?

Selena had heard Barney say these words before – both to her and others. But they never stung like they did this time. They never made her feel –

(weak alone under the bleachers and his pants around his ankles and his red shirt all I can see of him as he holds himself above me and hurts me)

262

– so weak and tired and afraid and disgusted as she now did.

Probably because every other time – even when the words *had* been directed at her – she had been able to shrug them off. To tell herself that he didn't mean it, or maybe he did but it didn't matter because she was the one using him so the joke was on him har, har, har.

No joke now. No jokes, no smiles. Just blood.

My mouth is so dry.

All dry, all empty, all gone.

Barney climbed upward. He tottered with every movement, but never quite fell. She was surprised how much she wanted to see him fall. How much she wanted to watch him tumble and disappear below and be consumed as he had consumed so many others.

Me, too.

She turned away from him, as though doing so would allow her to turn away from the thought that kept ringing in her mind: *I didn't eat people the same way he did, didn't chew them up and suck them dry and toss them to the side like he did... no, I did it my own way. And I fed off his scraps, too. Worse than him, because at least he had the guts not to pretend to be anything but a beast.*

The crack and rustle of dry branches sounded as the fat man – how could she ever have let him do what he so often did to her? – climbed higher. He would fall soon. He had to.

"Mind if I join ya?" he said suddenly. His voice was jovial; the tone he used for stars he was trying to get to sign onto his next picture, the one he famously schmoozed with at the Oscar after-party he hosted every year, a ticket so hot it made the Vanity Fair party look like a hillbilly hoedown.

The sound made Selena's hair stand on end. Not just because it was so out of place here, but because it was the tone he used whenever he was trying to *get* something. And here, what was there to get?

Nothing. Nothing to get.

She knew it was a lie. There was *always* something to get.

2

EVIE WATCHED BARNEY CLIMB, asking herself if she would really just watch if he fell. She'd tried to save him before; had almost fallen herself, trying to keep him alive.

But now… she didn't think she would do that again. She thought –

(feared worried HOPED)

– she would just watch him tumble downward like a ball bearing on a Plinko board, bouncing his way off branches until he hit the ground, then… gone, just like that ball bearing. Only there'd be no reappearing at the top of the board after that. He'd be gone for good.

She felt what happened next before she saw or heard it. A sudden heaviness came over her, and whatever traces of moisture the night might have trapped in the air dissipated. The tree crackled deep within itself, as though sighing out a final death-rattle.

Evie didn't know what was coming, but the same sense that told her something *was* coming also told her the direction it was coming from. She looked down. Queen was still directly below Barney, gaze fixed upward, jaws cranked wide as though she might just swallow him whole before he ever touched the dirt at her feet.

Queen watched Barney with the single-minded attention of a thing for whom all that matters is the hunt. But the focus that would allow the matriarch to survive in a place grown ever more hostile could also be her undoing. As Evie watched, a pair of hyenas crept forward.

These weren't Queen's daughters – apparently those two didn't have the same tenacity or interest as their mother, and were now dozing a good ten feet away. The newcomers were large, as all the females of the pack were. Not quite so large as Queen, but there was no mistaking the power in their muscles, the barely-controlled mayhem in their gazes.

They crept to within a few feet of Queen's hindquarters, then both lunged forward. Their teeth flashed, each of them going for one of Queen's rear legs. Evie knew she was witnessing an attempted coup.

The same thing that had alerted Evie to the attack also broke Queen out of her reverie. She swung about, her legs dancing out of reach of the others' teeth at the last second. And as fast as the attackers had come upon her, she was so much faster.

Evie had seen Queen hunt. This was the first time she saw the hyena fight. The matriarch wheeled away from two follow-up attacks – one of the would-be queens lashed out with a clawed paw, the other darted forward for another bite attempt – then returned the gifts. She batted aside the claws of the first, her own claws slashing out in a motion that seemed almost careless, but which was so fast Evie barely saw it before three long gashes opened on the side of the other hyena's face.

The one who bit at her fared worse. She jerked out of the way of the bite, then twisted around so she was behind the other female. She mounted her from behind, straddling her for a moment, then biting down onto the back of the hapless hyena's neck.

The hyena looked like its bones simply disappeared. One moment it was strong, powerful. Yowling with rage and the chance to take control of the pack. The next, it was a sack of loose flesh.

Queen kept her jaws locked around the attacker, riding the poor thing to the dirt. She shook it once, hard, and even if Evie hadn't known its neck was broken, she would have now as bullet-sharp cracks accompanied Queen's jerky movement.

266

Queen stood over the challenger's body. She let go of it, and the thing's neck and head, held aloft by Queen's jaws, tumbled down and became just one more lump in a grotesque pile of flesh and blood-matted fur.

Queen urinated on the body. She stepped away.

Chuffed.

The rest of the pack lunged forward and fed.

Evie turned back to the pack. In the short time she had turned away, the dead hyena had all but disappeared. She saw hyenas all around the tree, fighting over the bits of bloody flesh their sister had become. Queen's daughters were fighting over the severed head of their mother's attacker. The bigger of the two heaved, but the effort just resulted in the head tearing apart. All the bigger sister had was the lower jaw and tongue of the dead hyena, and the smaller hyena princess ended up with the larger portion.

The bigger sister seemed to shrug, then cracked down and Evie saw the dead hyena's jaw crushed within the jaws of its packmate. Queen's daughter pulped it, then swallowed it all – bones, tongue, and teeth – in a series of seizure-like swallows.

"What's wrong with these things?" came Selena's voice. Evie glanced over her shoulder and saw that the actress had come down to their level and now hunkered on the Naeku's branch.

When she responded, Naeku's voice sounded wetter than ever. Evie looked at the Maasai, trying to ignore the thin stream of blood that ran over the woman's lips as she talked. "There is nothing wrong with them. They are hungry, and we are food."

Evie shook her head. "This seems like more than that. It seems… personal."

267

Naeku nodded as though Evie had said something wise. "Life and death are always personal."

A resurgence of noise had accompanied Queen's dispatching of her rival. Now it surged again, and Evie looked down to see that the remaining would-be matriarch had returned to the fray.

This time Queen didn't attempt to avoid the attack. She met it head-on. The attacker's jaws gaped, but Queen's own mouth opened even wider. She turned her head to the side, and her jaws seemed to envelope the other one's gaping maw. She bit down, and the poor creature shuddered as its snout and face were crushed.

Awful *hrk, hrk, hrk* sounds came from inside Queen's mouth as her challenger suffocated while its head collapsed. Queen's paws dug into the ground, yanking the smaller hyena along, dragging it low. Evie saw with horror that Queen's pseudopenis had again grown erect and now scraped along the earth.

Queen lurched. The other hyena's shuddering changed to an electric shiver. Its brain fired a last confused jumble of impulses, and one leg rose in the air like an over-enthusiastic student who wants to answer the teacher's question. The others splayed to all sides. Its bladder and bowels released.

One more *hrrrrrrkkkkk.*

Queen opened her mouth, but the other beast's head was actually stuck in her jaws. She gagged it out, loosing a tumble of clotted flesh that no one could have recognized as the jaws and head of a once-strong hunter.

This time she didn't urinate on her fallen foe. She bit down on its belly, tearing it open. The hyena's recently-emptied bowels tumbled to the dirt in a spattered mass.

The other attacker had already been consumed. The pack was hungry again. It approached the new source of food, growling deep in their throats.

Queen stood over the carcass. She growled as well, then laughed the horrible laugh that had become to Evie a sound of nightmare. Another growl followed, and she took a step toward the rest of the pack.

The other hyenas all lurched backward as one. Queen growled again, and they lowered their heads. She kept growling until the entire pack had prostrated themselves.

Evie knew there would be no more challenges this night. All the hyenas wore a look she had seen in her own eyes, on those nights when Bill was angry and took out his anger on her and when he was done allowed her to go clean herself. She saw that look in the cracked mirror of their tiny bathroom. The look of something that has no more will to struggle. Who will live and die on the word of another, and never think to ask for more.

She had seen that look often, and despaired at it more than once. Now, though... she hated it. Hated it with a fire more intense than her fear.

SELENA HAD CREPT CLOSER as the struggle played out. It was horrifying, but at the same time familiar. The drama she saw every day, only now the masks and makeup were gone and only brutal reality remained. It was ugly and violent, but it was honest, too.

Honesty, though, could go too far. As the main bitch crushed her rival's head and then puked it up, Selena shuddered.

"God. Why... why are they..." She couldn't finish. She looked away. Her gaze went to Evie. The other woman wasn't

269

looking at her, which was good because there was such a depth of anger and revulsion in her eyes that Selena felt like she might have burned away to nothing had Evie been looking directly at her.

"It is their way," said Naeku. Selena looked at the Maasai woman, a sigh of relief on her lips that died when she saw just how bad Naeku looked.

"Hey," she said. "Hey, maybe you should just –"

Naeku continued speaking, talking right over Selena. Had this been a few weeks ago, especially on the set of a movie shoot, Selena would have laid into the woman and never mind that the footage and audio would have ended up on YouTube – publicity was publicity, and screaming obscenities at some uppity gaffer who got in her sightlines only made her Internet Movie Database rankings spike.

But Selena didn't scream. Didn't interrupt. She just listened to the words of the dying woman wedged into the crotch of a tree.

"It is their way," said Naeku. "It keeps them alive." She stopped speaking, though her mouth kept working, the jaw moving up and down as though trying to form new words and failing. Naeku inhaled, a bubbling intake of breath and blood that reminded Selena of things that frightened her.

Red blood. Red shirts and red on my hands –

"One year," said Naeku, "when I still lived in my village, before I fled that life, the lions started acting strangely." She looked around, and Selena wondered what the other woman was seeing, because she sure as hell looked like she wasn't seeing the tree or perhaps even the other women leaning toward her. "It was a dry year, like this. A year when the animals were mad with terror and hunger. But even for all that, the lions seemed... wrong." More mouth movements, more words drowning in blood before they could come out.

270

Evie moved to Naeku. She stood on another branch, but leaned in to take the woman's hand. "How so?" she asked.

Selena wanted to tell her to shut up, to let the girl just die – and there was no denying that *was* what was going to happen. But she didn't. Because if the guide wanted to tell one last story, who was Selena to say no?

"They would attack our men," said Naeku, "coming upon us like madness itself. This happens sometimes, but it is usually a lone lion, a rogue without family or pride." A bloody tongue licked bloody lips, and in that motion Selena could almost see the lions coming for her tribe. "But when our men hunted and killed the first lion, another took its place. Not outcasts, the pride itself had gone mad." She deflated a bit and said simply, "Eventually, the pride was dead. And that was when my father noticed…"

A long moment. "Notice what?" she finally asked, ashamed to be pushing a dying woman along, but not able to help herself. She could tell that Evie felt the same. She was a good enough actress to know when the audience was hooked, and Evie was just as tight on the line as Selena herself.

Naeku smiled a bloody, humorless grin. She looked in that moment more than a little like the big hyena that now hunkered below them, still waiting for Barney to fall. "He noticed that we had seen many lions, but we had not seen a single cub in over a year. We thought little of it, until my brother went hunting. He was looking for water, and found instead a place of death."

Naeku's gaze returned, if only partially, from the sight of whatever long-ago thing she had been watching. She looked down at the hyena queen below. "My brother found bones. Many different kinds, but mostly lions. The cubs. They had been eaten – all of them – by hyenas."

"I don't believe it," whispered Selena. She looked down at the creatures below. They were already done eating their kin. Most of them had muzzles now painted red, rouged by over-zealous makeup artists who were going for a strong look and only ended up creating something slattern – which meant the movie would probably do better, because sluts always sold better than female superheroes.

Naeku laughed grimly. "The lions are top predators, but so are hyenas. The hyenas will eat the lion cubs if they can. Lions would do the same in return. But hyenas are smarter than lions." Her eyes returned to that faraway place as she said, "Did you know that hyenas are even smarter than chimpanzees?" Again the Maasai woman's gaze came back, again she looked down. "So these hyenas found the cubs and killed them. Ate them, and fed their cubs on the flesh of their enemies' children. And it drove the lions mad. They lost their future, so they attacked anything that came near them, and died for it."

NAEKU HEARD THE SOUNDS of the hyenas below. She heard their breathing, their low chuffing. She heard everything so very clearly. The air, so still a bird would have had trouble staying aloft, nonetheless sighed in her ears. The tree in which she sat crackled, speaking in the dry tones of an elder, the whispered wisdom of ages so long past that no one remembers or cares about them.

She heard something else, too. Something low and keening. Terrible, yet...

"The lions went mad," she said again.

"That's horrible," said Evie.

Naeku's breaths came in shallow puffs. Each inhalation hurt. It was too thick, and she felt a warmth in her chest that she suspected was her lungs filling with blood.

"Yes. Horrible," she said. "And my father decreed that such must not go unpunished." She saw her father, crouched in the tree beside her. Only he wasn't here, was he? It was impossible.

Speaking without really hearing what she was saying – how could she focus on that, with her father so close, with so much sound everywhere? – she said, "My mother – and many others – counseled him to leave it alone. To let be what happened. But my father loved the lions, you see."

Her father beside her, dressed as he had been that morning, smiled. The smile widened as she said, "He went after the hyenas, he and the other warriors of the tribe. And when they came back, the ones who *did* come back, they told great stories of my father, and his bravery. But it was none of them who told what happened after they ran. It was a little girl who told the village of his last moments. Who told of him entering their den and cutting their leader even as she killed him."

Father's smile was still wide, but his skin split and blood ran. Gashes from phantom claws and teeth slashed through his flesh. He reached a now-bloody hand toward Naeku.

Come with me, he said. She heard it the same way she heard all the other sounds around her, the life that tumbled and keened in a clamor of noise.

Then Father disappeared. Not Father at all, Naeku realized. It was Evie, reaching for her with concern in her eyes. Her hand stopped midmotion, though, when Naeku mentioned what had happened to her father, and what he had done in return. Evie's eyes darted toward the hyenas below, to the one with the ruined face who still looked up and waited for food.

"Is that... is that the one..." Evie couldn't finish.

Naeku could have told her. Could have said, "Yes, that is her." But she didn't. She said what was more important; the greater truth that had brought them all here. "It does not matter. If she is that same animal, it does not make her evil, or make this something hateful. She is hungry, and she has her own children." Naeku lifted her hand – it seemed so heavy, that hand, and so far away – and pointed at the two hyenas that lay near their mother.

Before Naeku could say the words, Evie breathed, "Those are her daughters."

Naeku would not have expected any of the people with her to know that. But hearing Evie say it somehow seemed natural. Evie was a woman born far from the wild places... but she had lived in a wilderness of her own, a place where death was always near. Indeed, Naeku thought, the small, quiet woman had slept beside it and seen it come to her every day. She lived in its shadow, as none other Naeku had ever known.

"Yes. Her daughters. And that is what matters. Whether she hates us or is simply hungry are things that do not matter. Only this: she is protecting her family. She is protecting her pack. And that means she will hunt us, because she must. It is the way of things."

Evie's expression hardened – and for a moment, Naeku did not see her at all, but saw her father again, crouched in the place Evie had been. Then he faded away as Evie said, "It's not *my* way."

Naeku laughed. She couldn't help it, though it hurt. "What would you do if your child was dying? If you could save her by taking another's life?"

"I'd... I'd try to find another way."

274

Naeku chuckled again, and her eyes drooped with the effort of it. "'Try.' That is easy to say, but hard to do when the moment is staring you in the face."

"I *know*," Evie said, and something in her voice dragged Naeku back to full wakefulness.

Where am I?

For a moment she did not know. Then she saw the tree, the hyenas below. She was in this place, this last place. Father was gone.

But the sounds she had heard remained. They buzzed with life, and filled her heart. The one she had heard under everything, that low, rolling tone, grew louder as well.

She could almost place it. She could almost tell what it was.

Evie was speaking, and as Naeku listened the sound grew. And Evie's voice would lead her to what it was, and from that truth to the place past this place, this time past this time.

Naeku listened to Evie's story, and the sound grew all around, and she was glad of it.

3

EVIE HAD NEVER SPOKEN the words before, but once they started coming they wouldn't stop. She had told stories *about* this event, but those stories had always been fragments. Some truths mixed in with some lies. A few bits of honesty, but only enough to allay the suspicions of others and to silence the dark, nagging voice she heard inside herself.

What I deserve. It's all no more than I deserve.

"Bill," she began, "that's my husband –"

"I know who he is," said Naeku. Her voice, faltering before, suddenly punched through the air like a fist. Evie had heard this tone before – again, mostly with the ER doctors, but also from a few people who had tried to befriend her over the years before each and every one inevitably gave up on a lost cause. It was derision, scorn. Hatred.

Evie had heard those things in so many voices. She always assumed they were directed at her. But she didn't think Naeku was talking about her.

Bill. She hates Bill.

Evie turned away from that. Trying to bury the truth in a story, as always. But this time the story came out wrong. It came out *real*.

"When we were first married, it was different. Even after my first miscarriage, he was still *there*. It still seemed like us against the world. Then the next one came, and the next, and the one after that. Each time he got a little colder. Farther away. But he never hit me."

Those last four words – *he never hit me* – tasted suddenly like ash. How often had she said them over the years? Dozens? Hundreds?

276

And this time, they were actually true. He *hadn't* hit her. Not until…

She swallowed. The dryness still made speaking difficult, almost painful. And that was good, because some words could only be spoken in pain.

"The last time… the doctor told me the baby probably wouldn't make it. And if I kept her, he told me that I'd likely die."

"What did you do?" Selena's question startled Evie, mostly because the starlet sounded honestly interested. Evie looked at the woman and saw a reflection of herself. It was a warped reflection, a funhouse version where she took the pain, nurtured it, and instead of hiding from it tried to ride it to victory.

Evie shrugged and answered simply. "I wanted her." Another shrug, and another simple sentence. "I kept her." A final shrug, and this time nothing simple about it: "I didn't die obviously. But it didn't matter. Not for her."

And as always, the vision of the baby coming, dead only a few moments before living. The thought sounding in her mind: *I killed her. She was mine to protect and I didn't protect her I murdered her.*

The vision of Bill's eyes. Of something cold and reptilian that she'd never seen there before.

Something he came into the marriage with.

No, that's not true. I did it to him. I broke him. I –

NO! You never saw it until the babies died because that was the first time he wanted something and you absolutely did not *give it to him.*

Evie turned away from that line of thought. She focused on Naeku and felt her mouth draw into a tight gash on her face as she said, "So yes, I know a little about answering the

277

question of what I'd do. Of who I'd be willing to kill to give my child a life."

Selena spoke again, and now it wasn't interest Evie heard in her voice. It was *awe*. "That is bad-ass."

Evie laughed. "Yeah. So bad-ass that I let my own body kill my children."

"*Horseshit*," said Selena.

Evie blinked. "What?"

> ### Once Upon a Time,
> ### the Princess was full of horseshit.

Selena climbed closer, her eyes wide and full of something an earnestness Evie would never have suspected the other woman capable of feeling. "You didn't let it happen, it just *did*. Sometimes bad things happen, and sometimes they happen because the universe doesn't make a lick of sense and not just that but it doesn't even make *sense* that it doesn't make sense. Some things just *are*. So your babies die and what, that bastard uses it as an excuse to be an asshole? No, that's not your fault. Your only fault was in staying with that scumbag." Selena looked away, which was good because Evie suddenly felt short of breath.

Truth. This is what truth sounds like.

Evie clutched at the tree. Felt its rough, dead bark under her fingers. This was real. This was her life. This was what she deserved and what she –

Selena spoke again, a small voice that was textured by a Midwest twang Evie had not heard before. "There are people who stay with… people like that," said Selena. She was looking up now, and Evie didn't have to follow her gaze to know who she was looking at. "Some people do that because it lets us eat the scraps, or because we think it's better to be the predator's pet than the predator's prey. But you…" Selena's gaze lowered back to Evie's, and Evie saw a stranger there. The person

278

Selena actually was, instead of the one she pretended to be. "No, lady, you just got screwed by fate. Doesn't make you a bad person, but it *does* make anyone who hates you for it a bad person."

Grams' voice floated down from her perch in the tree. Evie hadn't known the old woman was listening, but she must have been because she said, "Amen to that, sister."

SELENA TILTED HER HEAD up and saw Grams looking down. The old woman, she realized, was beautiful. She hadn't noticed it before, because it wasn't the kind of beautiful Selena was. It wasn't the beautiful of a freakish mix of genes that created a face so many would look at and lust after. It wasn't the kind of beautiful made of makeup and soft lighting.

It was the kind of beautiful that came with living a good life, a life that let you look back and mostly smile.

Selena smiled now. She knew any agent or producer or casting director who looked at her right now would probably be shuddering. Her hair was a wreck, her clothes torn and bloody, and any makeup that made it through this far was probably more of the Heath-Ledger-as-The-Joker variety than the "And the winner for Best Actress is" type.

So why, looking up at this beautiful woman, did Selena Dancy herself also feel so suddenly beautiful? Why did she feel like she was young again, before red shirts and bleachers and even before she realized what kind of life Pa wanted for her?

Why?

Selena decided it didn't matter. She just rode the feeling, the truth of the moment. She looked away from Grams, and damn if she still didn't feel great. She looked at Evie and said the words that only someone like her – someone who'd never had a mother – could possibly speak with complete surety, honesty, and accuracy: "You would be a damn good mom."

For a moment, Evie's eyes shone. Selena was gripped with the insane certainty that if Evie could do what Selena was doing – if she could ride the wave of this moment and find her own moment of beauty – that they'd all be fine.

The glow in Evie's eyes became a glimmer. The glimmer became a spark. The spark died.

"I guess we'll never know," said Evie. "The last one, after... after she died... they had to..." She gestured at her belly, and Selena's own stomach tightened at the thought. She'd never wanted kids, oh hell no, but to have the ability taken away... to have it stripped from you, when all you wanted was that one thing.

She thought how badly she wanted that one gold statue. How much she hated the women who were nominated and won. She thought how bad that hurt, and how the pain would have been nothing compared to finding a man standing at the gates to every studio lot, the doors to every production company, holding out a warding hand and shaking his head and saying, "You won't win – ever – because you can't even act anymore. It's over. Go home. Find something else to be."

Selena, not sure whether she spoke to herself or to Evie, whispered, "Now that shit just ain't fair."

"Not many things are," said Naeku. "All we can do is try to –"

But she never got to finish the thought, because in that moment Grams began screaming. A moment later, so did Gale.

GRAMS HADN'T WANTED TO eavesdrop, but it wasn't like she could avoid hearing things. She was literally up a tree, and don't think she didn't hear how ridiculous *that* sounded to say, but ridiculous or not they were all in this together, and though she tried not to listen at first she gradually forgot to try and then leaned down to listen better.

When she said, "Amen to that, sister," it had been an unconscious moment. She didn't realize she spoke until the actress looked up at her, and something in Grams froze, like she was worried Selena would yell at her.

Ridiculous, because Grams had seen things much more terrifying than a spoiled brat of a woman hollering at her. But she *was* worried. Not about Selena, about the moment. About letting the story go on.

Selena didn't yell. She looked at her with a kind of... what? Love?

Maybe. As odd as that was, yes, Grams thought Selena had love in her eyes. Not a lustful desire, not even a look you might give someone you wished would be your friend. It was the look of someone seeing a cherished piece of art up close and real for the first time. Of someone leaning so far across the velvet rope that their nose almost brushed the canvas.

That's how Gale would have looked if we ever saw the elephants.

That brought thoughts of Craig. She didn't want to think about him – not now. Later, yes. Later she would cry and maybe scream. But not now. Now she had to keep focused on Gale, because that was the only way the girl would survive.

And she couldn't think of Craig because what the women below were talking about seemed, now, in this place, to be the most important thing in the world.

Grams fell into the words. She fell into Evie's story, and most of all into the fact that Selena Dancy, a woman who probably never had an unselfish thought in her whole adult life, was telling Evie, a woman who probably hadn't known

281

what a miracle she was, that she *did* matter. That she *was* worth something.

That's why Grams didn't notice the other thing that was happening. Not until it was too late.

Barney had *not* been listening to what was going on below. He probably wasn't hearing much of anything anymore. Just feeling the life ooze out of that hole in his shoulder, losing his grip on the empire of shit and terror he'd crafted for himself.

Below, Selena and Evie were finding truth. They were on the verge of realizing who they were. Grams had passed through a moment like that, long ago. She knew that this moment could be the most important thing that would ever happen to them, because this moment would show them who they really were.

Barney had discovered who *he* really was, too. She saw that in his eyes as he lurched toward her. He had come up level with her, and with the little girl who dozed fitfully in her arms, somehow managing to climb quietly in spite of his wounds and the way the tree creaked every time you looked at a branch cross-eyed. He had stolen up beside them and now he leaped toward them with a shriek.

Grams had one arm around Gale, and the other one went up in a warding-off gesture. Her entire body contracted, flinching away and finding nowhere to go. The motion woke Gale, who screamed her way out of one nightmare and into another.

Barney flailed at Grams' arm, knocking it away. She felt sure he was going to hit her, to beat her to death right there. Instead he swung his huge hands down toward Gale. Grams screamed. She howled as she felt her granddaughter torn away. Barney yanked Gale toward him, clutching at the screaming, flailing mass of limbs that the little girl had become.

Grams saw Gale's cane, folded neatly into short lengths of red and white, fall to the ground. One of the hyenas sniffed it, then looked up. It seemed to be grinning, knowing this was not all that would fall.

"Grams! Grams, Daddy!" Gale screamed, throwing her arms toward Grams. The old woman caught hold of one of them, her hand encircling the girl's thin wrist. Her other hand followed, both of them manacling the girl to her.

Barney yanked at Gale, trying to peel her away from Grams. "She ain't gonna make it anyway! Look at her, what chance does she have? Maybe we give her to them and they let us go! Maybe we – *ugh!*"

Barney cried out in pain as Grams, still holding Gale for all she was worth, kicked out as hard as she could. Her hiking boot caught Barney right in the center of the forehead, and his scalp split open. Blood washed over his nose, down his chin.

Barney didn't let go of Gale. The little girl used her free hand to rake her nails across his face, drawing furrows on his cheeks and forehead. Barney still didn't let go. He didn't even seem to notice the wounds. Just kept pulling, pulling. Grams was perilously close to falling right off the tree, and if that happened she knew Gale would come tumbling down right after.

She locked her legs around the tree limb they'd been sitting on. Barney kept pulling, drawing Gale away an inch at a time until Grams, who refused to let go of the girl's wrist, felt herself stretch parallel to the ground. The only thing anchoring her was her legs.

She had cursed the lack of water in her body only minutes before. Now life showed itself capable of cruel tricks, as sweat dampened her palms. She screamed as she felt Gale's wrist start to slip from her grip.

"She ain't gonna make it. Ain't gonna make it," Barney was saying. His voice was a snuffling, slurping thing that reminded Grams of the sucking sounds the mud had made when the survivors ran through the rain. It didn't sound human – and that, she realized, was Barney's truth. The thing he'd not just realized but embraced. Not human at all, just an animal willing to do whatever it took to survive. "Look at her," he mumbled, no longer speaking to Grams or anyone else. "We all don't have to die. We don't all –"

Grams was losing Gale. And she couldn't lose Gale. She'd already lost her son – three times, actually; once the first time the doctors told him he was doomed, then again when they repeated the same message (this time for a different reason) nearly a decade later, and a third time when he willingly gave himself to death in the hopes that he could trade his pain for a chance for Gale to live. He had sacrificed all, and Grams had seen her son die for her granddaughter.

She would *not* let Craig down. So she could *not* let Gale go.

She let her legs slacken, feeling the bark of the tree tear at her skin as Barney ripped Gale toward him. In the next instant Grams set her feet against the limb of the tree and shoved with all her might.

She didn't let go of Gale. She barreled right into the girl, now getting one arm around her little body, holding her better, tighter. The other hand went around Barney's neck. Her arm slid against his greasy, blood-slicked skin. The feeling revolted her, but she didn't push away. The bastard still had Gale, and she wouldn't let go until after he did.

She again pushed closer, not really sure what she could do with one arm around Gale and the other holding to Barney. He batted her with his free hand, but it was the hand on the side of his wounded shoulder, so the hits were glancing and weak.

Grams didn't know what she could do, so it was a surprise when she did it. She held the big man close, and Gale screamed as she was pressed between the two adults struggling over her. Barney jerked, and Grams fell forward, her face sliding into the hollow between his neck and shoulder.

Again, the slick wetness of his flesh on hers made her want to writhe away. But this time, there was the added bonus of his smell. She was right on him, her nose buried in his skin, and he stank. Sweat, blood, fear. All mixed together in a gruesome slime that pressed into her and made her eyes sting with tears.

She had no free hands. Her arms were wrapped around her granddaughter and the monster who was trying to steal her away. Her face was buried in his mass.

She bit him.

He howled as she did it, and howled louder when she released the bite, found a new one, and bit down again. This time she didn't let go, but ground her teeth together, sliding her jaw left to right as she tore into his flesh. Blood spurted, going up her nose and in her eyes.

Barney still didn't let go of Gale. He found some reservoir of strength and Grams felt herself being peeled away from Gale. She couldn't stop it. He was too big. Too strong. For the first time in her life, Grams hated the fact that she was old. "Age is just a number," she often said when friends her age bitched about their ever-advancing years and ever-sagging boobs. But now age wasn't just a number, it was muscles that weren't strong or quick as they had been and now needed to be. It was hands that couldn't hold as tight as they once did.

Age wasn't a number, it was your son's last breath on your cheek, and your granddaughter's screams as the monster fully and finally tore her from your arms.

4

SELENA FELT LIKE THE world skittered sideways when she saw Barney pulling at Grams, then it completely slipped its moorings and slid away from her for a moment when she heard his screams and realized he wasn't pulling at her at all. He was pulling *Gale*.

Even wounded, Naeku was quicker on the uptake than Selena. She lurched upward with a groan, then sank back again. Her eyes rolled back in their sockets and Selena thought for sure she was dead. Then they cracked slightly, and dull whites showed through the slits. Unseeing, but seeing enough, the Maasai whispered, "Save her."

Evie was already moving – another person who was faster than Selena when it mattered. She climbed to the next branch up, but the tree showed whose side it was on as the branch didn't just break but seemed to crumble in Evie's hands. A moment later Selena saw that for the trick it was: the branch hadn't dissolved, just some of the bark had peeled away.

It was enough. Evie fell, barely grabbing the branch below her before tumbling past it to where the hyenas were waiting, jaws open and panting and white-red ropes of bloody saliva jiggling back and forth like those fake jungle vines in *Me Jane* (two hundred million gross, world box office).

She remembered hating those vines. They looked so fake, so ridiculous. But when the editors and FX guys finished, she looked like she was swinging through the trees. It looked real.

Now it *was* real. Selena was flying through a tree of another sort, only this time she wasn't strapped to a thick safety harness that would be edited out of the final cut in post-production. She was barreling upward through the tree, tearing her way skyward. The tree cut her palms, her elbows, any and all skin that it could find. She didn't care.

Grams was hanging to Barney now, then Barney screamed and something came off him –

(Dear God she bit him good for her she bit that sonofabitch!)

– and then he reared back and slammed his elbow into Grams' face. The old broad didn't give an inch. She screamed but kept one arm wrapped around Gale.

Selena kept pulling herself up. Kept cutting herself apart in her hurry to climb. She saw Barney yank Gale mostly out of Grams' embrace. Heard him scream, "Why can't you just let… it… GO!"

Selena climbed a few branches higher, then her climb ended as she leaped onto Barney's back. She landed just as Barney tore Grams' arm away from Gale. He screamed – more in shock than in pain this time – as Selena's weight fell onto his back, and he dropped Gale.

The little girl hung there, trapped in space, a slow-motion non-descent that was all blood and fear and wide eyes behind dark glasses knocked askew.

The glasses fell. The girl would fall in a moment.

Selena lurched forward. She reached blindly, and felt something try to rip her arms from their sockets. She realized a moment later that it was Gale's weight, the girl's downward trajectory arrested only by Selena's grip.

Things returned to full speed, then vaulted into a stop-motion sequence where everything happened too fast and was too jerky for comfort. An action movie dialed up to "11," directed by a coked-up Michael Bay and edited by a speed addict.

CLOSE UP: Gale, swinging down in an arc, slamming into the trunk. Screaming.

REVERSE ANGLE: Barney, eyes rolling like a rabid animal, grappling with Selena, tossing her aside.

TWO SHOT: Selena, still holding on, letting him drop her, then catching the trunk with her free hand and crushing Gale to her, the little girl now caught between her and the trunk of the great dead tree.

EXTREME CLOSE UP: The little girl's eyes wide, staring at nothing but seeing death coming all the same.

REVERSE ANGLE: Barney, sliding down the tree, holding Selena, hanging off her like an anchor, dragging her away.

Selena saw the way this movie would go. She saw the tragic death of the little girl. The plucky actress trying her best to save her and then weeping as she realized she had failed, and the Oscar goes to –

"We don't gotta all die!" Barney was shouting. "We give the fuckers what they want and *we can GET THROUGH THIS!*"

The movie ended there, with his breath hot on her neck, his body writhing against hers. She saw his hand. It was red with blood. Red.

"No," Selena grunted. She pressed Gale against the tree. "Hold on," she whispered. Saw Gale's hands encircle the trunk as much as she could.

"Just let me do what I gotta do! Help me, Sel, you stupid bitch!"

Selena let go of Gale. She spun in Barney's grasp and had a glorious moment when she looked in his eyes and saw him realize what she was doing, know what was coming... and not be able to do a damn thing about it.

"I'm done helping you," she said in that beautiful, delicious moment that was better than any golden statue, better than any applause, better even than being the first woman to command twenty million as an upfront fee.

Selena locked her legs around Barney. He reached – maybe for her, maybe for something to hang onto – but she batted his hands away. She felt her legs clench around him, tighter than they ever had, because this time it was fully her choice and this time she was going to *enjoy* it.

She had ridden him up. Now she rode him down. The ride up had mostly been a patchwork of pain and lies and rationalized cruelties. The ride down, the part she'd written for herself… she smiled.

It hurt, slamming down the tree, and hurt worse when the earth reached up to grab them. The worst pain of all came next. But the smile just grew, because in a life where "not fair" had been her beginning, her middle, she had finally changed one thing:

Her end was *completely* fair.

That was all she had ever wanted.

5

EVIE REACHED GALE FIRST. She passed Grams in a few sharp vaults up branches that crackled and snapped, and grabbed the little girl just as her grip was giving way. Gale slid off the tree with a short, high shriek that ended as abruptly as it had come as she hit Evie's chest, then spun and threw her arms around her and cried.

"Shhh… shhh… it's okay. He's gone."

She looked down, where Barney and Selena had hit the ground. The bodies were already unrecognizable. More of the hyenas had painted faces, an ancient race of hunters getting ready for war.

Queen, her face buried in something large enough it could only have belonged to Barney, looked up. Her tongue lolled a moment, then she returned to her feast.

Gale was still weeping, but either she had no tears in her or they were so light Evie could not feel them on the hollow of her neck, where the girl had buried her face.

Not good. She's small, she has less time left than anyone else.

She felt arms sweep in, pulling Gale gently away. Almost Evie clutched the girl tighter, almost she spun away from Grams' reaching arms. *"Mine!"* she wanted to scream, and hold the girl and never let her go.

She forced herself to ignore that voice. Gale was not hers to hold, not when her own blood reached out to her. Evie swung slightly, awkwardly passing the little girl to Grams. Gale seized up for a moment, her arms clenching tightly around Evie's neck, then she must have realized who it was who wanted to hold her. She let go of Evie and leaped into Grams' waiting embrace.

Grams' eyes didn't leave Evie's. Even as she patted Gale's head, rubbed knobby fingers along her back in motions that were half massage, half checking the girl for injuries, she stared at Evie.

She's thinking the same thing we all are: how long until we do fall? Because we have to fall, and that's for sure. Sooner or later, we let go of the tree and just slip away.

Evie heard rustling and looked down to see Naeku slipping to one side as though she had heard Evie's thoughts and shrugged her shoulders and said to herself, "Well then, now's as good a time as any."

Evie lurched down the same branches she had just barreled up, now reaching down to keep the Maasai woman from falling. As always, the hyenas seemed aware of what was happening, and had clustered below Naeku.

Evie almost didn't make it. She grabbed a handful of Naeku's shirt collar at the last second. Even so, she felt herself going over with the guide. She planted her feet on the branch below Naeku, yanking hard and swinging her own butt out until it hung over empty space. The branch creaked but proved a sufficient fulcrum. Naeku slowly righted.

Evie pulled herself forward at the same time, landing straddled over Naeku. The guide blinked, eyes dull and listless, obviously not even aware of what had just happened.

"Naeku! Naeku, stay with us!" Evie remembered movies where someone was dying, on their last legs, and was brought back by a sharp slap to the cheek, maybe two. She knew that was just Hollywood hooey – she had been on the end of enough slaps to know that they brought pain, bruises, blood… but no life came with them.

The thought seemed important, even as it was sublimated by the more important task of trying to keep

292

Naeku from dying. She was the only one who knew where to go, the only one who knew what to do.

And more than that, Evie liked her. And wasn't that reason enough to want someone around? Forget the fact that there was no way she or Grams or Gale would survive without her, she just *deserved* to live.

THE ROAR NAEKU HAD heard was now everywhere. Low, rolling, it pulsed over her, covered her. It was a warm sound, if such a thing were even possible – not just the warmth of a loved one's call, but a physical warmth that spread over her.

That was good. Because she had been getting cold. So very cold.

Something in her mind started flapping its arms, calling for attention. It tried to tell her the cold was death, and she should fight it. But Naeku was too busy listening to the roar.

She floated in gray, nothing but her and that wonderful sound – a sound that was so familiar, so beloved, but one that she could not place. And then the floating shifted to a sickening lurch. She was falling through the gray, falling below the sound.

The horrible feeling of losing that noise brought her back. The gray dissipated, turning deep brown in the final darkness of a fading night.

I'm up a tree.

She didn't know where the thought came from and knew even less what it might mean. But she did know the shape that came close to her. A face.

"Father," she whispered. She frowned, wondering now if she heard… "The lions. Do you hear that, Father? Do you hear the lions?" She spoke as a child, the words the soft, nearly babbling procession of words that toddlers used when excited. But Father would understand her. He always did.

Father spoke, but his voice was strange. It was higher than it usually was. Not like he was stressed or strained, but as though it belonged to someone else. "Sweetie, I don't understand you."

The voice came in another language. Not the tongue of Naeku's childhood home. This was a cruder, harsher language. Something that took the rolling "r" sounds and converted them to plugs in her throat; something that made the friendly and evocative clicks and smacks of her birth language into sounds that locked themselves behind her teeth and refused to come without prodding.

Naeku tried to respond in kind. It was hard, and even in the gray-blue-brown where she and her Father now lived, she could hear that her voice was slurred and low. "Do you hear that?" she whispered. "Do you hear the lions?"

Father frowned. He *looked* different now, too. His skin was lightening, his features shifting and becoming somehow more petite.

Oh, how the men will laugh at you, Father! How they will make fun at the way you now look!

(only they're all dead – Father, the men who would have laughed, they're all gone)

Father's face finished its transformation, and in his place Naeku now saw the face of a white woman. "Sweetie," she said, "I don't hear the lions. But maybe you can show us where they are when we get down, okay?"

The woman had a strange expression. She looked like she was watching something die.

Me. She's watching me *die.*

That thought brought another: *Not me. I'm not dying; I* refuse *to die.*

294

And still one more: *But I* am *dying. I* will *die.*

The sound rose around her. Rushed, rolled. The lions, she was almost sure of it.

The woman still looking at her leaned close. "Stay with us, Naeku."

Naeku finally recognized her. Evie. Naeku reached out and grasped the woman's shirt. She pulled her close – not just physically, but mentally. The roar was so loud now, the lions so close that it was hard to concentrate on anything else. But there was still more to do. Maybe she was dying, but Naeku would not die without fulfilling her purpose.

She pointed up. She did not have to look where she was pointing; she knew the sky almost as well as she knew the land below. Knew that even though night was drawing to a close, what she pointed at would still be visible in the lightening twilight. "See those three stars?" she asked.

Evie just stared at her as though she had gone mad, and Naeku wondered if perhaps Evie couldn't even hear her. How could *anyone* hear her through the loud – and louder and louder – noise all around?

But she had heard. Evie glanced up, then looked back, confused. "Yes. Of course, we –"

"Follow them at night," said Naeku. She didn't like interrupting people, but she sensed that if she didn't get her message out *now* she might lose her only chance. "During the day, you will see a mountain in that same direction. Head toward its peak. There is a village that way."

Evie again glanced up, then her head tilted down and Naeku knew she was looking for the mountain. She must have seen it, for she nodded and turned back. "Got it, but why don't you just rest a minute and –"

Naeku waved her to silence, an almost violent motion that sent her lurching to the side once more. She managed to right herself with fingers and hands and arms that seemed so far away they almost could not be felt. "Before the village," she continued, "you will come to a gorge. It is a good sign, because the village is only two or three miles past that place." She swallowed, and now the sound that had blanketed all withdrew a bit. Even now, it seemed, the lions still feared some things. "Do *not* go in the gorge, even though going around it will take you out of the way. Go around the gorge, then go to the mountain. Follow the peak, follow the stars." She saw Evie was about to say something more, so she continued as fast as she could, "None of you has had water in half a day. In this heat, you have perhaps another twelve hours before your body just stops and dies of thirst. Less for Gale," she added in a whisper. Then, louder, "So get moving, and do not stop for anything."

Evie nodded. "Sure. Good, fine, we'll keep going. But you have to come. You've got to show us the village."

Now the lions surged in strength once again as Naeku shook her head. She realized they were coming for her. To take her somewhere.

"No," she said. "Never. The village is mine. A dying place. The old ways are passing on, and I have no wish to see the place I was born without my father or brother there."

She cocked her head. The roar had faded. Gone. She looked to the side, then down.

They were there. The lions she had seen so often as a child, the ones her father had gone to avenge. They hunched below, waiting for her. She would climb down to them and run and run...

Behind them, the world was gone. Just gray that she knew would not shift until she joined those silent lions who waited. Then, she somehow knew, the gray would part and

296

she would see not only the world she knew but vast, bright lands beyond sight.

And still one more thing. She saw a shape in the gray. Tall and thin, the shape she had known long and known well. She saw the shape and knew it, just as she knew she was seeing it as she had so long ago, when she was a tiny child and could always find that shape in the night and always climb up and be held.

"Father," she murmured.

The shape drew closer. Beside it, another shape, about the same size she now felt herself to be. Thin, with an almost defiant stance. Her brother.

And then, beyond both father and brother, a final shape. The one she had not seen for longer than any other. The shape was softer somehow, even through the veil of gray.

She was falling. She would join the lions. She would run with her father and brother, and would look over and see her mother, too, and would hold her hand.

Yes.

It was time to run with the lions, and with her family, and see all the universe and know the things she had always suspected.

"I am coming to you," she whispered, and did not know if she spoke to the lions, to father, to brother, or to mother. It did not matter. They were all the same, in some important way.

And a moment later, she was the same, too. She was with them and she was in them and they were in her and together... they ran.

6

GRAMS WATCHED AS EVIE adjusted Naeku's body. She wanted to cry, but no tears would come. Only a bit of moisture at the corners of her eyes, not even a single drop spilling.

Gale was silent in her arms. Grams thought maybe she should say something to the girl. She didn't, though, because what exactly would she say? "It's okay, sweetie – your dad's gone, your Grams feels like she could fall apart any moment now, our guide just died, and – oh yes – we're up a tree with a ravening pack of bloodthirsty hyenas just waiting for us to drop from exhaustion, but don't you worry I'm sure we'll all be fine"?

She just held her granddaughter, and felt the girl's trembling subside in stages. Below her, Evie pulled Naeku into a position where she would not fall. She had to shove the Maasai woman's body hard into the crotch of the tree, bending the corpse into an odd, awkward position, but Grams knew why she was doing it: it wouldn't do to watch her tumble to the hyenas. Not her. Barney and Selena had been bad enough – Grams hadn't liked either of them, but that didn't mean she wanted them dead – but to see the strong warrior woman torn apart would hurt so much it might just mark the end of the game.

So she was glad Evie pushed and prodded until the body was secure – or as secure as a body could be when it hung six feet above the living embodiment of Hunger.

Gale was silent. She no longer trembled. "You okay?" Grams asked. A dumb question, an absolutely *moronic* question, but she couldn't stay silent any longer.

Gale didn't respond. Grams worried that the girl might have gone catatonic. She glanced down and saw Gale's eyes closed, her little face slack. Grams didn't think that was a whole lot better than catatonic, though. Maybe she was asleep, just trying to evade reality as her body forced a few minutes or hours of exhausted slumber. But maybe she was unconscious. Maybe worse.

Grams was acutely aware that the sun had now climbed over the horizon. It was no longer twilight. It was day.

It was already getting hotter.

THERE WAS NO WIND to speak of, so Evie had no idea how the dust came to climb from the ground and coat her skin, her mouth – she even felt it in her nose. Maybe it was the motion of the hyenas below, stirring up a small cloud of red-brown each time they moved. Maybe it was just Africa letting them know that sooner or later would become part of her.

However it happened, it was a reality, as was the malaise that crept over her. She felt herself sinking into that dark place where she knew she was nothing and no one, a woman whose only great work in life had been to let baby after baby die within her, the final one far enough along that it must have felt those last few, awful moments within her as she died alone.

Evie shook herself. Looking down, she saw that the last traces of water from last night's storm had already been baked away. The ground was as rutted and cracked as it had been yesterday. The storm had not marked the end of the dry, hot seasons. It was a momentary reprieve. Maybe more rain would come, maybe it wouldn't.

Even if it did, Evie didn't know how they would get it. She supposed they could just cup their hands and hold them out and drink whatever they caught, but she knew that would prove only marginally better than nothing.

They needed to drink.

What time is it?

Another thing she did not know. Gale was still asleep in Grams' arms, and neither Evie nor the old woman had made a move to wake her – if they even could.

She looked at the body nearby. Naeku had slipped away without a murmur. Just a few last words, spoken softly in Swahili. She closed her eyes and sagged, but in the last moment Evie thought she saw the woman's lips curve up in the hint of a smile. She hoped she had seen that. She hoped Naeku had found a good place, if for no other reason than because the rest of them were liable to end up there soon.

She looked away from Naeku, knowing that if she kept following that reasoning she would end up just climbing down to the hyenas. Why prolong the inevitable? Why put herself through so much –

Shut up. Do something.

The thought was nearly alien. How often had she felt pain, how often had she been hurt… and how long had it been since she last felt the urge to resist it? A year? Six? Eight?

Yet she knew she *would* move. She would do something, even if it was only for the sake of resisting. Resisting pain, resisting defeat – weren't those enough of a goal in and of themselves to warrant the effort it took to pursue them?

She climbed to Grams. The old woman was looking into the distance, steadily avoiding any glances at the hyenas below – or at the girl in her arms, for that matter. Evie felt a momentary pang of guilt. Bill was gone, but was that really much of a loss? Certainly not compared to what Grams had already lost. Certainly not compared to what the old woman still stood to lose.

Grams' eyes flicked over to Evie as she approached. "How you holding up?" Evie asked.

With an absolutely straight face, Grams replied, "I don't like to complain, but I've never liked camping."

Evie had to smile. Hope tugged at her, and she followed that pull down to Gale. The little girl's eyes were open. Not seeing anything, of course, but she was *there*. The light in her gaze – the light that Evie had recognized from the first, and which she had so quickly loved – shone out. A bit diminished, a bit more ragged than it had been only twenty-four hours before. But the sight of it took the smile on Gale's face and turned it into a full grin.

"What about you?" she asked. "How are you feeling, kiddo?"

Gale didn't answer. Evie's grin disappeared. A girl awake but not answering – there was no scenario where that was good news. Shock? Total disappearance into someplace deep inside her?

Grams was looking at her granddaughter. The old woman shifted on her perch, and Evie got the impression the movement was less necessary than an excuse to jostle the girl, to see if she could be jounced into responding.

Gale didn't say a thing. After a long pause, Grams hugged her small form to her and said, "She'll be fine. She's a trooper." She shifted her gaze to Evie and said, "We have to get down from here."

Evie had to smile again, though for a different and darker reason this time. "I'm open to ideas," she said.

"I was about to say the same thing to you."

Another silence. Evie felt that dark place rising up within her. In a way, though, wasn't that good news? Wasn't it a good sign that the thing that had been a part of every waking moment for so long now had an ebb and flow to it?

She supposed it was.

She moved.

She dug into her pockets, pulling out everything she found. There was a flat stretch on one of the nearby branches, and she laid out the contents of her pockets there.

A small keyring. A lipstick tube. Bill's wallet – he had told her to get it only yesterday, but already it seemed like an alien relic from a world lost to time.

She didn't open it. Partly that was habit –

("Never touch my wallet, you cow! You might as well just cut off my balls and watch me bleed to death if you're going to steal into my private things whenever you want!")

– but much of her just wanted to forget the last years. Staring at Bill's wallet made that harder.

She looked at the other items. Nothing there; she didn't suppose she could bribe the hyenas away with the offer of a joyride in a fifteen-year-old Hyundai two-door, or the offer of an Extreme Hollywood Makeover.

Grams had followed Evie's lead. She didn't let go of Gale at any point, so it was an awkward process for the old woman to search her pockets, with much shifting and grunting. But she came out with a few things:

A bottle of prescription pills that rattled as she set them on the same branch with Evie's treasures. A lighter and half-crushed joint that surprised Evie – she knew that getting old wasn't the same as being dead, and that people still wanted the things that made them happy, but for some reason thinking of someone Grams' age lighting up a joint made her want to laugh.

She *did* laugh at the next thing Grams produced: a leather billfold not unlike Bill's own that flipped open when

302

the old lady put it down. Evie saw a few photos in those laminated windows that came with so many wallets, but which so few people actually used. She saw a driver's license – Grams was making a face in the picture, and Evie wondered how she'd convinced the DMV employee to let her get away with *that* one – and a prescription drug card.

She also saw the distinctive edge of a foil wrapper tucked in behind the pictures. She looked sideways at Grams, who shrugged. "Girl's always gotta be prepared to tame a wild beast, right?"

Evie laughed out loud at that. She picked up the prescription bottle and shook it. The *rat-tat-rattle* of the pills sounded dry and unpleasant, so she stopped quickly. She looked at the name of the medicine, printed on a laminated paper on the side of the bottle. She didn't recognize it, so cocked an eye at Grams.

Grams shrugged again. "Just antacids. Nothing we could drug them with."

Evie pawed at the small stash as though she hoped something else might appear there. "Anything else? Maybe a Taser or a small bazooka?"

Grams shook her head. Evie looked at Gale. "What about you, sweetie? You hiding anything we could use, Gale?"

Again, both women waited for the girl to speak. Once more, she did not. Grams hugged her in much the same way a proud parent might hug a precocious child who has just said something witty and true. "All she carries around is her phone – and who knows where that is now – and her cane."

She glanced down, and Evie followed the look. Gale's foldable cane lay at the base of the tree, the stark red-and-white color scheme bright even as a small, folded cluster of sticks below.

Queen strutted into view. Evie looked back at Grams, not wanting to fall into that creature's gaze. It was too strong, too much. "Not much to work with," she said.

She looked at Bill's wallet. She didn't think she'd find anything there – she knew she wouldn't, actually – but she still found herself reaching for it, found her fingers flipping it open.

She held her breath as she did so, and her shoulders twitched at the blow that she knew would come. But it didn't. Nothing happened.

She pulled open the small slits in the wallet. A few credit cards, his driver's license. A union card.

She pried open the back, where the bills would be. A few traveler's checks, a few dollars.

A paper.

She frowned. Everything else in the wallet was pretty much what she remembered being there in the old days, the days when he let her look at his things and didn't scream or hit her for the privilege.

But the paper... it looked odd. Just a white sheet, graying with age, darker gray at the folds that had been made to fit it into the slim compartment in the wallet.

She pulled it out. Her shoulders twitched again. Not fear this time, it was more the feeling a long-term jailbird might have walking out of the prison after being released. The prickle of expectation, the fear that comes with freedom.

She unfolded the page, recognizing that she was doing it without hope it would help them in their current plight. It was just something she was daring to do, and something she had to follow through to its end.

She looked at the open paper. A letter.

Dear Ms. Childs,

*We have received your manuscript, A PAPER
PRINCESS, and loved it. We have tried calling you at
the phone number you indicated on your submission
cover letter, but the person who answered indicated it
was a wrong number.*

*We are most anxious to talk to you about the
manuscript. We – not just me, but every agent at this
agency to whom I have shown the work – feel that it is
a great, wonderful piece, and that we can make a quick
and easy sale of it.*

*Please call us at your earliest convenience. And
(and this is something I've never said before, not in
twelve years as an agent), even if you don't end up
working with us, I want to thank you for the read. It
was wonderful.*

There followed a "Yours sincerely," and contact
information for the Write Brothers Agency. Evie barely saw
that. The paper was trembling too much in her hands for her
to see more than a sliding blur of ants crawling across the
graying skin of a corpse.

Bill's wallet fell from her other hand, numb fingers
opening and letting the thing tumble to the earth. The hyenas
did not notice. They did not care.

"What is it? Evie, what happened?"

Evie heard the words, but like the writing on the page,
they had become a meaningless nothing. Another nothing
joined it: a droning buzz that only gradually resolved in her
mind, and even more slowly did she recognize that she herself
was saying the words, over and over – "You sonofabitch, you
sonofabitch, you sonofa*bitch*."

"What is it? Evie, you're scaring me."

Those words penetrated, if only because they were so ridiculous. Certainly there were better things to worry about than one woman having a nervous breakdown over the contents of her dead husband's wallet.

Yet at that moment, Evie couldn't think of a thing that bothered her more. Not the heat, the lack of water, or even the hyenas with Queen at their head. Because those wouldn't last. A day at most, and all those problems would be gone. This, though...

She checked the date at the top of the letter, even though she knew what it would say. *A Paper Princess* had been her one attempt at a book, and Bill had forbidden her to keep sending it to agents and publishers. And she thought he did that was right about the time this letter was dated.

She saw it all clearly: him getting a letter. How much it would burn him. Then, worse, her getting a follow-up phone call. Him answering it on one of the increasingly frequent days he was sent home early from the construction jobs he worked. Answering smugly, "No, there's no one here by that name, sorry." Then the smugness turning to rage, and a burning desire to hurt her and – worse even than whatever he might do with his hands – to keep her down.

How dare she succeed? That's what he would be thinking, right? That's all he possibly *could* think.

She had lived in the darkness so long. She thought it came from her own mind, her own psyche just giving her what she needed as a just retribution for what she had done to her family, to her children. Now, with this letter, with the date on its heading, she saw the darkness with different eyes.

It was inside her, yes. But it wasn't hers. It was his. He had always seemed so kind during the early years of their marriage, so eager to please. She had thought the change that came over him was her doing, but now she started to see that as just one more part of the lie. He hadn't changed at all – it was just that as the babies died, he found himself in a world where he didn't get every single thing he wanted. And that was unforgivable. Not his fault – nothing ever was, ever could be – so the obvious culprit must be Evie.

There was a word for that, Evie knew. A word for someone who was all smiles and light so long as his every desire came true. But when such did not happen, his only response would be rage. Lashing out. Hurting those who denied him his dreams.

Sociopath.

She had researched that, too. She knew what it meant. A person who would go to any lengths to get everything he thought he deserved. A person who would hurt others around them just as a necessity, because if everyone around you was lowly and weak, didn't that mean he was mighty and strong? A person who would gradually self-destruct, who would lose job after job as he inevitably took shortcuts and easy ways out because why should he have to do so much when the universe already owed him everything?

A person like Bill.

The darkness was still there. But it was his. She knew that.

And that meant that maybe, just maybe, there was something that was still *her* below it.

The understanding didn't change her physical reaction. Probably a good thing, since if she hadn't twitched hard enough to knock the lighter and joint off the branch, she probably would have stayed there and kept on shaking until the end of time. But she did twitch, the lighter and the joint did fall.

She dropped the letter. It fluttered down and landed on the back of one of Queen's daughters. The hyena didn't move; the letter didn't bother her in the slightest.

Evie snatched for the other items, the things that had come from Grams' pockets and in that moment seemed beyond value or price. She got her hand around the lighter, snatching it out of the sky, but the joint continued down and disappeared to sight. Still there, but almost the same shade as the dry earth it had gone to meet.

Evie stared dully at the lighter. Then at Grams.

"Dammit," said Grams after a moment. "I was really looking forward to smoking that when we got back." Her voice carried the strained tone of someone trying for humor in an awkward situation.

Evie kept staring. A moment later, her mouth opened. A strangled sound came out that gradually became a bouncing, high-pitched laugh. The laugh became a near-hysterical fit.

She heard Grams laughing, too.

She looked down and saw the paper on the hyena's back. And laughed even harder.

GRAMS LAUGHED, NOT SURE what exactly she was laughing at, other than at Evie's own thundering explosion of mirth. She was glad Evie was laughing, though, she knew that much. She had worried when Evie read whatever was on that paper in the wallet. The look in her eyes – Grams had only seen that look once before, and it was on her own face on a day when she'd decided to die.

The laughter was better. Better than that already-dead look, better than the feeling that she was staring not at a friend and fellow survivor, but at just one more corpse in the tree.

The laughter petered out. Grams just didn't have the lung capacity anymore for sustained hysteria, so she grew quiet first. Evie's own return to silence came a moment later, but her eyes no longer looked dead. The eyes were brighter, more vibrant than Grams had ever seen them.

Not vibrant, angry.

She wondered why, and was suddenly afraid to ask. Rage was better than the death mask Evie had been wearing a moment before, but only a little. Rage was a dangerous thing at the best of times, and these were far from the best of times.

"You okay?" Grams asked.

Evie, her laughter done but her body giving out an odd hiccup every so often, as though still deciding whether to return to its amusement, coughed and said, "I'm fine." But she shook her head when she said it.

"What was it?" Grams asked.

Evie looked down at the paper lying like the world's most ridiculous baby blanket across the back of the slumbering hyena below. She shrugged. "A sign."

Grams wanted to say, "A sign of what?" but didn't. A lot of reasons for that, not least of which being that she knew from experience that that kind of living-death moment did not necessarily come with a need or desire to "talk it out," as she heard so many people describe it today. Sometimes you needed to be with your own thoughts, and getting in the way of that just created or prolonged pain.

And what's that sound?

She had heard it for a while now, she suddenly realized, though only a slight buzz at the very outer limits of her hearing. Unlike a lot of her friends, Grams still had full use of her ears – "twenty-twenty hearing," as she liked to call it. So the fact that she barely heard the noise meant no one else in the tree likely heard it at all. Evie was doing whatever Evie was doing, for better or worse, and Gale was in her own world –

(And please, God, let that world be a nice one, a happy one.)

– which meant Grams alone heard the almost angry buzzing.

The sound grew. And as it did it grew more and more familiar. She'd never heard the sound in person, but she watched TV and movies like anyone else. She knew that *chup-chup-chup* sound as soon as it came into focus with the ol' twenty-twenty ears.

A helicopter.

The sound grew louder, and she saw Evie look up, now aware of it as well. They both cast their gazes about the sky. Small sounds seem to come from everywhere and nowhere at once, so it wasn't until the sound had grown a bit more that Grams could pinpoint it. She turned toward it, Evie matching the movement.

It wasn't visible for a while. Long enough that Grams wondered if she was really hearing anything at all, or if the whole thing – the sound, Evie looking along with her, the child in her arms – as just the last fever dream of an old woman about to succumb to heat and thirst and drop right out of the sky into Hell itself.

Then she saw a dark spot in the otherwise empty blue of the sky. No clouds to get in the way, nothing but the sun so bright it hurt to look up, even though Grams was looking nowhere near that fiery orb. She squinted when she saw that dark pinprick in the blue, and as she did the pinprick grew to an ink spot, then to a blotch.

Grams started shouting, screaming, *shrieking*. She held to Gale with one arm as she waved the other frantically. Evie did the same, only she had both of her arms free, and waved them like a drowning woman feeling her breath start to go, the

310

last moments when salvation would be possible. Then Evie left off waving and started climbing, still shouting, stopping every few seconds to wave again.

"Hey! Hey it's us! We're here! We're here!"

Grams didn't know which of them shouted the words. Maybe they both did, because there were few words to choose from in that moment so it wouldn't have surprised her to find that both she and Evie shouted the exact same things at the exact same moments. "Help! Help us!"

Waving, waving. Calling down the thing that had come. The chopper, yes, but more than that, it was the thing that had to be in it.

It was help, come at last.

REGINA SQUINTED, ENGAGING IN that very human but equally ridiculous practice of trying to keep her eyes open by closing them halfway. Usually the noise of the chopper alone would have been enough to keep her six notches past awake and well into teeth-grindingly stressed. Now, after hours of looking, looking... the dull sound of the helicopter's rotors slashing the air was starting to sound more and more like a lullaby.

"Hey, boss. You spot anything that way?"

Regina started at Busara's voice. The woman was all business. She would have to be, Regina supposed; it wasn't often that you saw a native-born Tanzanian who owned her own chopper. There were a few, sure. Rich people existed in every corner of the globe, and the richer you got the more the whirlybirds started looking like something fun to own. But Busara wasn't rich, she was just a businesswoman who had parleyed a meager lot in life into something a bit less meager, then continued that pattern until she owned and operated her own helicopter charter.

Busara was a cunning businesswoman, too, which was one of the reasons that Regina hated having to call her. It wasn't enough that Happy Africa was going down in flames around her – now she was going to have to pay through the nose for Busara's services.

But there was no denying that Busara was the best at what she did, or that she provided value for her price. They'd been back and forth dozens of times, sweeping across the game preserve in long, carefully-plotted lines, and though Regina had felt her own concentration starting to drift only a few hours in, Busara looked as sharp-eyed and focused as she had when they began.

So when Busara asked Regina if she'd spotted anything, Regina knew it wasn't just idle chatter. She wanted a second pair of eyes on what she'd *already* seen. Regina shifted, turning to her right and following the invisible line extending from Busara's outstretched finger until it ended...

Regina squinted, this time not trying to chase sleep away but to make sense of what she saw. "The hell is that?" she asked.

"You want me to check it out?" Busara didn't wait for an answer. She just swept the yoke – or stick or handle or whatever the hell you called the steering wheel in these things – to the side. The chopper canted wildly, and Regina spent a few seconds convincing her insides to stay put before she managed to look back at Busara's target.

It was nothing but a dark blotch on the land, but it seemed to writhe. Regina couldn't get her head around it. She knew what herds looked like, knew the patterns one saw while watching a large group of animals following something as a single organism. This wasn't that. It was smaller, first of all, far

312

too small to be a group of Cape buffalo or some zebras. And there was an oddly stationary blotch in the middle, like half of whatever it was had congealed and become part of the landscape.

The helicopter sped toward the mystery, and a moment later – Regina was secretly proud that she was the one who first recognized what they were looking at – she said, "Hyenas. A bloody big pack of them, hanging out near a tree."

"What I thought, too," said Busara.

Regina was terrified at the thought of the many things – very few of them good – that might have happened to the guests and guides she last saw the night before. She genuinely liked the guides, of course – even Leg, who was a buzzkill from birth – but also liked some of the guests more than usual. The Jensen family in particular, with Gale being the central jewel in that particular crown. She didn't want anything to happen to any of the group that she had seen off last night… so why, amidst all those dire worries and concerns, did she feel so irritated that she hadn't been the first one to figure out what they were seeing after all?

She tamped her irritation down. Now wasn't the time. She could be irritated after all this ended, when she was dressing down Naeku and Leg for whatever ridiculous stunt had gotten them all in such hot water, or when she was talking to the desk clerk at whatever passed for the Tanzanian equivalent of the dole queue.

A pair of binoculars hung from a leather strap around her neck, and she held them to her eyes. She didn't hold out much hope that she'd see anything useful; the bumpy up and down of the chopper made spotting something with the field glasses something of an art – and one Regina had not mastered.

Besides, the little she had managed to pick out convinced her that she was looking at a pack of hyenas – a big one. They weren't likely to be sitting in a prayer circle with her guests and guides, sharing stories about the one time the pack matriarch got drunk and tried to shag a baby elephant.

No, hyenas didn't operate like that. Anyone they found to this point was likely good and dead, if not actually shat out in bits along the burnt African ground.

She looked anyway. It was something to do. It made her feel like she was accomplishing something, and Regina very much needed to feel like that right now. Otherwise she kept seeing images of the guests and guides – both groups which were, ultimately, her care and responsibility – torn and bleeding somewhere, mangled by a freak car crash or by some less freak but no less terrifying natural catastrophe.

The rain last night wasn't so bad. They wouldn't have been hurt because of the storm.

Then where are they, smartass?

No answer, other than to look. She tried to focus on the hyenas, but as she expected it was mostly just a jouncy blur of motion. Occasionally she thought she might be seeing a leg or a tail, maybe a snarling mouth or two. Other than that, it was just the tree. The ancient, dead thing almost appeared to dance, empty branch-fingers opening and closing as the chopper shifted its position relative to branches and the shadows they cast.

"Why do you think they're there?" she asked.

Busara shrugged. "It is hot."

"Don't have to remind me of that."

But Regina knew Busara was right: the creatures were just taking shelter from the worst heat of the day, resting in what shadows they could find out here.

"See anything?" asked Busara.

"Not a damn thing."

"Should I get closer?"

314

Regina pursed her lips. After a moment, she shrugged. "No, turn south. There's a gorge there, and maybe they –"

At that moment, the hyena pack seemed to explode. They ran in every direction as their fear of the oncoming helicopter finally overwhelmed their need for shade or for the company of the rest of the pack. She'd seen that before, so it wasn't a surprise. What was a surprise, though, was how fast the pack regrouped. Led by what looked like a single animal – the queen bitch of the pack, Regina guessed – they coalesced into a conical shape that wheeled back to the tree under which they had sheltered.

That's a big group.

It was true. At least fifty, maybe more. That wasn't unheard of, but it was veering toward an extreme end of the spectrum. Enough that they created a strange kind of camouflage for themselves, because as they joined into that big clot of movement their running kicked up a huge plume of dust that shot high enough that it obscured much of the pack beneath it. Even after the storm last night, the dust was so dry and fine it seemed to hang impossibly all around the beasties, rising so high in the still air that even the tree they had been resting beneath mostly disappeared in the dirty cloud.

"You want me to turn south?" Busara asked. Regina knew she'd heard her, but she also knew that the chopper pilot would double check everything. She wanted to get paid for her work, and that meant she would be careful to have Regina make every decision, no matter how small. That way when everything inevitably finished out as a tragedy of lost souls it wouldn't be the chopper pilot's fault.

No. Just mine.

Regina didn't answer Busara's question for a moment. Something about the sight of the cloud hanging near the ground, enveloping a tree whose highest branches only just

315

barely jutted out of the brown haze, momentarily hypnotized her. She might have just kept watching the cloud until either she or it melted away in the sun, but for the hyenas. They had decided they'd had enough of the chopper, apparently, because they came barreling out of their concealing dirt cloud, running west at a good clip. They outran their own dust, in fact. The leader of the pack –

(That's a big girl, isn't it?)

– pounded forward, following a straight course. Regina wondered suddenly if the pack wasn't fleeing the chopper after all. What if they were running *toward* something? What if they'd smelled blood?

Might that blood be coming from one of her people?

She pointed at the sprinting pack. "Follow them."

"Follow them?" Regina heard a trace of emotion in the woman's voice, one of the few moments she could ever remember hearing anything other than an emotionless cold that bordered on reptilian. Now, though, Busara was confused.

"Yes, follow them! See where they're bloody going!"

Busara shrugged. "You're the boss."

She swept the yoke/stick/steering wheel/thingamajiggy again, and Regina's insides swirled once more. Busara floated the chopper along after the running hyenas, staying back far enough to let them lead her rather than just running *from* her. The nose of the helicopter raised as she put a bit of vertical space between the hyenas and the machine.

Good pilot. She's worth every penny she charges.

She was so good, in fact, that she barely disturbed the dust cloud that still hung about that lone tree. It wafted back and forth, but other than that the tree was lost in dust and darkness.

316

BUSARA WAS SO GOOD, in fact, that even if Regina had been standing right on the top branches themselves, she probably would have missed the women waving desperately as their hope of salvation passed overhead, then disappeared from sight.

7

"THEY DIDN'T SEE US."

The words tumbled out of Evie's mouth, filthy and dark as the dust that obscured them from view.

They did it on purpose.

It was an insane thought. But Evie could almost imagine Queen, that hideous perma-grin she wore on the ruined side of her face stretching wider and wider as she laughed before telling her kin to *run run make the dust hide our food from the air-thing.*

"They didn't see us."

She didn't know who said it the second time. Maybe it was her, maybe Grams. Perhaps it was Gale. She couldn't tell because, after hours of listening to the constant barking and yipping and snoring and snarling of the pack only inches away, now that they were gone the silence was deafening.

The chopper was gone from sight, and the slap-slash of its rotors was gone now as well. A voice spoke in that deafening silence, and Evie knew beyond doubt now whose it was: it was the voice of her true self, the one that had hidden for so long in the years where she let her husband rule her.

Get moving. Now.

GO!

Without conscious thought, Evie started climbing down the tree. The dust still hung all around, but enough had settled that she could see enough to make her way down quickly.

"What are you –" Evie looked up to see Grams, still holding Gale, her face a study in shock and horror. "Are you crazy?" the old woman demanded. "We don't know if those things are coming back or not. And maybe the chopper will wheel around and this time they'll see us. We should –"

Evie didn't hear the rest. She just heard that voice inside, that true voice that had slumbered so long, saying, *Move. Or die.*

But it wasn't the voice that made her slash a hand through the air, silencing Grams. It was the image of Queen, grinning. Of her waiting until another helicopter came, then telling her pack to do what they had done before. To hide the food. To wait for it to fall.

To feed.

Evie shook her head as though to deny the images that came with those thoughts. "Maybe they *will* come back for us. But maybe they won't. What then?" She pointed at the tiny thing in Grams' arms. Gale seemed to have diminished in some important way, and now appeared to have the size and mass of a toddler. "We have to get her to water," she said. "We have to get *all* of us to water, or it won't matter who comes back for us."

Grams hesitated. In the hesitation Evie saw little of fear for her own safety. The old woman was hurting from her son's death, that was clear to see. She was hurting for her granddaughter's plight, too. She was afraid for the girl, not for her.

As she had several times since meeting the old woman, Evie thought, I want to be her when I grow up.

For the first time, the thought didn't seem hopelessly out of reach.

Grams nodded. She twisted, muttered a curse, then shrugged and said, "I can't get off this branch without moving her."

Evie wordlessly held up her hands, waiting for the old woman to pass down the elfin form in her arms. Grams shifted again – another curse following – then managed to get an arm hooked around Gale's shoulders, shoved a hand under the little girl's armpit, and lowered the precious package to Evie.

The motions seemed to wake the little girl from whatever trance had gripped her. She jerked, her sightless eyes spinning wildly in their sockets. "What are we –" she began.

"We're going, sweetie," said Evie.

Gale turned and began to claw at Grams, trying to burrow her way back into the comfort of the old woman's embrace.

"Don't wanna," she mumbled. "Don't – what about those *things*?"

Evie glanced at Grams. The old woman shook her head minutely, a message that Evie instantly understood: *"Don't you dare tell her what a mighty creek of shit we're paddling."*

Evie reached up and felt the little girl's dangling foot, touching it to show the little girl where Evie was; where she waited to help her charge. She reached higher. Squeezed Gale's thin calf. "They're gone for now," she said. Then, in direct disobedience to Grams' unspoken order, she said, "But we don't know how long they'll stay gone. So we're getting out of here." She felt Gale's leg twitch as she said that last, and wondered if she might have made a mistake telling the little girl that they were still in any danger. "Can you be strong for us, honey?" she asked.

The minute twitches and shivers that had rippled over and through Gale's form since the whole nightmare began suddenly disappeared. Her skin and muscles felt relaxed under Gale's hand. "They killed Daddy," she said suddenly. A moment later she said, "What if they come for us again?"

Evie climbed higher still. She perched on a branch near to Gale, then took the girl's face in her hands. She turned Gale to face her and pressed her forehead against the girl's far

320

smaller one. "Nothing is going to hurt you," she said. "Nothing. I promise."

It was the right thing to say. Gale nodded, and the little girl's skin suddenly felt less taut. Her expression unclenched. Evie took one of the little girl's hands in her own and started climbing the short distance to the base of the tree. She moved Gale's hands along as she did, guiding them to handholds that allowed the little girl to follow.

The last branch, and Evie dropped to the ground. Gale was still holding to the branch she had just left, and she reached up and touched Gale's leg. A soft tap, no words, but the little girl instantly understood what Gale meant. She swung her little legs over the side of the branch, her feet dangling.

Evie reached for her. Caught her elbow in her hand. Lifted. For a moment, Gale was in her arms. It felt so good, the sensation of the child caught up in an embrace of Evie's making. She smiled.

She lowered the little girl the rest of the way. As soon as Gale's small feet touched the dirt, the girl's brightness faded. She turned her head from side to side, listening. "What if they come back?" Gale asked again.

Evie looked around. She wasn't sure what she hoped to find until she saw it. Then she darted forward, picked up the object, and passed it to Gale.

"Now you have a weapon," Evie said.

As the girl had climbed down, her eyes had grown less listless and wild, her mouth had firmed from a slack pouch to a determined line. When she took the small bundle from Evie's hands, the determination became something more tangible. When her little hand jerked forward in a practiced motion that flicked the cane to its full extension, it morphed into courage.

Gale took a few practice swings, narrowly missing Grams as the old lady dropped to the ground nearby. "You just whack anything you hear that doesn't sound like us," she said.

Gale turned to face her grandmother. "You got it," she said. She smiled, and the sight of such a smile made Evie feel something she hadn't enjoyed in a long time.

She felt hope.

Once Upon a Time,
A Beautiful Princess showed her people
how to dream.

Evie needed to do one more thing. She turned to Naeku. The warrior woman looked peaceful, even jammed into the crotch of the tree. Evie didn't want to disturb that peace, but she needed the Maasai's knife.

Reaching up, she felt around Naeku's waist. The body started to shift, and Evie froze then repositioned Naeku once more. The warrior woman would fall eventually – everything did, sooner or later – but it would not happen today. Evie refused to allow it.

Once Naeku was steady in her final perch, Evie felt along her waist again. The knife was there, tucked into a sheath on the Maasai's belt. Evie tugged it free. She supposed she might have tried to get the sheath as well, but worried that reaching around the woman to undo her belt, then slide it out of her pants, might send her tumbling to the dirt. Evie doubted she would be able to get her back to the temporary sanctity of her makeshift grave in the sky.

She turned back to Gale and Grams, tucking the long blade into her belt as best she could. "Come on," she said. The dust had finally settled, and it was easy to see the landmark that Naeku had pointed out.

"During the day, you will see a mountain in that same direction. Head toward its peak. There is a village that way."

322

A village. People. Safety.

Evie took Gale's free hand. "Let's go," she said.

"Think we'll get there?" asked Gale. "To the village?"

Evie's eyebrows raised. She hadn't thought Gale heard Naeku talking about that. She would take it as a good sign, though, that Gale had.

Things aren't as bad as we thought. We're moving. We're alive. We're strong.

Out loud, she said, "Yes. I think we will."

Inside, she tried very hard to ignore the voice that screamed, *"You're a liar!"* She wasn't sure if it was the voice of her true self, that thing long asleep which now had finally awakened, or the other self – the dark thing that Bill had put in her, had infected her with, and had used so long to keep her under his thumb.

She worried it might be *both*. Because if they both said it… well, that could only mean one thing: the words must be true. She *was* a liar. And they were all going to die.

SIX:
water

Interlude

THE STORY CONTINUES, AND *the woman knows now that she is not telling the girl's story. She is telling her own, and despair creeps in. If the girl is not the real purpose of the story, then how can the woman hope to help her live?*

Then she realizes that the story can be for more than one person. It can be for all who hear it, each in their way, and each in their time.

She holds the thing in her hand now. She brings it to the girl. The girl's eyes are closed, and the woman whispers the story – the girl's story, the woman's story, the world's story – as she holds her gift to the girl's mouth.

THE COVE OF CREATION was old, yes. But there is old, there is *old*, and there is Old. The Cove of Creation was all three, which meant it was a place where danger and beauty sat side by side. It also meant that it was sometimes impossible to tell which was which.

Gale's thirst had grown, and now she could not even speak. She managed to keep walking, but only because she was such a bright, brave girl. Any other child would have fallen to her knees and given up, but not Gale.

She put one foot in front of the other, though sometimes she did so only with the help of Pebes' chocolate arms around her back. She kept moving, and soon enough she and Pebes found themselves in the Cove of Creation, that lightest-darkest, ugliest-most-beautiful place in the Magical Land of Piz.

Unlike the rest of the land, the Cove of Creation looked totally ordinary. But isn't that the way of it sometimes? Very often the most magic is found in the most ordinary spots.

"Why... why is it called... a Cove?" asked Gale.

Pebes was happy to hear her voice, even as weak as it was. He knew that meant that they were on the right trail. "Oh, this isn't the Cove," he said. "Or at least, not the Cove *Proper*. It's the gorge before the Cove."

"What's it called?" asked Gale.

"Why, the Gorge Before, of course."

"Of course."

They walked in silence for a while. Gale stumbled every so often, and once almost fell. The earth here was thick and brown, which Pebes knew was the color of life unborn. It was the color of seeds planted and ready to spring upward.

But this *was* still the Magical Land of Piz, so when Gale stumbled and nearly tumbled face first into the ground, she felt the soil with her hand. "This mud feels weird," she said.

"Yes," Pebes said slowly. "Weird indeed."

"Why does it feel like this?"

"Because it is not yet mud. It is UnMud, actually. It is the thing from which all Life comes, but it has not yet Become that thing which it will be."

"Oh," said Gale. Pebes could tell she didn't really understand what he had meant by that, but that was all right. Some things didn't have to be understood. They just had to be accepted.

He helped her stand, wiped the UnMud from her palms, and put his chocolate arm around her again. "Can you keep walking?"

She nodded, but didn't speak. She knew, just as Pebes did, that they were getting close to the end of the journey. And so she knew, just as Pebes did, that she had to find the cure for her ailment soon, or the journey's end would also be her own.

"The Cove of Creation is just ahead," Pebes whispered. He whispered because he had just told the truth. The Cove of

Creation *was* just ahead. That meant they were treading upon UnMud that was older than any to be found anywhere else. This was a holy place.

Holy places are good. They are places where we find power. Pebes hoped they would find the power he needed to help Gale.

Gale knew it was a holy place as well, if not in precisely the same terms as Pebes. And, because she was such a wise child, she also somehow knew that this was a place of power… but that not all power is good.

It was, she realized, getting dark.

And she was still so, so thirsty.

1

GRAMS, GALE, AND EVIE moved as quickly as they could, which, all things considered, Grams thought was pretty darn quick indeed. So long as she didn't look at the mountain too much – not really a mountain, actually, more of a tall hill, but that would do in a pinch – she could convince herself they were practically *flying* along.

Of course, she did have to look at the mountain quite a lot. Evie was taking the lead, and that was fine, but Grams had learned the hard way that letting someone else lead didn't mean you just turned over your universe to them. So she kept an eye on the "peak" Naeku had pointed out. That was depressing, because though it seemed they were moving along at a pretty quick pace, when she looked at the peak it never appeared to have grown any closer at all.

In spite of the fact that the mountain appeared to stay the same distance away from them at all times, she knew that they *were* moving. They had passed through a long grassland – the grass so dry and brittle Grams felt it might shatter into smoky brown shards as they walked through it. After the grass, a long stretch of nothing but dry waste: a patch of land that looked like an exceptionally dreary part of the dark side of the moon.

Now… trees.

The trees creeped Grams out. She didn't know why that would be the case – they'd just had their lives saved by a tree, after all. But there was no denying that walking among the trees made her want to shiver convulsively.

She wished she could have kept that joint. Not like she was going to smoke it in front of Gale or anything, but it would have been nice to have something to hold in hand and say,

"When I get done with all this, I'm gonna light this baby up and have myself a good quality toke."

Something to look forward to. That's what she wanted.

No. You want something that'll dull the pain. Something that will take you away from this place where everything you see reminds you of your son, and the way he looked in that last moment, when you were running and he stayed behind so you could live.

It was true. And as soon as she realized that fact, the desire for her joint disappeared. She would not blur the memory of what her son had done – not in the slightest. She wasn't saying she was swearing off pot, but she wouldn't light up just so she could avoid feeling or avoid remembering.

To do that would be to avoid feeling or remembering the life of her son. And that she would not do.

She glanced at Gale. The little girl still had one hand firmly in Evie's, and Grams was glad of that. She had thought she might feel a stab of jealousy, watching Gale cling to a relative stranger instead of her own grandmother, but the more she watched Gale walk with Evie, the more right it looked. The two of them were doll-like in appearance, fragile-seeming things that looked ever in danger when out in the world. But appearances lied, as Grams well knew. Dolls they might be, but they were the toughest damn dolls in the world.

Gale stumbled, and Grams leaped forward. The girl's shirt bunched between Grams' fingers as she grabbed a double handful of cloth. "Gotcha!"

Gale flashed a grin her way. "I know you do."

Grams let go of Gale's shirt. She noticed Evie looking at the two of them with undisguised affection. There was also melancholy in her eyes.

At least I got my boy. At least I had him for over three decades, and have his daughter still. What would it be like if he had never been born?

329

In some ways, she supposed that would have been easier. She never would have known his great spirit, quick wit, or big heart, so she wouldn't have felt the acute ache of their lack in her life.

But a good life was more than just a simple lack of pain. She hurt now because her boy was gone, but that pain itself brought smiles as they walked, because as soon as she thought, "I'll miss him!" she then had to think of *why* she would miss him.

And that brought so many more good things to mind. The memory of taking him out to teach him to drive for the first time, and how the next day her whole right leg throbbed because she'd spent the lesson with her foot jammed against an imaginary passenger's side brake pedal, even though Craig was a careful driver from the get-go and never gave her any cause to worry or fear. The memory of him bringing home the girl he would marry, her showing up posing as a delivery girl with a "special delivery" and that delivery ending up being Craig himself as he jumped out from the side of the house and screamed, "Mom, you just met my future *wife!*" The memory of him burying his guinea pig when he was ten, and saying a sweet little prayer that she could repeat word for word even now. The memory of his first date. The memory of his face on the night he came home and told her he'd been accepted to UCLA.

The memory of his smile and his embrace as he said goodbye and turned away to buy them a few seconds.

It was all there, so much so that she almost forgot where she was. The trees, so eerie when she first entered their midst, faded to insubstantial, flickering images at the edges of sight. Nothing was real but her memories of her son, and the reality of the gift he had left behind.

She was so deep inside herself that she didn't notice Evie and Gale stop. So deep inside herself that she didn't see what the other two saw, and nearly walked right into it.

Into *them*.

GALE FELT EVIE FREEZE, and went still herself. She couldn't see what Evie now saw, but even if she hadn't felt the woman's hand squeeze her own tightly she would have felt something change in the air.

Evie didn't move. Gale remained still. Grams also halted, though she kept walking a few feet farther than anyone else. That scared Gale, because what if Grams didn't stop walking? What if she kept on and just walked right into the middle of whatever it was that had stopped Evie?

Gale wanted to scream. She didn't know what was happening, but there was nothing good she could think of that would stop Evie dead in her tracks like this, or make Grams make an odd little noise that sounded like a perfect halfway mark between fear and laughter.

No one moved.

No one spoke.

Gale knew she shouldn't move, so she didn't. She knew she probably shouldn't make any noise either, but that was a taller order.

Don't talk. Don't make a sound. Just listen.

She listened. She heard nothing but the sounds she had already heard a million times during her time with Happy Africa, and a *billion* times (or so it seemed) on the long hike today.

She listened harder, straining to focus every single synapse on the sense of what might be out there. What might have stopped the women who were to take care of her?

Nothing. She heard nothing.

She relaxed a bit. *Nothing* was not something that came with the hyenas. It wasn't like they sat there howling at the moon at all hours of the day or night, but the whole time she'd been in the tree with Evie and Grams, Gale had heard a non-stop wall of noise below her. Sometimes loud, sometimes not-so-loud, but it was always there.

Here, in this suddenly motionless part of her universe? No sound at all.

She tried to be silent – tried hard. It seemed to go on forever, until she could bear it no more and finally said, "What? Is it them?"

No one answered.

Gale still remembered enough of a world before the darkness fell that she occasionally saw things in her mind. Memory images playing on an ever-fading TV in her head. Such an image exploded inside her now, one more powerful than any she'd had in a long time: Grams and Evie, both dead on their feet and Gale clinging to nothing but a pair of corpses.

She shivered, and wanted to start crying. But she didn't. She just said, "Is it *them*?" again.

This time she got an answer. Grams breathed in, hard and fast and jerky, like the air had turned into something thick and maybe a little sharp. In spite of the oddness of it, Gale didn't think it was a sad or afraid sound. Something else.

She was right. Grams spoke, and her voice, though it had that same sharp/choppy sound, was also happy. "No, sugarplum," she said. "It's not them." Then she said the words that, at least for a moment, turned nightmare to dream. "It's the elephants."

EVIE WASN'T SURE HOW it happened. The reality was that moving across dried grasslands and empty dirt spaces with a trio of exhausted, injured, and (in one case) blind females wasn't a high-speed event. It wasn't as though they were sprinting through a dark tunnel or something. They were *walking*. Through *Africa*.

Still, she hadn't seen them. Hadn't heard them. Hadn't even thought of them as a possibility in the most remote place in her mind. Not until she veered around a large tree – dead-looking, like everything else – and came up short when she found herself only ten feet from a herd of elephants that seemed to have materialized out of thin air.

After an infinite time span that probably lasted less than a second, she realized they hadn't materialized out of nothing. They were just so silent it made them almost invisible. They were so big they could not be seen by something as small as her. They were majestic, and even when the closest one turned its huge gray head toward her and flapped its right ear she felt oddly as though she had not fallen in among elephants, but among the wild gods that must have birthed this place.

"Is it *them?*"

"No, sugarplum. It's not them. It's the elephants."

Evie had forgotten that Gale and Grams were with her; that they even *existed*. The silence that cloaked the two dozen or so animals had fallen over all the earth, everywhere nearby. They were all in its folds, and the silence made everything seem like a dream.

That was why, she thought, Grams didn't move to stop Gale when the little girl stepped forward and held out her hand. It was most *certainly* the reason Evie didn't move to stop her. If Gale had pulled out tap shoes and danced a jig to a bagpipe version of the Pet Shop Boys' electronica classic "West End Girls," Evie probably still wouldn't have done anything.

The world seemed a faraway place, and this dream would not permit more than wonder.

The feeling disappeared in the next moment, though, when a big bull elephant stepped out of the group. Before Evie could process what was happening, it slid on silent feet across the space between him and the little girl whose hand still hung in space, whose face still shone in wonder. She didn't have time to speak or do more than inhale for the scream that she knew would come once the huge creature batted Gale to the side and finished the job the hyenas had started.

Only it didn't bat her aside. Its trunk rose, then fell in a graceful undulation. The trunk reached forward and touched Gale's small hand. Gale giggled in shocked delight. She didn't pull her hand back, though. She rubbed the bull's trunk softly.

"Gale, honey, you should back away," said Grams.

Evie, finding her voice, said, "I think so, too."

Gale didn't. She just stood there, grinning as the bull crept another step – another five-*foot-long* step – closer to her. Its trunk shifted away from her hand, and now it ran the appendage up and down her clothes. She giggled as it snuffled and snorked its way over her body. When it got to her head, the bull's nostrils flared and it inhaled so hard a handful of Gale's hair rose right off her head in apparent defiance of gravity.

She laughed. The sound was bright and beautiful.

Gale looked at Grams and saw that the old woman was crying. Surprising, because Evie really thought they would have run too low on water to do such a thing. Then she realized she was doing the same thing, their bodies calling up reserves of water – more magic in a thoroughly magical moment.

Gale giggled again, then gasped as the elephant's trunk dropped to her hand and held it again. They stood there like that for some impossible-to-name time, the little girl's hand held up and out, the huge creature's trunk wrapping around her arm like stripes on a candy cane.

Then, slowly, the bull's trunk loosed itself from Gale's arm. He backed away from the little girl, then its head lowered. Just for a moment – such a noble, great creature would not bow long to anyone, Evie somehow knew – but its forehead definitely dipped. And just as shocking, if not more so: Gale's own head bowed in return, as if her sight had returned for this moment so she could answer kindness for kindness, magic for magic.

The elephant paused as though considering. It turned its back to the three visitors to its realm. Its trunk extended again, this time to shove at the curious form of a baby elephant who clearly wanted to investigate what had so interested its daddy. The baby elephant bleated, and Gale gave a shock-bleat of her own: surprised, happy laughter.

The huge bull looked back again, staring at Evie with a face so expressive she could imagine what the elephant was thinking: *"Kids, ammaright?"* Then it turned to its offspring again. It shoved the baby until it had rejoined the rest of the elephants, then together they all plodded silently away.

As they left, Gale breathed, "I saw the elephants."

Grams, her voice no less hushed than that of her granddaughter, replied, "Yeah. You did, sugarplum."

Evie saw the brightness of the moment fall from Gale's expression. Her little shoulders slumped as she said, "I wish Daddy was here to see it."

Evie didn't know what to say to that. She knew she wanted to say *something*. Knew that to say nothing, to let the little girl descend from a moment of pure magic to one of plain misery, would be unacceptable. But knowing she had to say something was different than understanding what that something ought to be.

Something cracked. A branch snapped under the foot of the big bull, and it looked back at Evie. The moment felt purposeful, as though the creature had snapped the branch on purpose, had drawn her gaze for a specific reason.

And she knew what it was. The bull lowered its gaze, prodded its offspring once more, and continued away.

"I think your daddy *was* here to see this, Gale," said Evie. "I think maybe he was the one who made it happen."

Gale reached out a hand. This time she reached not for the elephants, but for Evie.

Evie took the little girl's hand. Grams was there a moment later, and she put her arm around both Gale and Evie.

They watched the elephants walk away; even – and perhaps most especially – the little girl who was blind.

2

GALE FELT FUNNY.

She kept seeing the elephants. She knew they were gone, moved on to wherever they had to go in this hot place, but they were still somehow here. She saw them everywhere, great gray things that flickered into life before her eyes, then were swallowed by the darkness that filled the rest of her vision.

But that was wrong, wasn't it? If she was seeing them, then why wasn't she seeing anything else? Why wasn't she seeing Africa, the great and beautiful place that Daddy had so constantly described? Why just the big gray blobs that bobbed in and out of her sight –

(not seeing they're not real I'm not seeing them at all)

– and nothing else?

She didn't know. She was blind, wasn't she? So why was she seeing them?

She felt so many things, as always. Most of all, though, she felt the heat. It made her skin feel tight and stretched, and the stretched feeling quickly became an uncomfortable warmth. Then pins, pricking every inch of her skin.

She would have shouted, but she didn't want to scare Grams. Grams had enough to worry about; Gale wouldn't add to it. But it was hard not to yell, because that was how bad her skin was hurting. She touched her forearm, in a place where it felt the worst. Instead of soft skin, she found a series of rounded lumps. They squished when she pressed them, but that hurt as well so she stopped squishing them.

She felt her other arm. More of the lumps. There were also some spots she barely recognized as her own arm. They were dry as sandpaper, and nearly as rough.

"Grams?" she finally said. "Grams, I think something's wrong."

Grams didn't answer. One of the big gray blobs did. "You know, I think you might be right!" it said. It had Daddy's voice.

Gale knew the voice was a lie. Daddy was gone now, and she wouldn't *really* hear his voice again until she died someday too and then he would talk to her in Heaven, which she knew because that's what Daddy and Grams both told her about Mommy. But even if she hadn't known what Daddy had done, and how he had died to save her and Grams and Evie, she would have known the voice was a lie. It wasn't her daddy's voice because Daddy *never* would have spoken to her like that.

The words themselves were words Daddy had often said. But he had never said them with such a sly, nasty tone. They sounded like the words of someone who was just talking to fill up time until you walked on the banana peel he left out and slipped and broke your leg all to pieces. The words of a nasty trickster whose best jokes all involved embarrassment or pain.

"In fact," said the gray blur with Daddy's not-voice, "I think Grams may *want* something to be wrong with you." The voice got even nastier. "After all, she got rid of your daddy, so as soon as she's got rid of you, she'll be able to have fun again!"

Over the years, Gale's cane had become less an arm or leg than a heart or lung. It did its thing whether she really paid attention to it or not, swinging back and forth, finding obstacles or drop-offs, things that needed avoiding or things that needed finding. It never stopped moving when she held it, and it almost felt like she wasn't moving it at all, but just holding onto it as it moved itself. A friend whose hand she

338

always held, and whose one purpose in life was to help her find her way.

But as the gray thing said those awful, hateful, harmful words –

(Grams wouldn't want me to die. She wouldn't want anyone *to die!)*

– the cane began jittering in a way it never had before. It wasn't finding things for her, it was having a fit. A silent temper tantrum in her hand that made it lash off to one side, then snap back to the other.

"Stop," she mumbled. She didn't know if she was talking to the thing that lied with Daddy's voice or to the cane.

The liar answered. "Make me," it said. Then it said, "*CIN*-der-*EL*-la, *DRESSED* in *YELL*-ah, went upstairs to *KISS* a *FELL*-ah," which was the beginning to a rhyme that Gale hated because it was the rhyme she always heard in her dreams while she jumped rope in the driveway right before the first time she fell asleep and woke up in the hospital and right before the first time she woke up in the hospital and couldn't see anything anymore.

"Shut *up!*" she shouted. She tried to get her once-faithful friend the cane to swing at the gray thing that was growing darker and darker as she watched. No longer a gray blob, but a shadow. No way she could hit a shadow with her cane, but she tried just the same. The cane swung, but felt like a dead thing in her hands. It hit something, and Gale heard a surprised little scream then heard the not-Daddy elephant say, "Oops, you've done it this time!"

Then she fell down. Just like that time jumping rope. Just like the time when she fell asleep in the dark and woke up to the darkest dark of all.

The darkness was back. So deep and complete that even the elephants were gone.

"Good night, sweetie," said her daddy's voice. Then nothing said anything at all, and she was glad of that and decided she would take a nap.

EVIE GLANCED AT GALE, then at Grams. She barely recognized either of them. Things had gotten cloudy in the last little bit. She kept putting one foot in front of the other, and every once in a while she even remembered to look for the mountain peak they were supposed to be following.

Other than that, there wasn't much on her mind.

That bothered her. Shouldn't there be something on her mind? There was Bill, for one thing. He'd be home soon, and he was going to be *so* mad at the mess.

Bill's gone. Flew right out the window, and him dying like that was the best thing that could have happened to you.

Evie blinked. Doing it hurt. She felt like someone had glued sand to the inside of her eyelids, and every blink felt like she was scraping a little bit of her eyeball right off. She blinked again, though, because the pain reminded her of something. She wasn't sure what it reminded her of, but...

Blink. *What was it I was supposed to be thinking about?*

Blink. *Grams and Gale are fine. Why worry? Why am I worrying?*

Blink-blink.

The double open-shut was enough to jerk her to something like thought. At least enough to realize what was happening.

She drew the back of her hand across her forehead. It reminded her of when she was a child, a Fourth of July party where she reached out to touch the barbecue her father had just loaded with coals. He hadn't lit them, so the barbecue was as safe as barbecues can ever be, but she still burned her hand.

340

Just the summer sun had heated the metal enough to raise blisters on her fingers.

She looked at the hand she had just wiped across her forehead. It was dry. Blistered, too, so that was just one more similarity to that until-recently-forgotten bit of her past.

Dry.

Blistered.

Again, she struggled with the meaning of it all. She was still there, still taking in information, so why couldn't she figure out what was happening?

Fourth of July. It's hot. It should be wet, you should be sweating up a storm.

Wunce Upon a Time,
a Prinsess feltt like she wuz –

She would wonder after that if the story was what saved her. If she had told it to herself so many times that she recognized the change in it; the change in *her*. She would never know for sure, of course, and didn't even think to wonder about it at all in that moment. She only knew that the story was wrong. She was thinking wrong.

Dry.

Blistered.

She looked at Grams, suddenly seeing the old woman with a focus that had been absent for some time. Grams was walking a straight line, one hand on Gale's shoulder, but her eyes were dull and seemed to see little. Her skin had turned red sometime in the tree, and now Evie could see that the red had brightened – at least in the good places – to a day-glo neon. In the not-so-good places, her skin had darkened to a shade that looked like leather with blotches of purple ink spilled here and there. In the straight-up-bad spots, Grams' skin had begun to blister.

Evie reached out and shook Grams. The old woman kept walking, but flinched as though she expected to be hit.

No. It was me who always got hit. Just me.

(where's bill?)

Focus.

"Grams," said Evie.

Grams blinked – probably those same sandpaper blinks that Evie was enjoying – and said, "Oh, hey, Evie," in the lazy tone of someone spying a passing friend while swaying back and forth on a porch swing.

"Grams, focus on me."

"Okay." The lazy tone didn't change.

Evie slapped Grams. Not hard, just enough to get the woman's attention. For a moment a fire blazed in Grams' eyes, then the old woman shook her head and blinked. She wiped her hand across her forehead, just as Evie had done.

"We gotta get water," she said.

"Yeah. Soon."

They were still walking in the direction Naeku had told them to go. Thank goodness for small favors – or large miracles. But they weren't going to last much longer. Their bodies couldn't go on like this, pushing on for miles without rest, without food, and – most importantly – without water.

Evie was surprised Gale was even standing, let alone moving forward. Though now she was watching – and thinking straight, at least for the moment – Evie noticed that the girl's cane, which had beat with metronome steadiness and regularity, now skittered up and down and sideways without apparent reason or rhyme.

The girl seemed to feel Evie watching her, because she turned her face toward her and mumbled, "Stop."

"What?" asked Grams. "Gale, what did you say?"

Gale cocked her head as though listening to something, then shouted, "Shut up!" and swung her cane hard to the side. The rod hissed through the air, then smashed into Grams' shin. The old woman shouted, but didn't remove her hand from Gale's shoulder.

That saved the little girl. Without that, she would have fallen hard. As it was, Grams was able to keep her upright for the extra half-second it took for Evie to leap forward and catch Gale as she slumped.

Evie didn't stop walking. On some level, she sensed that if she stopped walking now there would be no starting up again, so she just swept Gale into her arms, then lifted her into her chest.

The girl was burning up. She felt like a barbecue, but this one full of coals already glowing red hot and the last droplets of Kingsford Odorless Charcoal Lighter Fluid her father had always used flaring into bright tongues of flame that seemed to hover over the coals without ever quite touching them.

She's too hot.

She didn't say this. She didn't need to. She looked at Grams, and saw the old woman nodding. She knew, too.

Gale sighed against Evie's chest. "Are we almost to the store, Daddy?" she said. Her little girl's voice was even quieter than usual, and she seemed at once both terribly heavy and far too light in Evie's arms.

Evie lifted her hand, feeling for the first time how the blisters on her skin stretched and burst with every movement. Unlike that long-ago Fourth of July, these blisters trickled no wetness across her skin. Whatever water they might have held had been reclaimed by her body. But the blisters burst just the same, and trickled invisible streams of pain across her flesh.

"We need to get to the store!" Gale murmured.

"We'll be there soon," Evie said. "We'll meet your daddy there."

"Bring the elephants," said Gale. Then her eyes closed.

GRAMS HAD BEEN AFRAID plenty of times. Many of those times revolved around Jack, but there were others, too. Some might even say that she'd experienced more than her fair share of scares, and though Grams would have rebuked anyone who said that out loud, she occasionally had the same thought herself. She'd lost much. She had seen a lot of bad things.

Not one of those things held a candle to this one. Not when those bastards had pulled guns on everyone, not when the hyenas were racing after them, not even when Craig said his last few words of love and then turned away from her. The first ones had been terrifying, sure, but they were the kind of fear that is wholly In The Moment, and anything like that can't really be felt. Such fear was a stone skipping across her heart. Sharp and jagged, but it just dipped itself in a moment, then hopped away, then dipped, then hopped. Not enough time for her to fully understand it, which meant not enough time to come to an apex of fear.

And the last, with Craig... she *had* been afraid then. But that fear was tempered by love, by pride. And most of all, it had been less fear than sadness. Fear was anticipatory; it looked into the future to tell you all the ways that this moment might go bad, and all the ways you or your loved ones might come to harm. When Craig did what he did, fear wasn't much there because there was nothing to anticipate. There was no "possible outcome" because she knew from the moment she saw that expression on his face that "possible" had been replaced by "necessary and inevitable."

This fear was different. There had been hope, then hope lost, then hope found again. Now her hope was all but gone, because Gale was going to die. She knew it with every step that Evie took, and the way Gale's little head bobbed around like she was an infant again, her neck muscles too weak to hold up her skull. Gale mumbled as Evie walked, but after the bits about the store Grams couldn't make out any actual words. Just sounds, and a little gasp every so often that sounded like her granddaughter was having a cardiac arrest.

Grams reached for her, but that simple motion brought so much pain that she knew she wouldn't be able to hold her granddaughter for long, and maybe not at all. She let Evie keep Gale with her, though the emotional pain of *that* was nearly as bad as the physical pain blasting across her with every step they took.

Water. Have to find water.

Where, though? Grams wished that Helix had been the one to survive this far. What the hell kinda nerve did a withered old woman have surviving this long when someone like the YouTube celeb could have done more for her granddaughter?

Waste. Just a goddam waste.

That voice wasn't hers. It was Jack's.

Shut up, Jack. You're dead and gone and good riddance to bad rubbish.

Yeah. Dead. So... I guess I'll be seeing you soon.

The voice of the long-dead man wafted away, and as it left her thoughts cleared. Nothing like full operating capacity, as it were, but at least she managed to step over the next few bits of straggly brush, instead of plowing right through them and scratching up her shins in the process.

Another stray bit of shrub –

(How do so many plants manage to stay here so long and look so dead?)

– seemed to materialize in front of her and again she managed to sidestep it. She put her foot down wrong, though, her instep landing on a piece of loose rock that shifted below her. Her ankle twisted, and Grams shouted as pain arced through her nerves from there to her pelvis.

Thank goodness for dehydration. I might have peed myself just now if I had any water left.

Evie was moving stiffly, almost robotlike. Grams suspected that the other woman was operating only on autopilot, just as she herself must have been doing.

Evie was mumbling something. Hard to make out, and the little bit she *did* hear didn't make much sense.

"… *upon a time there was a little girl named Gale. She had a family, too: a father named Craig and a grandmother whom everyone called Grams. But this is not their story.*"

"Evie!" Grams shouted. Evie kept on going, holding the most precious package in the world like you would a soggy pile of blankets.

Evie kept mumbling. Trudging forward and murmuring odd snatches of phrases.

"Up, up, up she climbed…"

"Evie. Evie, stop…"

"… into the treehouse…"

Grams lost a chunk of time. No idea how long. She woke up stumbling, woke up to Evie still talking…

"… her world disappeared…

"Evie…" Speaking like this was almost too much. And they were almost too close. Almost *there*.

"… marshmallow… licorice… strawberry milkshake…"

"Evie!"

"…you're in the Magical Land of Piz, of course."

Grams spoke one last time, putting as much mustard into it as she could: "Evie!"

Evie slowed, then stopped. She turned, and said, "Grams?" in a tone so bemused it would have been comical in pretty much any circumstance other than the current one.

Pain still lanced up and down Grams' ankle and leg, and that was good. The pain of her burnt skin had become background noise, barely noticeable. The twisted ankle –

(Please just twisted not broke please, God, just let this one little thing go our way!)

– on the other hand, was digging jagged furrows in her mind, and the pain was keeping her awake. Agony became a surprising friend and ally, and Grams would take it gratefully.

"Evie, we gotta stop going."

Evie weaved back on her feet. Her eyes went in and out of focus. She turned away, and Grams thought she was going to start walking that herky-jerky robot walk again. Instead, Evie nodded ahead at something. "But we're almost there," she said. "We're close, we have to be."

Grams was relieved to hear that. Evie had enough unfried brain space to note that they *had* come closer to the mountain. The distant peak was still distant, but it was noticeably bigger.

Which was exactly why they *had* to stop. "Look around, Evie," Grams whispered between clenched teeth. "Look where we are."

Evie did. Grams saw general confusion (*what are we doing here?*) give way to a more specific confusion (*okay I know what we're doing here, but what is Grams telling me to look at?*) and that in turn to morph into –

"Oh, no," said Evie.

"Yeah," Grams agreed. Her ankle hurt so much that there wasn't much chance of her fading into insensibility anytime soon, but walking was becoming a problem.

Still, she limped over to Evie. "Give Gale to me," she said, thinking that as bad as she was, at least she was alert. At least she was seeing everything around her.

Not living in some weird place called Piz.

Evie started to pass the little girl over to Grams, then stopped and pulled her back to her breast. "You're hurt. There's no way you can –"

"I'm hurt," Grams snapped, realizing that Evie wouldn't pass Gale to her; realizing that if that was the case then she had to wake Evie up, "but at least I haven't been babbling nonsense about magic and milkshakes. Give me –"

"It's a milkshake *river*," Evie snapped right back. "And it's not nonsense, it's..." Her voice petered out and she grimaced, then laughed. "You are a mean old broad," she said.

Grams laughed, too. "The meanest ever." She took another step forward, her laugh dying as the ankle jammed another knife into her gray matter. "I got me a friendly neighborhood ankle pain, but you looked like you were a bit too comfy there." She laughed again – forced or not, she wanted to laugh right now, *needed* it – and said, "Forgive your dear old Grams for pissing you off, but sometimes being pissed off is what a woman needs to get moving."

Evie nodded. "I absolutely forgive you for pissing me off. Though we'll have to talk about your literary criticism style later."

Grams laughed again and took another twingey step and said, "It's a date." She looked around. "Now let's figure out how to get around this gorge Naeku warned us about." She looked at her granddaughter. Gale's skin was burnt and cracked and blistered like the rest of them, but she looked much closer to the point of no return than either Grams or Evie were.

Evie, also looking at the little girl, seemed to be thinking the same thing. "I don't know if she can afford the time it would take to go around."

Grams looked at the gorge, the mouth of which they now stood at. It wasn't much of a gorge, all things considered. Just a slit across the rocky land, a gash that led into a crevice with walls that never got more than fifteen or twenty feet high on either side.

I don't think Gale will last if we go around. Probably not even if we cut straight through and take the shortest path possible to the village.

Even so, Grams knew she was going to lead Evie and Gale around the gash. That would mean climbing, because the land humped around the sides of Naeku's gorge, climbing to a rocky hill of sorts on either side. That would be a pain in the ass to climb, and Grams really didn't know if she'd be up to the challenge.

But anything that put that much fear in the eyes of someone like Naeku... no, they couldn't go in there.

"Follow me," she said, and limped to the right. The rocky bits didn't look quite as bad on that side, so they'd have to try their luck there, and hope that the going was easy enough that –

"Stop walking."

Evie's voice was a whip that flailed Grams to a halt. Harder than Grams had ever heard Evie use that voice of hers, and with a steel that Grams would never have guessed the other woman had hidden in her soul.

Not true. You know exactly *what kind of steel a woman like Evie has buried in her.*

That wasn't relevant right now. They had to keep going. "Come on," Grams said, and turned to face the rocky terrain again. "We have to –"

"Shut up, Grams. *Now!*"

Grams shook her head. "What's gotten into –"

"*NOW!*"

This time, Grams did shut up, as much due to Evie's expression as her words. Evie's face had knotted with concentration, the skin drawing tighter and tighter as Evie strained against some internal burden. Evie's mouth puckered, then relaxed a fraction as she whispered, "Do you hear that?"

"Hear what?" Grams whispered back.

Then she heard it herself. It was quiet, but even if it had been louder she might have missed it if it hadn't been for Evie. It *was* the kind of sound that people tended to miss, after all. In fact, it was worse than merely "missable": it was the kind of noise that people actually paid to have in their rooms to lull them to sleep.

Craig had bought a white noise machine for Gale when she was first born, which Grams thought was just ten different kinds of silly. "So your plan is to get a baby to go to sleep by making it loud in her room?" she'd said when she first saw the gadget in her son's hands.

The Homedics White Noise Sound Machine looked like a flat gray speaker with white plastic trim, and that was pretty much exactly what it was. Several thin buttons were set around the speaker like gunmetal gray rays around an acne-pocked sun, and each activated a different sound: staticky white noise, thunder, ocean, rain, the sounds of a summer night… and one more, which put Gale to sleep instantly every time.

That last sound, the one Gale loved so much. That was what Evie had heard, and what Grams now heard as well. Gale hadn't liked any of the other sounds. But she *loved* the sound of the brook or country stream burbling along.

No. Not a brook. Definitely not a country stream. But water. It's water.

Grams looked at Evie. Evie was looking at Gale, and as Grams watched, the young woman shifted her gaze to the gash in the land. She glanced at the rocky rise on either side as well. Grams knew before Evie finally got around to looking at her what the young woman wanted to do.

That was fine, because Grams wanted to do it, too. Or perhaps better said, Grams and Evie both knew that they *had* to do it.

Something bad *might* be in there. But water *certainly* was. Just like they *might* put themselves and Gale in more danger if they went in, but the little girl *certainly* would die if they didn't get her water now.

Simple.

So in they went.

3

THE GORGE HADN'T SEEMED like much at first, a gully at best and perhaps not even that. But the farther in they went, the more Evie lost any sense that any other world existed. Part of that had to be the heat exhaustion – probably heat *stroke* – that still clouded her brain. Part of it was the way the walls of the gully rose around her. She couldn't tell if the hill climbed higher and higher, or if they were on a downward slope leading them to the center of the earth.

At least it was a few degrees cooler in here. That definitely helped. She put her feet down more surely with each step. She looked up, and realized that the slit in the earth had turned into their world, and the vast sky overhead was now the seeming-gash in creation. Just a thin, winding line of blue, like a river out of reach.

She realized another thing about the same time: she couldn't see the sun anywhere in that slim blue scar above. That meant that it was either earlyish in the morning, or well into afternoon. She didn't think it was morning – hadn't it been morning already? Up in the tree that saved them, then conspired to hide them?

Yeah. It's afternoon now. Maybe even later in the day.

That meant night was just around the corner. The African days were hot and long, but they didn't last forever. Evie didn't think they could walk through another night. She and Grams had been caught in opposing riptides of adrenaline and exhaustion, but sooner or later the stronger one would win. It would drag them away, and there would be nothing they could do to resist.

They would sleep. They would lay down and close their eyes and that would be the end of it. Either Queen would find them, or something else.

No. It'll be Queen. Not even her pack, *just her.*

Evie had no reason to believe that to be true. It made no sense, in some ways. The African wildlife had been hiding, many must be dead. But there were still creatures out there – the elephants had shown them that – and many of them would be only too happy to discover a trio of soft meat bags they came across in the night.

They had to stop.

They had to rest.

They had to keep going.

They had to find help.

The riptides swirled, but she felt that big mean current called Exhaustion starting to win.

Gale groaned in her arms. Evie started talking, dredging up the words from somewhere deep inside her.

"Gale turned around, afraid for a moment of what might be behind her…"

Bill had let her try her hand at writing in the early days of their marriage, which she now realized was just because he probably knew the odds were stacked against her. Failing would bring them closer, in his mind, because it would cement him as the most important part of her world, and the one thing that would always be there. Not that he actually intended her to rely on him or ask him for help. That would be inconvenient and so unacceptable to him. But knowing he held sole place as her hero… that would make him happy.

Or as close to happy as a sociopath like her husband – ex-husband, *dead* husband, *better-that-way* husband – would ever be.

"The creature gave a funny little bow, one thin chocolate arm crossing its center sphere (its body?), and it said, "I am the Peanut Butter Snowman." Then a jelly tear squeezed out to its cheek. 'I've lost my mommy and daddy. Can you help me find them?'"

Evie wanted to stop talking. To scream at herself to stop, because why in the *world* would she tell this little girl who had lost so much a story of loss? Why would she remind her – even in her delirious state – that her parents were gone?

But Evie couldn't stop. The story had her, and was taking her where it would. Coming from somewhere inside her, being born in a way both awful and miraculous.

"'I have looked all day, everywhere from the FlufferNutter Range to the Deep Fanta Sea. I can't find them.'"

Evie remembered all those mornings waking up with screams locked in her mouth. The dream-cries she thought came from a series of lost children, culminating in a lost daughter her own body murdered.

What if she'd been wrong? What if the screams were this? A Story, trying to be born.

And this final question: how could the Story that came from within her ever want to hurt her? Perhaps some stories *did* hurt – like all Bill's stories had been calculated to do. But not this Story.

"They talked of people they knew (Gale's parents and his, mostly), and of places they had seen (Gale had once been to Disneyland, and even a place called Africa, while the Peanut Butter Snowman had seen so many amazing sights that they cannot now be listed)."

Evie realized Grams hadn't spoken since before they entered the gully. She glanced back, afraid she would see the old woman stumbling forward in a state of shock that would be the last short layover before Final Stop Death. Or worse, that she would see no one; that she would have left the old woman

354

lying on the ground somewhere behind her, and not even realized it.

Grams was there, though. Not stumbling at all. It dawned on Evie that Grams was the only other person in camp who had heeded the instruction to wear a long-sleeved shirt, which might well have saved her. Her visible skin was darkening as sunburn deepened to sunscorch, but at least a lot of her had been protected.

Gale moaned, the first sound she'd made in a while. Evie kept speaking, even as she looked at the girl.

"…Gale realized she was suddenly very, very thirsty."

Evie knew the girl was dying. The story had her, too.

"And she thought she heard a laugh – something far away, but something she felt was the first and perhaps only dark thing in the Magical Land of Piz."

"Stay with me," she whispered. The middle of the Story, but Stories all paused occasionally, because they happened in the middle of Life. The two had to work together. "Stay, Gale."

She kept telling her story. The travel went quickly, and she wasn't sure anymore whether the speed was in the real world, or in that Magical Land.

"Gale knew it was a holy place as well, if not in precisely the same terms as Pebes. And, because she was such a wise child, she also somehow knew that this was a place of power… but that not all power is good.

"It was, she realized, getting dark.

"And she was still so, so thirsty."

GRAMS ALMOST SAID SOMETHING to stop Evie, when the story first started.

A story about lost parents? Good Lord A'mighty, what is she thinking?

But she didn't speak. She couldn't. The story Evie told was a good one, and she told it well. Grams almost forgot where they really were, at least for a blessed few minutes. She nearly forgot her terrible pain, her even-more-terrible thirst, and most terrible of all: the smaller and smaller movements Gale made.

She wanted to tear her granddaughter from Evie's arms. But what would that do? It wouldn't save her. If she was dead now, Grams couldn't stop that. If she *wasn't* already dead, her only chance was for them to find water. They couldn't spare even the moment or two it would take to shift her loose body from one set of arms to another.

They kept walking. And now her uninjured ankle, apparently jealous of the attention its twin was getting, had started to twinge as well. A few steps later it upped its Facebook status from Its Complicated to In a Relationship of Pain.

Is it still a limp if you do it on both sides? Probably not. Probably a hobble.

Evie would know.

Another odd thought, but there it was. Evie was it turned out, a storyteller, and the confident way she spoke during the story was totally different from her old voice. Maybe that was just all that had happened since they left Happy Africa and fell into Dark Pit of Pain and Nonstop Terror Africa.

But she didn't think so. She thought that, in telling the story, Evie was changing. She was becoming something she hadn't been – or maybe something she'd *always* been but hadn't been able to see.

The pain twinges didn't disappear. The stabbing stayed. But Grams floated above it. She, too, was in the story.

At one point she heard a *crunch*. It jerked her away from the Magical Land of Piz for a moment. Away from Pebes and Gale and their quest for the magic elixir that would save the girl.

She looked down, terrified that her ankle was no longer twisted, but shattered, and that she would see bloody bone poking through the skin of her foot or leg or both.

It wasn't her ankle. It was a stick. Not the burned gray-orange-yellow-black of every plant she'd seen. A whitish stalk poked out of the earth, coated in dirt. Life.

Grams smiled. She pushed on. *Crunch.* Then *crunch... crunch...*

Then *crunch-crunch-crunch* with every footfall. The stalks were still small, young. And if one young thing could survive in here, perhaps another could, too.

A few moments later, Evie said, "And she was still so, so thirsty," and Grams finally interrupted the story. She had to.

"We're here," she said.

EVIE ACTUALLY SAID, "THE Cove of Creation," when she saw the spring. She looked at Grams sheepishly, hoping she hadn't heard.

She had. But instead of laughing or mocking her, Grams just nodded somberly and said, "Indeed it is."

It wasn't a Cove, of course. Not even a stream or even a tiny brook. It was a spring. In the center of the gully, almost equal distance between the walls, a pool of water seemed to have simply appeared. Some deep subterranean river had pushed its way here, shoving through countless strata of dirt and rock until it pressed into a depression, and found the air.

Another miracle: it overflowed its bed. It pushed its way up then, needing somewhere to go, it slid down the floor of the gully, to the side, and slipped into a cave in the wall. There were several of these, pocking the stone on either side. Some were just indentations, some went farther into the walls and perhaps honeycombed the hills on either side of them. All of them must have been formed by the same river that no doubt cut this place open in the first place millions of years ago.

The river was gone, fled to easier paths and safer places. Only this small spring remained, burbling just enough to guide them here.

Evie looked at Gale.

The little girl was silent. Pale. Her eyes closed.

Dead.

4

"NO, NO, NO!" EVIE screamed. Grams heard the agony in her voice and knew immediately what had happened.

She wanted to scream, too, but forced herself forward. She took Gale – limp, lifeless Gale –

(Stop it. That's not helping.)

– from Evie's arms. She lay the little girl down. Her body seemed so light it might almost puff away. Again the life that was more and more abundant here gave Grams hope. Gale wasn't *that* light. The stalks crunched below Gale's back as Grams lay her down. She had to weigh *something* if she could make the plants crackle like that, didn't she? Her soul still weighed on her body, it must.

Grams felt the girl's neck. Felt no pulse.

She pulled her granddaughter close to the spring. She splashed water on Gale's face. Gale didn't move. Grams felt her throat. Still no pulse.

More hands came into view. Evie took Gale and slid her whole body into the spring. The bit of water wasn't big, and Gale's entry displaced enough of it that the dribbling burble they'd heard turned into more of a splash. Evie yanked Gale farther into the pool, then shoved the little girl completely under.

She pulled her out. Nothing.

Grams couldn't think of anything better to do than this strange baptism. There was nothing else they could try.

Another dunking. This time… nothing.

Another. This time… something.

Gale coughed. She didn't open her eyes, but she was alive. She was breathing!

Grams knew the water couldn't have started a stopped heart. She knew that her granddaughter must have been alive when she went in. Perhaps her heartbeat was so weak that Grams couldn't feel it. Maybe Grams was just so panicked her own fear masked what she *should* have felt. Either way, she had to have been alive, and had to have inhaled when Evie immersed her in the pool.

Grams' mind knew all this, but her heart – still perhaps in the grip of Evie's story – whispered to her. "The Cove of Creation," it said.

And that was what Grams believed.

EVIE GASPED AND SOBBED when Gale came up sputtering. She was alive!

Not out of danger, though. There was still another problem: she needed water. She was still unconscious, so she wasn't going to drink on her own. They couldn't feed her intravenously – Evie doubted that African gullies came equipped with IV stands or doctors hiding in their caves.

That would have been in the brochure for sure.

She stifled a giggle.

Don't do that. Don't retreat. Find a way.

Gale had to drink. That was the plot problem. She couldn't just dip her head and drink from the pool. Plot twist.

Solution…?

Grams had apparently realized the same thing, because she said, "Oh, you gotta be kidding me. She's going to die of thirst six inches from water."

Evie dragged the girl back to the edge of the spring. She pulled her out partway, putting her head on the small lip that marked the boundary of the water on that side, but leaving the rest of her mostly submerged. Evie dipped her hand into the water, trying to dribble some into Gale's mouth. It didn't work. Her hands shook, and her fingers were bloody and scarred. They shook, and the water didn't go where she wanted it to. Some got on Evie's cheek, but she was going to need water to go into her mouth in just the right amount, the perfect trickle that would encourage her to body to take over and drink.

Plot twist. Plot problem.

Would this be one of those stories Bill loved? Where the hero died for no other reason than because they dared to be the hero instead of Bill himself?

She couldn't let that happen. She had to figure out a better ending than that.

She felt her pockets – the impulse bred into *homo sapiens modernis* as the go-to response when faced with a nebulous need. She had left Bill's wallet behind, but she must have grabbed Grams' lighter and billfold, because they were still there. Naeku's knife, too, though it had started to cut at Evie's belt and looked about to fall out.

Lighter, billfold, knife. There was nothing useful there. Noth –

Evie dug in the pocket where Grams' billfold was kept. She pulled something out of it. Examined it. "Good, it's not lubed," she said, mostly to herself.

Grams' gaped at her. No tears; the old woman had drunk nothing yet so had no water to spare. But she was crying nonetheless – a strange sight, the tearless weeping. "What are you doing?" she asked with a strangled, hitching voice.

Evie didn't answer. She just tore the foil pack open. Pulled out the condom carefully – it wouldn't do to rip it, though not for the normal reasons.

She unrolled it. She heard Grams gasp and knew the old woman now understood. Evie dipped the floppy bit of plastic into the spring. It swelled, going from a dull yellow to a translucent tone as it went from prophylactic measure to water balloon.

Evie's hands still trembled. But not so much that she couldn't lift the makeshift canteen to Evie's lips. Not too much for her to squeeze the open end of the condom, allowing only a thin stream of water to emerge.

She dribbled the water on Evie's lips, a drop at a time. She tried to time the droplets so they fell into Gale's mouth between breaths. She didn't want to choke her to death, but she needed to wet the girl's mouth. A drop at a time. Two. She dared three drops between each breath.

She realized she was mumbling under her breath. The Story.

"The Cove of Creation was old, yes. But there is old, there is old, and there is Old. The Cove of Creation was all three..."

Gale's lips were cracked and parched. Their normally rosy hue had gone corpse gray, but as Evie dripped water into the little girl's mouth, as she told the Story and so spoke Truth, she thought she saw the lightest shade of pink creep back into those lips.

Gale's tongue lifted slightly. Evie looked at Grams, who pumped her fist at the sky and shouted, "Yes!"

Evie agreed with the sentiment. She dripped more water into Gale's mouth, directly on the girl's tongue this time. Gale didn't open her eyes, but her tongue curled. A small channel that guided the moisture to the back of her throat.

And she swallowed. Evie thought she had never seen anything quite so lovely as that simple movement. The girl swallowed the water, then her tongue stuck up and out, waiting for more.

Evie glanced at Grams. "You drink, too," she said. Grams hesitated and as Evie refilled the condom she added, "You won't help Gale much if you die."

Grams nodded. She fell to the ground and though she eschewed the full-body entry of Evie and Gale, she dipped her whole head into the spring. Came up wet, and did her best to wipe every escaping drop of water into her mouth.

"Not too much," said Evie. "You'll just throw it up and be worse off than before." Then she turned back to Gale's open mouth and still-questing tongue. "You're going to live," she said. She leaned in close and added, for Gale's ears only – and perhaps her own, "You found the Cove of Creation. You're not going to be thirsty anymore."

That thought dulled the happiness of the moment. In Piz, there had been that darkness that caused the little girl's torment in the first place. Would that darkness reach out of Story to find them here?

GRAMS ALMOST INSTANTLY FELT as though she might vomit. She might have kept going anyway, because no matter what she knew about drinking too much when dehydrated her body *wanted* that water and wasn't much listening to her brain at this point.

Then she thought of vomiting right in the pool. Would that foul it? Make it undrinkable? She didn't think so, but the idea that it *might* was enough to roll her on her back.

The sky was bright overhead. She couldn't see the sun, but there was no doubt it *was* there. It was still hot, and more sunlight – even of the indirect variety – was the last thing any of them needed.

She flopped back to her stomach, then hands and knees. Not the most dignified posture, but then she'd never been overly dignified herself, and at least this way her damn ankles wouldn't start screaming again.

363

She crawled over to Evie and Gale. Took the condom from Evie's hand. "Now you," she said. Evie didn't fight her. She saw the wisdom of what Grams wanted. She handed over the condom and then dunked her own head in the water.

Grams trickled water down Gale's throat. The older she got, the less use she had for a condom. Pregnancy was highly unlikely, but there were still all sorts of diseases out there, and Grams was careful. Still, careful with sex at her age was a lot like careful with fire in Antarctica: technically possible as a concern, but highly unlikely as a fact.

That used to bother her. Hell, it bothered her *yesterday*, when she looked at the Aussie kid – what was his name? Kip, she thought – and wished she was thirty years younger. Jack had been an ass, but he'd had good taste in beauty, and Grams had been a knockout well into her forties.

Now she was glad she had croned out. It meant she had that condom, unused and ready to save her granddaughter's life.

Now there's *a thought no one has ever had before. I should call Trojan and give them a new promo idea: "Trojan. The Brand You Can Drink."*

She giggled, and didn't care that Evie looked at her with concern. It made it funnier, in fact, and she laughed even harder.

Harder still when she realized that Gale was reaching up. Her eyes were still shut, but her hand *moved*. It felt Grams' arm, then traveled to the condom.

"Is that a water balloon?" Gale asked weakly.

Grams' laughter brayed so loud she worried she might cause the walls of the gully to fall apart and bury them.

She nodded. "You betcha. It's a water balloon."

GALE HAD FLOATED IN a strange place for a long time. Dark there, but a different kind of dark than the normal dark of her normal life. The normal dark wasn't scary. It had started out that way: a cold, somehow *wet* thing that made her feel like she was drowning. Then it warmed and became something she could stand. Eventually it became a companion. She didn't think of it as a friend – how could she when she would have been so glad to see it go? But at least it didn't generally make her feel afraid or stupid or angry anymore.

The other kind of dark, though... when she slipped away from the elephants and fell into *that* darkness, she felt that same cold, wet feeling again, only multiplied a thousand times over.

Worse, it was *inside* her. The other dark – the dark of her blind eyes – wasn't *her* – it was a thing outside her. But the new darkness pushed into her nose and ears and mouth. It forced itself into her throat, and choked her into deeper and deeper darkness.

She felt herself in that place, and knew she was dying. She couldn't see, she couldn't hear. Then she couldn't even feel. It was just a nothing version of her floating in this nothing version of the universe.

She was dying. *Should* have died. Only a sound came. A beautiful sound.

"Once upon a time, there was a little girl..."

Gale reached for the sound, knowing somehow that the words could save her if only she caught and held them. She missed.

"Once upon a time, there was a little girl..."

The words repeated, and Gale reached for them again. Again she missed, the words slipping away before she could properly take hold.

"Once upon a time, there was a little girl..."

The third time, she reached, she found, and she held onto the words. The darkness still had her, but the words were more than sound. They were a glimmer of light. They were hope.

The wet of the deep, dark cocoon, became a much wetter kind of wet. She gasped in surprise. She sputtered.

She heard laughter. She realized it was Grams. She felt wetness on her lips, and then felt something in her fingers. A water balloon?

She asked if it was. Grams answered. There was something in Grams' voice that told her it wasn't a balloon, just as there was something in her voice that told her she wasn't going to get a straight answer right now.

She drank from the "balloon." Feeling slowly returned. Her dark-enemy fled. Her dark-friend remained.

"Where are we?" she said. She had returned to feeling, but that feeling brought a return of pain, as well. She winced. "Something's poking me."

Grams laughed again. Gale had always loved that laugh. Now she positively *adored* it. It wiped away the last rotten wetness of the other-black. She was herself again.

"Sorry, your majesty, the Ritz-Carlton was booked, so we found this nice place."

Someone else laughed. The same voice that had thrown itself to her in the darkness. Evie. Gale had *thought* she was alive again, but now she knew. Grams laughing, Evie laughing.

She hadn't heard Evie laugh before. Not really. Not with her awful husband always so close. Even when he wasn't there, Gale could feel him hanging off his wife, covering her with something ugly which the kind woman did not deserve.

Now, though, Evie's laugh was strong. She was happy. That made Gale happy, too.

5

ODD HOW EVIE HADN'T noticed the heat toward the end of the walk between tree and gully. Shouldn't she have noticed it most there, at the end, when the moments between dry and dead were so few? When the African oven had turned up to flame setting High and almost seared them all away?

But there at the end, there was no sense of heat at all. Not until after she'd seen Gale drink, then Grams. Then herself.

"We should move soon, but let's get out of the sun for a bit."

No one asked what "move soon" meant. The trip wasn't over. Naeku said the village was only two or three miles past the gorge, but who knew how long that would take them? Three people, all of them hurt, all of them exhausted?

"Two or three miles" – it might well be a trip to the far side of Africa.

They had to rest, if only for a moment. And they couldn't do it in the sun. The caves were the best bet. Somewhere close to the spring, because she intended to keep filling and refilling the "water balloon" until everyone felt like they weren't on the verge of death – or until the spring ran dry, whichever came first.

She thought about going to the cave where the water burbled off to whatever place it was headed next, but when she took a few steps closer to it she smelled something nasty inside. Water meant life, sure... but it also meant it was that much easier for rot to set in.

She helped Grams sit Gale up. The girl seemed to handle it well enough – spectacularly well, in fact, considering her state only a few minutes before. Grams tried to lift her but couldn't. The old woman had held it together this long, but

Evie could see how her lips pressed together. The pain in her eyes.

Evie picked up Gale. Grams nodded thanks – even that small motion seemed to tire her out. Evie stood, feeling none too stable herself, and tottered with Gale in her arms toward a cave opposite the one she had decided against.

Grams followed. She didn't stand, just crawled on hands and knees.

Something poked Evie in the chest. She looked down and saw a miracle: Gale had somehow kept her cane through all this. The strap still lashed it to her wrist, and now she was curled up around it like it was a favorite teddy bear.

Evie shook her head. The world was an odd place. So many had lost their hold on life itself, but a girl's cane still held securely to her wrist.

She went into the cave with Gale. Gale's head craned. "We go inside something?" she asked.

Evie wondered for a moment if they really *had* found the Cove of Creation. Maybe the water was magic. Maybe Gale was starting to see again.

Stupid. She just felt the sun leave. She heard the sound change.

"We're in a cave," said Evie. As though to prove her words, she stumbled sideways. She couldn't see the back of the cave, which disappeared into darkness, but regardless how far back it went, it was a cozy fit here. One tumbling step to the side was all it took to fetch Evie up against the wall.

The whole thing seemed to shudder under her shoulder. Could there be a cave-in?

She saw the culprit, though. A loose stone was all it was. It tumbled to the ground and she kept moving into the cave. A glance behind showed Grams, still crawling gamely along, though Evie could see bloody tracks wherever Grams moved and knew her knees and palms must be bleeding.

We'll deal with that in a minute.

She moved into the cave. The ceiling got lower as she went, but she kept on as far as she could, because the air cooled the deeper she went. It wasn't until the ceiling lowered to the point that she might soon have to crawl herself that she lowered Gale to the ground.

"Be right back," Evie said.

"What? Where –" Gale sounded panicked.

"Just going to help Grams."

The little girl relaxed instantly. "Oh. 'Sgood," she said in a slurred voice.

They were all so tired.

Evie knew then that they couldn't wait here long. If they did they might fall asleep, then ride that sleep to oblivion. She wouldn't let that happen. Not with them "not very far" from Naeku's village.

She went to Grams. She didn't help her stand – she knew something was deeply wrong with the other woman's legs, feet, ankles, or perhaps all three. She got down on hands and knees as well, wrapping one arm around Grams' middle and pulling her forward, taking as much of the woman's weight as she could.

"Thanks," Grams grunted.

They both slipped sideways, maybe in the same spot that Evie had slipped before. This time it was the opposite direction. Grams was the one who impacted the wall. Dirt fell on their heads.

Grams looked up. "Maybe we shouldn't go in too far."

GRAMS DRANK FROM THEIR makeshift canteen. Three times she'd drunk, and she felt immeasurably better and immeasurably worse. Each time she drank, it brought a bit more focus. That meant that she noticed how badly banged up she was.

Taken hostage, crashed, run through miles of nowhere, up a tree, running again, heatstroke, sprained-maybe-busted ankles.

I guess a few pains isn't that bad. I'm a tough old broad after all.

She didn't know how she was going to keep going, though. Her legs and ankles throbbed, and she could feel her shoes pinching her so much she knew her ankles must be the size of basketballs.

She didn't want to stay here. This was the bad place Naeku had warned them about. But she didn't want Evie or especially Gale staying either. Neither of them would want to leave without Grams, she was sure, but it was the only play that made sense. Get going, find the village, find help, then hustle back and save her ass.

Something pinched her back. She stifled a curse, digging under her and yanking the thing out from where it poked her. She had occasionally sat on Gale's cane back home, and this felt a bit like that. For a moment she thought it *was* that, then remembered that Evie had taken the cane from the girl and laid it near one of the walls.

Idiot. It's one of those stalks. Must be some kind of fungus. Otherwise they wouldn't be this deep in the –

She froze, looking at the stalk. She looked around, seeing them everywhere. Mostly small, like the one in her hand. A few, though, were bigger.

Evie had seen her staring. She followed Grams' look, and pried up one of the bigger stalks. Grams was sure Evie must have seen them before, they were hard to miss, but they

370

had been preoccupied with saving Gale's life, then saving their own lives, then getting to shelter. They had seen the things, but hadn't really *seen* them.

Otherwise they would have realized they weren't plants. Weren't fungus, either.

"Oh, God," whispered Evie.

She looked at Grams, and Grams looked at her. Evie was closer to the mouth of the cave than Grams was, so looking at Evie meant Grams also looked out the cave. Into the gorge – and it was now a gorge again in her mind, because no gully could be this suddenly dark and full of threat.

The spring burbled.

Beyond it lay the cave where the spring ran away. Darkness within.

The darkness moved, just as Evie held out the cracked but still discernible rib bone and said, "We're in the den."

Evie must have seen Grams' expression shift. She turned and Grams knew she was seeing it, too. A few tiny forms tumbling out of the cave, wrestling with each other in a way that was too violent to be cute.

Hyena cubs. Two, then five, then ten.

Then a larger patch of darkness exited the cave. A full-grown female, left behind to guard the pack's children.

Even more terrifying: Grams heard laughter. Not from the cubs, not from the female guarding them. It came bouncing down the gorge, a keening, ever-hungry sound.

They were in the den.

And the rest of the pack had come home.

EVIE BARELY HAD TIME to throw herself across the floor of the cave and clap a hand over Gale's mouth. She didn't know how she knew that the girl was going to scream, but she did. The motion was almost too late. Gale managed a gasping inhalation, and Evie felt the little girl's breath on her palm as the scream tried to come.

Evie shook her head, put a finger to her lips, and a moment later realized how dumb it was to send visual cues to a blind girl. She leaned in close and whispered, "Quiet."

Gale shivered under her hand, but the heat of her breath on Evie's palm dissipated and did not return.

Evie turned back toward the mouth of the cave. The cubs were lapping at the spring, but the big female – not nearly the size of Queen, but more than a match for three exhausted females of a much weaker species – was staring right into their cave. She must have heard Gale. Or maybe Evie.

Maybe she just sensed *us.*

Small blessings: the female and the cubs must have been far back in that other cave. The female dozing while the cubs growled and snarled as they pushed for early dominance and so covered the sounds of the three weak creatures who had entered their domain.

The female knew they were there, now, though. Knew something was amiss, at least.

She stepped toward their cave.

Grams lay silent on the floor, her eyes so wide they looked like flash bulbs. Evie knew she must look the same.

One more step toward them.

This is it.

Then the laughter crescendoed, and the hyena sprang forward. Evie was surprised she didn't scream, but glad she hadn't. If she had, there was no way the female hyena wouldn't have come into the cave. As it was, the laughter saved them.

Alerted to the oncoming pack, the female quickly began yanking cubs away from the spring. Making room.

The rest of the pack swarmed into view then, appearing in the proscenium view afforded by the cave. Evie could only see twenty or so of the hyenas, but she could hear more beyond them. Many more.

The hyenas snarled and clawed at one another, none of them willing to give up their spot at the water for even a second. They were all hot from the hunt.

Then they quieted. Several of them moved aside as, of course, Queen pushed past. She glanced from side to side and Evie thought for one horrible second that she had seen what hid so close to her.

She chuffed. The pack moved back a few steps, so she was the only one drinking when she leaned her head down and began loudly lapping at the water. A moment later, her daughters pushed forward and joined her. Queen's head jerked up as they took their first drinks, but she apparently decided to allow the intrusion.

She leaned back to drink again…

Then jerked upright. Her one remaining ear pricked forward. She swiveled from left to right. Back again.

She stopped.

She was definitely staring into the cave. At Grams. Her head shifted and now she was looking straight at Evie. Another minute neck movement and her gaze fell on Gale.

She couldn't be seeing them – if she was, then she would have seen them earlier. But she felt them. She heard them. She *smelled* them.

Queen growled. The rest of the pack turned as one, their barks and yips silencing as they turned to the cave as well.

Queen sauntered toward the cave. Again, the other hyenas parted to let her pass. Her daughters followed, one on each side of the matriarch. Both of the younger hyenas bared their teeth. They growled.

Queen laughed as she entered the cave.

Grams scrabbled backward. Evie didn't move, willing Gale to stay silent and still and not knowing why because there was no way that would help anything.

Queen laughed again. She oriented on Grams. Her red tongue slid out of her mouth, rubbing across her thin lips and huge teeth. The tip of it jutted out of one of the holes in her ruined cheek for a moment. It made Evie sick to her stomach.

It affected Grams, too, though in a different way.

The old woman rolled to her belly. She grabbed something. Flicked it in her hand. She wasn't as practiced as Gale, but the motion still sent the red-tipped cane unfolding *flick-click-tick* to its full length.

Grams was on her feet at the same time, no longer seeming to notice the pain of her body. She wheeled to face Queen. Swung the cane. She missed by a mile, the cane whipping through empty air and bouncing off the side of the cave.

"Come on!" shouted Grams. She swung again. Missed again.

Or did she?

Grams took one more swing, but this one was different. She shoved the cane forward, jamming it into the wall of the cave. It caught on something and she turned to look at Queen. The hyena had a nearly human look of confusion on its face.

Evie realized what the old woman was doing. She thought she saw Queen realize it, too.

Grams spoke a single sentence. Her words clipped, like she bit each one off as it came, and her voice was bereft of fear or pain or anything at all but cold, sharp rage.

"You shouldn't have killed my boy."

Queen's face changed from confusion to fear. The hyena danced backward. The motion was awkward, those short back legs tripping over themselves as Grams used the stuck cane as a lever. She dug forward with it, leaning on it so it went deeper into the cave wall, even as she jerked laterally on the handle.

The cane snapped.

It didn't matter. It had done enough.

The cave collapsed. The mouth of the cave disappeared. In the penultimate moment of light, Evie hoped that Queen and her brood were caught and crushed. In the last moment of light, she saw rock and dirt tumble down and bury Grams.

SEVEN:
promises

Interlude

THERE ARE STORIES OF *girls and Princesses. There are stories, too, of Queens.*

QUEEN STEPS FORWARD, LIMPING slightly as she does. She hides the limp almost instantly. The crown is a tenuous thing, and any of her pack will be only too glad to take advantage of any weakness. Even her own daughters will kill her if they believe it will benefit them, just as Queen killed her own mother. Seasons ago, only a short time before the Tall Things came and one of them cut her.

Queen's muzzle twitches. One of the things in the tree had smelled like that Tall Thing, a little. Like an echo of a scent. Queen wanted to eat her. Wanted to bury her muzzle in her and chew and become full.

She was never full. She was always hungry.

Now, she was also angry.

She turned toward the spot the dark place had been. It was gone. Dust billowed out of its nowhere place. Rock had fallen. It had almost caught Queen – a sharp rock had hit her as she fled, the source of her limp – but she had gotten out. She would be Queen another day.

Not all had escaped. She saw a paw sticking out of the rubble. Queen licked it. It did not move. She bit it, the way she had bit it when her daughter had been a cub. Light enough not to maim, but hard enough to hurt. The pack life was painful, and a cub who did not learn to accept and embrace pain was doomed. Queen did not love her children, but they were important. Living children meant the pack would grow. Living children meant that Queen would have greater standing.

And now, one of her children was dead.

She could sense the pack gathering around her. On one side, her own daughter. Like her mother, the pack's remaining Princess licked at the paw of her sister. She did not bite down. There was no need.

Princess turned to Queen. Queen saw blood in her daughter's eyes. A glance showed that others in the pack had that same blood-look.

They were thinking. Thinking of Queen and her many seasons. Thinking perhaps now a new Queen might be better for the pack.

She growled. A few of the pack stepped back. Not enough.

The Princess actually stepped *forward*.

Queen growled again. Louder. She snapped the air. No motion directly toward her daughter, or any of the pack. To dart straight at one of them would be to admit she was afraid of that one. That would be the beginning of the end.

But she *was* tired. She couldn't let the others know that her leg hurt, or that she was still hungry hungry *hungry*.

She felt her seasons in a way she never had. But none of the pack could know that. She snapped the air, showing she still had teeth, and those teeth still had strength.

The pack bowed. Their heads dipped. Not low enough for her to be content, but enough to satisfy her for the moment. Later would be time to enforce her rule. She would mate with one of the curs who always watched, she would bear more children to replace the lost one.

Now, though, she had other things to attend to.

She was Queen. She had been insulted, and her offspring killed. To remain Queen, she must return the injury in kind.

She did not know if the three females were alive. She could not smell anything but rock and dust, and beneath it the familiar tang of her dead child's blood.

It did not matter. Alive or dead, she would find them. If dead, she would feast on them and all would see and know she was still Queen.

If alive, so much the better. A fresh kill tasted sweeter, and the kill itself would say everything she needed to say to the pack.

She turned her back on them. On the cubs, the curs, and her own daughter – time enough later to teach the Princess of the Queen's strength as well.

Now, though... the hunt. The first Tall Things had hunted the pack long ago. Now the pack would hunt the Tall Things.

Queen especially hoped their cub was still alive. She would eat it first. She still remembered feeding on the lion cubs so long ago. Nothing else had tasted quite so sweet since then.

But she thought, in her dark, primal way, that the Tall Things cub might taste even better.

She laughed. She ran through the gorge.

The pack followed.

The hunt was renewed.

1

I'M JUST LIKE GALE.

The thought was an odd one, bordering on insane. But odd or insane, it was the first thought Evie had as the light disappeared. The second thought was, I'm alive! The third: *Grams!*

Evie threw herself forward, peripherally aware that Gale was coughing and calling out. She sounded terrified, but the sharp tang of pain was absent from her voice. Evie figured – hoped – that meant the little girl was okay, so she kept on going forward.

She crawled forward, keeping as low as possible so as not to brain herself on the ceiling of the cave. Her hands swept from side to side as she searched for some trace of the old woman who had just saved their lives.

Be alive.

She didn't say it aloud. Saying it aloud meant admitting it probably wasn't going to happen.

"Grams?" Gale called. "Grams, are you there? Evie?"

"I'm going to get her, sweetie!" Evie shouted back. "Stay there and don't move."

"I won't," came the small reply.

Evie kept moving forward. She couldn't see a thing, and the dust was choking her. Everything was muddled. They were dying, then safe, then dying again. She didn't know how long she could keep whipping back and forth like this.

As long as you need to. Don't complain. Move.

She swept her hands again, and this time felt something. A limp crab in the darkness. The crab skittered, resolving into fingers that twitched. A groan sounded in the darkness. Grams was there – alive.

Evie felt up the old woman's grasping hand, to her arm, to her shoulder and her head.

"Ow!" Grams called.

Evie's hands jerked back. "Are you hurt?"

"Yes, and you poked me in the eye. Please lay off that."

Evie felt in her pocket, yanking Grams' lighter out of there while simultaneously cursing herself for not doing that first. She flicked it. Flicked it again.

The light sputtered to life. It wasn't much of a lighter – just your basic Flick-Your-Bic gas station model. But its light was worth more in that moment than the crown jewels. The dancing flame illuminated a small cave that had grown much smaller in the past few moments.

It also let Evie see Grams. The old lady was on her back, and as she watched she tried to lever herself up on her elbows, moving to a sitting position that got to forty-five degrees before she screamed and fell back.

"Grams!" Gale shouted.

Evie wheeled toward the sound. There was Gale, coated in dust but still leaning against the wall, still weak. She rolled to the side, feeling around and obviously readying to come closer.

"Stay there, sweetie!" Evie hollered. Gale stopped moving.

Evie turned back to Grams. The reason the old woman had cried out was easily apparent, since her legs were buried past the knees. The mouth of the cave had turned into a fourth wall, and Grams' legs went right up to that wall and then disappeared in them like the cave itself was trying to eat her.

Evie looked at Grams, who nodded. Evie nodded back. She returned the lighter to her pocket. The cave plunged into darkness again, but she didn't need to see to do what had to be done.

She found Grams' questing hands in her own. She adjusted her grip so they were each holding each others' wrists. A stronger hold was needed for what happened next.

Evie couldn't stand up straight. But she could shift her weight back over her hips, to lean backward and put nearly her full body weight into pulling Grams free.

The old lady screamed. Gale yipped in sympathetic pain, and Grams somehow managed to bellow, "It's okay, sugarplum!" in a voice that wasn't very convincing.

Evie said nothing. She made no sound, other than the grinding of her teeth as she leaned even farther back.

They had to get out of here. That meant they had to get Grams free. The old woman wouldn't make it without getting free, and Evie couldn't watch Gale lose yet one more person.

She pulled. Grams screamed. Gale started to cry.

Evie dug her feet in. They slid. She almost fell. She thought she'd have to get new footing, then realized she hadn't slid after all. Her feet were still firmly planted, but Grams was beginning to inch toward her.

She kept pulling, digging, pulling. A sudden image came, of Barney wheeling back and forth as he spoke on his sat-phone, kicking the ground away from him. For some reason that gave her an extra surge of strength, and she lurched back one more time.

She went down on her butt as Grams all but popped free. The impact felt like it compressed her spine to half its normal length, but it was worth it to hear Grams stop screaming wordlessly and shout, "Dammit, girl, easy! I'm old!"

Evie felt for the lighter. This time it took a dozen flicks to get it to come alive, and then it sputtered and weaved as though it had exhausted itself just watching Evie pull the other woman free.

Evie saw Grams' face. Gray with dust, but a thin rivulet of bright blood running down her cheek from a short gash on her temple. She looked down farther, at Grams' chest and waist. Everything looked okay there. Everything very quickly stopped looking okay after that.

Both Grams' legs were broken. The right one had grown a third joint just below the knee, her shin twisting off in the wrong direction halfway down its length.

The other leg was worse. The knee bent the wrong direction, and that was bad. Worse was the two bones jutting right out of her skin just below the wrecked joint. Blood wasn't pumping from the wound, and that was good, but it was pouring in a stream far too thick to be anything but bad.

Evie handed Grams the lighter. The old woman took it wordlessly, holding it high in a shaking grip.

"Are you okay?" Gale said.

"Fine and dandy," Grams responded. Then, morosely, she looked at her legs and said, "And I was looking forward to that marathon when I got back." She grimaced, then looked around, "Not that I'll be doing much running in here anyway."

Evie didn't say anything. She unbuttoned her shirt, feeling for Naeku's knife as she took it off. It wasn't there. Her belt had finally let go, the knife slicing it apart. Evie pulled her shirt off, casting around for the knife. She would need it to cut the shirt into strips she could use to bind Grams' wounds and hopefully make a splint as soon as they got out of this. In the movies people tore shirts apart easily, but she knew from years of mending Bill's clothes that such things really weren't possible. Cloth could be ripped, but it took a lot of effort and time unless you had something sharp to help the process along.

She spotted a glint. The knife lay half-buried, a macabre parody of the way she had found Grams. She didn't try to parse out the cosmic symbolism of that fact; just grabbed the knife and started sawing her shirt into strips.

Evie looked at Grams, wondering if the old woman's silence meant she'd fallen unconscious.

No one would blame you, lady. You've earned some shuteye if anyone has.

Grams' eyes weren't shut. They stared at Evie in a way that made her skin crawl. She wasn't sure why exactly, until she realized that she herself had caused the look. She had taken off her light overshirt, leaving only the tank top beneath.

"*He* do that?" Grams asked.

Evie had to will herself not to put the shirt back on. Bill was gone, but her body hadn't quite caught up to that fact. She still ached to cover the bruises that stretched across her back and upper arms. To hide the scars where more than one "lesson" had gone on a bit too long or gotten a bit too serious.

She couldn't hide her skin, so as she cut and tore her shirt to bandage length and began to bind Gram's legs, she hid her embarrassment in anger. It was mostly directed at herself. "If you're going to tell me all the reasons I should have left him by now –"

Grams surprised her by holding out the lighter, obviously wanting Evie to take it. Evie did, not sure what was happening, and less sure when Grams started wiggling painfully out of her own overshirt. "Not at all," she said. "You already know all the reasons." She twisted, pulling the shirt out from under her, tossing it aside. Then she rolled over more, exposing her back, and said, "We all know the reasons, but no one who hasn't been there can judge. Can *know*."

Evie stared at the long, thin scars on Grams' back. She thought suddenly of Gale's cane, and knew that something like that had been used. The old woman had been beaten, severely and often.

Grams rolled back over, looking up at Evie. She glanced at Gale. The little girl, Evie saw, wasn't paying attention to them. She was holding up her hand, wiggling her fingers. Evie worried there might have been some damage after all. But the little girl seemed fine other than the peculiar movements, and Evie looked back at Grams.

Grams jerked a thumb toward her back. "'Love of my life' did that. Until I realized what a shit he was –" Her gaze jerked to Gale. "Sorry, sugarplum."

Gale said, "It's okay," but was still fixated on her hand. She held it higher, then moved it from side to side across her face.

Evie turned back to Grams. The old lady spoke in low tones as Evie tied shirt strips around her wound, layering them so hopefully they could soak up the blood and give it a chance to clot.

"I got out," said Grams. "But it was hard. Hard to face something that's hurt you, and harder still to stand up to that thing and tell it you're not going to take its abuse anymore." She shrugged, a groan escaping her as Evie tied a knot in one of the bandages and moved on to another layer. "Wasn't until he hit my boy, though, that I found the courage and left."

Evie paused. As surprising as it was to hear that Grams had been beaten by her own husband, it was somehow more shocking to hear that her son had been abused as well. They seemed so... *normal*.

The most shocking thing of all, though, was the simple fact that Grams had *left*. Had gotten away.

"How?" asked Evie.

Grams knew what she was asking. "I just did. He tried to stop me, but he made the mistake of hitting Craig while I was making dinner. Hadn't put the skillet on the stove, but I was holding it tight enough, and I laid into him hard. It all came out at once, all those years. I broke both his arms." She looked at her legs. "Think this is karmic payback?"

Evie had to laugh at that. "No. I think you deserve to be showered in gold forever." But melancholy had a firm grip on the laugh. In Grams' question she heard her own long-held doubts and beliefs: that, somehow, she deserved whatever Bill doled out. She had had a good reason for that, she thought.

But surely Grams hadn't lost baby after baby after baby. Surely she hadn't killed her own children.

Yet, even after all these years, Evie heard shadows of shame in the old woman's question. Her husband had broken her flesh, but he had also broken something in her mind. It had mostly healed – Evie could tell that just by looking at the strong woman Grams had become – but there was still a loose wire somewhere. A lingering shame. A gnawing doubt.

Perhaps that loose wire would always be there. The *real* wound, the *real* scar.

Evie shook her head again. She tied the last knot and said, "Too bad you didn't kill him." Now it was her turn to jerk her head toward Gale. The little girl was still waving her hand like a magician rehearsing for a show.

Grams harrumphed. "I probably would have, if the skillet had been hot." She shrugged, and her body seemed to sink into the floor of the cave, as though talking of this had exhausted her in a way even the past day could not. "Still not sure how Craig turned out so well. But he did, didn't he, sugarplum."

Gale still didn't answer, and now that Evie had seen to the immediate problem of Grams' bleeding out, the buried worry for Gale came surging to the fore. "Sweetie?" she said.

Gale turned toward the two women. She held up her hand. "Do you feel that?"

Evie frowned. "Feel what?"

"Air."

Grams chuckled. "It's pretty much all around us." Then, in a low voce Evie suspected even she wasn't meant to hear, the old woman added, "Until we run out."

Gale shook her head. "No, fresh air." She waited a moment, then repeated, *"Fresh!"* in a voice full of meaning.

Evie blinked. The ceiling of the cave kept dropping the further back it went, and she had assumed it would eventually seal itself. But what if...

Gale started toward the back of the cave. She kept one hand stretched in front of her face, the other going from the wall beside her to the ceiling and back again. She shuffled forward, her feet never losing contact with the floor below.

"Wait!" shouted Evie.

Gale turned back. She put her hands on her hips and looked for all the world in that moment like an adult whose soul had somehow transported itself to the body of a child. "We have to get out of here. We have to get Grams to somewhere she can get help."

"I know," said Evie. "Just wait." She turned to Grams and hooked her hands under the woman's shoulders. She dragged the old lady a few inches. Grams groaned.

Evie stopped pulling, but said, "Keep going, kid. Don't let an old lady's pain stop you."

Evie kept pulling. Thinking as she did, We have to get out of here. We can't be this close only to get stuck in the dark.

2

GALE WAS THE LITTLE Elephant.

She could feel the air on her face, then on her hands as she waved them around – trying to ignore the sounds of pain Grams was making – but it was the smell that really convinced her.

She knew the instant they came into this place that she didn't like it much. It was probably as good as you could likely get in a cave in the middle of Africa right after waking up from some kind of sickness after being dunked in a pool of kinda stinky water. But something about the cave reminded her a little of the smell when Daddy –

(Daddy's gone.)

– found some roast beef in the back of the fridge that had been there, like, since the previous Christmas. She was glad she couldn't see it, based on his description, but the stink was bad enough. It had been well-sealed in a plastic bag, but somehow the smell of rotted meat had made it out – it was what alerted her to it, and she told Daddy, and he found the gross stuff.

The smell in the cave was like that. Like old meat, rotted away so long ago everyone had forgotten about it. She didn't say anything, though, because she got the sense that if they didn't get in here and drink some water and rest they were going to get even sicker.

So she went. She drank. She did feel better. Not well, but good enough (she hoped).

And then *they* came.

She heard a series of shouts and growls. Then a crash and the dull thud of rock hitting the ground. More screams, and she heard Grams cry out in pain, heard Evie helping her.

She liked Evie. She wasn't Daddy, but Gale didn't much remember Mommy anymore – killed her to say it, but it was true – and she figured Evie would do in a pinch. Maybe even not in a pinch.

So she was glad Evie was here. Glad enough that even after the sound of the cave falling apart and Grams' screams, Gale knew somehow that Evie would take care of it. She would watch them all.

That knowledge let Gale retreat into herself. Not in a sick way, but in the way she did when most frightened. A lot of the time that fear came when she was in a new place, somewhere full of things she didn't know about and which could reach into her darkness and smack her if she wasn't careful.

Gale's first teacher after she went blind – Mrs. Peacock, a beautiful name that belonged to woman who was blind herself and to whom Gale still sent a braille Christmas card every year – had told her what to do. "Step away. Take a breath. Then reach out and feel what you can feel. Figure out what you can. Just listening and holding out your hand will tell you a lot. Sometimes more than you need, and usually at least *enough*."

That was what Gale did now. She smelled that yucky smell, still, and so much dust. She thought at first that was all she would be able to pick up. Then she got a whiff of fresh air.

After that, she got another. She held out her hand. Another thing Mrs. Peacock had shown her: rooms had their own, specific air. It was like fingerprints, with no room quite the same. The smell, yes, but also the little currents in them. The placement of the air conditioner, whether there were windows, whether any such windows faced the sun, and a thousand other details. Gale had learned to discern those different rooms, and often could tell so much about those rooms she walked with confidence even in new places.

This cave was a kind of room, she figured. A room that she now realized was an abandoned living room or nursery for hungry hyenas.

Hungry Hungry Hyenas, she thought. Then thought, What an awful game *that* would be.

In the middle of that random thought, she caught another hint of fresh air. *New* air. Which meant this room had a window. Or perhaps, even better, a door.

She held up her hand. Moved it from place to place. She felt air blow across it. Always on the same side. She hadn't felt it before, of course, because the front of the cave continually got fresh air. It wasn't until she had the dust and closed-in feeling to sharpen her focus air that she recognized the air came not only from the front of the cave, but the back.

As soon as she realized it, she started crawling. She was the blind girl and though she heard Grams' lighter rasp to life a few times –

(*I wonder when Grams ever uses the thing, I don't think I've ever seen her use it.*)

– she figured things were mostly pretty dark. That meant, for maybe the first time since going blind herself, she was the closest thing to a sighted person in the group.

She started crawling. Evie and Grams followed, and that was nice. The air got fresher, and that was even nicer.

The ceiling lowered as they went, and that wasn't so nice at all.

Soon she had to crawl. She kept forward, though, even though she could tell that moving along like this was hard for Evie and maybe straight-up *hurt* Grams.

We'll get her help when we get out.

390

She kept pressing forward, finally having to just wriggle along on her stomach, the cave had closed in so much around her, until she heard Evie shout, "Hold on!" A second later she said – to Grams, Gale figured – "Give me the lighter."

Chk. Chk. Chk.

Evie flicked the lighter, the wheel rolling along whatever scratchy thing caused the sound and the spark. Evie whispered something to Grams.

Grams said, "We don't have much choice, do we?"

That scared Gale. What if they were deciding whether to keep going?

They *couldn't* decide that. Because Gale felt something else: warmth. The kind of warmth that came from the sun. They were getting close to the end, she thought. She hoped.

"Come on!" she shouted. "We're almost there."

Scrabbling sounds answered her. She had heard those sounds all along, and now realized they weren't the sounds of two women crawling. That would have been little thuds, hands and knees then maybe elbows and knees. Then slithery hisses as Grams and Evie kept on moving on their tummies.

She thought about the sound. Pictured what must be happening.

Grams was hurt. She knew that. So probably she couldn't crawl. Wriggling might hurt worse, though. So that left the obvious: Evie was pulling her. Only there wasn't enough room to grab Grams by the hands or arms and yank her along. Maybe at the beginning, but not now for sure.

So Evie... what?

She scootched.

That was the sound. As soon as Gale figured the way their bodies must lock into each other in relation to the cave – another skill you developed as a blind person, being able to sense the geography of a room and how it related not just to you in general, but to your hands and arms and head and each *piece* of you – she "saw" them.

Evie was on her back. Probably with her legs spread wide so Grams was sitting between them, right up against Evie's privates.

She blushed at that thought. She guessed it was all right though. This *was* an emergency.

So… Grams is back against Eve. Evie wraps her arms around Grams, scootches her butt back a few inches, then pulls Grams those few inches as well. Rinse, lather, repeat, as Daddy liked to say.

Used to like to say.

For a moment, she wasn't sad about Daddy. She knew what he had done. Daddy was, she realized, a hero. Better even than a police officer or even a fireman. He had saved them all, even though he knew how bad it would be for him to do that.

So she wasn't sad, and she *wouldn't* let Evie and Grams stop. She couldn't do that, and still be as good as she knew Daddy would want her to be. He was watching her now, she had no doubt.

"We're almost there, Grams," she said quietly. The whispers paused, then started up again.

Gale thought some more about the cave, and their relation to it. She herself was sliding forward on her tummy now. Gale and Grams were both pretty small, and she figured they had enough room to keep crawling forward. But if Grams couldn't move anymore, there was no way Evie could pull her. Not enough room. They needed to tie a rope to Grams and just drag her.

We don't have any rope.

The whispers stopped. Gale got ready for what was coming. For Grams to say, "Sugarplum, your ol' Grams is gonna rest here a while."

Grams spoke, but not to Gale. "Don't you dare. No way you're going without that."

Gale's heart sank. Grams *had* decided to stay. "Don't do this, Grams," she said.

"Gotta, sugarplum." Grams didn't sound surprised that she had figured out what was going on, in broad terms if not the details – the deets, as the other kids at school always said. Grams always sounded like Gale was brave and smart and had lost nothing of importance when she lost her sight.

Gale couldn't lose that voice.

"Come on, Grams. Just a little further."

"That's a little further than the furthest I can go, kiddo," said Grams. Then she said, in a tone Gale knew meant she was talking to Evie again, "I said *no.* You take that. Maybe you'll find a tree or something you can light on fire. Make that Bat-Signal Helix talked about." She sighed. "What a beautiful kid *he* was."

Evie must be trying to make Grams take the lighter. Grams was refusing. So like her. Brave, but also sensible. Because if Grams really *was* stuck, really *couldn't* continue – and much as Gale didn't want to think that, she knew that if Grams thought that was the case, then it likely was – then her only hope was for Evie and Gale to find help as fast as possible, then get back in here and rescue her with that help.

She realized she was thinking of Evie and herself *both* going. That was going to happen, for sure. She didn't want to leave Grams here, but no way would Grams let Gale stay.

So I'll rescue her. I'll be a hero like Daddy.

She pictured Daddy wrapping a cape around her shoulders. She'd be the Blind Avenger, and she'd make him proud. He'd been the hero of the family for a long time, but it was her turn now.

She began wiggling her way backward. They must have seen it or sensed it, because Grams said, "You keep going, sugarplum," in her Command That Must Be Obeyed voice. Gale ignored it. " Gale, I'm warning you…"

Grams sighed. She must have realized the same thing Gale had: that there was no good end to an "I'm warning you" sentence out here. What was she going to do? Send Gale to her room?

Yes. Send me to my room. I'll go there and stay forever, so long as there are no caves, I have air conditioning, and I never get near to a hyena or hear that awful laugh again.

Grams spoke to Evie again. "You get her out of here. Get to that village and bring back help."

"No, we can stay," Evie said. "We can get you –"

"Only way I get out is if you *get help!*" Grams barked. She had moved from her Command That Must Be Obeyed voice to her Your Butt Is About To Be In REAL TROUBLE voice. "And only way my girl makes it is if she stays with you."

"What if they find their way in here?" Evie asked quietly.

Gale, still shimmying her way backward, halted for a moment. She hadn't thought of that.

"Then I reckon I'm old and cranky enough I'll at least poison a few of 'em."

That was when Gale reached them. She felt something spongy-but-hard with her feet and knew that must be Evie's shoulder or back. She turned her head toward the two women who had done so much for her. "Grams?" she said.

"Now, don't you start –"

"I love you. Evie and I are going to save you."

When Grams spoke again, her voice sounded all cry-ey. "You do that. Works out better that way anyhow. I'm tired and dusty and I'd rather lay down a few minutes. Always been a lazy gal, you know."

"Don't die," said Gale.

Grams cry-ey voice went away, and a new voice took its place. She'd never heard this voice before. No, wait, that was wrong. She'd heard it only a few minutes ago, when Grams shouted, "You shouldn't have killed my boy!"

The new voice instantly had a label: Grams Booty-Kickin' Voice.

"I won't die," said Grams. "I refuse to do that. And I'm too stringy to eat." Again her voice shifted, now Grams' voice was back to normal. The voice that Gale loved most of all, because that voice told her with every syllable that Gale was good and strong and could do anything she would ever want or need to do. "You get Evie out of here, Gale. You found the way, you realize that? We couldn't have seen it – only you. So you have to bring Evie along a bit farther. Go get some help, and then you come right back here and dig me out or pull me out with a rope or whatever works best. If you want to bring some gorgeous rescue worker along to do the job, so much the better." Gale knew Grams wanted her to laugh at that part. She didn't. Now was not a time for laughing.

Gale reached back as far as she could. She felt Evie's hand on hers, and felt it guide her to another hand: Grams'.

Evie didn't let go. She held them both together. A chain of grandmother to kinda-mother-and-good-enough-to-count... to Gale.

"We'll get you," Gale said.

Grams' hand dropped away. "Get going. Daylight's burning."

Another moment. Grams said, "You take that, too. Might need a knife, you know."

"We run up against something that needs knifing..." Evie didn't finish the sentence, which Gale knew meant she didn't want to say something terrible.

Grams sighed. "And what exactly will *I* do with that?"

"Take the knife, Grams," said Gale. "Or we're not going."

Grams sighed. "You are a stubborn girl."

"And where in the whole wide *universe* would I have gotten that from?" asked Gale.

Another sigh. "Fine. I've got it. Now get going."

Gale nodded, though no one probably saw it. Then a thought struck her. "You aren't lying are you? You have the knife?"

Grams' sigh turned into a cough of irritation. "I have *never* lied to you. Maybe haven't told you a thing or two, but that wasn't because I was lying, it was because it wasn't something you needed to know."

Gale didn't really understand what Grams was talking about there, but the important thing was that Grams had the knife. Grams was, as Helix had said, a tough ol' broad. She would be okay.

I hope.

Gale started moving forward.

EVIE FOLLOWED THE LITTLE girl, trying not to think about Grams, laying in the dark, waiting.

She felt something when Gale said, "I love you," then that feeling grew to something so great and hot that it was like the sun had followed them in here. Only unlike the sun outside – the light of which Evie now saw – this thing inside her wouldn't burn. It would warm. It would guide.

And this blossoming power came when Gale said, "Evie and I will save you."

Evie didn't say anything. She couldn't, in that moment. She would have started crying if she tried.

"Evie and I will save you."

"Evie and I."

Evie.

She was going to save someone. The darkness that lived so long within her pushed back more. Still there, still lingering in the background. But weaker.

I'll save them.

A bad moment came a few moments later, when the cave ceiling dropped so low it pinned her. But she refused to stop.

I'll save them. I'll save them both.

She pushed and scrabbled. She felt skin raking off her back in long strips. She didn't care. She kept forward.

She got free. The tunnel grew lighter.

She could see the tunnel's exit. The little girl standing there.

Gale outside, Grams still inside. Evie the link between them.

I.

Will.

Save.

Them.

EIGHT:
final hunt

Interlude

FAIRY TALES ARE SO often dark. They are horror stories dressed in bright, shining clothes. Gold and silver drape them, but beneath are corpses. The world knows this. That is why the tales prevail: because as bad as they are, they are less terrifying than the world itself often manages to be.

THE PACK HAS BEEN cowed to submission. But Queen must always pay to keep that submission. The price is blood.

She sniffs, trying to smell her prey. The ones who killed her daughter.

Her remaining daughter sniffs as well, but both know in that deep place that says who is great, who is the prime huntress, she who must be Queen, that only the matriarch will catch the scent.

She is quick.

She is cunning.

Her nose is keen.

And, most of all, Queen *always* leads the pack to prey.

But in that same deep part, she wonders if this is the end. The pack demands blood, and what if she cannot pay it? Such a thing *will* happen sooner or later – that is the way of it.

But she has not reached that place, and this is not that time.

She races forward, acting as though she has caught the scent. She has not, but appearances matter. The visibly weak are the first culled.

She runs into the wall-darks. The den is a place of mystery, with many places that seem to lead out of the hiding spot, but there are only two ways in or out. She knows this.

But still she enters the wall-darks. She enters and sniffs her way through each. She doubts she will find anything in any of them. But then, there *was* something in one of the wall-darks, hiding and then bringing the rock down on her and her kin.

Perhaps now they hide in another one.

She checks them all. She urinates often, reminding the pack that follows that all this – the den, the wall-darks, the whole *world* – is hers.

Still they grow restless. They laugh, and that laugh troubles her. For the first time, she fears the laugh is for her. The laugh is always the last thing the prey hears before the sound of their own blood emptying on the ground.

She searches, searches. The sun has fallen. The dark time comes. That is fine. She will find the scent, she must find it. Darkness will not stop her.

The pack laughs again. She snaps at her daughter as she leaves the last wall-dark. Her daughter will be Queen, but not today. The someday-Queen leaps away from the now-Queen's teeth, but too slow. She yips, and when Queen lets her go she tries to lap the blood streaming from the punctures in her leg.

Queen's own mother lapped her own blood. Queen slit her belly, and her mother's insides tumbled out. The then-Queen was strong, though. She kept fighting until the sight of her own intestines transfixed her. She ate them herself, dying as she did, her face coated with her own blood and coils of guts still hanging from her slack jaws when the rest of the pack fed.

A good way for a Queen to die.

But not this Queen. Not today.

She leads the pack out of the den. They stream between the high walls and a faded image comes to the deep places of Queen's mind. The man she fed on here. His sharp thing. The pain in her face. The satisfaction as she fed.

She bays. She laughs.

Atop the high places that make the den safe, she sniffs again.

Something… something…

She turns, moving slowly, her snout going now to ground, now to the sky. Something *is* here.

She follows the smell. It grows stronger.

She finds a hole. Large enough for her to squeeze in, easily. The smell comes from there. It moves away from the hole. Moving toward a place of Tall Things.

Too many Tall Things will mean she cannot kill them and show the pack she is strong. She has to stop her prey before they –

She freezes. Sniffs at the hole. Realizes that not *all* of them came out. Just the young one, and the cub.

But the old one…

Another sniff…

The old one is still inside the hole. And –

(sniff)

– she still lives.

Queen thinks. She could kill the old one. But then the younger one and the cub might find other Tall Things. She cannot allow that, but nor can she let the old one live. Not the one that killed Queen's own child.

She looks at several females of her pack. Captures their eyes with her own. A quick exhale, and they bow in the way they must. They turn to the hole.

Queen's remaining daughter takes a step that way, too. Queen chuffs. She wants her child with her. To see Queen kill the Tall Thing's cub and feed on her flesh.

It will be good for the someday-Queen. She will see her mother kill the cub, and the other one, and will know she still has much to learn.

The females Queen has chosen to be honored with this part of the hunt look at her once more. She shakes her fur, indicating they should go.

They enter the hole.

A few minutes later, the screams come, but Queen barely hears them. She is leading the pack, running as fast as they can after the young female and the cub.

The pack laughs. It is now a good laugh. The blood-laugh of the final hunt.

1

NEITHER OF THEM WAS well enough to do this. They were dehydrated, burnt.

It would be so easy for Evie to stop. She had let Bill do what he wanted to her for so many years. Eventually she came in a strange way to welcome it.

So why not welcome this? Why not just stop? A bit of rest and then... would it be so bad?

As Evie was thinking that, Gale stopped walking. She was done, Evie knew.

Evie scooped her up. No time to stop. Had to keep on.

I made a promise.

The sun was gone now. Twilight was bad, because the mountain she was supposed to follow had disappeared, but the stars weren't out yet. Or were they?

There they were.

She trudged forward.

Gale started moaning. Evie was glad. Moaning was better than the deathly silence into which the little girl had slipped earlier.

Or maybe she's not making that noise at all. Maybe it's me.

Evie wasn't sure. She was so... so... tired.

It was night.

The stars were the only light.

The wind rose. The grasses around them whispered. Evie had thought about setting fire to some of the grass – she thought she had heard the sound of a helicopter once, and maybe she could signal it.

But there was that wind. She worried that if she set fire to something, they might have traded one death for another.

Night.

Keep going.

Made a promise.

"The elephants," Gale whispered/moaned.

Evie didn't say anything. That was Gale speaking. Wasn't her, she was sure of it. The girl was still alive. Grams was, too. Had to be.

Grams is alive. Gale is alive.

Promised I'd save them both.

Promised.

2

WHEN IT FINALLY CAME into view, Evie didn't understand what she was seeing. She thought the thing beside her was the mountain. But if that was the case, then they had passed by it – and so passed the village as well. She must have wandered in the night, must have –

She froze.

The mountain wasn't to her left. It was too small. Too uneven.

It was the village.

3

A *BOMA* SURROUNDED THE village. But beyond it, instead of tents, Evie could see the tops of huts. Huts meant people. People meant help.

They had made it.

Evie ran, holding Gale as carefully as she could, but running just the same.

"Help! Please help!" she screamed. She tripped on something, tumbled forward in the fast-pedaling run of someone who is trying to convince gravity to give her a break.

Gravity relented. Evie kept running.

A narrow opening in the gate looked like the only way in. Only a few feet wide, but easy enough for her to run through, and it never even crossed her mind to ask why the *boma* had been left open to the night and the wild.

She stumbled again as she ran through. Lurched to the side this time, and screamed as thorns bit into her arm and shoulder. She had to physically lean away to unstick herself – the thorns were sharp, hardened by sun and age.

"Help!" she screamed again. She was all the way in the village now. All the way, and something terrible had begun to coalesce in her mind.

There were no lights here. And, less obvious but more important, there were no sounds. No snores, no low murmurs of late-night conversation.

There was only darkness. Silence.

"The village is mine. A dying place. The old ways are passing on…"

She heard Naeku's voice, and despaired. All this way, and the thing that was supposed to save them had died long before Evie or Gale or Grams had even set foot on the continent. How long before could not be said, but long enough that some of the huts leaned to the side, the roofs of many had disintegrated, and there were a few piles of branches and mud she guessed had once been huts that since gave up and simply let themselves fall and die.

She understood the feeling. That was what she wanted, too.

The end. No way she could save herself or Evie now. She didn't have enough left in her.

She had broken her promise.

And then she heard the voice.

4

"EVIE?"

At first she couldn't believe what she was hearing. It couldn't be – she was imagining. She was seeing things in the last moments of her life.

But no. Her imagination would never come up with something like this. No story would be so strange. Only life could play this particular, cruel joke.

All their work and struggle, so many dead to get here, and here *he* was.: the one who had died first. Only he wasn't dead, he had flown out the window and gotten up and stumbled blindly and ended up here.

He ended up here *first*. And though he was abraded – she could see the cuts on his arms and hands where he must have hit the ground and rolled, and the left side of his face was a mask of bruising and congealed blood – he wasn't near as bad off as she was, not to mention Gale or Grams.

If Grams is even alive.

"Bill?" Evie managed.

"It is you! You're real!" Bill stumbled forward, arms outstretched and a look of such joy on his face. She saw him as she had seen him at first. She was his world. She made him happy.

She could forgive him.

"Bill," she breathed. A smile started to grace her face. It hurt, her face was so burnt that the expression burst her split lips. Blood streamed over her chin. Bill didn't seem to notice.

He's back.

The thought shattered as he reached her. His hands held her, but not in an embrace. He jerked her from side to side, looking her up and down. Only that wasn't quite right either, was it? He wasn't looking at her, he was looking *for* something.

"Water! Food!" he shouted. The expression she had seen – longing, love – had been only for the rescue she represented. She was nothing more than what she had always been: something to feed him and bring him a cold beer when he called. "Evie, what did you bring me?" he demanded plaintively. He sounded like a spoiled child, his voice high and wheedling. "I need help!"

She shook her head. Her shoulders began that old twitch, that hitching together to shield from the angry blows. She spoke anyway, holding Gale out like an offering. "She needs help, Bill. We need help and –"

Bill's laugh was shrill. He sounded –

(Like one of them.*)*

– hysterical. "*You* need help?" he demanded. "Do you know – do you have *any idea* – what I've been through? What –"

Another laugh came. It silenced Evie, and made the whole night stand still. It wasn't Bill laughing this time.

They're here. She's here.

Bill still had his hands on Evie's shoulders. Now he jerked them back and forth. He was still strong, so strong, so when he did that she felt her head snap backward, then whip forward again. It hurt, though less than anything else in the past thirty hours or so. She gritted her teeth against the pain.

"What the hell did you do?" Bill shrieked. "What did you bring here?"

He gazed at her, petulant and lost, then let go. He started limping to the wall. Toward the opening that would let him out, let him run.

She almost let him go, knowing he would die.

But then we'd die, too. Maybe he can help us survive.

409

It was the first time she'd had a thought like that. The first time she'd *ever* thought of Bill not as a friend or lover or – in later years – a false protector and owner, but as a *means*. He might be able to help them. And that was what she said. "Bill, wait! We have to stay together. Maybe we –"

The laughter came again. Just like that first night, only there was no one left to buy them time, and no tree to hide in. The huts here would not save them – no doors, hardly any *walls* left. Just dry sticks supporting disintegrating clumps of thatch. She could hide behind one of them, but they'd find her. They'd tracked her so far, it was ridiculous to think of finding safety here.

Bill was still moving toward the opening in the *boma*. Evie couldn't let him leave. She had to have his help or she wouldn't be able to keep her promise.

She remembered something Naeku had said that first night. The moment when the pack flowed around them, leaving them for the bodies on the ground and then for the beautiful, arrogant, and ultimately unlucky Gunnar Helix.

"We will not run, because that is what the food does... and there is nothing we can outrun in this place anyway."

"Bill!" Evie shouted as he reached that open gateway to death. "Wait! Your only chance is with us! You can't outrun them!"

He stopped. He sagged, leaning a hand on the *boma* as though too exhausted to stand. He yelped and turned back to Evie. She saw blood dripping from his hand.

But he was coming back.

As he walked toward her, the laughter outside grew to a thundering peal. It seemed to push Bill forward, like he was drawing strength from it.

She realized her mistake too late. "You're right," he said, and flecks of dried spittle appeared on his lips. His curled fist leaped forward, and Evie felt it like a hammer on the side of her head. She fell, stunned. Her arms opened and Gale tumbled away and to the side.

Bill stood over her and said, "But I bet I can outrun *you*. And while they're busy with you…"

5

BILL'S SENTENCE TRAILED OFF into a wheezing whistle. The whistle turned to a shriek

His words hadn't done it. Not even his expression, still so spoiled, so Everything Is About Me.

It was just that she'd finally had enough. She imagined this was what Grams felt when she went after her husband with a skillet. The moment where yet another thing broke inside her. Only this time it wasn't a piece of her soul, it was the dam that had been holding back all her resentment, all her rage at the woman she had lost and the things that Bill constantly did to the woman she now was.

The floodgates opened while Bill was speaking. He stood over her, legs wide so he straddled her in the ultimate position of power. Back home, he usually walked away after that – he'd already knocked her down, already proven he was The Man.

Sometimes he kicked her. That was worse.

Sometimes he got down on the floor with her. Worst of all.

This time he didn't do any of those things. He whistled and shrieked as Evie channeled every bit of rage and pain into the moment and kicked upward and felt his balls explode under her power. She thought Bill's feet left the ground as she lifted him up, carried his weight one last time.

This time, though, she really and truly enjoyed the lift.

Bill fell, and exhibited a kind of strength and self-control she had never seen before, because he managed to get one hand away from his crushed testicles –

(I hope they're permanently damaged. I hope you have a ballsack full of jelly.)

– and fall directly on her. She was already turning as it happened, an instinctive part of her understanding what he was going to do. She crawled, but he got his hand on her leg.

Evie reared around instantly. She heard a gasping snarl escape her lips and had a moment to wonder if the real beast wasn't the thing climbing on top of her; wasn't even the surging shadow drawing near to the *boma*.

Maybe it was her.

She kicked, the flat of her heel catching Bill directly on the jaw. She saw the whole bone shift to the side, his leer becoming a grotesquely off-center mask of blood and shattered teeth.

Outside, the pack roared. Laughed.

Bill managed a laugh, too. He pulled her toward him, flipping her over as he did so she was on her belly.

So strong. How is he so strong?

Evie scrabbled at the ground, feeling her nails break as she tried to find purchase and failed. He yanked her closer, riding her now, one hand between them, still clapped to his gonads.

Evie couldn't do anything. He was winning again.

She saw Gale nearby, eyes closed. So still.

I promised.

Her screams cut off. Her expression hardened, and she felt no pain in her face as her jaw set and blood flushed her cheeks. She knew that anyone watching her, anyone who had known her in the past decade, would have flinched. They would have pulled away from the wild animal that had just appeared in their midst.

Evie reached behind her. She caught Bill's left ear and twisted. Yanked. Tore. The ear came off in her hand and now the pressure on her back alleviated.

413

Evie didn't try to crawl away. She was done with crawling. She flipped over and wriggled closer to Bill. One hand still on his nuts, the other had gone to his ear. That one came away as she closed in, and batted at her. Wrapped around her throat. Pressed.

Evie couldn't breathe. Darkness gathered at the corners of her vision.

She didn't care. The animal didn't know death was coming, it only knew there was an enemy to face, to conquer.

The animal Evie reacted with quiet ferocity. She lifted her right hand, threading it past Bill's arm. Her palm on the left side of his face, with its bruises and gashes. The wounds opened and slicked her hands. She didn't care about that, either.

His eye was almost swollen shut. Her thumb found it anyway. The blood-filled bag of his eyelid burst under the thumbnail she had just inadvertently sharpened on the ground. She dug further. Bill screamed through an open mouth whose lower portion now lay almost on his chest, the unhinged jaw wagging back and forth, the tongue lolling loosely.

Evie dug further. He tried to pull away. She grabbed the jaw with her other hand, feeling the looseness of it, the way it was barely attached to his face.

Bill leaned closer to her. He couldn't help it, with her dragging the slack looseness of his jaw toward her. He had to bow toward her, or have his face ripped in half. She was vaguely aware that his hand had come off her throat. He was hitting her, panic and pain maddening him and giving him strength.

The right side of her vision disappeared as one of his blows landed. She felt something crack in the socket on that side. She didn't care. She just dug her thumb deeper and deeper. Liquid washed down her arm.

Bill rolled away. She followed him, now on top of *him* but not riding him, no she was riding the wave of his pain and her power and still digging into him, her thumb disappearing up to the second knuckle.

The laugh came. The pack was nearly here.

Queen had arrived.

Evie came to her senses. She rolled off Bill. Looked at him for a moment the way she might have looked at a piece of moldy bread: disgusted, viewing it as nothing more than trash that had outlived its usefulness.

Bill wasn't moving. Just whimpering. The sound disgusted her.

She stood. Looked around. One of the huts that had surrendered lay in a pile only a few feet away. She walked quickly to it, reached down, and pulled a wrist-thick branch from the mess.

She went back to Bill. Remembering what Grams had said in that moment the old woman had faced her enemy, had brought the walls crashing down around her, Evie spat, "*You never should have hit me.*"

She stabbed downward, leaning on the stick with all her might, feeling it sink into him. He screamed. Blood burst from his mouth.

The beast inside her smiled. She let it grin through her, and felt her mouth stretch wide. The last thing Bill would see, she knew, was grinning teeth.

She grinned all the wider at that.

6

BUT THEY WOULDN'T BE *her* teeth.

She didn't want him dead, not this way. She had bigger plans. She jerked the stick out of his stomach. Blood gouted and Bill found a scream somewhere deep inside.

Without letting go of the stick, she knelt and pushed her fingers deep into him. The hole she had made opened, and she got her whole hand in there. She grabbed a handful of wetness and yanked as hard as she could.

Her hand came out of the hole, bits and pieces of her husband dangling from her grasp. Bill screamed again, but the scream was weaker.

Evie stood. She dragged the bloody stick along the ground, leaving a trail of blood behind.

She dropped the stick halfway between Bill's quietly weeping form and the gate of the *boma*. She kept walking toward that opening, squeezing her gory gift in her hand. It made a sucking sound as it disintegrated and fell in sticky clumps to the ground.

She kept some of it in her hand. Enough to rub it all over the sides of the *boma* opening. The thorns bit into her again, and she felt like vomiting for the first time. Not because of what she had done, what she was doing, or what she then intended to do. It was because she knew that Bill's blood was mingling with hers. It made her sick.

The last time. Never again.

Her job done, she ran back to Bill's body. She glanced at him. He was trying to turn over, perhaps to crawl away. It didn't work. Blood welled, and dark coils poked out of his rent belly.

She didn't kick him. Why bother?

She ran to Gale and picked up the little girl. "Hold on, Gale," she said, and ran, holding a treasure that sparkled, even when asleep. Evie would not let that light go out.

7

EVIE CARRIED GALE AS fast as she could. She could see the darkness writhing, and knew the pack was finally, truly here. She didn't have much time.

She didn't try to run away. She knew she wouldn't have been fast enough in any event, and besides, only food ran out here.

Evie was done with crawling, and was just as done being food.

She sprinted around the *boma*, following its curve, trying to get as far around as possible before they arrived.

Now. Far enough.

She sensed them. Knew they were here. Knew they would see her if they looked this way.

She dropped to the ground, hoping and praying that she had gone far enough; that the curve of the high *boma* would hide her from them. And more important, that any scent they might catch of her would be masked or overwhelmed by the fresh trail of blood and meat.

She heard them. So close. Snuffling and yipping. Shuffling as though unsure what to do next.

Something barked. A yip. The laugh that she had grown to know and hate – but also, in a strange way, love. Hadn't that same laugh been inside her when she smiled at Bill? When she tore off his ear, then blinded him, then gutted him and left him as an offering.

Not an offering…

… the snuffling ceased…

… the creatures ran inside the boma…

… Bill's screams began…

… *not an offering. Bait.*

8

EVIE PUT GALE DOWN. letting go of the girl for even an instant sent a near-physical pain surging through her. But it had to be done. She needed to be able to move fast.

She ran straight at the opening in the *boma*. Not to go in, though. She was done with that, too. She dug in her pocket as she ran.

She fumbled it out.

Chk. Chk. Chk.

The wheel spun. A spark lit. The flame leaped into view.

The second the Bic flicked to life, Evie shoved her hand deep into the *boma*. She kept running, dragging her hand – and the lighter – through the branches as she went. The thorns slashed her, she felt more blood spattering as she did it. She held on, refused to let the pain dull her or force her to let go of the lighter.

As she followed the curve of the thorns the *boma*, aged and dried to perfect kindling by the dry seasons, exploded into flame. The fire followed her as she ran.

Bill had stopped screaming. She thought she heard confused snuffling.

She ran faster. The *boma's* opening came into view. She hit it with her shoulder. This time the pain almost made her drop the lighter. But she didn't, and the wall sagged sideways when she hit it. It didn't fall, but the opening shivered and closed from several feet to only a single foot wide.

She grabbed the other side. A thorn impaled her hand, jutting right through it. She didn't notice. It was just a better anchor now, and that was all.

She yanked that side of the *boma*. It tumbled toward her. The gate was sealed.

She yanked her hand away and kept running with the lighter, stopping only when she realized the flame had already outpaced her.

She turned and hurried back toward Gale. She glanced over and saw that several of the huts were burning as well; embers had flown to them, and now it wasn't just the wall. The village was burning.

The pack was burning.

Evie heard yelps, yips of fear and pain.

Her animal self smiled.

As she passed the swirling flames that marked where the only way in or out had been, what looked like a ball of living flame erupted right through the slim opening.

Evie jumped backward, barely avoiding a collision with the tumbling mass.

The thing rolled, and the flames that rode it mostly snuffed away. But smoke still curled from what was left of her fur, and she seemed not at all weakened by the pain she must be feeling.

Queen bared her teeth. And *laughed*.

9

EVIE LAUGHED RIGHT BACK. She threw back her head and barked at the sky. She knew she sounded insane – she probably *was* insane by now – but she howled and it felt so good, so right.

She looked back down. Saw Queen.

She also saw something else. A paw, blackened and charred, jutting out of another part of the wall. Queen sniffed at Evie then did something strange. She went to that charred foot. She licked it. She nipped it.

Then she turned back to Evie. The scars on the left side of Queen's face were gone, along with much of the skin there – and everywhere else. Skin sloughed off in peeling chunks that were little more than wet clumps of ash. What remained of her left eye had burned away, sooty bone visible around the socket.

Her right eye was somehow completely untouched. It stared at Evie, and the frightful appearance of the hyena was not what scared her. It was the look in Queen's eye.

Somehow she knew that the leg sticking out of the village turned funeral pyre belonged to the Princess. Queen's daughter was dead – probably the other one as well, dying or dead inside the *boma*.

Queen wanted to kill Evie in return. Not for food. Evie didn't care what Naeku had told her in the tree – sometimes it wasn't about survival. Sometimes even the crudest of beasts would thirst for revenge, as Queen now did.

Evie felt fear wriggle through her. The dark place inside her exploded upward, trying to control her one last time.

She fought it down. She grinned her own terrible grin, then held her hands wide. "Come on then. *COME ON!*" she shrieked.

Queen attacked.

10

QUEEN RUSHED HER, BUT Evie didn't move. Didn't so much as flinch. She just leaned forward, her hips moving back and her center of gravity directly over her knees. Her arms widened further, as though to embrace an old friend.

Maybe, in a way, that was what she was doing.

Evie expected Queen to bite her, to slash at her with her claws. Instead, the hyena lowered her head at the last moment. She hit Evie with the force of a battering ram. Something cracked loudly inside her. Pain coursed through Evie – a rib going, maybe several. She couldn't breathe as well, either. Worried maybe the rib had punctured her lung.

She screamed, but even as she did she wrapped her arms around Queen. Embraced her, dragged her down. They fell together.

She let go with one arm, managing to get it between her and the hyena just in time. Instead of tearing out her throat as she had obviously intended, Queen clamped down on the arm. Another *crack*. The arm broke. Evie screamed. Didn't let go of Queen.

Queen bit down harder, then something lit in her remaining eye. Evie wasn't letting go. Wasn't trying to get away. She saw it in the matriarch's eye: the realization that this was *wrong*. The prey was not doing what prey should.

"That's right, you *bitch*!" Evie screamed. She rolled then. Queen had been on top, but Evie pitched to the side, tumbling through the dirt, and now Queen was below *her*. She kept rolling. Drawing Queen atop her once more. Then another half-roll.

Queen yipped, then barked, then *screamed* as Evie continued her course, shoving Queen away at the last moment, getting her feet up and kicking the creature right into the flaming *boma* she had rolled them to.

Queen's screams loosed Evie's arm. She didn't try to escape. She shoved her feet against Queen. Pushed deep into the fire. She felt her pants burn, her feet explode in pain as they began to burn in their shoes.

She kept pressing.

Yips. Whimpers. Murmurs.

After that: nothing.

Evie pulled her feet out of the pyre. She looked at them, fearing she would see nothing but charred nubs. They weren't that bad after all; apparently she hadn't pushed Queen as deep into the fire as she had thought.

But she had pushed her far enough.

Evie grabbed handfuls of dirt, patting it against her pants where they smoldered. The smell of cooking meat assailed her nostrils.

Then she turned and got slowly, painfully, to her feet. They hurt, but she wouldn't stop now. She had to get Gale to a safe distance. The grasslands they had walked through had thinned the closer they got to the village, so if she could just move Gale away far enough, they should be safe from the fire.

And the burning village was a hell of a Bat-Signal.

11

EVIE KNELT BESIDE GALE, intending to pick her up, when a sharp crackling arrested her attention. She turned and saw a ten-foot section of the wall fall apart. It just tumbled in on itself, disappearing in the blink of an eye.

A new opening had come into being. Like the doorway to the Magical Land of Piz, it simply appeared in the *boma*. And just as in her story, something came through from the land beyond.

The hyenas.

Not all of them, not by far, and the ones who leaped past the flames were, like Queen, burnt.

One at first. Two more. Five threw themselves through the flame.

A dozen of the beasts made it out. They turned to Evie and Gale. They bared their teeth.

Evie looked at Gale. She wasn't checking for life. She knew the girl was alive. Like Evie, Gale had made a promise. She would return. She would save her Grams.

Evie would make sure of it.

She turned to face the hyenas. They had fanned out, partially surrounding her. Their muzzles – those that remained and hadn't been burnt away in the fire – wrinkled and their teeth showed in full. They growled. One laughed.

Evie laughed right back. She half-turned, not showing her back, but enough to jam her much-abused hand back into the still-burning *boma*. She yanked, coming away with a three-foot length of wood, two feet of which burned. She raised the stick high, tongues of flame leaping even higher.

One of the hyenas took a step back. Just a small step, and then it growled and stepped forward again, even closer this time.

Evie didn't know what she was doing. She just did it. It came from that part of her that had lain under the dark for so long. That dark was gone. She couldn't see the future, but she could see *herself* again, and trusted what that self told her to do.

She waved the stick. The hyenas followed it with their eyes, hypnotized by dancing flame. Evie pointed with the stick. The hyenas followed the motion again... and that brought them around enough to see what lay so close nearby.

Queen. The wall had collapsed around her, but Evie could make out her shape, and knew the hyenas would see it as well. They wouldn't understand what she wanted to say – not completely. But they would see Queen, dead. They would see her burning. They would see the flame Evie held.

While they were still looking at their dead pack leader, Evie listened to herself once more. She looked up at the moon and shrieked a wordless cry. She turned to the hyenas and laughed and laughed. A merciless, biting laugh that spoke not of joy, but of her own pain and hunger and rage.

The hyenas turned toward her. Not laughing, not snarling. Teeth now hidden.

One by one, the hyenas dipped their heads. One by one, they whimpered.

One by one, they ran.

426

12

CHUP-CHUP-CHUP.

Evie held Gale in her arms. Waiting.

The chopper landed. The camp manager, Regina, was out before it had fully set down. She ran for them, head bowed against the wind of the chopper's rotors.

"Good God, dearies!" she screamed. She moved as though to hug Evie, then thought better of it and stood back. Evie appreciated that. She didn't want anyone touching her. It would hurt too bad. Regina gestured toward the helicopter. "Let's get you back to camp!" she shouted, the sound small against the thrum of the helicopter's blades slashing through the air. She didn't move, though. Neither did Evie, waiting. She knew what was coming next. "Naeku? Leg?" asked Regina. Evie shook her head. "Anyone else?"

Evie nodded.

13

EVIE WATCHED AS THE helicopter pilot, Busara, disappeared into the hole in the ground where Evie and Gale had escaped the cave. Where Grams still was.

There had been IVs with saline solution for emergency hydration in the back of the chopper. They got one in Gale, strapping her to the long bench at the very rear of the helicopter's passenger space. Regina turned to Evie and repeated the motions. The solution burned, but she really couldn't complain – everywhere else burned far worse.

"We'll get you back to camp, then –"

"No."

Regina looked at Evie, surprised. "No? You need medical attention, and the girl –"

"Made a promise," said Evie. Regina wouldn't understand that, she knew, but she also knew that time was short. They had to get to Grams, and there would be no way to do that without Evie's help. Even *with* her help, she hadn't known for sure if they could find the gorge or the entrance to the cave.

She told all this to Regina, who told it to Busara. The chopper pilot nodded and said, "That is a bad place," once Regina explained what they needed to find.

"What? You knew about that place? Why the hell didn't you take me there?"

Busara turned in her seat and looked at Evie, who was sitting on the floor beside Gale, holding the little girl's hand. "Because nothing that goes to that place ever lives."

She said it admiringly, but also as a warning. Regina didn't catch it, but Evie did. The woman was telling her that Grams must be dead.

Evie shook her head. Busara turned back around and the chopper took off. It landed only a few minutes later, but even in the darkness Evie could tell they were at the right place.

Busara insisted on being the one to go into the cave. "They are small, the passages like this," she said. She glanced at the sturdy shape of Regina. "You are too fat," she said, then, looking at Evie, "And you are in no shape to do so."

Evie agreed. They had put a sling on her broken arm, and she hurt every time she took a breath. Busara would go.

She did.

And came out shaking her head. "I'm sorry. It's just blood and death down there."

Evie shrieked. Not the mad howl of a beast in its strength. She had become a creature who swam in agony. The pain she felt was far worse than that of her broken arm or the ragged shards that pressed her every time she breathed.

I didn't save her.

Regina put her hands on Evie's shoulders, trying to steady and calm her. "I'm sorry, I'm so –"

Evie shrugged away from the woman, and from her words. She couldn't hear that, couldn't accept that.

She ran. The IV bottle they had lain over her shoulder when she insisted on getting out of the chopper fell away, and she felt its weight tear the needle tear from her arm. She ducked around Busara, who tried to catch her as she passed by. Busara had been holding a rope as she went in – the hope being that they would find Grams and the old woman would have the strength to tie the rope around her and draw her out – and Evie snatched it away from her.

She ran the last few feet to the hole. Dove in.

I. PROMISED.

The climb in was worse than the climb out had been. Climbing away from the safety the helicopter promised. But the promise had been made here; it must be kept here.

She pulled herself deeper. The cave walls didn't press around as closely as she remembered, and she wondered that she must have lost so much weight in so short a time. Her broken arm got pinned beneath her, her whole body laying on it. Agony lanced through her body with every inch she thrust herself forward. She didn't care.

Her lead hand, the one pulling her forward even as it kept the rope in a death grip, came down on something wet. She let go of the rope long enough to grab it. A leg. Severed. She screamed and threw the thing to the side. There was enough room for it beside her, she could crawl past it, but it brushed against her as she did.

She kept crawling, and there were more and more of the bloody chunks of flesh. More and more things that were less and less identifiable. She grabbed something she thought might – *might* – be a skull, all its flesh shredded away. Another thing that was half fur and half torn gristle. Another handful of something that might be a thin, cold paw that –

– that *twitched* in her hand. It turned, and it wasn't a paw at all, it was a hand, and it grabbed hers and her own fingers tightened as Grams said, "Took you long enough," in a weak voice. Then added, dreamily, "You don't have any weed on you, do you?"

NINE:
Queen

Postlude

THE GIRL IS NO longer afraid. She is sad; she has lost so much more than a girl like her should ever have to lose. But she is safe, and even in her sadness she smiles often. The young have that power. They can always find it in themselves to go on.

Sometimes, so can the old. Like the woman who lays on the seat near the girl. Their seats are folded down, and they hold hands across the short aisle between them as the vehicle bumps its way from the helipad where they landed to the nearby hospital.

Also in the aisle: the woman. The storyteller. The protector.

The new Queen.

The girl looks at her – even with sightless eyes, the Queen would swear she looks right at her – and says, "Can you finish the story?"

The Queen smiles. She knows what the little girl is asking.

AFTER THEY ARRIVED AT the Cove of Creation, and Gale drank her fill of the waters that would save her, there was still more to do. There always is. They had not yet found Pebes' parents, for one thing. Gale knew they would, of course – she had told him she would help him do just that, and she was a girl who kept her promises. But even after they did, there would be more. There would be light to enjoy, and darkness to fight. There would be adventures, because that was the way of things.

They were alive. And for the living, every day is an adventure.

They traveled. There was darkness. There was loss. There was even some pain – for even in Piz, that also was the way of things.

But they also found laughter, and smiles. They found much magic, and even greater joy...

NOVELS BY MICHAELBRENT COLLINGS

THE DARKLIGHTS

THE LONGEST CON

THE HOUSE THAT DEATH BUILT

THE DEEP

TWISTED

THIS DARKNESS LIGHT

CRIME SEEN

STRANGERS

DARKBOUND

BLOOD RELATIONS:

A GOOD MORMON GIRL MYSTERY

THE HAUNTED

APPARITION

THE LOON

MR. GRAY (aka THE MERIDIANS)

RUN

RISING FEARS

THE COLONY SAGA:

THE COLONY: GENESIS (THE COLONY, VOL. 1)

THE COLONY: RENEGADES (THE COLONY, VOL. 2)

THE COLONY: DESCENT (THE COLONY, VOL. 3)

THE COLONY: VELOCITY (THE COLONY, VOL. 4)

THE COLONY: SHIFT (THE COLONY, VOL. 5)

THE COLONY: BURIED (THE COLONY, VOL. 6)

Made in the USA
Middletown, DE
15 September 2019